SAVE ME

SAVE ME

Mandasue Heller

MACMILLAN

First published 2017 by Macmillan
an imprint of Pan Macmillan
20 New Wharf Road, London N1 9RR
Associated companies throughout the world
www.panmacmillan.com

ISBN 978-1-4472-8836-7

1 3 5 7 9 8 6 4 2

A CIP catalogue record for this book is available from the British Library.

Typeset by Ellipsis, Glasgow
Printed and bound by CPI Group (UK) Ltd, Croydon, CR0 4YY

Visit **www.panmacmillan.com** to read more about all our books
and to buy them. You will also find features, author interviews and
news of any author events, and you can sign up for e-newsletters
so that you're always first to hear about our new releases.

For my Mum and Dad, with all my love
RIP
xxx

Acknowledgements

As always, love to my beautiful family: Win; Michael, Andrew and Azzura; Marissa, Lariah and Antonio. Ava, Amber, Martin, Jade, Reece, Kyro and Diaz; Aunt Doreen, Pete, Lorna, Cliff, Chris and Glen; Toni, Natalie, Dan, Joseph and Mavis, Valerie, Jascinth, Donna and their children. Also Liz and family, Rosemary and Graham, and my lovely re-found family, Uncle Brian and Auntie Joyce, Brian Jr, Julie, Ian, Amanda, etc; and our Heller clan in the US. Love you all.

Love also to Norman, Betty and Ronnie, Katy and John, Kimberley, Brian and Jac, Ann Mitchell, Colin and Amanda, Jayne and Nev, and the rest of my friends – past and present; and eternal gratitude to my mum's church family, Chris and Allan, Ann, Sylvia, Rick, Keith and Carol, Dr Sue Burke and Judith.

Also, Carolyn Caughey, Cat, and Nick.

Huge thanks to my editor, Wayne Brooks; Alex, Jez and the rest of the brilliant team at Pan Mac. Also my agent, Sheila Crowley.

And, lastly, a massive thank you to the sellers and readers of my books; the bloggers, librarians, Facebook and Twitter friends. You're all wonderful!

Prologue

The girl's breath plumed around her pinched face as she hopped from foot to foot, and she clapped her skinny arms with her hands.

'Hurry up. I'm freezing to bleedin' death here.'

'I'm going as fast as I can,' the lad grunted, yanking the crowbar backwards and forwards. 'The fucker who put this sheeting up must have used foot-long screws, it's that tight.'

'I should have done it myself,' she sniped. 'I'd have had it off ages ago, me.'

'If you reckon you can do it any faster, be my guest.' The lad paused and offered the crowbar to her. Sneering when she flashed him a dirty look, he said, 'Thought not. Now shut the fuck up, or I'll sack it off and go home. You're the one who's rattlin', not me.'

'Just get on with it and quit being a dickhead,' she muttered, hunching her bony shoulders.

The lad repositioned the end of the crowbar in the gap between the metal sheet and the wall and gave one last tug. Almost falling off the wheelie bin he was perched on when a rivet popped out and the corner of the sheeting sprang away from the wall, he dropped the bar onto the grass and pulled it the rest of the way off with his hands.

'And we're in!' he said when he'd unveiled the broken window in its rotten frame. 'Happy now?'

'I will be when you find something to flog,' the girl replied, casting a nervous glance back at the road when he elbowed the rest of the glass out of the frame. 'What's in there?' she asked when he'd hauled himself up onto the sill. 'Can you see anything?'

'Nah, it's too dark,' he said. 'Chuck us the lighter.'

'Don't waste the gas, 'cos there's not much left,' she cautioned, tossing the disposable lighter up to him.

The lighter flared like a beacon in the pitch darkness, momentarily illuminating the lad's gaunt features before he dropped down off the sill, landing with a thud on the other side of the wall. A car turned onto the lane and drove slowly past the overgrown hedge-row fronting the old cottage. As its headlights pierced holes in the dense thicket, the girl pulled her hood up and squatted down in the shadows of the bin.

Standing up again when the car had passed, the girl listened for sounds of movement inside the cottage. Unnerved by the absolute silence after several minutes, she was about to climb up onto the bin to see what was taking the lad so long, when his face appeared at the window.

'What's happened?' she asked when she saw the panic in his bulging eyes. 'You didn't get caught, did you?'

'There's a fuckin' stiff in the cellar!' the lad hissed as he struggled to push a holdall out through the gap. 'I went down there to have a mooch, and found it trussed up on a mattress with gaffer tape over its fuckin' gob!'

'You're kidding?'

'Do I look like I'm fuckin' kidding? Come in and take a look for yourself if you don't believe me.'

'Fuck off!' she cried, buckling under the weight of the bag when it landed in her arms. 'Shit, this weighs a bleeding ton. What's in it?'

'No idea; I didn't stop to check,' the lad said, breathing heavily as he scrambled out and dropped down beside her. 'We'll check it when we get back to the gaff.'

'What about that in there?' She jerked her head in the direction of the cottage. 'Was it a man or a woman?'

'Dunno,' he muttered, already kicking a path through the tall weeds to get to the gate. 'I shit myself when I saw it and the lighter flew out of my hand, so I couldn't get a proper look.'

'But it was deffo dead?' she asked, stumbling along behind him.

'Looked like it,' he said, turning to take the bag off her and looping the strap over his shoulder. 'Smelled like it, an' all.'

'Don't you think we should call the police?' she asked, banging into him when he stopped to yank the broken gate aside before stepping out on to the pavement.

'What, and have 'em think I had summat to do with it?' he grunted. 'No chance! Let's just get the fuck out of here before we get caught.'

PART ONE

1

Ellie Fisher's train was idling at the platform, and she heard its heavy doors slamming shut as she raced across the metal foot-bridge and clattered down the steps at the far side. Letting out a wail of frustration when it began to slide smoothly away before she reached the bottom, she paused to catch her breath before continuing on down; cursing her boss with every step for making her stay behind to file some invoices. It wasn't even her job to deal with the stupid invoices, but the girl whose job it *was* had pulled a sickie today, and the other two girls who shared the office had disappeared as soon as the clock hit five thirty, so she'd been a sitting duck.

Dismayed to see that she had a thirty-minute wait for the next train when she checked the electronic timetable above the shuttered coffee-shop door, Ellie reached into her handbag for her phone as she heard it ping. There was a message from her husband, Matt, on the screen, reminding her to pick up a couple of bottles of wine on the way home. She contemplated calling him to let him know she was going to be late, but immediately changed her mind. He was going to be mad enough without pre-warning him and giving him time to stew on it.

A train whizzed by on the opposite side of the tracks, leaving an icy gust of wind in its wake that snatched the hair off Ellie's shoulders. Shivering, she pulled her collar up around her chin and gazed out over the tracks. The nights were drawing in much earlier as autumn gave way to winter, and the sky was already a stormy slate-grey. Unnerved by the deepening shadows, she was toying with the idea of heading out onto the road to catch a bus instead, when she heard footsteps on the bridge. Glancing up, she frowned when she saw a hooded figure in dark clothes climbing over the barrier rail.

The ghostly wail of a train horn in the distance reached her as she watched the figure find its footing on the narrow ledge that ran along the outside of the bridge, and the hairs on the back of her neck bristled as she instinctively guessed what was about to happen. Heart in her mouth, she looked around for a guard, or even a cleaner, but the station was deserted.

'Hey . . . !' she yelled when she looked up at the bridge and saw the figure holding onto the rail and leaning out over the tracks. 'What are you doing? Get down from there!'

Her words were whisked away by the wind, and the figure didn't look round. Panicking, Ellie fumbled her phone back out of her bag and dialled 999 as she ran toward the steps.

'Police!' she spluttered when her call was answered. 'I'm at Long Lane train station, and someone's just climbed over the railing on the bridge. I think they're going to jump!'

After giving her name and explaining that there was no one else around – and that, *no*, she did *not* think it was a railway employee doing maintenance work – she thanked the operator when he assured her that a unit was on its way, and shoved the phone into her pocket.

The figure turned its head when she reached the top of the steps, and she saw that it was a young man. Dark hollows surrounded his eyes, his cheeks looked gaunt, and he seemed to be shaking even more violently than she was. Afraid that she might spook him and cause him to lose his footing, she held out her hand as she slowly approached him.

'Please don't jump; I only want to talk to you.'

'Stay back!' he ordered, readjusting his grip on the rail. 'I mean it . . . stay back or I'll do it right now.'

'My name's Ellie,' she persisted, edging closer. 'I want to help.'

The man let out a low growl and stared up at the sky for a moment before looking down at the tracks. 'Leave me alone.'

'*No!*' she cried. 'Whatever's wrong, it can't be bad enough to kill yourself over.'

'What would you know?' he grunted. 'You've got no idea how shit my life is.'

'So tell me,' she urged. 'I bet it's not half as bad as you think, and problems are always easier if you share them.'

The sound of a high-speed engine heading their way cut through the howling wind, and she swallowed nervously.

'Okay, you obviously don't want to tell me your problems,

so I'll tell you mine . . . I've got a really boring job, and my boss kept me behind today to do some work that someone else was supposed to do, so now I've missed my train and I'm going to be late home, and my husband's going to go mad, 'cos I've got my sister and her new boyfriend coming round for dinner and he can't stand her. I know she can be a bit of a witch, but I haven't seen her in months, so I'm hoping we—'

Ellie's words had been shooting out like machine-gun fire, but she abruptly stopped speaking when she saw the man's body tense, and her legs turned to jelly when she looked in the direction the train was coming from and saw the beam of its headlights slicing through the darkness.

The man's eyes were squeezed shut when she turned to him, and his fingers were loosening their grip on the rail. Aware that she had no time to waste, she lunged at him and threw her arms around his neck, yelling: 'If you jump, you'll take me over with you, so you won't just be killing yourself, you'll be killing me as well! Is that what you want?'

'Let go,' he croaked, his voice strangled by the pressure of her arms crushing his windpipe. 'I need to do this.'

'No you *don't*,' she cried, her face contorting with pain as her muscles began to cramp. 'Stop this now, I'm begging you. *I DON'T WANT TO SEE YOU DIE, YOU SELFISH BASTARD!*'

Her last words came out on a scream, but they were swallowed up by the wind and the thunderous roar of the express train rushing by below. Almost losing her grip when the man's body suddenly sagged, she cried out with relief when he turned and scrambled over the barrier.

'Oh, thank God!' she gasped, slumping down beside him when he sank to his haunches. 'It's okay, you're safe now. It's going to be all right.'

'No, it's not,' he groaned, wiping his nose on his sleeve. 'You should have let me jump.'

'I couldn't have lived with myself,' Ellie said, releasing a shaky breath as her racing heart began to slow down. Casting a sneaky glance at her watch and wishing that the police would hurry up, she asked, 'Why did you want to do it? Is it money? A girl? Drugs?'

The man rested his elbows on his knees and dropped his face into his hands. 'Forget it. It's not your problem.'

'I think it kind of is, seeing as you nearly took me with you,' Ellie reminded him. 'At least tell me your name so I know who to curse when I have nightmares about this in the future.'

'Just leave me alone,' he moaned. 'There wasn't supposed to be anyone around when I did it, so why did you have to turn up and ruin everything?'

'I'm glad I did,' Ellie said unapologetically. 'And when you get over whatever's making you feel like this, I'm sure *you*'ll be glad, too.'

'No, I won't,' he said. 'Everything's fucked up.'

Ellie saw the yellow stains on his fingers and, figuring that he probably needed a smoke as much as she did, reached into her handbag for her cigarettes. 'Here,' she said, lighting two and passing one to him.

'Cheers,' he muttered.

'You're welcome,' she said, sighing as the nicotine soothed her jangling nerves. 'I'm actually supposed to be giving up,' she admitted, squinting when the wind blew the smoke into her eyes. 'My husband thinks I've already stopped, so I have to buy them on the sly and hide them. Almost thirty years old, and I'm sneaking around like a naughty schoolgirl. Crazy, or what?'

The man gave her a puzzled look and took a deep drag on his cigarette.

Jumping when her phone suddenly started ringing, Ellie muttered, 'Speak of the devil,' when she took it out and saw Matt's name on the screen. Unable to face talking to him, because he'd want to know what she was doing, and she could hardly explain while she was sitting right next to the man, she pressed *Ignore* and switched it to silent before shoving it into her pocket.

'That your hubby?' the man asked.

Ellie nodded and took another pull on her cigarette as the phone began to vibrate against her hip.

'Why didn't you answer it?'

'I'll talk to him when I get home,' she said, wondering where the police had got to. They might no longer be needed, but *they* didn't know that, and she dreaded to think what could have happened if she hadn't been here.

'Sorry if I scared you,' the man apologized quietly. 'I honestly didn't think anyone would be around.'

He was staring down at his filthy trainers as he spoke, and Ellie's heart went out to him when she heard the misery in his voice. She'd once read that the people who threatened to commit suicide were the ones who didn't mean it. The fact that they'd pre-warned others of their intentions was a sign that they desperately wanted someone to talk them out of it, whereas the ones who *really* meant it told nobody; they simply crept away and did it.

'My name's Gareth,' he went on. 'And my nan died last week.'

'I'm so sorry,' Ellie said softly. 'Were you close?'

'Yeah, very.' He sniffed. 'She was more like my mum than my nan. I could tell her anything, and she never put me down or made me feel stupid.'

'Is that why you tried to jump?'

'Part of it, yeah. That, and finding out my girlfriend's been screwing around behind my back.'

'That's awful.' Ellie frowned. 'But now you know she's a cheat, is she worth losing your life over?'

'She was all I had left,' Gareth said plaintively. 'No one else gives a toss, but Lynn's been great, and I really thought we had something – you know?'

Ellie nodded and waited for him to go on.

'The council turned up at my nan's this morning and gave me a week to get out,' he told her. 'I went round to Lynn's to ask if I could stay there for a bit, but she didn't answer the door, so

I figured she'd probably gone shopping. I know where she keeps her spare key, so I let myself in. And that's when I caught her – in bed with some bloke.'

Ellie heard the bitterness in his voice and sneaked a glance at her watch. Her train was due in ten minutes, and she absolutely couldn't miss it. But she didn't want to leave him while he was still feeling like this.

'I know it's painful,' she said. 'And you probably won't believe me when I say that it'll get easier in time, but I promise it will. I've lost people I cared about, and it feels like you're never going to smile again. But life does go on. It *has* to.'

'Easy to say when you've got somewhere to live,' Gareth muttered. 'This time next week I'll be homeless.'

'Isn't there someone you can stay with?' Ellie asked. 'What about your parents?'

'They've never given a shit about me.'

'Friends, then? Or how about a hostel?'

Before Gareth could reply to that, he heard the wail of a police siren in the near distance and gave Ellie an accusing look. 'Did you call the pigs?'

'Sorry, but I had to,' she admitted. 'Don't worry; they'll probably go once they've seen that you're okay.'

'No they won't,' he said, scrambling to his feet. 'You don't know those bastards like I do. They'll have me sectioned for this.'

'I'm sure they won't,' Ellie said, frowning as she too got up. 'Look, my train will be here soon and I'll have to get going, but

14

I can spare a few more minutes if you'd rather not speak to them on your own?'

'Nah, I'd best go before they get here,' he said, taking a last drag on the cigarette before flicking the butt over the railing.

'Will you be okay?' she asked. 'You're not going to try anything like this again are you?'

Gareth shoved his hands into his pockets and shook his head. 'I've lost my nerve now. Anyhow, I reckon my nan must have sent you to save me, so I can't, can I?'

'Anyone would have done the same,' Ellie said modestly.

'No they wouldn't,' he countered. 'You're one of the good ones, and I won't forget this.'

When he turned and walked away, Ellie watched until he'd been swallowed by the shadows and then started making her way down to the platform. Her phone began to vibrate again as her train came into view, and she quickened her step as she pulled it out of her pocket. Sure that it would be Matt, and that she was about to get an earful for ignoring his calls, she was relieved to see an unknown number on the screen.

It was the operator she'd spoken to when she rang the police. After apologizing for the delay and explaining that the officers had been diverted to an emergency in the town centre, he asked what was happening.

'Everything's okay now,' she told him. 'I talked to the man and he climbed over the railing. He was upset about something, but we had a chat and he seemed fine when he left.'

'Did you get his name?' the operator asked.

'I think it might have been Dave,' Ellie lied, remembering Gareth's reaction when he'd realized she had reported him to the police. 'Anyway, sorry for wasting your time, but my train's here, so I'll have to go.'

As soon as she'd cut the call, her phone vibrated again. It was a message from Matt.

They're here! it read. **Where the fuck are you????**
Sorry, train delayed, she replied. **Be home soon xx**

Sighing, she slipped the phone into her bag and wearily boarded the train. Glad that the carriage was empty, she flopped into a window seat and rested her head on the glass of the window. She had never experienced anything quite as terrifying as that in her entire life before, and she was still shaking from the rush of adrenalin that had coursed through her body when she'd thrown her arms around Gareth's neck. She could only imagine how low he must have been feeling to contemplate killing himself, and she hoped his girlfriend would be ashamed of herself when she realized how deeply she'd hurt him. But, more importantly, she hoped that Gareth had meant it when he'd said he didn't have the nerve to try it again, because it would be a tragedy if he lost his life at his young age.

2

Ellie called in at the local off-licence after getting off the train, and bought two bottles of wine before walking the rest of the way home. A familiar sensation of gloom settled over her when the high-rise block of council flats where she and Matt lived came into view. They'd moved on to this estate shortly after getting married, and it was only meant to have been a temporary stop-gap until they had saved enough to put down a deposit on a house of their own. But things hadn't worked out quite as planned, and they had been stuck here ever since. And, sometimes – *often* – Ellie wondered if they were ever going to escape.

A row of vandalized garages lined the ground floor of Ellie's block, and she saw the silhouetted figures of several hooded youths huddled in the mouth of one as she approached the communal door. The few residents who could afford cars had taken to parking in the open car park at the side of the block, because they were sick of coming down in the morning to find their vehicles looted or burnt out. The garages now served as a meeting point for junkies and winos, and a couple of prostitutes had set up shop in there at the end of summer, so used condoms had joined the syringes, empty cider bottles, crushed beer cans and fast-food wrappers that spilled out of every doorway. It was a depressing sight, and Ellie averted her gaze as she hurried past.

A flashy silver car was parked in one of the disabled bays close to the door. She glanced at it as she let herself in, and shook her head at the stupidity of the owner for leaving it there. With those youths hanging about, it was likely to be stripped of anything remotely saleable as soon as the coast was clear.

Surprised to hear the sound of laughter drifting out from the living room when she entered the flat a few minutes later, Ellie put the wine bottles down on the hall table and quickly took off her coat before heading in.

Her sister, Holly, was lounging on the sofa with her legs draped over the lap of a man who Ellie assumed must be the new boyfriend. Matt was sitting in his armchair facing them, and he looked remarkably relaxed, Ellie thought, considering he claimed to hate Holly and had been sulking ever since he'd heard they were coming round. Hoping that it was a sign that he was coming out of his recent slump, she leaned down and kissed him on the cheek.

The smile didn't leave Matt's lips, but it wasn't reflected in his eyes when he looked up at her. 'What kept you? I was worried.'

'Sorry,' she apologized. 'I got caught up in something, and it all went a bit crazy.'

'Never mind all that!' Holly leapt up and spread her arms. 'Come and give your baby sister some love.'

Ellie winced when Holly gave her a rib-crushing hug. There were only three years between them, but they couldn't have been more different if they tried. Ellie had always been the quiet, responsible one; Holly the gregarious fun-time girl. And little had changed, because Holly, despite being almost twenty-seven, still dressed and acted like a teenager.

Holly pushed Ellie away after a moment and looked her up and down. 'You've put weight on. You're not pregnant, are you?'

'No, I'm not!' Ellie spluttered as a blush seared her cheeks. Holly had always been tactless, but this was a new record even for her, because Ellie had only been in the room for a matter of seconds before the first insult had landed.

'Well, you're definitely bigger than you were last time I saw you,' Holly went on obliviously. 'You should try going to the gym, like me; it doesn't half tone you up.' She slapped her own flat stomach to emphasize how taut it was.

'You've been going to the gym?' Ellie's eyebrows rose in surprise. 'Since when?'

'Since I went with Tony and saw all the fit birds giving him the eye,' said Holly. 'Not that I'm worried, 'cos he knows what'll happen if I ever catch him looking back.'

'Why would I be interested in anyone else when I've got

you?' the man on the sofa drawled, his eyes twinkling as he grinned at her.

'And you just make sure it stays that way, or there'll be trouble,' Holly warned playfully. Then, to Ellie: 'This is Tony, in case you hadn't guessed.'

'Pleased to meet you.' Ellie extended her hand.

'You, too.' Tony leaned forward and shook it.

'That's not your car by the door, is it?' Ellie asked when she saw a set of keys on the table beside him. Grimacing when he nodded, she said, 'You might want to think about moving it. Some lads were eyeing it up when I came in.'

'It's okay,' Tony replied unconcernedly. 'I said I'd slip them a few quid if they look after it for me.'

Ellie was about to point out that the lads would get far more if they stripped it, but Matt said, 'Everyone ready to eat?' before she had the chance, and Holly and Tony both declared that they were starving.

'Did you get the wine?' Matt asked Ellie as he pushed himself stiffly up to his feet.

'It's in the hall,' she said, guessing from his tone that he'd expected her to say she'd forgotten it.

Holly sniffed the air when Matt opened the kitchen door. 'That smells lovely. What are we having?'

'Spag bol,' he told her over his shoulder.

'My favourite,' she grinned. 'I'd eat it every single day if I could cook.'

20

'You should have paid more attention when Mum was trying to teach you,' said Ellie. 'It's really easy.'

'Sack that!' Holly snorted. 'Why do it myself when I can pay someone to do it for me?'

'You always were a lazy mare,' Ellie teased. 'That's why I was surprised when you said you'd been going to the gym.'

'I could do with a hand in here,' Matt called out.

'Sorry, won't be a sec,' Ellie called back. 'Just getting the wine.'

She went out into the hall and picked up the bottles. Holly and Tony were talking quietly when she returned, and she felt a tug of envy when she saw the loving way they were gazing at each other. They were a good-looking couple: Holly slim and pretty, with expressive brown eyes and thick honey-blonde hair that had been restyled into a bob since Ellie had last seen her; Tony dark-haired and handsome, with friendly blue eyes, a toned physique, and an affable manner. He was actually pretty much a clone of all the men Holly had dated before him, and she didn't have a good track record when it came to maintaining relationships, so it remained to be seen if he would last any longer than his predecessors. But they seemed happy enough right now.

Wistful for the days when she and Matt had looked at each other with anything remotely resembling intimacy or love, Ellie placed the bottles on the drop-leaf dining table and went into the kitchen to help him.

'About time!' he hissed, pushing the door shut behind her.

'Keep your voice down,' she whispered. 'They'll hear you.'

'Should have thought about that before you decided to leave me to entertain them on my own.'

'Please, Matt, not now. We can talk later. Let's just have dinner and—'

'Knock, knock!' Holly popped her head around the door. 'Anything I can do to help?'

Glad of the interruption, Ellie nodded at one of the cupboards. 'You can get some glasses out of there, if you don't mind?'

Matt had gone back to plating up the spaghetti. Edging past him, Ellie opened the fridge and took out the bowl of salad she'd prepared before leaving for work that morning and then quickly followed her sister into the living room.

When they were all seated and had helped themselves to salad, Holly said, 'Matt tells us you've got a new job, Ells?'

'Yeah, that's right.' Ellie twisted the top off one of the bottles of wine and glugged a measure into her glass before offering to pour one for Matt.

'How come you left your last one? I thought you liked it there?'

'I fancied a change.' Ellie passed the bottle to Tony when Matt shook his head. 'And my new place is closer to home, so I don't have to set off quite so early in the morning.'

'I don't know how you can stand being stuck in an office all day.' Holly pulled a face. 'They reckon your periods start to coincide when you work closely with other women, and my moods are bad enough without having to put up with some other bitch's PMT. I'd end up killing someone.'

'It's not that bad,' said Ellie. 'But they annoy me when they pull sickies, like the one who's supposed to deal with the invoices did today. That's why I was late: because I had to stay behind to deal with a pile she'd left and ended up missing my train. Then someone tried to jump off the bridge, and I had to talk him down, so I nearly missed the next one as well.'

'Seriously?' Holly's eyes widened.

'Mmmm.' Ellie nodded and took a swig of wine before continuing: 'I saw him climb over the railing, and you know how you just know something bad's about to happen? Well, I *knew* he was going to jump, so I called the police and went up to talk to him. He was only young, and he was in a right state, poor thing. It turned out his nan died last week, and the council came round this morning and gave him a week to get out.'

'Was he living with her?' Holly asked, smiling at Tony when he filled her glass and passed it to her.

'I think so. But that's not the worst of it. After the council came, he went round to his girlfriend's to ask if he could stay there, and caught her in bed with another man!'

'Wow, what a bitch,' said Holly. 'But that's no reason to try and kill yourself,' she added unsympathetically. 'We've all had our hearts broken, but we don't all lose the plot like that. Sounds like a right loser, if you ask me.'

'I think it knocked him for six, so soon after losing his nan,' said Ellie. 'I felt sorry for him.'

'That's 'cos you're a bleeding heart,' Holly scoffed. 'Remember when you brought that tramp home that time and asked Mum if he could live with us?'

'Oh, don't,' Ellie groaned.

'What's this?' Tony asked, smiling curiously as he ate.

'She found this old tramp rooting through the skip behind Sainsbury's,' Holly explained. 'He absolutely reeked of shit, and I swear you could see fleas leaping about in his hair. My mum had an absolute fit and chased him down the road with the hoover pipe. It was so funny, I nearly wet myself!'

'It wasn't my fault,' said Ellie. 'Mum was always telling us to be kind to people who are less fortunate, so I thought she'd want to help him.'

'What, by letting him move in and infest the house with fleas?' Holly snorted. 'But that's you all over, that: always picking up lame dogs.'

Out of the corner of her eye, Ellie saw Matt's cheek muscles twitch and guessed that he probably thought Holly's comment had been aimed at him. Hurriedly changing the subject, she said, 'I'm sure Tony doesn't want to hear all that old rubbish, so tell me about you two. Where did you meet?'

'We bumped into each other on the Tube,' Holly told her. 'And when I say bumped, I mean *literally*, 'cos he nearly knocked me right under the bloody thing! When I'd stopped shouting at him, he took me for a drink, and one thing led to another – like it does. We've been together ever since.'

'The Tube?' Ellie repeated. 'As in London?'

'Yeah, I've been living there for six months. Thought I'd told you?'

'No. Last I heard, you were moving to France to live with ...' Ellie tailed off, unsure if she should mention in front of Tony the name of the man Holly had been raving about the last time Ellie had spoken to her.

'Pierre?' Holly wrinkled her nose in distaste. 'Nah! He turned out to be a right tosser, so I binned him off and came home. I stayed at Mum's for a few nights, but she did my head in, so I called Marie – remember her from school? The fat one with big tits?'

'All your friends looked like that,' Ellie said, remembering that Holly had deliberately chosen bigger girls to hang around with, because she'd enjoyed being the slim, good-looking one of the bunch.

'No they didn't,' Holly argued. 'Jackie's boobs were smaller than mine, and Keira's were practically non-existent. Marie's were massive, but she had them reduced a couple of years ago, so now she's just fat. Anyway, I heard she'd moved to London, and I fancied a change, so I rang her and asked if I could stay at hers for a bit. I met Tony a few days after I got there, and he asked me to move in with him the same night – didn't you, babe?'

'Sure did,' said Tony, winking at her as he shovelled a forkful of food into his mouth.

'You don't sound like a southerner,' Ellie commented, trying to ignore the waves of contempt she could feel coming from

Matt. He hated it when people talked with food in their mouths, and she was sure he'd add it to his list of things to moan about when they'd gone.

'That's 'cos he's from Wigan,' said Holly. 'And that's why we get on so well: 'cos I'm a down-to-earth northerner, and not some *up-my-own-arser*, like London girls.'

'You always say that, but they're not that bad when you get to know them,' Tony said as he scraped up the last bit of food on his plate. Sitting back when he'd swallowed it, he said, 'Thanks; that was delicious.'

'There's plenty left if you'd like more?' Ellie offered.

'No, he doesn't,' Holly answered for him. 'I don't want him getting fat.'

Ellie flashed Tony a *poor you* smile before asking Holly, 'So what have you been doing with yourself in London? Are you working?'

'Mmmm.' Holly nodded as she took a swig of wine. 'I've started a fashion and beauty blog.'

'Really?' Ellie was curious. 'I didn't realize you could get paid for that.'

'You don't get a wage, as such,' Holly explained. 'But if you get enough followers, companies pay you to advertise their shit. I haven't made any actual cash yet, but I get loads of freebies, so I can't complain.'

'*I* can.' Tony rolled his eyes. 'You can't move in my place for boxes of face-cream and smelly stuff.'

'You love it,' Holly said dismissively. Then, to Ellie: 'Hey, you haven't mentioned my hair yet. What do you think?'

'It's lovely,' Ellie said truthfully, wishing she had the time and money to restyle her own boring straight brown hair.

'I wasn't sure what I wanted, so Tony persuaded me to let the stylist loose on it,' Holly went on. 'She's supposed to be one of the best in London, and it cost an absolute fortune, so it's a good job it suits me or I'd have sued the arse off her!'

She paused to take another swig of wine, and then tilted her head and peered at Matt. 'You're being very quiet, brother-in-law. Not boring you, am I?'

'Not at all.' He replied coolly. 'It's my favourite subject.'

'Wow, talk about facetious!' Holly laughed. 'I hope he shows more enthusiasm when *you* make an effort to tart yourself up, Ells?'

Ellie smiled and carried on eating. It was a long time since she and Matt had been able to afford to go out, so she'd had no reason to get dressed up. And the way things were going, she sometimes wondered if she would ever see the inside of a nightclub or restaurant again.

Determined not to start thinking about their money worries, because she was likely to burst into tears if she thought about the bills that were building up in the drawer, Ellie finished her meal and reached for the wine bottle to refill her glass.

'Go easy,' Matt said quietly.

Holly caught it and drew her head back. 'Who put you on

booze patrol, Mr Killjoy? She can drink as much as she likes.'

'No, he's right,' Ellie said, putting the bottle down. 'I've been working all day, and I have to be up early in the morning, so I probably shouldn't have any more.'

'God, when did you get so *boring*?' Holly sneered, snatching the bottle up and emptying the contents into her own glass. 'I remember when you used to outdrink the lot of us.'

'That was a long time ago,' Ellie said quietly.

'Not that long,' said Holly. 'You're getting old before your time, Sis.'

'You're not that far behind me,' Ellie reminded her.

'No one would ever guess it to look at us,' Holly snorted. 'I'm not being funny, but you haven't half let yourself go.'

'Holly,' Tony cautioned quietly.

'*What*?' she asked innocently. 'I'm not lying; she *has*.' Then, turning to Ellie, she frowned. 'You're not ill, are you?'

'No, of course not,' said Ellie. 'Why would you think that?'

'I don't know . . . ' Holly peered at her thoughtfully across the table. 'I could always tell when you were hiding something, and you're being well cagey tonight. It's not us, is it? Were you supposed to be doing something else and we've ruined your plans?'

'We didn't have plans,' Ellie assured her. 'And I've been looking forward to seeing you, so I don't know where all this is coming from.'

'It's coming from you acting weird.'

'But I'm not.'

'Yes, you *are*!' Holly slapped her hand down on the table-top, causing wine to jump out of her glass and soak the tablecloth. 'I'm not stupid; I've got eyes. Matt was absolutely fine before you got home, now he's clammed up, and you're not being yourself. If you didn't want us here, why did you invite us over?'

'You're imagining things,' Ellie insisted, smiling to lighten the dipping mood. 'If I'm acting weird – which I don't think I am, by the way – it's probably 'cos I'm a bit tired. And I'm still thinking about that lad on the bridge.'

'Well, stop it, 'cos he's not your problem,' Holly grunted. 'This is supposed to be a special occasion, so get drinking and let's start having some fun!'

Ellie frowned when Holly swallowed her wine and then immediately opened the second bottle to pour another glassful. She'd hardly touched her food and would soon be steaming if she carried on knocking it back at this rate. And that wouldn't be good, because she could be an unpleasant, argumentative drunk.

'Are we all done?' Matt abruptly stood up.

'Need a hand?' Tony offered when he started gathering the plates together.

'I've got it,' Matt said, waving for him to stay seated.

Holly watched through narrowed eyes as Matt limped into the kitchen. 'Why's he walking like that?'

'His leg's been playing up, and I don't think the painkillers are working as well as they used to,' Ellie said quietly, hoping that Matt couldn't hear them.

'Don't tell me he's still milking that old shit?' Holly sneered. 'It's four years since the crash; surely his leg's healed by now?'

'It's five, actually,' Ellie corrected her. 'But it was a complicated fracture, so it might not get any better than this.'

'Bollocks! I bet he's been better for ages, and he's stringing it out to punish you.'

'Don't be ridiculous.'

'Oh, come on . . . it's obvious he blamed you for crippling him. Mind you, it's his own fault for getting in the car in the first place, if you ask me, 'cos you always were a shit driver. How many times did you take your test before you passed? Three . . . four?'

'I think we should go.' Tony pushed his chair back. 'It's been a long day.'

'Aw, not yet,' Holly complained, looping her arms around his neck to prevent him from standing up. 'We've still got to tell her about—'

'It can wait,' he interrupted, giving her a meaningful look.

'Yes, *sir*!' Holly giggled and gave a salute. Then, turning to Ellie with a gloating smile on her lips, she said, 'See how much my man loves me? Bet *Brat* doesn't take care of you like my Toe takes care of me?'

Tony spoke quietly into her ear before she could say anything else, and she held up her hands in a gesture of contrition before pushing herself up to her feet.

'Sorry, Sis,' she apologized, walking clumsily around the table. 'My big gob's running away with me, but you know I love you really, don't you?'

'Yeah, I know,' Ellie said, sighing when Holly dragged her up off her seat and hugged her. 'Why don't you go and sit on the sofa while I put the kettle on? You'll be fine once you've had a coffee.'

'Only if you put booze in it,' Holly grinned, swaying on her feet when Ellie broke free of the embrace. 'And none of this cheap shit . . .' She flapped her hand at the wine bottles. 'It's time to break out the champers, 'cos we gotta celebrate, baby!'

Tony jumped up to catch her when she lost her balance. 'Sorry, but I reckon I should get her to bed,' he said to Ellie. 'We had an early start this morning, and she had a few drinks before we left the hotel this evening.'

'You're probably right,' Ellie agreed when Holly laid her head on his chest and closed her eyes.

'Come on, you.' Tony guided Holly out into the hall as if she were a child. 'Let's get your coat on.'

'Matt . . .' Ellie called through the kitchen door. 'Holly and Tony are leaving.'

Matt wandered out to join them in the hallway. 'Going already?' he asked, as if he'd been having a great time.

'She's had too much to drink, so I'm taking her back to the hotel to sleep it off,' Tony explained. 'Sorry for ruining dinner.'

'You haven't ruined anything,' Matt assured him as they shook hands. 'It was good to meet you.'

'You, too,' said Tony. 'And dinner's on me next time. When Holly sobers up, I'll get her to ring Ellie to arrange it.'

When Matt opened the front door to show them out, Holly threw her arms around Ellie again. 'Love you, Sis.'

'Love you, too,' Ellie said amusedly as she disentangled herself. 'Now go and get some sleep. We'll talk tomorrow.'

Shaking her head as she watched Tony lead her sister away down the corridor, Ellie said, 'It's been a while since I've seen her in that state. I hope she doesn't get sick in the car.'

She turned to Matt, but he'd already gone inside. Sighing, she followed him in and closed the door. He was in the bathroom, so she made her way to the kitchen and picked up the dirty plates he'd left on the ledge. She'd just scraped the remnants of spaghetti and salad into the bin and was about to put them in the sink when he appeared in the doorway.

'That was nice, wasn't it?' she said, giving him a tentative smile.

'Why do you do that?' he demanded.

'Do what?'

'That thing you do when you know I'm pissed off. Acting normal, because you think it'll make me forget about everything.'

Ellie put down the plates and leaned wearily against the countertop. 'Okay, let's get it over with. What have I done this time?'

'Oh, I don't know . . .' Matt narrowed his eyes. 'How about

we start with ignoring my calls, when you know that drives me crazy? And then leaving me to deal with those two on my own?'

'You seemed to be getting along fine when I got home,' Ellie pointed out.

'Only because, unlike *you, I've* got manners,' said Matt. 'Would it have killed you to let me know what was happening? Or were you too busy sticking your nose into that other idiot's business to worry about me?'

'He was going to kill himself,' Ellie reminded him. 'And I'd already missed my train, so what was I supposed to do - sit there and watch him do it?'

'Oh, yeah, the *missed train . . .*' Matt drew quotation marks in the air with his fingers. 'How very convenient.'

'I didn't miss it on purpose,' Ellie protested. 'Richard asked me to stay behind to do some work, so—'

'*Richard*?' Matt raised an eyebrow. 'What happened to Mr Brown?'

Annoyed with herself for blushing when she had done nothing wrong, Ellie said, 'Everyone calls each other by their first name.'

'Really?' said Matt. 'And was *everyone* there when you stayed behind today, or was it just you and *Richard*?'

'Please don't do this,' she groaned, massaging her temples when they started to throb. 'There is nothing going on between me and my boss.'

'Like you'd admit it if there was,' he sneered. 'I should have known you were screwing around behind my back again. No wonder you're enjoying your new job so fucking much. God, I'm such an idiot!'

Ellie's patience snapped, and she banged her fist down on the ledge. 'I have *never* screwed around behind your back, and I'm not doing this again, Matt, so you'd better stop it right now. I lost my last job because of your paranoia, and I can't afford to lose this one as well.'

'Don't try to twist this round and make me out to be the bad one,' Matt shot back. 'I'm not the one who goes around flaunting myself every chance I get.'

'*Flaunting* myself?' Ellie repeated incredulously. 'Have you actually looked at me lately, Matt? I dress like a flaming fifty-year-old so *you* can't accuse me of trying to attract attention to myself. It's no wonder Holly said I've let myself go. I look disgusting!'

'It's better than dressing like a tart, like her.'

'*Stop it!*' Ellie yelled, conscious that the neighbours could probably hear every word, but too upset to care. 'I've had a shit day, and all I wanted was to have a nice catch-up with Holly, but you couldn't let me have that, could you? And God knows what she thought when you went quiet as soon as I walked in. It was embarrassing!'

'I'm surprised she noticed, considering all she did was talk about herself – as usual.'

'She was telling us what she's been up to. It's called having a conversation.'

'That wasn't a conversation. She was just bragging to make you think she's got a great life.'

'Maybe she *has* got a great life. She certainly looks happy. And Tony obviously thinks a lot of her, so—'

'Oh, I wondered when we'd get round to *him*,' Matt pounced. 'Fancy him, did you?'

'You can't be serious?' Ellie gasped. 'It's the first time I've ever clapped eyes on the man.'

'And you couldn't have made it more obvious that you liked what you saw,' said Matt. 'Don't think I didn't notice the sneaky smiles you kept giving each other. *Oh, yes, Tony, I'd love to have dinner with you,*' he mimicked. '*And I'll bring some wine to get Holly pissed again, so I can have you all to myself.*'

'You're losing it, Matt, you seriously are,' Ellie said quietly. 'I didn't say a word when he mentioned going to them for dinner. And he invited *both* of us, not just me.'

Matt twisted his lips into an ugly sneer and marched out, and Ellie muttered 'Shit!' when he slammed the bedroom door so hard it rattled the crockery on the draining board.

She hadn't meant to fly off the handle like that, but it was hard not to retaliate when Matt accused her of things she hadn't done. Her boss was gay and pushing sixty, so it was laughable that Matt thought something was going on between them. As for Tony, he was her sister's boyfriend, so Ellie would never look at him in that way. And she wouldn't have been interested even if he hadn't been with Holly, because she loved Matt. She only wished Matt would remember that and stop accusing her of lusting after every man who crossed her path.

3

Matt's side of the bed was empty when Ellie woke up the next morning. He'd left a note on the bedside table telling her that he'd gone fishing but would be home in time to make dinner. It was signed with a kiss, and a wave of relief washed over Ellie at the sight of it. His back had been turned when she came to bed after cleaning up, and he hadn't responded when she'd said goodnight. It wasn't unusual for him to ignore her for several days following an argument as heated as the one they'd had last night, but that kiss told her she was forgiven. For what, she wasn't quite sure; but it was easier to let it go than demand answers and risk setting him off again.

Long Lane station was always busy in the morning, and Ellie was jostled from all sides when she stepped off the train a short time later. Carried along to the exit by the crowd, she glanced up at the footbridge and shuddered when she recalled the events of the previous night. Holly had been right when she'd said that Gareth wasn't her problem, and God knew Ellie had enough worries of her own without adding to them by worrying about a stranger – an unstable stranger, at that. She had acted on pure instinct when she'd thrown her arms around his neck, but now, in the cold light of day, she realized she was lucky he hadn't dragged her over with him. It was a sobering thought, and she vowed to keep her nose out of other people's problems in future.

A huge stack of pallets was blocking the pavement when Ellie reached the office, and she had to squeeze past them to get inside. Two of the three girls who worked alongside her were seated at their desks: Jackie applying make-up; Sue painting her nails. Adele was missing again, and Ellie was irritated to see another stack of invoices sitting on her desk. A glance at the other desks told her that neither of the other girls were sharing the load, and that pissed her off even more. They were all younger than her, but they'd worked here for longer and clearly thought that gave them superiority. If she didn't need the job so desperately, she'd have told them to stop taking the piss. But she couldn't afford to jeopardize her position by kicking off, so she kept her mouth shut.

'Something wrong?' Sue asked innocently when Ellie picked up the invoices and slapped them down on the other side of her desk.

'No, everything's fine.' Ellie forced a smile. 'Just hate these cold mornings.'

'Get a brew and warm yourself up,' Sue suggested.

'Ooh, yes please,' said Jackie, her gaze riveted to the mirror in her hand. 'Tea, two sugars.'

'If you're making one for her, you might as well make one for me as well,' Sue said, as if she hadn't planned it that way all along.

Still smiling, determined not to let them think they'd got one over on her, Ellie made her way into the kitchen and filled the kettle. In her last job, she had been one of the girls, but she felt like an outsider here – and the way they treated her, she couldn't see that changing anytime soon.

A gust of cold air snaked around her ankles when the main office door opened, and she sighed when she heard her boss ask 'Where's thingumajig?'

'In the kitchen,' Sue said, to the accompaniment of drawers opening and closing as she and Jackie quickly put away their cosmetics.

Richard popped his head around the door and smiled at Ellie as he unwound the long scarf that was wrapped around his neck. 'Coffee for me; strong, black, no sugar. And when you've finished, I've left a couple of cassettes on your desk. Could you get them typed up ASAP?'

Teeth clenched, Ellie nodded and took another cup out of the cupboard.

The girls had their heads down when she carried their drinks through, so she placed their cups on their desks before taking Richard's into his office. Then, sitting down at last, she

39

worked her way through the invoices before making a start on her own job.

Headphones on, she slotted the first of the microcassettes Richard had left on her desk into the audio transcriber, and spent the rest of the morning typing out the letters he'd dictated – which was no easy job, because he had a speech impediment that made his words indecipherable at times.

Desperate for a smoke by lunchtime, Ellie downed tools, grabbed her bag and coat, and rushed outside before her co-workers had even registered what time it was. Pausing to light a cigarette, she puffed on it as she walked down to the grubby cafe at the opposite end of the road from the pub where the other girls always opted for a liquid lunch.

After ordering her usual tuna sandwich and coffee, she took a seat at a pavement table and fished her phone out of her bag to check for messages. Holly had rung an hour earlier, so she rang her back.

'Hey . . .' Holly answered sheepishly. 'How are you today?'

'A lot better than you sound,' said Ellie. 'Got a hangover, have we?'

'Oh, don't,' Holly groaned. 'I was sick as a dog all night, and I woke up with a banging headache.'

'Serves you right for drinking so much.'

'Yeah, well, never again. I'm going teetotal from now on.'

'You always say that.'

'I mean it this time,' Holly insisted. 'Anyway, shut up about that, 'cos it's making me feel sick just thinking about it. I rang to ask what you're doing tonight?'

'Having a quiet night in,' Ellie told her, hoping that she wouldn't ask if she and Tony could come over again. 'Matt's cooking.'

'Well, ring him and tell him not to bother,' Holly ordered. 'You're eating with us tonight.'

'I can't,' Ellie said. 'He's gone fishing, and he never takes his phone.'

'Why not?'

'Because he doesn't like to be disturbed, and he reckons it scares the fish.'

'Whatever,' Holly said dismissively. 'Send him a message for when he gets home, then. The table's booked for eight, so be here by quarter to.'

'I don't know where you are,' Ellie reminded her. 'And I'm not promising we'll make it. I'll have to let you know when I've spoken to Matt.'

'We're at the Lowry,' said Holly. 'And we're going home in the morning, so you'd better come.'

Sighing when Holly abruptly hung up, Ellie sent a quick message to Matt before reaching for her sandwich. She didn't really fancy going out tonight, and she was pretty sure that Matt wouldn't be overly keen to see Holly again so soon. But if they were going back to London in the morning, she supposed she didn't have much choice.

4

Matt was standing at the cooker stirring a bubbling pan of chicken curry when Ellie got home. When he heard her come into the kitchen, he turned his head and smiled.

'Good day?'

'It was okay,' she said, going over and kissing him on the cheek. 'Didn't you get my message?'

'I haven't checked my phone since I got home. I was a bit late, so I thought I'd best get on with this. Was it important?'

'I spoke to Holly at lunchtime, and she invited us over to the hotel for dinner.'

'Oh, yeah?' Matt tasted the food and reached for the pepper pot. 'When?'

'Tonight.'

'*Tonight?*' He looked back at her and frowned. 'But you knew I was cooking. I left you a note.'

'Yeah, I know, and I told her we'd have to do it another time. But they're leaving in the morning, so there won't be another chance. I did tell you in the message.'

'I see.' Matt put down the pepper and started stirring again.

Aware that he wasn't happy, Ellie said, 'Don't worry about it; I'll ring her and tell her I've got a migraine. She knows how sick I get with them.'

Matt sighed and put down the spoon. 'No, it's fine.' He switched the cooker off and placed the lid on the pan. 'This will keep till tomorrow.'

'Are you sure?' Ellie asked. 'I don't mind giving it a miss if you'd rather stay in.'

'I'm positive,' Matt insisted. 'It's been ages since we've been anywhere nice. And Flash Harry's paying, so we'd be stupid to turn it down, wouldn't we?'

He grinned, and Ellie gave him an uncertain smile in return. His mood had definitely lifted, but the 'Flash Harry' comment didn't bode well. Needing to know if he was genuinely feeling better, or was only making an effort because he felt guilty, she said, 'What did you think of Tony, by the way?'

'Seemed okay.' Matt shrugged. 'Better than the last loser she brought round.'

'Yeah, he was a nightmare,' Ellie agreed. 'So you're sure you don't mind going tonight?'

Matt shook his head and glanced at the clock. 'What time are they expecting us?'

'Quarter to eight.'

'Okay, you go and get ready while I clean up in here,' Matt said, pushing her toward the door. 'And wear that purple dress I like.'

'Really?' Ellie hesitated. 'You don't think it's a bit low-cut?'

'It's perfect,' Matt insisted.

'Not sure it still fits, but I'll try it,' Ellie said, giving him one last searching look before she left the room. If he was putting on an act, it was very convincing.

Ellie had struggled to get into the purple dress and had wanted to change into something else, but Matt had told her she looked beautiful, so she'd left it on. She regretted that decision as soon as they walked into the Lowry Hotel, because there was some sort of function taking place and the foyer was swarming with men in expensive-looking suits and women with immaculate hair and make-up wearing designer dresses and shoes. Ellie's clothes looked cheap in comparison, and the sleeves of her dress were so tight her arms were beginning to go numb.

Matt looked handsome in his only suit. It was dark grey, but there were faded patches on the shoulders from being hung in the wardrobe for so long, and Ellie guessed that he felt as out of place as she did when she saw him tugging nervously at his shirt collar as he surreptitiously eyed the other men. But just as she was about to suggest that they sneak out and go home, her sister appeared at the top of the staircase.

'Hey, you made it!' Holly called, not seeming to care that everyone had turned to look at her as she made her way down the stairs in a floaty turquoise dress and silver stiletto-heeled shoes. 'I was about to send out a search party.'

'You look amazing,' Ellie said when she reached them and hugged them both. 'I love that dress.'

'Tony bought it for me in Paris,' Holly said, giving a twirl. 'Gorgeous, isn't it?'

'Lovely,' Ellie agreed.

'You look very nice, too.' Holly repaid the compliment. 'Is that a new frock?'

'No, I've had it for ages,' Ellie said, wishing that she hadn't chosen to wear her fake-fur jacket over it, because she was already sweating.

'Suits you,' said Holly, before turning to Matt. 'And you're looking rather dapper, too, brother-in-law. Isn't that your wedding suit?'

'Mmmm,' he murmured, shoving his hands into his trouser pockets.

Holly spotted Tony at the top of the stairs and waved to him before linking one arm through Ellie's and the other through Matt's. 'Come on, you two; let's go and get a drink.'

'I'm so glad you came,' Tony said, greeting them with hugs and handshakes when they joined him on the first floor. 'I was worried you might have been annoyed with us after last night.'

'Not at all,' Ellie murmured, stepping away from him in case Matt accused her of standing too close.

'What's everyone having?' Tony asked, leading them to the bar.

'Me and Ells will have white wine,' Holly said, perching delicately on a bar stool.

'This is so posh,' Ellie whispered, feeling like an elephant as she clambered onto the neighbouring stool and gazed around the room. 'Don't you feel weird staying here?'

'It's not that good,' Holly replied breezily. 'Not compared to some of the other places we've stayed in, anyway. Tony took me to a castle in Scotland last month, and it was absolutely heaving with millionaires. You should have seen the diamonds the women were flashing. I've never seen so many outside of a jeweller's window. And I'm not talking your little chips, I'm talking serious *bling.*'

Ellie saw Matt roll his eyes and guessed that he was wishing he hadn't agreed to come. She didn't blame him, because she'd have given anything to be at home right now; cuddled up on the sofa, watching TV as they tucked into the curry he'd made.

When the barman placed their glasses in front of them, Ellie grabbed hers and swallowed a mouthful.

'Thirsty or hot?' Holly asked, sipping her own.

'Boiling,' Ellie admitted. 'Don't suppose you've got a cardi I can borrow?'

'Do I look like Mum?' Holly snorted.

'A wrap, then?'

'Just take your jacket off, you dozy cow.'

Before Ellie could explain that she didn't want to, because she could feel sweat-stains forming on the underarms of her dress, someone came out of the dining room and signalled to Tony that their table was ready.

Relieved that the seat she was shown to was against a wall,

Ellie slid the jacket down off her arms as Matt took the seat beside hers. 'How are you holding up?' she asked him quietly.

'Oh, I'm hunky dory,' he grunted. 'Tony's been telling me all about his fascinating life as a jet-setting playboy.'

'Seriously?'

'Nah, I'm exaggerating,' Matt whispered. 'But not half as much as *he* was.'

'I hope no one wants a starter?' Holly said loudly as she settled in the seat facing Ellie. 'I've been stuffing my face all week and it's starting to show, so I'd rather go straight to the main if no one minds?'

'Suits me,' Ellie agreed.

'Me, too,' said Matt.

'Well, I can't sit here eating a starter by myself, so I guess that's all four of us,' Tony said resignedly.

When they had all decided what they wanted and the waiter had taken their order, Holly leaned towards Tony and whispered, 'Can I tell them now?'

Ellie caught the exchange and gave her sister a curious look. 'Tell us what?'

Holly bit her lip and waited for Tony to give her the go-ahead. Squealing excitedly when he nodded, she said, 'We're going to Barbados for Christmas!'

'Lucky you,' said Ellie.

'Lucky you, too,' Holly grinned. ''Cos you're both coming with us!'

'What?' Ellie frowned.

'No, we're not,' Matt said.

'Sorry, but there's no way we can afford it,' Ellie added.

'Don't be daft,' Holly said dismissively. 'We're paying.'

Ellie felt Matt bristle beside her, and shook her head. 'It's a lovely offer, but we can't accept. I'll be working right up to Christmas Eve, and it's a busy time for the company, so there's no way my boss will let me leave any earlier.'

'You've got to come,' Holly insisted. 'We're getting married, and you're going to be my maid of honour.'

'Wow.' Stunned by the news that her sister had decided to settle down after years of hopping from one man to another, Ellie sat back in her seat. 'That's fantastic, and I'm really happy for you both. But why Barbados?'

'Because it's hot and exotic,' Holly said dreamily. 'And everything's booked, so you can't say no. We're having the ceremony on the beach at sunset, followed by a champagne barbeque with a live band. It's going to be amazing, and I've already picked out our dresses. Mine's white, obviously, and yours is peach with this big satin sash and—'

'Holly, stop,' Ellie cut her off. 'I honestly can't do it. Why don't you get married here and then go there for your honeymoon instead?'

'*No!*' Holly was no longer smiling. 'This is the biggest day of my life, and I want it to be special. And we're paying, so what's your problem?'

'*That*, for starters,' Matt said coolly. 'We're not charity cases.'

'Mate, that's the last thing we meant by it,' Tony tried to placate him. 'I'm paying for everyone, not just you.'

'Mum and Billy are fine with it,' Holly added, as if that made all the difference.

'You've invited *Billy*?' Ellie frowned.

'He's Mum's husband, and she's not going to go without him, so of course I invited him,' said Holly. 'Just like I'm inviting Matt.'

'What do you mean by that?' Ellie demanded.

Scowling at Tony when he nudged her with his elbow, Holly said, 'I didn't mean anything. I'm only saying I invited Billy 'cos of Mum, and I'm inviting Matt 'cos of you, that's all.'

'Cheers,' Matt muttered.

'What *is* your problem?' Holly rounded on him. 'You were fine last night, but now you're back to your usual sarky self. And you wonder why I wouldn't invite you to my wedding if I didn't have to?'

'Don't talk to him like that.' Ellie jumped to his defence.

'I'll talk to him any way I like,' said Holly. 'You might be scared of him, but I'm not.'

'What are you talking about?' Ellie stared at her in disbelief. 'I'm not scared of him.'

'Come off it,' Holly snorted. 'You'd have jumped at the chance to come to Barbados if it wasn't for him, and don't say you wouldn't. It's like you can't even breathe without asking his permission.'

Ellie could feel her blood pressure rising. 'You're going too far,' she said quietly. 'And you'd better stop before you say something you regret.'

'I'm only saying what everyone else already thinks,' Holly said bluntly. 'We've all had to walk on eggshells around him since the accident in case he gets upset, and you spend all your time making excuses for him. You've totally changed, and it pisses me off.'

Ellie gritted her teeth. She couldn't outright deny what Holly had said, because part of it was true. But she would never admit that out loud and risk having Matt think she was siding with her sister over him.

'Maybe I have changed,' she said. 'But it's not Matt's fault, it's called growing up. It hasn't been easy for either of us these last few years, but it's been a damn sight harder for him because he's the one who had to spend weeks in hospital and then lost his job over it.'

Tony had looked uncomfortable throughout the exchange, but he smiled when he saw the waiter heading their way with plates in his hands.

'Food's here,' he said. 'Let's eat; then we can talk about this later when everyone's calmed down.'

Matt hadn't spoken a word while Ellie and Holly were arguing about him, but he pushed his chair back now, and said, 'I've lost my appetite. You stay if you want to, Ellie, but I'm out of here.'

Glaring at her sister when Matt stalked out of the dining room, Ellie said, 'Thanks a lot!'

'Hey, it's not my fault he's got a massive chip on his shoulder.' Holly was unrepentant. 'And don't go giving me that old crap about him being depressed, 'cos he's *not*. He's just a moody shit!'

'Oh, so now you're a doctor as well as a bitch?'

'I might be a bitch, but at least I'm honest. He's a miserable git, and he's dragging you down with him.'

'If he's miserable, he's got good reason,' Ellie replied tersely. 'He was earning good money before the accident, and he feels like he's letting me down because he can't find another job. But you didn't think about that before you started bragging about staying in swanky hotels and jetting off on foreign holidays, did you? And I wouldn't mind, but you've never even worked a day in your whole flaming life!'

'I *am* working,' Holly reminded her.

'That's not work, it's a hobby,' Ellie said scathingly. 'But, then, why *would* you work when you've got a rich man to keep you in the lap of luxury?'

'You cheeky bitch!' Holly spluttered. 'Tony's not my sugar daddy, he's my fiancé.'

'Whatever you want to call it, it amounts to the same thing,' Ellie retorted, shoving her arms back into the sleeves of her jacket. 'If he wasn't paying your way you'd still be living on the estate with Mum, not sitting here like some pampered little princess.'

'You're just jealous,' Holly snarled, her eyes glittering with anger.

'Of *you*?' Ellie snorted, snatching her handbag up off the floor. 'In your dreams!'

'Ladies, please,' Tony implored as people from the surrounding tables began to look their way and the waiter hovered behind him, plates still in hand. 'Ellie, I honestly didn't mean to offend you and Matt, and I'm sorry you took it like that, but please, take some time to think it over before you say a definite no to Barbados. Holly's really fond of you, and I know how important it is for her to have her family around her on her big day.'

Ellie dragged her gaze away from her sister's furious face and gave Tony a tight smile. 'I'm sure you're a very nice man, and money clearly isn't an issue for you like it is for us. But there's no point asking us to think about it, because we're not going to change our minds.'

'Good!' Holly said sharply. 'You've always been a selfish bitch, and we'll have a better time without you. Go on, then . . .' She flapped her hand dismissively. 'Run after your man, like you always do, you pathetic lapdog.'

'Do yourself a favour and keep her away from the best man, if you're having one,' Ellie said to Tony as she rose to her feet. 'She'll probably end up screwing him in the bogs, like she did at my wedding. And, yes, he was married, before you ask. It was his *wife* who caught them!'

'You bitch!' Holly squawked.

'Takes one to know one,' Ellie retorted before stalking out.

Matt was waiting outside the main doors, and Ellie could see that he was still seething by the way he was pacing up and down. The adrenalin that was coursing through her was making her feel sick and she desperately wanted a cigarette, but Matt would be furious if she lit up in front of him after pretending to have stopped, so she pushed it out of her mind and slid her arm through his.

'You okay?'

'Oh, yeah, I'm happy as fucking Larry,' he muttered, almost pulling her off her feet when he set off briskly down the steps.

'Take no notice of Holly,' she said, struggling to keep up as he marched away from the hotel and out onto the road.

Matt abruptly stopped walking, causing her to crash into him. 'Why not? She was only telling the truth, wasn't she? You *would* have jumped at the chance to go on holiday if it wasn't for me.'

'No I wouldn't,' Ellie insisted. 'I'd rather be at home with you, because you're my husband and I love you. Anyway, you know what she's like. She'll probably ring tomorrow and say they've decided to get married in Manchester instead.'

'It wouldn't make any difference, 'cos I still won't be going,' said Matt.

Sighing when he started walking again, Ellie cursed Holly under her breath as she hurried to catch up with him.

After a silent bus ride home, Matt claimed he had a headache and went straight to bed. Too agitated to think about sleeping at such an early hour, Ellie went out onto the tiny balcony and closed the door quietly behind her. Matt had been in a good mood when they'd set off for the hotel, and she'd really hoped they would have a nice time. But her insensitive sister had ruined everything – *again* – and she felt like she'd been pushed back to square one. It was so unfair, and she struggled to hold in the tears as she lit the cigarette she'd been craving.

A car pulled into the car park below, and she watched as a man stepped out from behind the wheel and ran around to open the door for the woman in the passenger seat. Their laughter drifted up to her as they walked toward the door with their arms around each other, and she felt a stab of pure envy in her gut. It had been a long time since Matt had showed her any kind of affection, and she couldn't help but wonder if Holly had been right about him punishing her. The anger, the paranoia, the unfounded accusations, the days when he refused to communicate or even wash . . . She'd been putting it all down to depression, but what if it was actually resentment, because she'd walked out of the crash without a scratch while he'd been left with serious injuries?

Annoyed that she was allowing Holly to make her question Matt's feelings for her, Ellie flicked the cigarette over the balcony and went inside. None of this was Matt's fault, and she refused to give up on him – no matter how much of a struggle it was at times. And if Holly couldn't understand why she chose to put Matt's needs before her own, then God help Tony if he ever needed *her* like Matt needed Ellie.

5

As Ellie had expected, Matt barely spoke to her that weekend, and it took every ounce of willpower she possessed not to scream at him to pull himself together as he slunk from bedroom to living room and back again in his pyjamas. Aware that she would make things worse if she said anything, she left him to it and got on with cleaning the flat around him. But she was desperate to escape the claustrophobic atmosphere by the time Monday morning came.

Already on edge, her hackles rose when she walked into the office and saw her co-workers huddled over Sue's desk, looking at something on the screen of the mobile phone Sue was holding.

'*What?*' she snapped when they all gazed up at her with sly smiles on their lips.

'You on Facebook?' Sue asked.

'No. Why?'

'Jeez! I'm only asking.' Sue rolled her eyes at the other girls. 'No need to bite my head off.'

Scolding herself for taking her frustrations out on them, Ellie took a deep breath. 'Sorry. I'm not feeling too well today. Think I might be due on.'

'Join the club,' Adele said wearily. 'That's why I was off last week. The cramps were so bad I couldn't get out of bed.'

'More like the man was so hot you didn't *want* to,' Jackie countered knowingly.

'Shut it, you!' Adele laughed, letting them all know that Jackie had hit the nail on the head.

Annoyed to think that she'd been held up that evening and missed her train because this girl had been busy screwing whichever random man she'd picked up the night before, Ellie turned her back on them and sat down.

She'd just taken her headphones out of her drawer and was about to put them on, when Sue said, 'Here, Ellie, come and look at this.'

Sighing, she got up again, and went over to see what they seemed to be finding so fascinating.

'It's a Facebook page for people who are looking for someone they've lost touch with,' Sue explained when Ellie stared blankly at the screen. 'And someone's put up a post looking for someone called Helen.'

'And?'

'And we think it's you. It mentions Long Lane station, and that's where you catch your train, isn't it?'

'Yes, but so do loads of other people. And that's not my name.'

'No, but Helen sounds a bit like Ellie, and the description fits you to a tee,' Sue persisted. 'Listen, I'll read it to you. It says: *"I'm looking for a girl called Helen. I met her on Thursday at Long Lane train station in Manchester, and I've been back there every day since but I haven't seen her. She looks like she's in her late 20s, early 30s, and she's really pretty, with long brown hair and greeny-blue eyes. If anyone knows her, can you ask her to message me? She'll know what it's about. Cheers. G."'*

All three girls stared at Ellie when Sue had finished reading, but she avoided their gaze as an uncomfortable heat surged up her neck and spread across her cheeks.

'It *is* you!' Sue crowed, her eyes widening.

'No, it's not,' Ellie lied. 'It's not my name, and I never speak to anyone at the station.'

'Methinks someone's telling porkies,' Adele teased. 'You look exactly like the description, *and* you use that station, so it's way too much of a coincidence for it to be anyone else. And you couldn't be blushing any harder if you tried. So, come on, who is it, you naughty girl? Did you have a quickie behind the ticket booth?'

'I'm married,' Ellie snapped, wishing that Adele had stayed off a while longer, because she was even worse than the other two when it came to taking the piss.

'So was Jackie, but it didn't stop her from having a bit on the side,' said Adele.

'Hey, my marriage was over way before I decided to have a

bit of fun,' Jackie protested. 'And John had been at it for months behind *my* back, so he deserved it.'

'Well, my marriage is fine,' Ellie said defensively. 'Whoever this *G* person is' – she flapped her hand at Sue's phone – 'it's not me he's looking for.'

'If you say so,' Sue murmured. 'Soon find out, though, won't we? There's tons of comments, so someone's bound to figure out who it is before too long.'

Ellie returned to her desk and placed her headphones over her ears to block out the girls' voices as they continued to speculate about the identity of the mysterious Helen. But as hard as she tried, she couldn't keep her mind on her work as the day progressed.

It was obviously Gareth who had put up that post, and she could only assume that he wanted to thank her for saving his life. The girls, however, clearly thought she'd been messing around behind Matt's back. And Matt would definitely jump to the same conclusion if he were to hear about it.

As soon as the clock hit five thirty, Ellie was up off her chair and out of the office as if the Devil was on her heels. Remembering that Gareth had written that he'd been looking for her at the train station, she took the bus home instead.

Matt was slumped in his chair in front of the TV when she got there. He was still wearing his pyjamas, and she wrinkled her nose at the smell of stale sweat. There was a thick sheen of grease on his hair, and he hadn't shaved in days, so he was now sporting a straggly half-beard. It wouldn't have been so bad if it was neat, or even the same colour as his hair which was a lovely shade of chestnut; but this was a speckled mess of browns and grey, and it made him look like one of the winos who hung out in the garages below.

'Have you been sitting there all day?' she snapped, struggling to mask her irritation as her patience sank to an all-time low.

When Matt gave an unintelligible grunt in reply, she tutted and stomped into the kitchen. He hadn't taken anything out of the freezer for dinner, and she wasn't in the mood for making anything from scratch, so she bunged a frozen pizza and some chips into the oven and then went to get changed out of her work clothes while she waited for them to cook.

After dinner, which they ate in silence, Matt shuffled off to bed. Glad, because she was sick of looking at his miserable face, Ellie went out onto the balcony to have a smoke. She'd been thinking that she should probably tell him about Gareth's post in case he heard about it from someone else, but he'd lost touch with most of his friends after the accident, so there was no danger of any of them telling him; and, apart from fishing, which he did alone, the only place he ever went to nowadays was the job centre. He was hardly likely to hear about it in either of those places, so she decided it would probably be best to say nothing and wait for Gareth to forget about her when he got no response to his post.

6

Ready for work the following morning, Ellie was in the kitchen drinking a cup of coffee when Matt joined her.

'Sorry,' he murmured, coming up behind her and resting his chin on her shoulder as she prepared a cup for him.

'It's okay,' she said.

'No, it's not,' he countered guiltily. 'I've been treating you like shit, and you don't deserve it.'

'It doesn't matter,' she insisted, wriggling free when his sour breath began to turn her stomach. 'I just want you to feel better.'

'So do I,' Matt said, leaning back against the ledge when she handed his cup to him. 'My moods are getting worse, and I know I'm the only one who can sort it out, so I'm going to ask my GP to put me on antidepressants.'

'If you think it'll help,' Ellie said, trying not to sound as pessimistic as she felt. He'd had them before, but had stopped taking them because he claimed they didn't work, so what was to stop him doing the same this time?

'It can't be any worse than this,' Matt said, raking his fingernails through his beard. 'And I think it's time I started looking for another job while I'm at it. I know I can't go back to building, 'cos it's too physical, but there must be something I can do.'

Grimacing when flakes of dead skin landed on the floor between their feet, Ellie stepped around him and tipped the last of her coffee into the sink. He sounded keen, but they had been down this road several times before, and she knew that his enthusiasm would die out as quickly as it had flared to life if he got any knockbacks.

'I'd best get going, or I'll miss my train,' she said, drying her hands on the tea towel after rinsing her cup out. 'And you'd best ring the surgery before all the appointments get taken. If you manage to get one, make sure you take a shower before you see the doctor,' she added as she slipped her coat on.

'Are you saying I stink?' Matt asked.

'A bit,' she said, kissing him on the cheek. 'But I still love you. See you later.'

'Yeah, see you,' Matt said distractedly, raising an arm to sniff his pit.

The other girls were already at their desks when Ellie reached the office, and she frowned when she noticed them exchanging furtive glances as she took off her coat.

'Not brewing up, Helen?' Sue asked when she sat down. 'Oops, sorry! I meant, *Ellie*.'

Gritting her teeth when the others started laughing, Ellie gave them a fake smile, and said, 'No, but mine's a coffee if anyone else is,' before turning her back on them and getting down to work.

At lunchtime, she walked down to the cafe and bought her usual sandwich and coffee. But just as she'd sat down and was about to start eating, someone called her name, and her heart sank when she looked up and saw the man whose life she'd saved waving at her from the other side of the road, a huge bunch of flowers in his hand.

'Oh, wow, I can't believe I've found you,' he said when he ran over. 'I've been looking for you for days.'

'Let me guess . . .' she said, scowling when she glanced back down the road and saw her co-workers spying on them from the doorway of the office block. 'Someone replied to your Facebook post and told you where to find me?'

'Yeah, that's right,' he confirmed. 'I got a message last night, telling me that you have your lunch here every day, but that your name's Ellie, not Helen. Sorry about that, I obviously wasn't listening properly that night. Do you mind if I join you?'

Ellie wanted to tell him to go away, but he was being so polite she couldn't bring herself to be rude, so she waved for him to take a seat.

'Thanks,' he said. 'Oh, and these are for you.' He handed the flowers to her.

Laying them on the table, she said, 'They're lovely, but you really didn't have to.'

'It was the least I could do,' he smiled. 'I'm going to get myself a coffee. Can I get you a fresh one?'

Ellie shook her head. 'No, thanks; I've only just got this one.'

'Okay. Won't be a sec.'

No longer hungry, Ellie pushed her plate away and looked to see if the girls were still watching when Gareth went inside the cafe. They had obviously seen enough, because they were walking off in the direction of the pub, but she had no doubt that she would be the sole topic of their lunchtime conversation today.

Gareth was carrying a take-away cup and a wrapped sandwich when he came back out. 'Thought I'd best get something for later,' he explained. 'I'm still sorting through my nan's stuff, and I'll forget to eat if it's not sitting right in front of me.'

'Sensible,' Ellie said, sipping her coffee.

'So did you get home all right the other night?' he asked when he'd sat down.

'Mmmm.' She nodded. 'I was late, obviously, but I got there.'

'Hope I didn't get you into trouble with your hubby?'

'What do you mean?' Ellie frowned.

'You were ignoring his calls,' he reminded her. 'So I thought things must be a bit awkward between you.'

'Not at all,' she lied. 'I just didn't want to tell him what was going on while I was sitting next to you. You were already upset, and I didn't want to make you feel worse.'

'Thanks for caring,' Gareth said. 'And I'm sorry for acting like such a prick.' Grimacing as soon as the word left his mouth, he said, 'Sorry; didn't mean to say that. I don't usually swear in front of ladies.'

'I've heard worse,' Ellie assured him, amused that he thought she was a lady.

'Well, I'm sorry for putting you through all that, anyway,' Gareth said. 'I hardly slept that night, 'cos I kept thinking about the look on your face when you grabbed me. I'm totally disgusted with myself.'

'You don't need to keep apologizing,' said Ellie. 'Like I told you at the time, anyone would have done the same.'

'Maybe,' he mused. 'But I still reckon my nan sent you to save me. She was funny like that: always banging on about seeing ghosts, and getting feelings about things. Do you believe in that sort of stuff?'

Ellie pursed her lips. 'I've never given it much thought, to be honest. I suppose there must be something in it if so many people reckon they've seen things, but I never have.'

'I always thought it was rubbish, but I believe in it now,' Gareth said.

A little unnerved by the intensity of his gaze as he peered at her, Ellie dropped hers and took another sip of coffee.

'You look tired,' Gareth said. 'I hope I haven't given you nightmares?'

'No. I've got a bit of a headache, that's all.'

'Good. Not about the headache, obviously; just that it's not my fault. I've been thinking about what you said that night, and you were spot on when you said I was being selfish. It didn't feel like it at the time, but you don't think about the people who'll have to deal with it when it's over.'

'I don't suppose you would,' Ellie murmured, pushing her sleeve back to check her watch. 'Wow, is that the time? I'm going to have to get going in a minute.'

'Oh, sorry. Have I taken up all your lunchtime?'

'It's okay. I wasn't that hungry, anyway, so I'll finish my coffee and head off.'

'I should probably make a move, as well,' Gareth said, picking his sandwich up. 'I need to call in at the supermarket and get some boxes for my nan's stuff, then I've got an appointment with the housing.'

'Good luck,' Ellie said, smiling when he stood up.

'Thanks,' he said. 'And thanks again for what you did. I know you think it was nothing, but it meant a lot that you cared enough to sit and talk to me.'

'I'm glad it helped,' she said. 'Take care.'

'You, too.'

He nodded goodbye at that and walked away, and Ellie thought about the change in his appearance as she watched him go. He was still wearing the same dirty trainers and grubby jacket he'd been wearing the last time she saw him, but his dark hair looked glossy today, so he'd obviously washed it, and he'd shaved off the stubble that had made his cheeks look so gaunt. His mood seemed to have lifted considerably, too, and she hoped that the council would offer him somewhere to live before they took the keys to his nan's place, because it was a miserable time of year to be made homeless.

*

Ellie's co-workers were waiting when she got back to work, and they bombarded her with questions as soon as she walked through the door.

'Well?' Jackie demanded, while Sue said, 'It *was* you he was after, wasn't it?'

'He was a total *babe*,' Adele added incredulously. 'How the hell did *you* get off with *him*?'

If Ellie had been interested in Gareth, she'd have been offended by the insinuation that she wasn't attractive enough for him. But she wasn't interested, and it tickled her to see the envy in young, gorgeous Adele's eyes. So much so, that she was almost tempted to string it out and let them think that something *was* going on between her and Gareth. But she couldn't disrespect Matt by allowing them to think she was having an affair, so she held up her hands.

'Okay, yes . . . it was me he was looking for. But it's not what you think.'

'Course it isn't.' Sue smirked.

'Go, Ellie!' said Jackie, with something approaching admiration in her eyes. 'I always suspected there was a cougar hiding behind that little mouse facade.'

'No, honestly, it isn't,' Ellie insisted. 'I saved his life. That was the night he was talking about in that Facebook thing you showed me. I missed my train and saw him climb over the bridge.'

'You're kidding?' Adele gasped. 'He didn't look like a suicidal nutter.'

'That's 'cos he's not,' said Ellie, feeling suddenly protective of Gareth. 'He's just a kid who's going through a tough time.'

'So when you say you saved his life, what did you actually do?' Sue wanted to know.

'I grabbed him and stopped him from jumping,' Ellie explained. 'Then I sat and talked to him till he'd calmed down. But anyone would have done the same,' she finished modestly.

'I wouldn't,' Adele snorted. 'I'd have been terrified of going over with him.'

'I didn't think about that until the next morning,' Ellie admitted. 'I just acted on instinct at the time. Anyway, that's all there is to it, so can we forget about it now?'

'I suppose so,' Sue agreed, sounding disappointed that there would be no more gossip. 'I might start calling you Helen, though,' she added playfully.

Ellie smiled and carried the flowers through to the kitchen to put them in water as the other girls went back to their desks. The Gareth situation had been dealt with, so there was no longer any danger of Matt hearing about it and jumping to the wrong conclusion. And it seemed to have broken the ice between her and the girls, so now – hopefully – she wouldn't have to dread coming to work each day.

7

Matt had taken Ellie's advice and showered after she left for work that morning, and she was glad to see that he had shaved off the awful beard. He'd also ironed his clothes, and had aired out and tidied the living room.

'You've been busy,' she said, taking in the freshly polished surfaces, neatly arranged scatter-cushions and crumb-free carpet. 'Are they for me?' she asked when she saw a vase of flowers standing on the dining table.

'Roses for my rose,' he said, grinning as he added, 'They were in the bargain bin at Abdul's, so they didn't cost much, and probably won't last very long. But I thought you deserved something nice.'

'They're lovely,' Ellie said, smiling as she sat down and kicked her shoes off. She couldn't remember the last time anyone had bought flowers for her, and now she'd been presented with two bunches in one day. Not that Matt would ever find out about Gareth's, because she'd deliberately left them in the office.

'You look exhausted,' Matt said as he made his way into the kitchen to check on dinner. 'Hard day at work?'

'A bit,' she said. Then, 'How was yours? Did you manage to get an appointment with the doctor?'

'Yeah, they had a cancellation, so I went in at lunchtime. He's put me back on Prozac.'

'That's good,' Ellie said, thinking: *As long as you give them a chance to work this time.*

'Why don't you go and get a bath,' Matt suggested when he came back into the room and caught her yawning. 'Dinner's nearly ready, but I can keep it on a low light till you come out.'

'Best not, or I'll probably fall asleep,' she said, pushing herself up to her feet. 'I'll just get changed into my night clothes.'

In the bedroom a minute later, she had no sooner got undressed than her phone started ringing, and she sighed when she saw her mother's name on the screen. Her mum rarely rang, but when she did it was usually an excuse to complain about something or somebody.

'Hello, Mum . . .' she said, sitting down on the bed and reaching for her pyjama bottoms. 'What's happened, and who did it?'

'Don't play the innocent with me, Eleanor Louise Fisher,' her mum replied curtly. 'You know exactly why I'm calling.'

'I take it you've spoken to Holly?'

'Yes, I have, and she's upset. Matt's got no right to stop you from going to her wedding. It's the biggest day of her life, and she needs you there – just like she was there for you on yours. Or have you forgotten everything she did for you that day?'

'Oh, I haven't forgotten,' said Ellie, thinking that her mother obviously had, or she wouldn't be crediting Holly with doing anything apart from cause uproar.

'Yes, well, it's time you got your priorities right and stopped putting Matt before your own family all the time,' her mum went on angrily. 'Billy wouldn't dream of interfering, and Matt shouldn't either.'

Too bloody right Billy wouldn't dream of interfering, Ellie thought angrily. *He wouldn't dare, in case I let slip about him trying to interfere with me.*

She had never told her mum about that, and didn't want to blurt it out now in anger, so she gritted her teeth until the temptation had passed. It had only happened once, and Billy had been drunk so she had fought him off more easily than she might have had he been sober. He'd acted as if he didn't remember anything the following morning and, for her mum's sake, Ellie had kept her mouth shut. But she had despised him ever since.

And the feeling was clearly mutual, judging by the scathing tone of Billy's voice when he piped up in the background now, saying: 'I don't know why you're bothering. She's always been a selfish cow, so just leave her if she doesn't want to go.'

'No, I will not leave her,' her mum replied. 'It's our Holly's big day, and I won't have it ruined because that bloody husband of Ellie's thinks he's calling the shots. I'm sick of it.'

'*MUM!*' Ellie yelled as her mother and stepfather continued to discuss her. 'If you're not talking to me, I'm going to hang up ... Can you hear me?'

'Yes, I can hear you,' her mum said sharply. 'And I hope you heard me, too, because I meant every word. We've all made allowances for Matt since the accident, but this is the last straw, and you'd better sort it out before I come over there to give him a piece of my mind!'

Tutting when the phone went dead, Ellie threw it down on the bed and cursed Holly for dragging their mum into their fight. Matt already thought her family hated him, and he'd take this as confirmation that he'd been right all along.

Still thinking about the situation after she'd donned her pyjamas and gone back into the living room, Ellie wondered if she ought to try and persuade Matt to go to Holly's wedding, after all. If they didn't go, her family would never forgive him, and that would make future get-togethers extremely awkward. But how could she persuade Matt to change his mind without telling him why she'd suddenly changed hers? He was in a positive frame of mind right now, but that could change in an instant if he heard what her family were saying about him.

'You still awake?' Matt asked when he came in from the kitchen carrying two bowls of stew and found her curled up on the sofa.

'Just about,' she said, smiling when he sat down beside her instead of going over to his chair.

'Good, 'cos I've got something to tell you,' he said. 'Remember that campsite we stayed at last time we went to the Lakes? Well, I went online when I got home from seeing the doctor, and they're doing some great Christmas packages, so I thought I'd book us in for the holiday weekend. What do you think?'

'I think it's a lovely idea, but there's no way we can afford it,' said Ellie.

'Yes we can,' he argued. 'You get paid next week.'

'And as soon as it goes in, it'll be going straight back out to pay the bills,' she reminded him. 'And then we'll have to scrape by till next month, when it'll happen all over again. So, like I said . . . lovely idea, but not gonna happen.'

'I've already made the provisional booking.'

'Well, you'll just have to unbook it, then, won't you?'

'But I don't want to,' Matt protested. 'We haven't been away in years, and you deserve a break. I know it's not in the same league as Barbados, but it'll be gorgeous down there at this time of year.'

'We can't *afford* it,' Ellie reiterated.

'We could if we sold something,' he replied, gazing around the room in search of inspiration. 'My records!' He slammed his bowl down on the table and jumped to his feet. 'I'll sell my records.'

Rushing over to the cabinet in which his collection of rare vinyl albums was housed, he kneeled down in front of it and carefully lifted out the first stack.

'This would probably fetch thirty or forty quid,' he said,

holding up a Pink Floyd album that had been signed by Roger Waters. 'And this is an absolute beauty.' He held up a limited-edition Rolling Stones album. 'A collector would pay fifty quid for it any day.'

'Matt, stop,' Ellie urged. 'I don't want you to sell your records.'

'Oh, wow, I'd forgotten about this one,' he went on, as if he hadn't heard her. 'I need to go on eBay and start listing them.'

Ellie put down her bowl when it occurred to her that this was starting to look like a manic episode rather than a simple lift in mood. If she was right and she didn't stop him from sell-ing his records, an extreme low was sure to follow.

'Matt, put them away,' she said, going over and squatting beside him. 'I don't want you to sell them.'

'We need the money,' he argued, still sifting through the pile. 'You're always wiped out from working, and you deserve the chance to relax. I'm sorry it's not as fancy as Barbados, but—'

'Will you be told, I do not want to go to Barbados,' Ellie interrupted, pushing all thought of the wedding out of her mind. 'My mum and Holly can say whatever they like, but I'm perfectly happy to stay right here with you.'

'Your mum?' Matt paused and looked round at her. 'I didn't know you'd spoken to her about it?'

'She rang when I was in the bedroom,' Ellie admitted. 'But there's nothing for you to worry about. She only wanted to know why I'm not going to the wedding, and I told her it's because I don't want to.'

'Did she blame me?'

'No, she blamed *me*, because it was my decision.'

'It wasn't, though, was it?' Matt said dejectedly. 'It was mine, because I wouldn't let Tony pay our way. If I was any kind of man, I'd have had the money to take you there myself, but I'm a complete waste of space.'

'No, you are not,' Ellie said firmly. 'And please don't let this set you back, because you were doing so well before you got it into your head that I need a break.'

'Don't worry, I'm not going on a downer,' Matt promised, slotting his albums back into the cabinet. 'I said things were going to get better, and I meant it.'

Praying that it was true, Ellie patted his arm and pushed herself up onto her feet.

'Come and finish your dinner, then let's have an early night, eh?'

'Sounds good to me,' Matt said as he too stood up. 'Or we could skip the first and go straight to the second?'

Ellie drew her head back and gave him a questioning look. 'Are you saying what I think you're saying?'

'Might be.'

Surprised, because it had been ages since they had made love, and she'd started to wonder if they ever would again, she said, 'Are you sure you're up to it?'

'Only one way to find out.' He grinned.

*

'I'm sorry,' Matt said, rolling off her after twenty minutes and flopping against his pillow.

'It's okay,' Ellie murmured, resting her head on his chest. 'It was lovely, even if we didn't finish.'

'Yeah, but . . .'

'*Ssshhh!*' She placed a finger over his lips to silence him. 'We're both tired, so I think we did well to last as long as we did. Now stop worrying, and let's get some sleep.'

As soon as the words had left her mouth, her phone started ringing on the bedside table, and she groaned when she rolled over and saw Holly's name on the screen.

'Aren't you going to take it?' Matt asked when she told him who it was.

Ellie contemplated it for a moment, then reached out and switched the phone to silent. She knew she would have to speak to Holly eventually, but for now, she just wanted to cuddle up to Matt and go to sleep.

8

'Why have you been ignoring me?' Holly demanded when Ellie answered her call on the train the following morning.

'I wasn't ignoring you, I was busy,' Ellie said quietly, conscious of her fellow passengers. 'What's up?'

'We need to talk about my wedding. Have you climbed off your high horse and decided to come yet?'

'Holly, I can't. I would if I could, but it's just not possible. You know Matt hasn't been well, and I—'

'Oh, for God's sake, it's all Matt, Matt, fucking Matt with you, isn't it?'

'He's my husband,' Ellie reminded her.

'And I'm your *sister*,' said Holly. 'But if you won't do this for me, do it for Mum, 'cos this might be the last Christmas we're ever going to have with her.'

No longer caring that the other passengers could hear every word, Ellie demanded, 'Is something wrong with Mum? Is she ill? Tell me, Holly; I need to know.'

'No, she's not ill,' Holly grunted after leaving her hanging for several seconds. 'But that's no thanks to *you*, 'cos you've stressed her right out.'

Angry now, Ellie said, 'If she's stressed out, it's your fault, not mine. I've done nothing wrong, and I won't be blamed for this. You should have asked me if I could go, but, as usual, you made your plans without consulting anyone, then expected us all to go along with it.'

'This is your last chance,' Holly warned. 'You either come to my wedding, or you can forget you've got a sister. *Or* a mum, 'cos she'll never speak to you again if you let me down!'

'I don't get why you want me there so badly, when all you ever do is put me down,' Ellie snapped. 'Or is it because you think that having your fat, ugly sister there will make *you* look better?'

'You *are* fat and ugly, but I don't need anything to make me look good,' Holly retorted nastily. 'And just so you know, it wasn't my idea to have you there in the first place, it was *Tony's*. But now he knows what a selfish bitch you are, I'm sure he'll be as glad as I am that you're not coming. And I'm especially glad that Matt isn't, 'cos he's even uglier than you!'

Furious when Holly hung up on her, Ellie shoved the phone into her handbag and glared at the man sitting across the aisle, who had obviously been listening and was still staring at her.

'*What?*'

Embarrassed, he quickly looked away, and Ellie turned her glare out through the window as the coffee she'd drunk before leaving the flat began to churn in her stomach. Holly had always been a bitch, but this was a whole new level of bitchiness, even for her. And now she'd dragged their mum into it, Ellie's name was going to be mud within the family.

Still thinking about her dilemma at lunchtime, Ellie groaned when she saw Gareth strolling along the pavement in her direction.

'Fancy seeing you here again,' he quipped when he reached her. 'I'll have to watch it, or you'll start thinking I'm doing it on purpose.'

'Not at all,' she said, dropping her half-eaten sandwich onto the plate and wiping her mouth. 'How did you get on at your appointment?'

No longer smiling, he said, 'Not too good, to be honest. They want me out of my nan's place ASAP, 'cos they've got someone lined up for it; but I'm not classed as vulnerable, so I've got no priority points.'

'So where are you supposed to go?' Ellie asked.

'Into a hostel, if I'm lucky enough to find a place with vacancies,' he said. 'If not . . .' He shrugged. 'I'll just have to find somewhere by myself.'

Ellie felt sorry for him, and also a little guilty that she hadn't wanted to talk to him and would have preferred for him to keep on walking. Looking at him as he was right now, it was easy to forget that, only a few days ago, he'd felt so desperate and alone he had tried to kill himself. And now he was faced with imminent homelessness, she wondered how long it would be before he felt that desperate again.

Her coffee was forming an unappetizing skin. Gazing down at it, she made a snap decision, and said, 'Do you want to join me for a coffee? Mine's gone cold, so I'm going to get another.'

'Thanks, but I can't,' Gareth said, looking suddenly embarrassed.

'I'm buying,' said Ellie, guessing that he had no money. 'You bought me those flowers, so this will make us even. Please . . .' She stood up and gestured for him to sit down.

At the counter a few seconds later, Ellie studied Gareth through the window as she waited for their drinks. Adele had called him a babe, and Ellie had to admit that he was quite handsome. *Very* handsome, actually, with his glossy black hair and soulful green eyes. She would put him in his mid-twenties, at a guess, but he had an air of vulnerability that made him appear younger.

Gareth was slouched in his seat when she came back outside, but he straightened up when he saw her, and said, 'Thanks,' when she passed his cup to him.

Ellie sat down and took her cigarettes out of her handbag. Passing one to Gareth, she lit her own and sat back.

'Can I ask you something?' Gareth said, peering at her thoughtfully when he too had lit up. 'Are you happy?'

Thrown, because it was such an unexpected question, Ellie said, 'Yes. Why? Don't I look it?'

'Not really,' he replied. 'You look kind of . . . *weary*, I suppose; like you've got the weight of the world on your shoulders.'

'You hardly know me,' she reminded him. 'And I can assure you that I am *very* happy. I have a good job, a wonderful husband, and a lovely home, so why wouldn't I be?'

'I've upset you, haven't I?' Gareth said guiltily. 'I should have kept my stupid mouth shut.'

Aware that she was being spiky and defensive, Ellie said, 'I'm not upset with you; I'm just sick of people telling me I don't look well, or happy, or whatever.'

'So it's not just me, then?'

'No, I've had it from my sister, as well. She's never been particularly tactful, so you'd think I'd be used to it by now; but she still manages to get to me.'

'Are there just the two of you?' Gareth asked, gazing at her over the rim of his cup as he took a sip of coffee.

'Yeah, just me and her,' said Ellie. 'What about you?'

'I had a brother, but he died.'

'Oh, I'm sorry.'

'It's okay. He was a lot older than me, so I don't remember much about him. Him and his mates went swimming in the canal, and he got his foot stuck in an old bike or pram, or something, and drowned.'

'That's awful.'

'It was his own fault,' Gareth said, shrugging. 'My mum told him not to go there, but he ignored her, so that's what he got.'

Thinking that an odd thing to say considering his brother

80

had lost his life, Ellie didn't say anything else, and they finished their coffees in silence.

'I'd best get going,' Gareth said, pushing his chair back after a while. 'It was nice to see you again.'

'You, too,' Ellie said, relieved that he was leaving because the atmosphere had become a little strained.

9

Gareth didn't turn up at the cafe again, and Ellie quickly forgot about him as Christmas drew closer and her thoughts turned to Holly's wedding. She hadn't heard from her sister or their mother since the last argument, and neither had answered their phone when she had swallowed her pride and tried to call them, so she guessed they weren't talking to her.

As sad as she was at the thought of not seeing her family at Christmas, she was determined not to let it ruin the day for Matt, so she went shopping after leaving work on Christmas Eve and, using the £100 bonus Richard had given her, bought all the ingredients she needed to replicate the dinner her mum usually cooked.

Later that evening, when the joint of beef was in the oven and the turkey crown and veg had been prepared for cooking in the morning, she and Matt ate dinner and then changed into their nightclothes before settling on the couch to watch a film. But it hadn't been on for long when the intercom buzzed.

Wondering who it could possibly be, because they rarely got

visitors and never at this time of night, Ellie got up to answer it. Shocked to hear her sister's voice, she pressed the door-release button and rushed back to tell Matt who it was.

'Aw, no, seriously?' he groaned. 'I thought she was supposed to be in Barbados?'

'So did I,' said Ellie. 'She's probably on her way to the airport and thought she'd call round to see if I've changed my mind. But, don't worry; I doubt she'll stay too long when I tell her I haven't.'

'I hope not,' Matt said grumpily.

Ellie went back out into the hall and opened the front door. Chilled by the icy air in the communal hallway, she wrapped her dressing gown tighter around herself and hopped from foot to foot as she waited for her sister.

Holly was dragging a huge suitcase behind her when she came round the corner a minute later, and Ellie frowned when she saw that she was crying.

'What's wrong?' she asked, rushing out to meet her. 'Has something happened? It's not Mum, is it?'

'The wedding's off,' Holly wailed, falling into her arms. 'He – he's already *marriieeed . . .*'

'Who, Tony?' Ellie asked, wondering if she'd heard right.

Unable to make sense of Holly's reply because she was sobbing so hard, Ellie reached for the suitcase and guided her inside.

'What's all the noise about?' Matt asked, coming into the doorway when he heard the commotion.

'The wedding's off,' Ellie told him quietly. 'Go and watch the film; I'll talk to her in our room.'

'No, take her in there, I'll watch it on the portable,' Matt said, already heading for the bedroom. 'And don't forget to turn the oven off before you come to bed,' he added, letting her know that he had no intention of coming back out again.

'I know he doesn't want me here,' Holly whined when he stomped into the bedroom and slammed the door shut. 'But I had nowhere else to go.'

'He doesn't mind,' Ellie lied, leading her into the living room. 'We just didn't expect to see you tonight. Now take your coat off and sit down. I'll make a drink, then you can tell me what's going on.'

Holly's tears had stopped when Ellie came back a few minutes later carrying two cups of cocoa, and she'd taken off her coat and shoes and was huddled in the corner of the sofa with a forlorn look on her face.

'So what happened?' Ellie asked, sitting beside her. 'Did you even get to Barbados?'

Holly nodded and clutched her cup between both hands. 'We flew out on Thursday, and everything was lovely. The hotel was amazing, with a swimming pool, and a Jacuzzi; and it was all-inclusive, so we could have anything we wanted.'

'Go on,' Ellie urged, hoping that she wasn't going to go all around the houses before getting to the point.

'The vicar, or pastor, or whatever he's called, took us down to the beach for a rehearsal yesterday afternoon,' Holly continued plaintively. 'And right as we were about to start going over our vows, *she* turned up.'

'*She?*' Ellie repeated.

'His *wife*,' spat Holly. 'The sneaky bitch had logged into his emails and got all the details, then used his credit card to book herself onto a flight so she could come and wreck it.'

'Didn't you know about her before that?' Ellie asked. 'Surely Tony must have mentioned her?'

'Kind of,' Holly admitted. 'I mean, he told me he'd *been* married, but he said they were divorced. She reckons they're only separated, though. *And* she said they're still sleeping together. All those times when he had to go away for work and said I couldn't go with him, she reckons he was with her.'

'No way,' Ellie murmured, wishing she'd been there, because she'd have told Tony exactly what she thought of him. 'What a bastard.'

'You should have seen her,' Holly went on bitterly. 'She came strolling over to us with her nose in the air, like she thinks she the Queen of fucking Sheba, or something, and looked me up and down like I was something she'd stepped in. And her kids were giving me proper evils, the snot-nosed brats.'

'He's got kids?' Ellie raised an eyebrow.

'Yeah, a boy and a girl. Never told me about *them*, either.'

'Wow, what a scumbag. So what happened then?'

'She started mouthing off about how he can't get married to me 'cos he's still married to her, so the vicar took off. Then her and Tony got into a massive argument, and the kids started bawling so Mum and Billy took them to get some ice cream. That's when she told me about them still shagging – and Tony went beetroot, so I knew it must be true.'

Shaking her head in disgust, Ellie said, 'Well, at least you found out before you got married, 'cos you'd have come home thinking everything was perfect and he'd have ended up getting arrested for bigamy.'

'I hate her,' Holly snarled. 'She's ruined my life.'

'No, *Tony* has,' said Ellie. 'But you'll find someone else in time.'

'I don't want anyone else,' Holly protested. 'I want *him*. But you wouldn't understand, 'cos you don't know how good it feels to have a gorgeous man treat you like a queen. Your Matt's not—'

'Don't start,' Ellie warned before she could go any further. 'Matt was fine till you started being funny with him, so whatever you've got going on in your head about him, it's your fault, not his.'

'S'pose so,' Holly conceded. Then, flopping her head back against the cushions, she moaned, 'What am I going to do, Ells? I need to talk to Tony, but I don't want to ring him in case *she's* there.'

'Why would she be?'

''Cos I left him there with her. He said he needed time to think, so I packed my bag and caught the first flight back.'

'Good for you,' Ellie said approvingly. 'And what did Mum have to say about it?'

'She was fuming,' said Holly. 'So I left her there to keep an eye on them. That slapper will probably try and turn it into a nice family holiday now I'm out of the way, but Mum won't give them a minute's peace. I almost pity the bitch.'

Ellie envisaged the scene and smiled to herself. Their mother wasn't the kind to go looking for trouble, but God help anyone who brought it to her door, because she would give them absolute hell.

'So what now?' she asked.

'Who knows?' Holly sighed. 'I'll have to wait till I've spoken to Tony.'

'As long as you don't let him sweet talk you into taking him back,' Ellie cautioned, guessing that it would take very little persuasion on his part. 'If he's serious about you, you need proof that he's finished things with his wife.'

'Yeah, I know,' Holly agreed. 'And I'll tell him that when he calls. He will call, won't he?'

'I don't know,' Ellie said, half hoping that he wouldn't, because she was annoyed with him for treating her sister so badly. Not that Holly hadn't hurt or betrayed her fair share of men in her time, because she absolutely had. But Tony had strung her along to the point of almost marrying her, knowing full well that he wasn't legally entitled to. *And* there were young children involved, which was unforgivable in Ellie's eyes. But Holly would do whatever her heart dictated when – *if* – Tony got in touch.

'I know Matt was pissed off to see me,' Holly said after they'd sat in silence for a while. 'But do you think he'd mind if I stayed for a few days? Mum said I could take her keys and stay at hers, but I forgot to bring them. I've still got Tony's credit card, so I could book myself into a hotel, but I don't want to spend Christmas on my own.'

'Of course you don't,' said Ellie. 'And don't worry about Matt. I'm sure he won't mind.'

'Thanks,' Holly said gratefully. 'And if you need me to do anything – cooking, or whatever – just let me know.'

'No need, it's all sorted,' Ellie assured her. Then, glancing at her watch and seeing that it was almost eleven, she said, 'Right, I'm going to turn the turkey off, then I need to get some sleep. Go and get the spare quilt out of the airing cupboard and make up a bed on the couch.'

Holly was lying down with her eyes closed and the quilt pulled up around her throat by the time Ellie had finished in the kitchen. Saying goodnight, Ellie switched off the light and went to her bedroom.

Matt was propped up in bed, watching TV. 'Has she gone?' he asked, peering at Ellie as she shrugged out of her dressing gown.

'No, she's on the couch,' she told him as she slipped into bed beside him. 'I said she can spend Christmas with us.'

'You're kidding?' he groaned. 'What did you do that for?'

'I could hardly say no, could I? She's really cut up about Tony.'

'Serves her right. I'm sorry, I know she's your sister, but she treats people like shit, so I've got no sympathy.'

'Don't worry, I'm sure you won't have to put up with her for long. She'll be out of here in a flash if Tony gets in touch.'

'Good!' Matt muttered, aiming the remote control at the TV to turn it off before rolling onto his side.

'Can we please try and get through tomorrow without an atmosphere?' Ellie begged, talking to the back of his head when he drew the quilt up over his shoulder. 'I know you don't like her, but it's Christmas, and she's just had to cancel her wedding because she's found out that Tony's still married to someone else.'

Matt stayed silent for several moments. Then, sighing heavily, he said, 'Okay, I'll play nice. But if she starts any of her usual nonsense, I'm out of here.'

Thanking him, Ellie lay down and, squeezing her eyes shut, prayed that Holly wouldn't do anything to upset him and ruin the day.

10

Holly was sitting up when Ellie walked into the living room the next morning; mobile phone in hand, a deep frown creasing her brow.

'Happy Christmas,' Ellie said as she passed by on her way to the kitchen. 'Did you sleep okay?'

'Did I hell,' said Holly without raising her eyes. 'This sofa feels like a pile of bricks. And why's the reception so bad in here? My signal keeps cutting out.'

'It's better on the balcony,' Ellie told her as she switched the kettle on after filling it. 'But close the door behind you if you go out, 'cos it's been snowing.'

'Great!' Holly muttered. 'I hate snow.'

'Good job you don't have to go out today, then, isn't it?' Ellie said, hoping that she wasn't going to keep this moaning up for too long.

'Rub it in, why don't you?' Holly replied miserably, reminded that she was supposed to be in Barbados getting ready for her wedding. 'I hate my stupid life.'

'I know it's difficult, but try to put it out of your mind,' Ellie counselled as she spooned coffee into three cups. 'Give it a few days, and you'll wonder what you ever saw in Tony in the first place.'

Holly twisted her head and stared at her sister. 'Sorry, but did you actually *look* at him when you met him? He's gorgeous.'

'Looks mean nothing, it's what's on the inside that counts,' said Ellie. 'And from what you told me, it sounds like he's been getting inside his wife every chance he gets.'

'Why would you say something like that, on today of all days?' Holly complained.

'Because it's the truth,' Ellie said bluntly. 'And the sooner you accept it, the sooner you'll get your life back on track.'

Before Holly could say anything to that, Matt walked in.

'Morning.' He nodded at her.

'Morning,' she replied politely.

Grateful that he was honouring his promise to be civil, Ellie kissed Matt on the cheek as she passed a cup of coffee to him before handing Holly's to her.

When Ellie went back into the kitchen to make a start on the veg, Matt switched the TV on and sat down. Glancing over at him as he flicked through the channels, Holly said, 'Thanks for letting me stay, Matt; I really appreciate it.'

'No worries,' he said. 'Ellie's told me what happened, and it's natural you'd want to be with family at a time like this.'

'That's so true,' she said. 'And I, um, meant to say I'm sorry for what I said last time I saw you. I didn't mean any of it.'

'Yes you did,' Matt said flatly. 'But it's done now, so forget it.'

Holly gave him a guilty smile and looked back down at her phone. Tutting when she saw that the battery had died, she said, 'I don't suppose you've got a charger I can borrow, have you? I think I might have left mine at the hotel.'

Matt leaned over and peered at the phone, then shook his head and turned back to the TV.

'Oh, God, this is all I need,' Holly moaned, slamming the phone down on the quilt. 'How's Tony supposed to get hold of me now?'

'It's probably better that he can't,' Ellie said, coming out of the kitchen carrying three sets of cutlery. 'It'll give you a chance to get over him.'

Giving her a dirty look as she started laying the table, Holly shoved the quilt off her legs and dropped her feet to the floor. 'I'm going for a shower.'

Irritated to see that she'd slept in her blouse and knickers, the latter of which were on plain view, Ellie said, 'Get dressed before you come back in. Your case is in the hall.'

'Okay,' Holly drawled, pausing to stretch before strolling out.

Matt gave Ellie a pained look when she'd gone. '*Seriously?*'

'I'll make sure she's decent before you get up tomorrow,' Ellie promised, glad that he wasn't the kind of man to appreciate her younger sister's lithe body and lack of inhibition. It was bad enough that Holly made her feel fat and frumpy without having to worry that her husband's head was being turned, as well.

Fully clothed when she came back some time later, her hair still damp from the shower, Holly held her phone charger up in the air. 'Panic over. It was in my case.'

'Great,' said Ellie, wishing that the charger *had* been left in Barbados, because Holly would no doubt check her phone every two seconds while they were eating, which would infuriate Matt.

'Will Abdul's be open today?' Holly asked as she settled on the couch to apply her make-up after plugging the phone in.

'Probably,' Ellie said. 'Why? What do you need?'

'Fags and booze,' said Holly. 'No offence, but that cheap wine you buy gave me a rotten hangover last time I was here.'

It was on the tip of Ellie's tongue to remind Holly that, without Tony to pick up the tab, cheap wine was all *she* would be able to afford from now on. But she didn't want to start an argument, so she kept the thought to herself.

Finished with her face half an hour later, Holly got up and checked her reflection in the mirror. After fluffing her hair up, she pulled her jacket on and slipped her feet into her shoes before looping her handbag over her shoulder.

'Take my keys so you can let yourself back in,' Ellie said, picking them up off the table and tossing them to her. 'And be careful in those heels,' she added, eyeing Holly's stilettos. 'I don't want to spend the day in A and E if you break your neck.'

'Yes, Mum,' Holly drawled, waving over her shoulder as she sashayed out.

'Thank God for that,' Matt said when she'd gone.

'She hasn't been that bad,' Ellie scolded.

'*Yet*,' he muttered, glancing at the clock. 'How long till dinner?'

'We'll be eating at two, as usual. Why?'

'So I know when to be back.'

'Back from where?'

'I thought I might nip down to the canal for a couple of hours,' Matt said, pushing himself up to his feet.

'You're going fishing on Christmas day?' Ellie frowned. 'In the snow?'

'I probably won't catch anything, but it beats sitting here listening to your sister talk about herself,' said Matt.

'Fine, go,' Ellie said. 'But make sure you're back on time, 'cos I won't be pleased if you're late and dinner gets ruined.'

Abdul's Hypermarket was a five-minute walk from the flats, but it took Holly twice as long to get there as she picked her way carefully along the snow-covered path and over the slushy main road. Stamping her feet on the mat when she got there, to dislodge the snow that was sticking to her heels, she headed for the alcohol display at the back of the shop and picked up two litre bottles of Courvoisier. Taking them to the till, she plonked them down and peered at the rack of cigarettes behind the man who was serving.

'These, and sixty Richmond Superkings, please.'

After paying with the credit card Tony had given her – which she'd half expected him to have cancelled, and thanked God he hadn't – she pulled the collar of her jacket up around her chin and left the shop.

Colliding with a youth who was on his way in, she said, 'Watch it, you idiot!'

'You what?' He stopped in front of her and gave her a fierce look.

Unfazed, because she had tackled bigger and harder men in her time, Holly stood her ground. 'I said watch it, *idiot.*'

The youth smirked and looked back over his shoulder. 'Have you heard this tart mouthing off?'

Holly followed his gaze and snorted softly when she saw two clones of him standing by a low wall. 'Who are they? Your bodyguards?'

The thug snapped his head back around and thrust his face into hers. Laughing when she jerked away from him, he said, ''S'up, gobby? Ain't scared, are ya?'

'Grow up,' she spat, trying to shoulder past him.

Crying out when he shoved her roughly back against the wall, causing the bag to smash against her shin, she yelped, 'Pack it in, you dickhead!'

'Or what?' he sneered.

'Or you'll have *me* to deal with,' a man said, striding up the path and putting himself between them.

Forced to look up, because the man was a good foot taller

than him, the youth puffed his chest out. 'And what are *you* gonna do?'

'Why don't you test me and find out?' the man said quietly, sliding his hand into the inside pocket of his jacket as he spoke. 'And don't think your mates will help, 'cos I'll take the lot of you out,' he added when the boy looked round for support.

The blood drained from the youth's face, and he held up his hands and backed away. 'All right, mate, take it easy . . . I'm going.'

Leaning down to rub her sore shin when the boy and his friends walked quickly away, Holly said, 'Thanks, but you didn't need to get involved. I was handling it.'

'I'm sure you were,' the man said amusedly. 'But there were three of them and only one of you, so I thought I'd best even things up.'

Holly straightened up and gave him a curious look. 'What did you do to make him take off like that?'

'I flashed my gun at him,' he told her.

'Seriously?' She frowned.

Laughing softly, he shook his head. 'I haven't got one. I just made him *think* I did.'

Holly studied his face properly for the first time. With his dark hair, twinkly eyes and sexy smile, he reminded her a little of Tony – which, in turn, reminded her about the aborted wedding.

'Hey, what's up?' the man asked when he noticed the change in her expression. 'That little shit didn't hurt you, did he?'

'A bit, but this isn't about him,' Holly said, blinking to clear the tears that were clouding her eyes. 'I was thinking about something I was supposed to be doing today. But don't worry about it. I'll be fine once I've had a drink – or four.'

'That bad?' He raised an eyebrow.

'Worse.' She sighed. 'I was supposed to be getting married today, but my fiancé forgot to mention that he hasn't divorced the last one yet.'

'Wow, that's rough. No wonder you need a drink.'

'Yeah, well, I intend to have a *lot*,' said Holly. 'That's *if* I manage to get home without breaking the bottles. I'd never have worn these stupid heels if I'd known it was this icy.'

'I see what you mean,' the man said, looking down at her feet. Then: 'Tell you what, why don't I carry the bag home for you?'

'Ah, thanks, that's really kind,' Holly said. 'But I don't want to keep you from your family on Christmas day, so get yourself off home.'

'I'm not doing Christmas this year,' he told her.

She gazed up at him and pulled a face. 'You can't not do Christmas. What about your family?'

'Haven't got one,' he said, reaching for the bag and offering his arm to her.

'That's so sad,' she murmured, linking him. 'I'm Holly, by the way.'

'Gareth,' he said. 'Which way are we going?'

11

Ellie popped her head out of the kitchen when she heard the front door opening.

'You took your time,' she said when Holly stepped into the hall. 'I was starting to think you'd got lo—'

The word died on her tongue when Gareth appeared in the doorway behind Holly, and she felt as if her stomach had dropped through the floor.

'This is Gareth,' Holly said as she slipped her jacket off. 'I got into a bit of bother with some lads at the shop, and he saved my life. He hasn't got anyone to spend Christmas with, so I've invited him to have dinner with us. You don't mind, do you?'

'I'm, um, not sure we've got enough to go round,' Ellie lied.

'Don't be daft, there's loads,' Holly contradicted her. 'That turkey crown's massive, and you've prepared more veg than Mum usually makes for the whole family.'

'I should probably go,' Gareth said, looking as uncomfortable as Ellie felt.

'You're going nowhere,' Holly said firmly, seizing him by the arm and pulling him into the living room. 'And *you* stop being so selfish,' she admonished Ellie. 'He's got no family, and he'd be spending the day on his own in some dreary hostel if I hadn't brought him back with me.'

Ashamed, because she knew exactly how difficult Gareth's life had been, Ellie blushed, and said, 'It's fine by me, but you'll have to explain it to Matt when he gets home from fishing.'

'That's the miserable brother-in-law I told you about,' Holly said to Gareth, rolling her eyes.

'I really think I should go if it's going to cause trouble,' he reiterated.

'And *I* really think you should sit down and let *us* worry about Matt,' Holly said, pushing him toward the sofa.

Gareth flashed Ellie a look of apology as he sat down, and she dipped her gaze and bustled back into the kitchen.

She was still in there when Matt came home a short time later, and she took a deep breath when he joined her and pushed the door shut.

'Who the hell's that?' he demanded.

'Holly met him at the shop,' she whispered. 'She was having trouble with some lads and he rescued her, so she invited him to have dinner with us.'

'Cheeky bitch!' he spluttered. 'And what did you say?'

'She put me on the spot,' said Ellie. 'And I could hardly say no after he'd put himself out for her, could I? But at least he's taking her mind off Tony and the wedding, so you won't have to suffer her going on about it,' she added, trotting out the line she'd rehearsed.

'Okay, he can stay for dinner,' Matt grunted. 'But he's out of here as soon as it's over.'

'Absolutely,' Ellie agreed.

Holly had already told Gareth all about herself, so when dinner was served and they joined Ellie and Matt at the table, she started quizzing him about his life.

'So, you say you're living in a hostel?'

'Yeah, that's right,' he said, helping himself to some roast potatoes. 'I was living with my . . .' He paused and flicked a surreptitious glance at Ellie from under his lashes, before continuing: 'I was staying with a mate, but we fell out, so now I'm waiting on the council to find me a place.'

'We'll have to swap numbers,' Holly said. 'Then you can let me know when you're sorted, and I'll come and visit you.'

'Yeah, course,' Gareth murmured, casting another quick glance at Ellie.

'How old are you?' Holly went on, watching as he poured a liberal helping of gravy over the food on his plate.

'Twenty-five.'

'Two years younger than me.' She grinned. 'Have you ever been with an older woman?'

Ellie felt something brush against her leg and frowned when she guessed that her sister must be trying to play footsie with Gareth under the table. Considering she was supposed to have been marrying the so-called love of her life in a matter of hours, she was doing a damn good job of getting over it.

'Age means nothing,' Gareth said, with yet another hooded glance at Ellie. 'If you make a connection with someone, nothing else comes into it.'

'I couldn't agree more,' Holly purred, giving him a seductive smile.

Gareth ignored it and looked at Matt. 'Thanks for this, mate. It beats the hell out of the pot noodle I was going to have.'

'Thank Ellie, not me,' Matt replied. 'She's the one who did all the work.'

Gareth turned to Ellie and smiled. 'You're a great cook, Mrs . . . ?'

'Ellie's fine,' she murmured.

'Is that short for something?' he asked.

Annoyed that her sister was taking his attention away from her, Holly said, 'It's short for Eleanor. Eleanor *Louise*, if you please,' she added with a smirk. 'I'm just Holly, thank God. Nothing pretentious about me.'

'Eleanor's a beautiful name,' said Gareth.

Ellie carried on eating without replying. She'd never felt more awkward in her life, and she wished that Holly would stop chattering, because the sooner dinner was over, the sooner Gareth would leave.

Holly had other ideas, and she kept up her questioning all the way through dinner. When they had all finished eating and Matt and Ellie began to clear the table, she opened one of the bottles of brandy she'd bought and poured large, neat shots into hers and Gareth's glasses before leading him over to the sofa.

'I'd best get going when I've had this,' he said.

'Aw, no, stay a bit longer,' she wheedled, cosying up to him and swigging a mouthful of brandy. Shuddering as it went down, she giggled and clinked her glass against his, saying, 'Bottoms up!' before downing the rest of her drink.

'Take it easy,' Ellie cautioned, watching as her sister reached for the bottle and poured another neat glassful.

'God, you sound like *him*,' Holly sniped, nodding at Matt who was carrying the plates into the kitchen. 'If that's what being an old married couple does to you, thank God I escaped when I did.'

Matt slammed the plates down on the kitchen ledge. 'I'm getting a headache,' he muttered to Ellie. 'I'm going for a walk.'

Following him out into the hall, she closed the door, and whispered, 'Have you really got a headache, or are you just trying to get away from them?'

'What do *you* think?' he grunted, yanking his coat on. 'She doesn't even know him, and she's practically dry-humping him. It's disgusting.'

'I'll try and get rid of him while you're out,' Ellie promised.

'Don't try, *do* it,' Matt said as he opened the front door. 'And don't leave them on their own,' he added as he stepped outside. 'The way she's going on, she'll probably drag him into our bed the minute your back's turned.'

Ellie nodded and watched as he strode away. Closing the

door when he'd turned the corner, she went back into the living room, where Holly was now quizzing Gareth about girlfriends. He glanced up at Ellie with a strained expression on his face, and she sensed that he wanted her to intervene and get Holly to back off, but she walked on into the kitchen, closing the door behind her.

She was washing the dishes when the door opened a few minutes later, and she frowned when she turned her head and saw Gareth standing behind her.

'Holly's gone to the loo, so I thought I'd sneak out while the coast was clear,' he told her. 'I just wanted to apologize if I've made things awkward for you. I had no idea she was your sister, or I wouldn't have come.'

'You weren't to know,' Ellie replied quietly. 'But thanks for not letting on that you know me.'

'I kind of guessed you didn't want Matt to know,' he said. 'Anyway, thanks for letting me stay for dinner. It's been great to see you again.'

Ellie said, 'You, too,' and was about to show him out when the doorbell rang.

Holly came out of the bathroom and answered it, and Ellie frowned when she heard her say, 'What the hell are *you* doing here?'

'I needed to see you,' Tony replied. 'Can we talk?'

Brushing past Gareth, Ellie marched to the front door and glared at Tony.

'You've got a bloody nerve coming here after what you did.'

'It was a misunderstanding,' he insisted. 'I honestly thought my divorce had been finalized.'

'Of course you did,' she sneered, not believing a word of it. 'Holly's told me everything, so do yourself a favour and get lost, 'cos you're not welcome here.'

Tony turned back to Holly and held out his hands. 'Just talk to me, baby. I love you, and I know we can get past this.'

'If you loved me, you wouldn't be shagging that whore behind my back,' she spat, angrily slapping his hands away.

'It only happened once,' he said. 'I went round to see the kids, and things got out of hand. But I've thought about it, and I know you're the one I want.'

'You had to *think* about it?' Holly squawked. 'Oh my God, I can't believe you said that! Get the fuck away from me!'

'Don't do this,' he pleaded. 'We're good together, you know we are.'

'What part of *FUCK OFF* do you not understand?' she screeched, taking a swing at him.

'I'm sorry,' he cried, shielding his face with his arms as she rained slaps and punches down on his head. 'I'll tell Suzie I can't see her again.'

'What do you mean you'll *tell* her?' Holly repeated furiously. 'Why haven't you already told her?'

'He was probably hedging his bets in case you turned him down,' Ellie said, poised to jump in if Tony tried to hit her sister back.

'I didn't mean it like that,' Tony insisted. 'I mean I'll tell her

I'm not coming to see the kids again, if that's the only way to prove to you that I'm not interested in her. You're the only one I want.'

'Tough, 'cos I don't want *you*!' Holly said, taking a step back when she noticed Gareth standing behind Ellie in the doorway. 'This is my man now.' She slipped her arm through Gareth's. 'And he's worth ten of you, so sling your hook.'

'Hey, this has got nothing to do with me.' Gareth raised his hands. 'I'm out of here.'

'Yeah, you'd better be,' Tony snarled as his rival stepped out into the corridor. 'And don't ever let me catch you near my woman again.'

Gareth hesitated and peered down into the other man's eyes. 'Don't threaten me, mate. You've got no idea who I am, or what I'm capable of.'

'I'm not your mate,' Tony spat, squaring up to him.

Afraid that they were about to start brawling, which wouldn't go down too well with her neighbours, Ellie stepped between them, and said, 'Just go, Gareth. And *you* can go, as well,' she added to Tony. 'You've done enough damage already.'

Shoulders sagging when Gareth walked away and Holly trounced back inside the flat, Tony said, 'Please don't look at me like that, Ellie. I feel terrible about what happened, and I'll do anything to make it right. Will you talk to her for me? She'll listen to you.'

Ellie sighed when she heard the sincerity in his voice and

saw it in his eyes. 'You took too long to think about it, so I doubt it'll make any difference; but I'll see what I can do.'

'Thank you,' he said gratefully. 'I've booked a suite at The Lowry. If she agrees to talk, tell her to ring me and I'll come and pick her up.'

Holly was sitting on the sofa with a fresh glass of brandy in her hand when Ellie went back into the living room.

'What did he say?'

'That he's sorry, and he wants to talk to you.'

'How did he sound?'

'Upset, and guilty, obviously. He said to give him a ring when you're ready to talk and he'll come and pick you up.'

'Wanker!' spat Holly. 'As if I'm going to go running back to him just like that. He must think I'm as stupid as that ugly bitch wife of his!'

Before Ellie could respond, the front door opened, and Matt came in.

'Has Tony been here?' he asked as he took off his coat. 'I'm sure he drove past me just now.'

'Yeah, he was here,' Ellie said. 'He was trying to talk Holly into giving him another chance.'

'Oh?' A flash of hope flared in Matt's eyes.

'And I told him to fuck off,' said Holly. 'I've got a good mind to go and find that Gary and shag the arse off him,' she added bitterly. 'That'll show him.'

'His name's Gareth,' Ellie corrected her. 'And you're going nowhere until you sober up.'

Disappointed that his sister-in-law had decided not to leave with her boyfriend, Matt said, 'I'm going to lie down for a bit.'

'Moody shit,' Holly muttered, slumping back against the cushions and putting her feet up on the coffee table when he stomped into the bedroom.

'Don't start,' Ellie warned, reaching for Holly's cigarettes.

'Thought you'd given up,' Holly said as she slid one out of the pack.

'As far as Matt knows, I have,' Ellie said quietly, picking up Holly's lighter. 'Stay there and warn me if he comes back out.'

It was only 5 p.m., but it was already pitch-dark outside, and the temperature had plummeted. Shivering when she stepped onto the balcony, Ellie lit up and took a deep drag. It was the first smoke she'd had that day, and she felt light-headed as soon as the nicotine hit her. About to take another drag, she looked round guiltily when the door opened behind her.

'What are you doing?' she hissed when Holly came out to join her. 'I thought I told you to watch out for Matt.'

'I need a cig,' Holly said, pulling the door to behind her. 'If he comes out, you can tell him you were keeping me company.'

Nodding her agreement, Ellie watched as Holly lit up and exhaled her smoke into the air. 'So what did you make of what Tony said?' she asked. 'Did you believe him about it being a mistake?'

'I don't know.' Holly shrugged. 'Half of me wants to believe him, but the other half is telling me to forget him and move on.'

'Can you do that?'

'I don't know. It's been great living with him and not having to worry about money, but I'm not sure it's real.'

'What do you mean?' Ellie peered at her. 'I thought you loved him?'

'So did I.' Holly sighed. 'But then I met that other guy and fancied the arse off him, so it made me wonder. You know what I'm like. I can be madly in love with a bloke one day, and hate his guts the next.'

'You were about to marry Tony,' Ellie reminded her. 'So you must have thought it was more serious than your other relationships.'

'Yeah, I did. But he looked so old next to Gareth, it kind of turned me off.'

'Christ, you're fickle!'

'It's okay for you. You've been married forever, so you don't care how old Matt looks.'

'Excuse me?' Ellie drew her head back.

'Oh, you know what I mean.' Holly flapped her hand dismissively. 'You and Matt are nearly the same age, but Tony's nearly forty. *Forty*,' she repeated, as if she'd only just realized and was horrified. 'Look at me . . .' She held out her arms. 'I'm young and gorgeous, and I could have any man I want, so why am I going to settle for *him*?'

'Forty's hardly ancient,' Ellie pointed out. 'And you looked so happy when you brought him round to meet us. I can't believe your feelings have changed that fast. You're only lashing out because he's hurt you.'

'I know,' Holly conceded. 'And I do still feel something for him, but I can't forget the way that bitch and her brats looked at me on the beach. It was like she was laughing at me, telling me I mean nothing 'cos he always goes back to her in the end.'

'She's a woman,' said Ellie. 'That's what we do when we feel threatened by someone younger and prettier.'

'It still pisses me off,' Holly muttered, taking another drag on her cigarette. Looking at Ellie when she'd exhaled the smoke, she said, 'Don't you ever wonder how *your* life might have turned out if you hadn't got saddled with Matt?'

'I'm not saddled with him,' said Ellie. 'I love him.'

'But is that enough?' Holly asked. 'I mean, you're not exactly passionate about each other, are you? It's more like you know this is your lot, so you've accepted it. But there's got to be more than *this*.' She flapped her hand at the balcony door, indicating that she was talking about the life Ellie was leading behind it.

Frowning, Ellie said, 'Why do you do that? I know you're hurting, but that doesn't give you the right to pick holes in mine and Matt's life.'

'Sorry.' Holly held up her hands. 'I know it's a touchy subject, but you're my sister, and I just think you deserve better.'

'I'm perfectly satisfied, thank you,' Ellie said tersely, taking one last drag on the cigarette before flicking the butt over the balcony. 'I'm going back in.'

'I think I'll go for a walk,' Holly said.

'In this weather?' Ellie hesitated. 'You'll freeze to death. And this isn't one of your posh London suburbs, don't forget. You're likely to get mugged if you walk around in the dark on your own round here.'

'I'll stick to the main road,' Holly assured her. 'I just need to be on my own for a bit, to think things over.'

'Well, if it's Tony you're thinking about, he's at the Lowry,' said Ellie. 'And I wouldn't leave it too long if I were you, or he might decide to cut his losses and go back to his wife.'

She knew it was a bitchy thing to say, but she was sick of Holly putting Matt down, so she figured it was deserved.

'Have you got some flats I can borrow?' Holly asked when she followed Ellie inside a few minutes later. 'My shoes aren't really made for this kind of weather.'

'Why don't you ring Tony and get him to pick you up, like he offered?' Ellie suggested.

'I'm not going to see him,' Holly said, already slipping her feet into a pair of shoes she'd spotted at the side of the sofa.

'Who *are* you going to see, then?' Ellie demanded, although she'd already guessed it was Gareth.

'No one,' Holly lied. 'I just fancy a walk.'

Tutting her disapproval, Ellie said, 'Don't do anything stupid. He might be good-looking, but he's homeless and broke, so there's nothing he can give you.'

'It's not all about money,' said Holly, reaching for her jacket.

'I hope you remember that when you've blown it with Tony and you're forced to move back in with Mum and Billy,' Ellie said piously. 'But it's your life.'

'Yes, it is,' Holly agreed, smiling as she zipped the jacket up before picking up the unopened bottle of brandy. 'I'll take these,' she said then, scooping Ellie's keys up off the table. 'And don't bother waiting up. I could be a while.'

12

Holly did a quick Google search when she left the flat, and was pleased to find that there was only one hostel in the area – and that it was only a ten-minute walk away.

On the way there, she told herself that she was doing nothing wrong; that she was only doing to Tony what he had done to her, and when she'd had her fun she would call him and make him grovel before graciously agreeing to give him another chance.

Holly began to reconsider her decision when she arrived at the hostel and saw the heavy-duty security door and steel-barred windows, but a vision of Tony's wife smirking at her as she'd announced that she and Tony were not only still married, but were also still screwing, renewed her determination, and she marched up to the door and jabbed her finger down on the bell.

'Does a man called Gareth live here?' she asked the scruffy man who answered.

'Who wants to know?' he asked, looking her up and down.

'None of your business,' she replied frostily. 'Is he here, or not?'

Telling her to wait there, the man closed the door and she heard him shuffle away. A few minutes later, Gareth appeared.

'Oh, it's you,' he said, folding his arms when he saw her. 'What are you doing here?'

'Thought you might like to help me finish this.' She held up the bottle.

'We're not allowed to bring booze inside,' he told her. 'And we can't have visitors, either. Unless they're family.'

'Tell them I'm your cousin and I've come with terrible news about your auntie,' Holly said, slipping the bottle inside her jacket. 'I can cry, if you like? I'm really good at putting it on.'

Gareth ran a hand through his hair and gazed out over her shoulder at the dark road beyond. Then, sighing, he said, 'Wait there a sec.'

He left the door ajar, and Holly heard him asking someone if it was all right for his cousin to come in. Figuring that he'd been given permission when he came back and gestured for her to come inside, she stuck close to his side when he ushered her through a musty-smelling reception area and down a long corridor, past a series of doors which all seemed to be decorated with footprints and fist-sized indentations.

Gareth unlocked a door at the end of the corridor and waved her into a tiny box-like room, containing a wardrobe, an ancient armchair minus its seat cushion, a single bed, and a table on which an old portable TV sat among a mess of tea-making equipment and empty Pot Noodle cartons.

'It's like a cell,' she said, trying not to pull a face as she eyed the stained pillow-case and grubby duvet cover.

'Better than sleeping rough,' he replied.

Wondering again what she was doing here when she could be lounging on a king-size bed at the Lowry, drinking champagne while Tony begged for forgiveness, Holly let out a little squeak of fear when she spotted a movement in the corner.

'What was that?' She clutched at Gareth's arm and pointed over at it. 'Something just ran behind the wardrobe.'

'It'll be Quasi,' he said, smiling as he sank down onto the bed.

'Quasi?' she repeated, frowning as she perched beside him and looked nervously around.

'It's a mouse, and it's got a hump on its back like Quasimodo,' he explained. 'The hunchback of Notre Dame,' he elaborated when she gave him a blank look.

'I've got no idea what you're talking about,' she muttered, slapping herself on the thigh. Giving him a disapproving look when she saw amusement in his eyes, she said, 'It's not funny. I feel like I'm being eaten alive.'

'No one asked you to come,' he reminded her.

'Yes, well, I'm starting to regret it now.'

'I'll show you out, then.'

'It's okay,' Holly said, touching his arm when he made to

stand up. 'I'm here now, so we might as well have that drink. Have you got glasses?'

'No, but I've got a cup,' he said, leaning over and picking a stained mug up off the table.

Holly's skin was already crawling, and she grimaced at the thought of her lips touching the chipped rim of the cup. But she didn't want Gareth to think she was being a snob, so she handed the bottle to him.

'Ladies first,' he said, handing the cup to her when he'd filled it.

Shivering when she felt the heat of his thigh against hers, Holly turned the cup round to the least chipped section and swallowed a mouthful before handing it back to him.

'How long have you been living here?' she asked as he took a swig.

'A few weeks,' he said, resting on his elbow when he'd taken a drink and passed the cup back to her. 'So what happened with your fella after I left?'

'I told him to fuck off,' Holly said, shuffling further up on the bed until her back was propped against the wall.

'He seemed pretty cut up.'

'He deserved it.'

'So is that it?' Gareth asked as she took another swig. 'You're finished with him?'

'Depends,' Holly said, slipping her jacket off after handing the cup back to him.

'On what?'

'On whether I decide to get with someone else,' she said, smiling seductively as she added, 'Someone *better*.'

Gareth swallowed the rest of the drink and sat forward to refill the cup. 'Was Ellie okay after I left?' he asked, passing it to her.

'She was fine,' Holly said dismissively. 'But I don't want to talk about her, I want to know about *you*. You didn't answer earlier when I asked if you had a girlfriend?'

Gareth smiled but didn't reply. Holly took it as a yes, but she didn't care. She was here to get revenge on Tony for cheating on her, and if some girl she didn't know and was never likely to meet got hurt in the process, it wasn't her problem.

'You're lucky to have Ellie looking out for you,' Gareth said. 'I wish I had someone who cared that much about me.'

Irritated that he was still talking about her stupid sister, Holly swallowed the rest of the brandy and shivered when it burned her throat and brought tears to her eyes.

'Your Ellie's husband seemed a bit quiet today,' Gareth went on. 'Was that because I was there?'

'No, it's because he's a miserable git,' Holly said, tossing the empty cup aside and grabbing his arm. 'Now shut up about them and kiss me . . .'

Matt had stayed in the bedroom after Holly left, so Ellie had settled on the sofa to watch TV by herself. She had fallen asleep in the middle of a film, but she was jolted awake some time later by the sound of the doorbell ringing. Going out into the hall, she peeped through the spyhole and tutted when she saw Gareth struggling to hold Holly up in the corridor outside.

'There she is!' Holly said loudly when Ellie opened the door. 'My big sis, Ellie, with her big fat belly. *They call her Ellie belly . . .*' she sang. '*Smelly Ellie belly . . .*'

'Shut up before you wake the whole block,' Ellie hissed.

'Ah, fuck 'em, loada stuck up auld bastards!' Holly drawled. 'Yeah, I'm talking to *you* . . .' She pointed at one of the neighbouring doors. '*And* you . . .' The next.

Ellie glared at Gareth. 'Why the hell did you let her get this drunk?'

'I couldn't stop her,' he replied apologetically. 'She turned up at the hostel with a bottle, and the next thing I knew, she'd finished it. If I'd known she was going to get like this I'd have poured it down the sink.'

Ellie breathed in deeply and reminded herself that her sister wasn't his responsibility. 'Sorry for snapping,' she muttered, pulling Holly in over the step and shoving her in the direction of the living room. 'And thanks for making sure she got back all right.'

'No worries,' Gareth said. 'I'm sorry it's so late, but she fell asleep and I couldn't wake her for ages.'

'Nothing happened, did it?' Ellie asked. 'I mean, you and her didn't . . .'

Gareth looked confused for a moment, then horrified. 'God, no! We were only talking.'

Shamefaced, Ellie murmured, 'Sorry, that was out of order.

You're both adults, so it's none of my business. It's just that . . . well, you saw her boyfriend earlier. She's angry, and I wouldn't want her to use you to get back at him.'

'I'm not stupid,' Gareth said quietly, gazing down into her eyes.

'No, I know you're not,' Ellie said, glancing round when she heard a bang coming from the living room. 'I'd best get inside before she wakes Matt. Thanks again.'

'Wait,' Gareth said when she went to close the door. 'I've got something for you.'

Frowning when he pulled a slim box out of his pocket and handed it to her, Ellie said, 'What is it?'

'Just a little something to say thank you for everything you've done,' he said. 'I was going to bring it to the cafe when you went back to work, but now I've seen you, I thought you might as well have it now.'

'Thanks, but I can't take it.' Ellie handed it back. 'You already gave me those flowers, so there's no need for anything else.'

'It was my nan's, and there's no one else for me to give it to,' Gareth said. 'It'll only end up getting nicked if I have to keep it at the hostel, so I'd prefer it to be with you where I know it's safe.'

Sighing when he held it out again, Ellie said, 'Okay, I'll take it; but I'm only looking after it till you get a place of your own. And Matt can't know about it, so please don't mention it if you ever see him again.'

'It'll be our little secret,' Gareth assured her. 'But make sure you look inside the box.'

Feeling guilty when he gave her a conspiratorial smile, Ellie muttered goodnight and quickly closed the door.

Holly was flat out on the sofa when she went back into the living room, so she gently slipped the shoes off her feet and covered her with the quilt. About to go into the kitchen to find a temporary hiding place for the necklace, she jumped when Matt appeared in the doorway behind her and asked what was going on.

'Nothing,' she whispered, shoving the box down the side of a cushion before turning to him. 'Holly's drunk, so I was just covering her up.'

'I thought I heard a man's voice?' he said, yawning and rubbing at his eyes.

'It was only one of the neighbours, making sure she got in okay,' she lied. 'Go back to bed. I'll be in when I've switched everything off in here.'

She turned back to the sofa when Matt shuffled into the bedroom, but as she was trying to slide her hand down the side of the cushion, Holly rolled over and pushed her away, mumbling: 'Gerroff, Tony . . . I'm not in the mood.'

Unable to get at the box without disturbing Holly again and potentially bringing Matt back into the room, Ellie decided to leave it till morning and switched off the TV and lamp before heading to bed.

13

Holly was gone when Ellie got up the next morning, but she'd left a note and an unopened pack of cigarettes on the coffee table. Annoyed that she'd left the latter on plain view, because Matt would have thrown them away if he'd seen them first, Ellie slipped them into her cardigan pocket before reading the note.

Sorry for sneaking out, but I can't remember getting home last night and I'm guessing you're probably pissed off with me, so I've gone to sort things out with Tony. Thanks for putting up with me, speak soon, Holls xxx

Relieved that she'd gone, because it was exhausting having to deal with her dramas, Ellie chucked the note into the bin and went out onto the balcony to have a quick smoke before Matt got up. The snow had melted, so the estate was its usual drab grey, and as she gazed at the shabby buildings with their peeling paintwork and grimy net curtains, she wondered how long it would take Holly to forgive Tony. It wouldn't be easy for her to turn a blind eye to what he'd done, and she would be suspicious of every phone call he made from now on; every trip he took without her, and every unexplained receipt she found in his pocket. But Ellie suspected she'd find a way to live with it if finishing with him meant losing out on his money and being forced to move back to the ghetto.

Finished with the cigarette a few minutes later, Ellie was about to go back inside when she spotted a hooded figure standing among the overgrown bushes by the gate. She couldn't be certain from that distance, but she suspected it was Gareth, and that made her wonder if he had lied when he'd told her that nothing had happened between him and Holly last night. If so, and they had arranged to meet up today, he was in for a long wait. But it wasn't her problem, and she wasn't about to put herself out by going down and telling him.

Matt came into the living room as Ellie stepped back inside, and she felt a guilty blush heat her cheeks when he asked, 'What were you doing out there?'

'Just wanted to see if the snow had stopped,' she said, aware that she could easily have checked by looking out of the window instead.

'Where's your sister?' he asked, looking round.

'She's gone to see Tony,' Ellie told him, walking around the far end of the couch and pausing to plump the cushions so he wouldn't smell the smoke on her clothes.

'*Yes!*' he crowed, punching the air as he flopped into his chair. 'Kettle on?'

'I'll do it in a minute. I need a wee first.'

Ellie dashed to the bathroom and quickly sprayed herself with perfume. Alarmed when Matt suddenly bellowed her name as she was flushing the toilet, she rushed back into the living room.

'What's wrong? Have you hurt yourself? It's not your leg, is—'

Tailing off when she noticed the cigarettes sitting on the coffee table, she patted her cardigan pocket, and guessed, when she found that it was empty, that they must have fallen out when she'd run to the bathroom.

'Okay, you caught me,' she admitted, holding up her hands. 'Holly left them, and I smoked one. That's why I was out on the balcony.'

'I don't give a shit about that,' Matt replied icily. 'I'm more interested to hear what you've got to say about *this*.'

Momentarily confused when he thrust a slim box under her nose, Ellie felt her stomach do a little flip when she remembered, and she swallowed nervously when she glanced at the sofa and saw that the cushions had been moved.

'I was looking for the TV remote, but I found this instead,' Matt told her. 'Care to explain?'

'It's not mine,' she lied. 'It must be Holly's.'

'Is that right?' he said. 'So why does it say Dear *Ellie* on this?' He flapped a piece of paper in front of her face. '"*Dear Ellie*,"' he

SAVE ME

read it out loud. '"*Thanks so much for letting me spend Christmas with you, it meant the world to me. I hope you'll love this necklace as much as my nan did, and I'll see you at our usual place in the new year. All my love, Gareth . . .*"' He spat out the name, before finishing through clenched teeth: 'Kiss, kiss, fucking *kiss!*'

The blood had drained from Ellie's face, and the room felt as if it had gone into a spin. Unable to think up a reasonable explanation, she croaked, 'It's not what you think. He was just . . .'

'He was just *what?*' Matt yelled when she faltered. 'You'd better start fucking talking, or so help me . . .'

He left the threat hanging, and Ellie sensed that he was struggling to control his rage when she saw him ball his hands into fists. Scared, because she'd never seen him as angry as this before and really thought that he might hit her if she said the wrong thing, she took a step back.

'He was just th-thanking me,' she stuttered. 'He – he's the lad I told you about that time: the one who was going to throw himself under the train.'

'You already fucking *knew* him?' Matt's eyebrows shot up in disbelief. 'And you let him sit at my fucking table without telling me?'

'Only because I knew you'd react like *this,*' Ellie spluttered. 'I was shocked when Holly brought him in. I had no idea he lived round here. You've got to believe me.'

'Why should I?' Matt snarled. 'You've probably been screwing him behind my back for months, for all I know.'

123

'I haven't, I swear,' Ellie insisted. 'It's not like that.'

'Don't fucking *LIE TO ME!*' Matt roared, spittle flying from his mouth and spattering her cheek. 'I'm not stupid. Men don't give presents to women they hardly know!'

'Matt, don't!' Ellie cried when he yanked the necklace out of the box and tore at the chain, causing crystal beads to fly around the floor. 'It was his grandmother's, and you've got this all wrong. There's nothing going on with me and Gareth.'

'Do *not* say that man's name in my presence, or I swear to God I'll kill someone,' Matt warned.

'But I'm telling the truth,' Ellie persisted, desperate to make him understand. 'And I didn't tell you I'd seen him again because I knew you'd think the worst. He walked past the cafe where I have lunch and recognised me, so he stopped to thank me. That's all there was to it, I swear.'

'If it was only once, why did he say he'd see you in your *usual place*?' Matt made quote marks in the air with his fingers.

'Because it was twice,' Ellie admitted. 'But—'

'I *knew* you were lying!' Matt yelled, seizing her by the wrist. 'So how long has it been going on? I said HOW FUCKIN' LONG?'

'Matt, stop it!' she cried, wincing when he twisted her wrist. 'You're hurting me!'

He let out a roar of anger and tossed her arm aside, then stalked out of the room, pausing to yank his jacket off the hook before leaving the flat. Legs trembling when he'd gone, Ellie ran over to the window to check if the man she'd seen in the bushes was still hanging around. If it *was* Gareth and Matt saw him, she dreaded to think what would happen.

Relieved to see that the man had gone, she watched as Matt emerged from the main door and strode down the path, heading in the direction of the canal. Going into the kitchen to get the dustpan and brush when he'd disappeared from view, she came back into the living room and set about sweeping up the scattered beads with tears of shame in her eyes. The necklace was old, and she could only imagine that Gareth's grandmother must have treasured it to have kept it for so long. Determined to get it fixed and give it back to Gareth, she placed the beads into a plastic bag along with the chain, and had no sooner stashed it in the zip pocket of her handbag than the doorbell rang.

Thinking that it was probably one of the neighbours come to complain about the shouting, she groaned when she looked through the spyhole and saw Gareth standing there.

'Holly's not here,' she said without preamble when she opened the door.

'I came to see you, not her,' Gareth said. 'I just saw Matt, and he looked angry, so I wanted to check you were okay.'

'I'm fine,' Ellie said, wondering why he'd been watching the flats if he wasn't looking for Holly.

Gareth spotted a red mark and the beginnings of a bruise on her wrist. 'Did *he* do that?' he asked, frowning.

Embarrassed, Ellie pulled the sleeve of her cardigan down over it. 'No, of course not. I banged it on the door.'

'I don't believe you,' Gareth said.

'I don't really care *what* you believe,' Ellie snapped. 'It's none of your business.'

'Sorry,' he said quietly. 'I wasn't trying to interfere. I just worry about you, 'cos I know I made things difficult between you and Matt.'

Feeling guilty for snapping at him, because he looked like a puppy who'd been kicked and had no idea why, Ellie said, 'Don't apologize; you've done nothing wrong. I'm in a bit of a funny mood today, that's all.'

'It's okay, I understand,' said Gareth. 'But if you ever need to talk, or whatever, I'm only ten minutes down the road; Lockwood Court.'

Grateful that he cared, but nervous that Matt might come back at any minute, Ellie said, 'Thanks, but I promise I'm okay.'

When at last he'd gone, Ellie closed the door and leaned wearily back against it. Her arguments with Matt usually blew over pretty quickly, give or take a few days of sulky silences, but she had a horrible feeling that this one was going to be worse than usual. This time, Matt didn't merely *suspect* that she was cheating on him, he thought he had actual *proof*; and it would be difficult to convince him otherwise, because she'd lied and he had caught her out.

14

Matt still hadn't come home or answered any of her calls by midnight, so Ellie went to bed; but she hadn't been asleep for long when she was woken again by the sound of muffled voices. Jumping up when she heard a girlish giggle, she pulled her dressing gown on and marched out into the hall. Stopped in her tracks by the sight of Matt slobbering over a scantily dressed young girl who had her arms around his neck, she squawked, 'What the *hell* is going on?'

'Oh, fuck, I thought you'd be asleep by now,' Matt grunted, turning drunkenly round to face her as the girl tugged the hem of her short skirt down to cover her panties.

'Who's *that*?' Ellie demanded through gritted teeth.

'Her name's Barbara,' Matt said, grinning nastily as he added, 'Your replacement.'

'It's Belinda,' the girl corrected him, giving him a playful slap on the arm.

'At least I got the initial right,' he joked, pinching one of her buttocks and making her squeal.

Ellie's head felt as if it was about to explode. 'Get . . . her . . . *out!*' she snarled.

'Fuck you,' Matt drawled. 'I invited her, and she's staying.'

Belinda looked from one to the other of them and mock-grimaced. 'Oh, dear . . . are you having a domestic?'

'Take no notice of her,' Matt said dismissively. 'She's just my ex-wife. Or, at least, she *will* be my ex when I've seen my solicitor in the morning and divorced her cheating arse.'

'Gerroff!' Belinda snorted, pushing him away when he nuzzled her neck. 'You're drunk.'

'Yes I am,' he agreed, giving her a leery grin. 'And I didn't splash out on all that fizz for nothing, so we'd best make the most of it before it wears off.'

'Not in front of *her*.' Belinda flicked a glance at Ellie when he moved in to kiss her. 'Isn't there somewhere more private we can go?'

'Bed,' he said, grasping her by the hand and pulling her toward the bedroom door.

'Don't even think about it!' Ellie warned, blocking their path. Then, glaring at the girl, she hissed, 'Get out, and don't ever let me catch you near my husband again!'

'Oh, so I'm your husband again, am I?' Matt snorted. 'Pity you didn't remember that when you were busy screwing the arse off that cunt!'

'I haven't screwed anybody, but we'll talk about that when you've sobered up,' Ellie retorted angrily. 'Right now, *she* needs to go before I do something I regret.'

Matt swayed on his feet and stared at her for a few seconds. Then, muttering, 'Whatever,' he dropped the girl's hand and, pushing past Ellie, stumbled into the bedroom.

'Hey, what about me?' Belinda called after him. Pulling a face when Ellie glared at her, she said, '*What?* It's not *my* fault. *I* didn't know he was married.'

'And the wedding ring didn't alert you?' Ellie asked sarcastically.

'I wasn't exactly looking at his hands,' Belinda replied cockily.

'Just get out,' Ellie hissed.

'Not without my money,' said Belinda. 'He said he'd give me twenty quid to get a cab home in the morning.'

With her lips pursed in defiance, and her hands on her non-existent hips, the girl reminded Ellie of the teenagers who hung around in the park drinking cheap cider.

'How old are you?' she demanded.

'Seventeen,' said Belinda. 'Why?'

'For God's sake, you're not even old enough to get into a nightclub, never mind cop off with a stranger,' Ellie said irritably. 'What if he'd spiked your drink and raped you, you stupid girl.'

Belinda's eyes widened. 'You saying he's a rapist?'

'Luckily for you, *no,*' said Ellie. 'But he *could* have been, and you'd have been trapped in here with him. Didn't your mother warn you about things like this?'

'You'd best not be dissing my mum?' Belinda retorted churlishly.

If Ellie hadn't been so angry, she'd have laughed in the girl's silly little face. But she wanted rid of her, so she said, 'Wait there,' and marched into the living room to get her purse.

'Here . . . get a taxi home,' she said, thrusting a ten-pound note into her hand when she came back and ushering her out into the communal hallway. 'And stick to boys your own age in future,' she added tartly before slamming the door in her face.

Desperate to have this out with Matt, she marched into the bedroom. He was sprawled face-down on the bed, still fully clothed and snoring his head off, and he didn't stir when she shook his arm. Doubting that she would get any sense out of him even if she did manage to rouse him, she gave up and went back into the living room.

After falling asleep on the sofa in the early hours, Ellie was aching and cold when she was woken by the sound of the toilet flushing the next morning. Sighing when Matt came in a couple of minutes later and walked through to the kitchen without looking at her, she pushed herself wearily up to her feet and followed him.

'We need to talk,' she said, shivering in the doorway as he carried the kettle to the sink and poured water into it.

Matt switched the kettle on and reached into the cupboard for a cup.

'Don't you think this is a bit childish?' she asked as he

spooned coffee into it before taking the milk out of the fridge.

Matt resolutely ignored her and kept his gaze on the kettle until it had boiled. After making his drink, he went back to the bedroom and closed the door, and Ellie tutted when she heard him push the little bolt into place. Unwilling to sit around and wait for him to snap out of his strop and talk to her, Ellie had a quick wash and brushed her teeth, then pulled her coat on and headed out for a walk to clear her head.

The local park wasn't the nicest of places at the best of times, and it was especially bad during school holidays when the local gangs used it as a hangout. Ellie usually avoided it like the plague, but she had nowhere else to go, so she found herself heading in through the gate. Surprised to find it deserted, for a change, she walked round to the duck pond and, taking a seat on one of the graffiti-scarred benches, lit a cigarette.

She hadn't taken two drags on it before she heard her name being called, and she muttered, *'You've got to be fucking kidding me!'* under her breath when she looked round and saw Gareth jogging toward her.

'Wow, what a coincidence,' he said, grinning widely when he reached her. 'I walk through this park every day, but I've never seen you here before.'

'I needed a bit of peace and quiet,' she said, hoping he would take the hint and go on his way.

He didn't.

'How are things with you and Matt?' he asked, sitting down beside her. 'Did you manage to sort things out with him?'

'Yeah, everything's fine,' she lied, avoiding his gaze as she took another pull on her smoke.

Gareth drew his head back and gave her a searching look. 'Are you sure? You don't look very happy.'

'I said I'm fine,' she muttered. 'So don't let me keep you if you were on your way somewhere.'

'I was, but it's not important,' he replied softly. 'You know you can talk to me, don't you?' he went on after a moment. 'I probably wouldn't be here right now if you hadn't let me get all that stuff off my chest, so why don't you let me do the same for you?'

Ellie shook her head and dipped her gaze as tears pricked her eyes.

'Take it from someone who knows, you'll feel better for it,' Gareth persisted.

'What's the point?' She sniffed. 'I'll still have to go home, and Matt still won't be talking to me.'

'Why isn't he talking to you?'

'Because he found the necklace and your note.'

'Ah...' Gareth grimaced. 'He wasn't meant to see that. Sorry.'

'It's not your fault, it's mine,' she said, rooting in her pocket for a tissue. 'I should have told him I'd seen you again after that first night, but he can get a bit jealous, so I thought it'd be better if I didn't say anything. Then you turned up with Holly, and now he thinks I arranged the whole thing so we could spend Christmas together. I told him he'd got it all wrong, but he didn't believe me. Then last night he . . .'

'What?' Gareth prompted when she tailed off and blew her nose.

'He brought another woman back to the flat,' Ellie said, her cheeks flaring with embarrassment.

'You're kidding?' Gareth frowned.

'I wish I was,' Ellie said miserably. 'She was only seventeen, and I doubt she'd have looked twice at him if they hadn't been so drunk. But she was that cocky, I could have slapped her.'

'So what *did* you do?'

'I gave her a tenner to get a taxi home, and told her to stick to boys her own age in future.'

'You're better than me, 'cos I wouldn't have given her a penny,' Gareth snorted. 'And what did Matt have to say about it?'

'Nothing.' Ellie sighed. 'He'd passed out by the time I got rid of her, so I couldn't have it out with him. And now he's ignoring me.'

'Wow, what a bastard.'

'Oh, don't say that,' Ellie groaned. 'He's only being like this because I lied. If I'd been honest from the start, he wouldn't have reacted so badly.'

'That's no excuse to use you as a punching bag,' said Gareth. 'And don't say he hasn't, 'cos I've seen the bruises.'

'He didn't hit me,' Ellie said truthfully. 'He grabbed me a bit harder than he realized, that's all.'

'If he was any kind of man, he would never put his hands on

you in anger,' Gareth argued. 'He's lucky to have you, but if he can't see that, he doesn't deserve you.'

Feeling uncomfortable, and more than a little disloyal, Ellie took one last drag on her cigarette and, dropping the butt to the floor, ground it out with her heel.

'I'd best get going. Thanks for listening.'

'Anytime,' Gareth said softly.

Ellie nodded goodbye and walked quickly away. He meant well, but this wasn't his business, and she should never have confided in him like that.

Matt was sitting in the living room when Ellie got home; agitatedly drumming his fingertips on the arm of his chair.

'Decided to come back, then, did you?' he said when she walked in. 'Thought you'd have run off with lover boy by now.'

'We need to sort this out once and for all,' she said, perching on the sofa and resting her elbows on her knees. 'Will you talk to me?'

'Depends if you're going to tell the truth this time?'

'I'm sorry I didn't tell you I'd seen Gareth again, but I honestly didn't think it was important at the time. And I didn't want you to jump to the wrong conclusion – which is exactly what you *did*.'

'Can you blame me?'

'Probably not,' Ellie conceded. 'But I swear on my life there's nothing going on with me and him.'

'So you keep saying. But I can't get past the fact that you've been meeting up with him behind my back.'

'It wasn't like that. He stopped to talk to me at the cafe, but I didn't see him again until Holly brought him here that day. I tried to get rid of him because I knew you'd be upset if you knew who he was, but she begged me to let him stay. That's all there was to it, I swear. You do believe me, don't you?'

'I don't know what to believe,' Matt murmured. 'And I honestly don't know if I'll be able to forgive you this time. I need space to get my head around it.'

Irritated that he was acting like the victim when he was the one who had almost slept with someone else, Ellie said, 'Okay, I'll give you space, if that's what you need. But don't take too long, because I've done nothing wrong and I won't be treated like a criminal in my own home. Oh, and just so we're clear,' she added as she rose to her feet. 'If you ever bring another woman into my home again, it'll be *me* who puts in for a divorce.'

15

Matt didn't mention Gareth again, and Ellie didn't mention the girl he'd brought home, and by the time she was due back at work the following week, things were pretty much back to normal. Better, in fact, since Matt had been invited to an interview with one of the companies he'd sent his CV to, which had given his confidence a much-needed boost.

On the morning of the interview, Ellie was getting dressed when Matt's phone started ringing. He was in the shower, so she went round to his side of the bed and picked it up, but it went dead as soon as she answered it.

'Was that mine or yours?' Matt asked, walking in with a towel round his waist and another in his hand which he was using to dry his hair.

'Yours, but they hung up,' Ellie said, handing the phone to him and walking over to the dressing table to brush her hair.

'No number,' Matt said after checking it. 'Hope it wasn't that woman trying to rearrange the interview.'

'I'm sure she'll ring back if it was,' Ellie said, watching him through the mirror. He'd been a builder before the accident, and his torso and arms were still surprisingly muscular. Reminded of the younger, sexier Matt who had swept her off her feet and promised her the world, she felt a rush of longing for the life they had lived back then.

'What's up?' Matt asked when he noticed her staring at him.

'Nothing,' she lied, smiling as she put down the hairbrush and reached for her handbag. 'Just thinking how good it'll be if you get this job.'

'Yeah, well, don't bank on it,' Matt cautioned. 'It's been a long time since I worked; they might not think I'm worth the risk.'

'I'm sure you'll do great,' Ellie assured him, kissing him on the cheek. 'Text me when it's over and let me know how it went.'

Ellie checked her phone at regular intervals throughout the morning, but when Matt still hadn't messaged by lunchtime, her hopes began to fade. Taking his silence as a sign that the interview hadn't gone well, she rehearsed what she would say to him as she made her way down to the cafe. He would undoubtedly be gutted, so she would try to make him see the positives rather than focus on the negatives. She would remind him that it was a massive achievement to secure an interview after being unemployed for so long, and that the effort he'd made to sort out his depression and get himself back out into the real world was a testament to his strength of character, so all he had to do was keep moving forward and something was bound to come good in the end.

Matt rang as she was finishing her coffee.

'Hey . . . how did it go?' she asked, keeping her tone light.

'Where are you?' he demanded, sounding more angry than disappointed.

'At the cafe, finishing lunch,' she told him. 'Why?'

'You need to come home.'

'I can't, we're really busy at work with all the post-Christmas stuff. What's wrong? Has something happened?'

'I said come home,' Matt repeated tersely.

Frowning when the phone went dead, Ellie slotted it into her handbag and gathered her things together. Matt had been really looking forward to this interview, but she had been secretly worried that a knockback would send him back down – and it seemed she'd been right to be concerned. But, however bad he was feeling, she couldn't ask her boss to let her leave work early on her first day back after the holidays, so he would have to wait.

Matt was sitting in darkness when Ellie got home that evening. Almost jumping out of her skin when she turned the light on and saw him, she clutched at her chest.

'Christ, you scared the bloody life out of me! What are you doing?'

'I thought I told you to come straight home?' he said, eyeing her coldly.

'I tried, but I couldn't get away,' she lied, putting her bag down and slipping her shoes off. 'I take it the interview didn't go too well?'

'I didn't go.'

'Why not? I thought you were looking forward to it?'

'This isn't about me, it's about you,' Matt said, rising to his feet and shoving his phone into her hand. 'Read it.'

Confused, Ellie looked down at the phone, and her blood ran cold when she saw a text conversation on the screen.

Your wife's having an affair, the first message read.

Who is this? Matt had replied.

Wouldn't you like to know? the messenger had taunted. **Just ask her what she did when you went out the other night.**

Clearly furious by then, Matt had written: **Go fuck yourself you sick bastard!** which had resulted in a flurry of emojis of crying-laughing faces and broken hearts.

'This is bullshit,' Ellie gasped, gazing up at him when she'd finished reading. 'Please don't tell me you believe it? Someone's obviously trying to wind you up.'

'And why would anyone do that?'

'I don't know? But it's not true, I swear.'

'So what *did* you do when I went out?' Matt asked, his eyes never leaving hers.

'Are you serious?' She frowned.

'Just fucking *tell* me!' he barked.

'I sat here and waited for you, like an idiot,' she barked back. 'While *you* were out picking that tart up – remember?'

'She meant nothing, and you know it,' Matt said dismissively.

'Don't you dare make out like you did nothing wrong that night,' Ellie shot back angrily. 'I've kept my mouth shut about it to keep the peace, but that doesn't mean I've forgotten what you did.'

'But I didn't actually *do* anything, though, did I?' Matt replied self-righteously. 'Whereas *you've* been at it with any random dick you can get your hands on by the sound of it. No wonder you can't be arsed to make any effort with me any more, you're too fucking tired from screwing your way around Manchester!'

'How dare you!' Ellie gasped. 'You're the one who brought another woman into my home.'

'And you brought that bastard into *mine*!'

'That had nothing to do with me – and he'd tell you the same if you asked him.'

'Like I'm going to mug myself off by asking the cunt if he's *FUCKING MY WIFE!*' Matt roared.

Taking a stumbling step back when he fisted his hands, Ellie cried out when she almost fell over the coffee table.

'For fuck's sake!' he hissed. 'I wasn't going to hit you.'

'You *looked* like you were,' she said shakily, wrapping her arms around herself.

Matt took a deep breath and ran his hands through his hair. Then, quietly, he said, 'I can't keep doing this. I've got to get out of here.'

'Good idea,' Ellie agreed. 'And don't come back till you've calmed down.'

'I won't be coming back.'

'What?' She frowned. 'Don't be stupid.'

'I mean it,' Matt said wearily. 'I've been trying really hard to get my life back on track, and I can't keep letting you hold me down like this.'

'*Me* hold *you* down?' she repeated incredulously. 'Are you kidding me? I've run myself ragged trying to keep a roof over our heads while you've moped about in your pyjamas for the last few years. I've lost touch with most of my friends, and I hardly even see my own family because you're so paranoid. And now you've got the cheek to say *I'm* holding *you* down?'

'You certainly know how to stick the knife in, don't you?' Matt said coldly. 'Do you think I've enjoyed being stuck in this shithole while you've been out there having fun? 'Cos I'm telling you now, I've *hated* it. And that's why I need to get out of here – before I start hating *you*, as well.'

'You're not seriously blaming me for you being unemployed, are you?' Ellie asked, going after him when he stalked into the bedroom. 'What did you expect me to do, Matt? Give up my job so we could *both* sit here doing nothing?'

'At least you had the choice,' he said, dragging his holdall down off the top of the wardrobe.

'So did *you*,' she argued. 'But you refused to get help when I asked you to; and when you finally did and they gave you antidepressants, you stopped taking them before they had a chance to take effect. How is that my fault?'

'You made me feel worthless,' Matt said as he started throwing clothes into the bag. 'You *and* your family,' he went on bitterly. 'Do you think I don't know they've been chipping away at you to leave me ever since I lost my job?'

'No they haven't,' Ellie argued. 'It's all in your head – just like all the other stuff you've accused me of doing behind your back. You were so convinced I was cheating with my last boss, you spied on me; and even though you had no proof whatsoever, you tried to start a fight with the man in front of the whole office. He only agreed not to report you because I told him you were clinically depressed, and now you're going down the same path with Richard – and he's *gay,* for Christ's sake!'

'So *you* say,' Matt muttered. 'But you've told so many lies, I don't even think you know the truth any more.'

'I haven't lied,' Ellie insisted.

'Is that right?' Matt raised an eyebrow. 'So I suppose I just imagined all that shit with your latest bit on the side, did I? The necklace, and the little love letter that came with it?'

'I only didn't tell you about that because I knew you'd blow it out of proportion,' said Ellie. 'But that's nothing compared to you bringing that girl home and trying to screw her in our bed.'

'Yeah, well, I wish I had now,' said Matt. 'At least then you'd know how it feels.'

'Is that where you're going?' Ellie demanded when he continued to pack. 'To your floozy?'

'If I was, it'd be none of your business,' Matt said coolly. 'And you've got your little toy-boy to keep you occupied, so don't worry about me.'

'Oh, this is ridiculous,' Ellie said irritably. 'I haven't done a damn thing, and I won't let you throw our marriage away over some stupid, vindictive messages, so put your stuff away and let's discuss this like adults.'

'There's no point,' Matt said, zipping up the bag and looking round to see if he'd missed anything. 'You lied about meeting up with that dickhead behind my back, and I've been battling with myself to forgive you, but I can't.'

'You can't just give up on us,' Ellie pleaded, following when he brushed past her and headed out into the hall. 'At least tell me where you're going? Please, Matt; I need to know.'

'I'm going to Dave's,' he said, reaching for his jacket.

'Dave?' she repeated, confused. 'But you haven't seen him in years. What if he's moved?'

'Which only goes to show that you never listen when I talk to you,' Matt said, opening the door and stepping outside. ''Cos if you did, you'd remember me telling you that I bumped into Dave and his missus at the surgery a few months back, and me and Dave have been meeting up at the pub on his days off.'

Sighing when he'd gone, Ellie went into the living room and gazed out of the window. She had no recollection of Matt mentioning that he'd bumped into his old workmate. If he had, she'd have been pleased for him, and would have told him to invite Dave and his wife round for dinner. She was also sure that he'd never mentioned going to the pub, because it was a long time since she'd enjoyed sharing a drink with friends, and she would definitely have asked to join them if she'd known.

When Matt emerged onto the path a couple of minutes later, Ellie frowned as she watched him stride off in the direction of the canal with no hint of the limp that usually dogged him. It reminded her of what Holly had said the night she brought Tony round to meet them, when she'd accused Matt of dragging his injuries out in order to punish Ellie for crippling him. Ellie had dismissed it at the time, but it seemed that her sister might have been right, after all. Matt *did* blame her, and had probably only stayed with her for this long because he'd had no job and nowhere else to go. But now that he'd reconnected with Dave and had a place to stay, he'd decided to drop the pretence and leave. So much for knowing her husband better than he knew himself; after what he'd said to her tonight, Ellie was beginning to wonder if she'd ever known him at all.

16

Matt's side of the bed was empty when Ellie woke the next morning. Disappointed, because she'd hoped that he might have come home while she was sleeping, Ellie reached for her phone to check if he'd tried to ring her. He hadn't, but Sue from work had left a voicemail, asking where she was and warning her that Richard was on the warpath. Cursing herself for forgetting to set her alarm when she saw that it was almost 10 a.m., she rang Sue and told her that she'd caught a virus and had been throwing up all night. Then, swallowing her pride, she called Matt and left a message when it went to voicemail, asking him to come home and talk, or at least let her know he was okay.

Showered and dressed a short time later, she'd just switched the kettle on to make herself a coffee when the doorbell rang. Muttering, 'For God's sake, what *now*?' when she looked through the spyhole and saw Gareth on the step, she yanked the door open and folded her arms.

'Yes?'

'Sorry, is this a bad time?' he asked, frowning as he shifted the rucksack he was carrying onto his other shoulder. 'I actually thought you'd be at work, but I was passing, so I thought I'd call round on the off-chance.'

'I woke up late, so I took the day off,' she said, making an effort to temper her tone when she saw the uncertainty in his eyes.

'Ah, I see. No worries, I won't keep you long,' he said. 'I'm on my way to Wythenshawe, but I didn't want to leave without saying goodbye.'

'Oh, have the council found you a place?' Ellie asked hopefully, thinking that Matt would settle down a lot faster if Gareth was out of the area and there was no danger of them bumping into each other.

'Not yet,' Gareth said, looking sheepish, as he added, 'I've been kicked out of the hostel.'

'Really?' Ellie frowned. 'Why?'

'It was a stupid misunderstanding. Some lads were fighting and I tried to split them up, but the manager got the wrong end of the stick and thought I was involved, so I got the boot.'

'That doesn't sound very fair. Didn't you tell him he'd got it wrong?'

'I tried, but he's had it in for me from the start, so he jumped at the chance to get rid of me. It's okay, though, 'cos I didn't like it there, anyway; too many alkies and nut-jobs.'

'So what's in Wythenshawe?'

'My mate lives there, so I'm going to see if he'll let me kip on his couch for a bit. That's *if* he's still there, mind. It's been a while since I've seen him, so he could have moved by now.'

'Wouldn't you be better ringing him before you set off, then?'

'I would, but I lost his number when my last phone got nicked,' Gareth said. 'But, never mind, the walk'll do me good.'

'That's a long way to go on the off-chance,' Ellie said. 'Can't your family help?'

'Nah, they don't really bother with me,' said Gareth. 'But it's all right; I'm used to being on my own. Anyway, you get back to whatever you were doing. I've taken up enough of your time already.'

Concerned for him, but aware that there was nothing she could do to ease his troubles, Ellie said, 'I hope you find your friend.'

'Me, too.' He smiled. 'Take care, then.'

He turned to leave, but Matt walked around the corner at that exact moment, and Ellie's heart sank when she saw the suspicion in his eyes.

'What's this?' he demanded, marching up to them and looking pointedly at Gareth's rucksack before turning to Ellie. 'Sneaking him out before I got home, were you?'

'He hasn't been inside,' Ellie replied truthfully. 'He's been kicked out of his hostel, and he's on his way to stay with his friend, so he came to . . .' She tailed off, unable to come up with an explanation that wouldn't make Matt even more suspicious than he already was.

'I wanted Holly's number.' Gareth came to her rescue.

Matt's lip twisted into a sneer, and he turned on Ellie, spitting, 'Christ, you must think I'm stupid. When did it start?'

'What do you mean?' She frowned.

'I mean how long have you been *fucking* him?' he yelled, grabbing her arm roughly.

'Leave her alone!' Gareth pushed himself between them. 'She's telling the truth.'

'You keep your fucking nose out of this,' Matt snarled. 'This is between me and my wife.'

'I'm the one you've got a problem with, so take it out on me, not her,' Gareth challenged.

Matt didn't need asking twice. Tossing Ellie aside, he punched Gareth full in the face.

Horrified at the sight of blood spurting from Gareth's nose, Ellie screamed at Matt to stop.

The men went down onto the floor, and started grappling. Unable to get out of the way in time when they rolled towards her, Ellie fell heavily against the doorframe, smacking her head on the wood before landing awkwardly on her hip.

Her cries of pain brought Matt to his senses and, disentangling himself from Gareth, he rushed over to help her up.

'Don't touch me!' she gasped, slapping his hand away as she pulled herself to her feet. 'I've done nothing wrong; it's all in your head.'

'What was I supposed to think?' Matt asked defensively. 'I'm gone for one night, and I come back to find *him* here.'

'Just because *you're* a cheat, that doesn't mean she is as well,' Gareth said, wiping his bloody nose on the sleeve of his jacket as he, too, stood up.

'I've never cheated on her,' Matt protested. 'And this has got nothing to do with you, so fuck off.'

'Oh?' Gareth raised an eyebrow. 'That's not what Holly said.'

'Holly?' Ellie was confused. 'What's she got to do with this?'

'They had an affair,' said Gareth. 'She told me at Christmas, when she came round to the hostel and got drunk.'

'Don't tell me you believe this shit?' Matt spluttered when Ellie stared at him. 'You know what Holly's like when she's been drinking; she talks absolute crap.'

'Oh, my God,' Ellie croaked, holding onto the door frame as the strength drained from her legs. 'It's true.'

'No, it isn't,' Matt insisted, stepping toward her with his arms outstretched. 'Come on, sweetheart . . . you know I'd never do anything to hurt you.'

'Why don't you ring Holly and ask her?' Gareth suggested.

'And why don't *you* fuck off?' Matt roared, turning on him and shoving him roughly in the chest.

Afraid that they were about to start fighting again, Ellie stepped in front of Gareth and glared at Matt.

'He's not going, *you* are. And, this time, don't bother coming back.'

'I'm going nowhere.' Matt stood his ground. 'This is *my* flat, too, don't forget.'

'Not any more it isn't,' said Ellie. 'You walked out, so now you can *stay* out. And you can give me your keys while you're at it.' She held out her hand.

'No chance.' He shook his head. 'This is all lies, and I'm not going anywhere until we've talked about it – in private.'

'I don't want to talk,' said Ellie. 'Not until I've heard Holly's side of the story.'

'She's as much of a liar as *him*.' Matt jabbed his finger at Gareth. 'They're just trying to split us up; can't you see that?'

'I think you're doing a good enough job of that on your own, mate,' Gareth interjected sarcastically.

'You'd better get out of my fucking face,' Matt warned him.

'Is everything all right?' someone called from the other end of the corridor. 'Shall I call the police?'

Ellie snapped her head round and saw that two of her neighbours had come out and were watching from their doorway.

'No, it's okay,' she called back. 'He's leaving. When I've got my keys,' she added, turning back to Matt and holding out her hand again. 'I mean it, Matt; either give them to me, or *I'll* ring the police and get them to take them off you.'

'Here, take the fucking keys!' Matt yanked them out of his pocket and threw them at her. 'But don't think I'm coming back after this. You've had your chance.'

He marched away at that, and Ellie scooped the keys up off the floor before scurrying inside. Going after her before the door slammed shut, Gareth dropped his rucksack in the hall and followed her into the living room, where she was already stationed at the window, waiting to make sure that Matt left the building.

'Are you okay?' he asked.

'No,' she muttered.

'You've had a shock,' Gareth said, coming up behind her and squeezing her rigid shoulders. 'Why don't you go and sit down while I make you a cup of tea?'

'I need something stronger than that,' Ellie said, twisting away from him and heading into the kitchen when she saw Matt emerge from the main door and stride off down the path.

She came back a few seconds later with two glasses and the half-full bottle of brandy Holly had left behind. Slumping down on the sofa, she sloshed a large measure into each glass and shoved one into Gareth's hand when he took a seat beside her.

Downing her own in one, she immediately refilled it, muttering, 'All those times he's had me in tears, accusing me of sleeping with any man who came within a mile of me, and it was *him* who'd been cheating all along. Bastard! And that bitch is no better,' she went on after taking a swig of her fresh drink. 'But I should have known she couldn't be trusted, 'cos it's not the first time. She went after every lad I was interested in when we were growing up, and they all chose her, because *she* was drop-dead gorgeous and *I* was fat and spotty.'

'I can't believe that,' Gareth interjected quietly when she paused to swallow another mouthful. 'You're beautiful.'

'No, I'm not,' she countered, without a hint of false modesty.

'I'm overweight, and my skin's shit, but I honestly don't care about any of that any more. Back then, though, it was soul-destroying to be compared to her all the time, knowing I could never match up. And she still lords it over me to this day – can you believe that? Take the night I met you . . . I hadn't seen her for months, but do you know the first thing she said when I walked in? She said: *You've put weight on; you're not pregnant, are you?*'

Another pause, another swig.

'Just wait till I tell my mum what she's done. Mind you, I wouldn't put it past her to have screwed my mum's husband, as well, knowing her. And she's such a slut, he wouldn't even have had to force himself on *her*.'

'What do you mean by that?' Gareth asked, frowning.

'What do I mean by what?' Ellie asked, licking her hand when she raised her glass too quickly and brandy sloshed out.

'What you just said about your mum's husband not having to force himself on Holly,' said Gareth. 'Are you saying that he *did* force himself on *you*?'

'He tried.' Ellie shrugged. 'But he was drunk, so nothing happened.'

'And your mum's still with him? Knowing he'd done that to her own daughter?'

'She didn't know, 'cos I didn't tell her,' said Ellie. 'Matt's the only one who knows. And now you,' she added, frowning at the realization that she'd just revealed one of her darker secrets to a virtual stranger. 'You can't tell anyone, though.'

'Of course I won't,' Gareth reassured her, resting his arm along the back of the sofa. 'So what are you going to do about Matt?'

'I don't know,' Ellie admitted, her chin wobbling as the anger was replaced by a wave of white-hot pain. Overcome by a sudden longing for Matt to walk through the door, take her in his arms and tell her that nothing had ever happened between him and Holly, she bit down hard on her lip.

'Hey, don't cry,' Gareth said, taking the glass from her hand and placing it on the table. 'I know you're hurting, but this will get easier, I promise,' he went on, pulling her into his arms. 'That's what you told me when I was at my lowest, and you were right.'

'How could he do that to me?' Ellie whimpered. 'After everything I've done for him, how could he cheat on me with my own sister?'

'Because he's an idiot,' Gareth said, raising her chin with his finger and gazing down into her eyes.

Ellie's breath caught in her throat when he gently kissed her. She wanted to let him, to get her own back on Matt for betraying her; but guilt overrode the desire for revenge, and she pushed him away and ran into the bathroom when bile flooded her mouth.

Gareth was standing by the window gazing down at the parking lot when she came back a few minutes later. Turning when he saw her reflection in the glass, he gave her a tentative smile.

'Better?'

'A bit,' she mumbled, unable to look him in the eyes. 'I'm really sorry about that. It should never have happened.'

'Don't apologize,' he said, coming over to her. 'You must know how I feel about you by now?'

'I'm married,' she reminded him, stepping behind the table to put a barrier between them. 'And I'm too old for you. You should be with someone your own age.'

'Five years is nothing,' he argued. 'And Matt's done far worse, so you've nothing to feel guilty about.'

'He's still my husband.' Ellie folded her arms. 'And, whatever he has or hasn't done, I can't just stop loving him.'

'You're not thinking about taking him back, are you?' Gareth asked.

'I don't know *what* I'm thinking,' she admitted. 'My head's in a mess, and I need to be on my own.'

'I'm sorry I had to be the one to tell you about them, but I couldn't stand there and let him talk to you like that when I knew what he'd done,' Gareth said. 'Please don't hate me.'

'I don't,' Ellie assured him. 'And I'm glad you told me, but I need you to go now. *Please.*'

'Is that what you really want?' Gareth asked.

Sighing when she nodded, he went out into the hall and picked up his rucksack. Then, glancing back at her after opening the front door, he gave her a sad smile.

'Take care.'

Ellie nodded, and stayed where she was. Shoulders slumping when he'd gone, she went out and clicked the deadlock into place before going into the bedroom. She would have to speak to Matt at some point, but she couldn't face him again today. Not in this state.

Still nauseous, she kicked off her shoes and climbed into bed, hoping to fall asleep and never wake up again.

17

The buzzing of the intercom woke Ellie, and she groaned when she squinted at the alarm clock and saw that it was 2.15 a.m. She pulled the pillow down around her ears and tried to go back to sleep, but as soon as the buzzing stopped, it immediately started again; and by the third time it happened, she was wide awake.

Angrily shoving the quilt off, she went out into the hall and jabbed her finger down on the intercom button.

'If that's you, Matt, I've got nothing to say to you, so—'

'It's me,' Gareth croaked. 'Help me . . .'

Alarmed, Ellie pressed the door-release button and ran out into the corridor and around the corner to the lift.

A minute later the door slid open and Gareth fell into her arms. As she staggered back under the weight, she saw blood on the front of his jacket and cried, 'Oh my God, what's happened?'

'I've been stabbed,' he gasped, clutching at his stomach.

The main door slammed shut down below, and Ellie stiffened with fear when she heard the sound of footsteps in the stairwell. Scared that Gareth's attacker had followed him here to finish the job, she half-walked half-dragged him back to the flat and dropped him onto the sofa before running back to peer out through the spyhole. A figure strolled around the corner a few seconds later, and she almost wet herself with relief when she saw that it was the Polish man who had moved into the flat at the other end of the corridor a few weeks earlier.

After waiting a few more seconds to make sure that nobody else was coming, Ellie went back to Gareth and asked him to show her where he was hurt. He unzipped his jacket and gingerly raised the edge of his blood-soaked T-shirt, revealing a small wound in the flesh above his hip-bone.

'It isn't very long,' she said as she peered at it. 'But I can't tell how deep it is, and you've already lost a fair bit of blood, so I think you should go to hospital. I'll call for an ambulance.'

'No!' Gareth said when she stood up. 'They'll fetch the police.'

'Good,' Ellie said over her shoulder as she headed into the bedroom to get her phone. 'The sooner they start looking for whoever did this, the more chance they'll have of catching them. Did you see their faces?'

'It was Matt,' said Gareth. 'That's why I don't want the police to get involved.'

'What . . . ?' Ellie came back into the room and stared down at him in disbelief. 'Don't be ridiculous. Matt would never do anything like this.'

'You didn't think he'd sleep with your sister, but he did,' Gareth reminded her, gritting his teeth as he struggled to sit up.

Fresh blood seeped from the wound and snaked down into the waistband of his jeans. Telling him to keep still, Ellie went into the kitchen, coming back a few seconds later with a bowl of warm water and a bag of cotton wool.

'Where did it happen?' she asked as she tore a wad off the roll and started gently cleaning the wound.

'In the park.'

'So it must have been dark?'

'Not so dark that I couldn't see his face,' said Gareth.

Unable to believe that Matt was capable of doing something like this, Ellie chewed her lip as she continued tending the wound.

'I'm sorry,' Gareth said quietly. 'I shouldn't have come here and put this on you, but I panicked.'

'It's okay,' she said, folding a wad of cotton to use as a dressing when she'd wiped the blood off. 'Why are you still here, though?' she asked as she secured the edges of the dressing with a couple of plasters. 'I thought you were going to Wythenshawe?'

'I did, but my mate wasn't in, and I don't know his area very well so I figured it'd be safer to head back over here for the night,' Gareth explained. 'Thanks for this,' he went on as he gingerly sat up. 'But I'll get off now.'

'Don't be daft, you can't go out there again tonight,' Ellie said, getting wearily up to her feet. 'You can sleep on the couch.'

'What if Matt comes home while I'm here?' Gareth asked when she went out into the hall. 'He already thinks there's something going on between us.'

'He can't get in,' Ellie reminded him, coming back with the spare quilt. 'But even if he could, I doubt he'd show his face round here tonight if he did do this.'

'*If*?' Gareth repeated flatly. 'Don't you believe me?'

'To be honest, I'm too tired to think about it right now,' Ellie sighed. 'And I'm sure you must be tired as well, so let's just try to get some sleep. We'll talk properly in the morning.'

'I don't want to cause any more trouble, so I'll be gone by the time you get up,' Gareth said, pulling the quilt up around his throat.

Ellie opened her mouth to tell him that there was no rush, but decided against it and nodded goodnight before heading into her bedroom.

After a fitful few hours of sleep, Ellie was woken by her alarm at 7 a.m. Gareth was still huddled beneath the quilt when she went into the living room after getting dressed and, thinking that he was asleep, she was about to tiptoe past the sofa to make herself a coffee when she heard him groan.

'Are you okay?' she asked.

'I don't know,' he replied weakly. 'I feel a bit weird.'

Concerned when she switched the lamp on and saw how pale he was, Ellie came round to the front of the sofa and asked to see his stomach. Trying not to inhale too deeply when he moved the quilt aside and a cloud of warm, stale sweat wafted over her, she lifted his T-shirt and carefully peeled off the make-shift dressing.

'It's scabbing over, so it must have closed,' she told him. 'But I still think you should get it seen to, especially if you're not feeling well. It might be infected inside.'

Gareth shook his head and squeezed his eyes shut, as if in pain, nauseous, or both. Aware that she couldn't force him to get treatment if he didn't want it, Ellie said, 'All right, stay there for now. But if you're any worse by tonight, I'll be calling an ambulance. Okay?'

'Okay,' he agreed, shivering as he pulled the quilt back over himself.

Ellie gave him a couple of paracetamol and then made him a slice of toast and a cup of tea – neither of which he touched before drifting off to sleep again.

After ringing work to let them know that she was taking another day off, she spent the rest of the morning alternating between watching TV and watching over Gareth.

When her phone rang at lunchtime, she went out into the hall to answer it, closing the door quietly behind her.

'What do you want, Matt?'

'Where are you? I came to your office to talk to you, but they said you rang in sick?'

'That's right.'

'Why? What's wrong?'

'Nothing, I'm just tired.'

'Okay, I'll come there, then.'

'No, don't,' Ellie said, irritated that he still thought he could call the shots after everything he'd done. 'I'm not ready to talk to you yet.'

'Is *he* there?' Matt demanded. Furious when she didn't answer, he spat, 'You're unbelievable, do you know that? You kick *me* out and let *him* stay, and you seriously expect me to believe there's nothing going on?'

'I wouldn't have had to let him stay if you hadn't attacked him,' Ellie hissed.

'I hardly touched him,' Matt scoffed. 'You were there, you saw what happened. And he's lucky that's *all* he got, considering what he's done.'

'I'm not talking about the fight; I'm talking about you jumping him in the park last night.'

'I haven't been anywhere near any parks.'

'Just like you didn't go near my sister?'

'Right, I've had enough of this,' Matt said angrily. 'I'm coming home, and he'd best be gone when I get there!'

'Do not come here, or I'll call the police,' Ellie warned. 'I mean it, Matt.'

'Go for it,' he challenged. 'They can't do anything. I've got rights.'

'No, you haven't,' she argued. 'You lost them when you walked out and told me you weren't coming back. Go back to Dave's and sort your head out. I'll call you when I'm ready to talk.'

'Fuck you!' Matt roared. 'You think you can push me out of my own home and move that cunt in and I'm just going to roll over? Well, fuck you, and fuck *him*! I'll kill you both before I let you—'

Shocked by the venom in his voice, Ellie cut the call and switched the phone to silent when it immediately started to ring again. Laying the now-vibrating phone face-down on the hall table, she checked that the front door was still securely locked before going back into the living room. Gareth was snoring softly, so she took her cigarettes out of her handbag and let herself out onto the balcony.

Still shaking, she lit up and took a deep drag. In all the years she had known Matt, she had never heard him speak like that before. It was so unlike him, she wondered if the antidepressants he'd been prescribed were having an adverse effect on him. She'd done a google search of the possible side-effects when he'd first started taking them, and had read a discussion on a forum between people who were on them and others who lived with someone who was. While the majority seemed to have been affected positively, others claimed that their loved ones had undergone an extreme change of personality – and she suspected that Matt fell into that category. It was the only explanation she could think of for his recent behaviour.

'Don't suppose you've got a spare one, have you?'

Turning her head at the sound of Gareth's voice, Ellie saw him shivering in the doorway.

'I thought you were sleeping?'

'I woke up when you opened the door,' he said, stepping out to join her.

'Sorry.' She passed a cigarette and the lighter to him. 'How are you feeling?'

'A bit better.'

'That's good. I was starting to get worried about you.'

'I've survived worse.' Gareth smiled and lit up, then rested his elbows on the rail and gazed out over the estate. 'I didn't realize you had such a great view from up here.'

Acutely conscious of his arm almost touching hers in the confined space, Ellie said, 'You should see it at night when the city's all lit up; it's amazing.'

'I bet it is,' he said, sucking on his cigarette. 'How long have you lived here?'

'Seven years. It was supposed to be temporary, until we'd saved enough to buy one of them.' She nodded toward a clutch of semi-detached houses on the other side of the fence that encircled the parking lot. 'They were getting built when we first moved in, and I set my heart on the one on the corner with the big garden. It would have been a great place to start a family, but hey-ho . . . .'

'What happened?' Gareth asked.

'Life got in the way,' said Ellie. 'We had a car crash and Matt was badly hurt, so we had to put trying for a baby on hold. I used to tell myself it would happen when he was better, but it never did.'

'Would you try again, if you and Matt manage to sort things out?'

'Probably not. I don't think he wanted it as much as I did, so it's probably just as well it didn't happen.'

'Lynn was pregnant,' Gareth said quietly. 'But she got rid of it without telling me.'

'Oh, no, that's awful.' Ellie frowned. 'How did you find out?'

'She admitted it when I caught her in bed with that bloke. I could have forgiven her for cheating, but not for that.'

'I'm so sorry.'

'I'm not.' Gareth turned his head and peered into her eyes. 'I know what it's like to grow up with a mum who doesn't give a toss about you, and I don't want that for my child. I'd want it to have someone decent like *you* for its mother.'

Ellie looked away and took another drag on her cigarette. Before that kiss yesterday she would never have dreamed that Gareth was attracted to her, but she wasn't so sure any more. And she also wasn't so sure that it wasn't mutual. She'd tried to convince herself she was just flattered that a good-looking younger man was paying attention to her, but it was more than that. It had been a long time since Matt had looked at her in the way that Gareth often did – and even longer since he'd made love to her without losing his erection halfway through. She knew that shouldn't matter, and she'd tried hard not to let Matt see how much it affected her, but it hurt. And each time it happened, she felt that bit less desirable than the time before.

'That's not Matt, is it?' Gareth asked when he spotted a

man walking along the path that led to the estate from the canal.

Ellie looked and shook her head. 'No, but we should probably go in when we've finished these. He's already mad at me for letting you stay last night, and it'll only wind him up if he turns up and sees us out here together.'

'Sorry, that's my fault,' Gareth said, taking one last drag on his cigarette before flicking the butt out over the balcony ledge. 'I'll get going and leave you in peace.'

'Stop blaming yourself,' Ellie said as they went back inside. 'Me and Matt were having problems long before you came along.'

'Yeah, but I'm the reason he's pissed off right now,' Gareth countered. 'And you're never going to get it sorted while I'm still here, are you?'

'I suppose not. But let me make you something to eat before you go. You must be starving.'

'A bit. And if it's not too cheeky, can I take a quick shower?'

'Of course. The clean towels are in the airing cupboard in the hall. Just be careful you don't open the wound up again. You don't want it getting infected.'

'Thanks, Ellie,' Gareth said softly. 'I really appreciate everything you've done for me. I wish I could turn back time though, 'cos I'd never have helped your Holly out that day if I'd known it was going to come to this. But that's fate for you, eh? What's meant to be will be.'

Ellie didn't believe in fate, but she knew he did, so she murmured, 'I guess so,' before heading into the kitchen.

Gareth had changed into clean clothes when he came back into the living room after showering a short time later, and with his skin glowing from the heat, and his wet hair as glossy as treacle, Ellie was struck afresh by how handsome he was. Most of the good-looking men she had met throughout her life had been a little self-obsessed, but Gareth had a gentle, caring nature, and she couldn't understand what had possessed his ex to cheat on him.

After eating the pizza she'd made, Gareth got ready to leave. Concerned about him walking all the way to Wythenshawe so soon after being stabbed, Ellie took some money out of her purse and pushed it into his hand.

'I can't take that,' he said, trying to give it back. 'You've done enough for me already.'

'I want you to have it, so you can take the bus to your friend's place,' she insisted. 'I'll only sit here worrying about you if you don't. And if he's not there, come back, because I don't want you sleeping in the park in your condition. Okay?'

Gareth gazed down at her and sighed. 'Okay, but only 'cos I don't want you worrying. And I'll pay you back next time I see you.'

Telling him to forget about it, Ellie saw him out and waved him off. The silence pressed down on her like a lead weight when she had closed the door, and a wave of loneliness washed over her when she went into the living room and saw the spare quilt lying in a crumpled heap at the end of the sofa. But being alone was something she would have to get used to if she didn't get this mess with Matt sorted.

After folding the quilt and putting it into the cupboard, she made a cup of coffee and sat down on the sofa. She had intended to call Matt, but after bringing his number up on her phone and staring at it for several moments she cleared the screen. What was the point? He'd already denied sleeping with Holly, and he wouldn't change his story now, so she would never get a straight answer out of him. She needed to speak with Holly first – but not on the phone. Her sister was a born liar, but Ellie could read her like a book, and if she could look her in the eye when she confronted her, she would know in an instant if Holly was lying. But she would have to be crafty in her approach, because Holly would avoid her like the plague if it was true and she suspected that Ellie had found out. So, as difficult as it was to pretend that everything was hunky dory, she made the call, and left a breezy little message when it went to voicemail, asking Holly to call her so they could arrange to meet for a catch-up.

18

Holly didn't reply to Ellie's message, and Matt didn't call again either. Alone with her thoughts, since Gareth was no longer around to talk to, Ellie's resolve began to waver; veering from believing it one minute, to wondering if Gareth might have got it all wrong the next. Holly was a vain, self-centred bitch who had made a play for every boy Ellie had ever made the mistake of revealing that she fancied when they were younger; but was she really wicked enough to sleep with her sister's husband? And if Matt *had* slept with her, why had he stayed with Ellie when he could have run off into the sunset with her younger, prettier, and no doubt a lot more adventurous in bed sister? It didn't make sense.

Desperate for answers, Ellie swallowed her pride and tried to call Matt at the end of the second week of him being gone. As had happened with Holly's phone, his went straight to voicemail, so she was forced to leave a message asking him to get in touch so they could talk.

She didn't hear back from him that night, but her phone

started ringing as she was making her way to the train station the following morning. Hoping it was him, she stopped walking and, ignoring the grumbles of the people who had to swerve around her, quickly rooted the phone out of her bag.

Disappointed to see her mum's name on the screen, Ellie hovered her thumb over *Ignore*. Apart from Gareth, she hadn't told anybody that she and Matt were having problems, and she especially didn't want her mum to know, because she didn't want to give her the satisfaction of saying *I told you so!* But her mum rang her so rarely, and never this early, so she decided she'd better answer it.

Determined not to give anything away, she said, 'Morning, Mum; how are you?'

'Don't pretend everything's okay when we both know it isn't,' Kath Thompson replied bluntly. 'What's this I hear about you and Matt splitting up?'

'Who told you that?' Ellie asked, prepared to lie through her teeth if need be.

'He did, so don't bother denying it,' said Kath. 'Billy saw him in town last night, and he said he's putting in for a divorce because he caught you with another man. Is it true?'

Annoyed that Matt had chosen to discuss their business with her stepfather, knowing that the man would run straight back to her mother, Ellie said, 'No, it isn't, and Billy shouldn't be so quick to spread gossip when he's only heard one side of the story.'

'He wasn't gossiping, he was defending your honour,' Kath

berated her. 'You might not be his, but he's always looked out for you, so there was no way he was going to let Matt swan around with another woman behind your back without pulling him up about it.'

Ellie's throat constricted, and she felt as if her legs were about to buckle beneath her.

'Are you still there . . . ?' Her mum's voice floated to her through the fog of shock. 'Ellie? *Ellie* . . . ?'

'Yes, I'm here,' Ellie said when she found her voice. 'Was – was Billy sure the woman was with Matt? There's no way she could have been with someone else?'

'Well, considering he had his tongue down her throat when Billy walked into the pub, I'd say it was a fair bet they were together,' Kath said disapprovingly. Then, sighing, she added, 'I'm guessing you didn't know?'

'No, I didn't,' Ellie murmured, biting down hard on her lip when tears scorched her eyes. She didn't know why she was surprised, considering how they had left things the last time they had spoken; but it hurt nevertheless.

'I feel bad now for blurting it out like that,' Kath said guiltily. 'But the way he came out and told Billy about the divorce, I assumed you knew. And you're saying it's definitely not true about you and the other fella?'

'No, it's not,' Ellie sniffed.

'I wonder where he got that from, then?' Kath mused. 'It's not the sort of thing you pluck out of thin air for no reason, is it? *Some*thing must have put the idea in his head.'

Reluctant to discuss it any further, because her mum would undoubtedly jump to the same conclusion Matt had if she heard about Gareth, Ellie said, 'Nothing's happened, and I've got to go now or I'll miss my train.'

'Okay, get yourself off, then,' Kath said. 'But call me as soon as you get home, because we need to start making plans. I'll ring your Auntie June and get the number of that solicitor who handled her divorce. She must have been good, 'cos our June ended up with way more than Col was trying to palm her off with.'

'I'm not ready for that,' Ellie said, feeling sick at the thought of it.

'Look, love, no one likes to think this will ever happen to them, but it can and it does,' Kath said sagely. 'And if Matt thinks you're cheating, he's going to try and take you for everything you've got, 'cos that's what men are like when their egos are knocked. *They* can mess about and think nothing of it, but God help the woman who does the same to them.'

Desperate to get off the phone, Ellie muttered, 'I've got to go, Mum. We'll talk later.'

Unable to face going to work after ending the call, Ellie walked home in a daze. She had thought there was nothing else Matt could do to hurt her, but the knowledge that he was seeing another woman *and* intended to divorce her was devastating.

Struggling to hold it together when she arrived back at the

flats a short time later, she was fumbling in her handbag for her keys when Gareth strolled around the corner.

'You're going to be late if you don't get a move on,' he said, grinning as he approached her. 'I thought you'd have left ages ago.'

'I did, but I needed to come home,' she said, trying and failing to slot her key into the lock.

'Hey, what's up?' he asked, no longer smiling when he noticed the tears in her eyes. 'Has something happened?'

'I don't want to talk about it,' she sniffed.

'Here, let me,' Gareth said, scooping her keys up off the floor when she dropped them. 'Is Matt in?'

'No.' She shook her head. 'He hasn't come back yet.'

'What?' Gareth frowned. 'Since I was last here?' Shaking his head when she nodded, he said, 'Come on, let's get you inside.'

Settled on the sofa a short time later with a cup of tea, Ellie relayed what her mum had told her.

'Wow,' Gareth said when she'd finished. 'Didn't waste any time, did he? How long's that been going on, then?'

'I've got no idea,' Ellie said miserably. 'Years, for all I know. It's like our entire marriage was a lie.'

'Hey, it's his loss, not yours,' said Gareth. 'He was lucky to have you, but if he can't see how special you are, he doesn't deserve you.'

Ellie gazed despondently down into her cup. Gareth was wrong; she wasn't special, she was plain and boring, and Matt had probably only stayed with her for as long as he had because he'd needed a nursemaid. And now he'd found someone else to fill that role, he was cutting Ellie out of his life as if she'd never existed.

'Hey, come on, he's not worth getting upset about,' Gareth said, tilting his head and gazing up into her downcast eyes. 'He's an idiot, and you deserve someone who treats you better. You know what they say . . . the best revenge is to show them you're happy without them. And the more you act it, the more true it becomes, so stop dwelling on it and smile.'

Ellie pursed her lips and thought about what he'd said. Then, nodding, she said, 'Yeah, you're right; I do deserve better.'

'That's my girl,' Gareth winked at her.

Smiling, because he always made her feel as if he really cared, Ellie twisted round in her seat, and said, 'So how have you been getting on at your friend's place?'

'Yeah, it's good,' he said. 'Or, should I say, it *was*, until the bailiffs turned up this morning and kicked us out.'

'You're kidding?'

'Nope.' He shook his head. 'That's why I'm back here today: to see if my housing officer's found anything for me yet. I doubt she has, or she'd have rung me; but I'm hoping she might be able to get me into another hostel while I'm waiting.'

'What if she can't?'

'I'll have to kip in the park,' said Gareth. 'But I've done it before, and it's not that bad. You just need to know the best places to hide if any gangs come through looking for trouble.'

Horrified by the sound of that, Ellie frowned. He had suffered so much hardship in the short time she had known him, and yet he always put his own problems aside to offer her comfort. He was one of the most unselfish people she had ever met, and she was truly grateful for the support he'd given her throughout this ordeal with Matt, so the least she could do was offer him a helping hand in *his* time of need. Matt would be furious if he knew what she was about to suggest, but she didn't give a toss what he thought. He'd moved on, and it was time she did the same.

Decided, she said, 'You could always stay here while you're waiting for your housing officer to find you something. I know it's not the comfiest sofa in the world, but it's got to be better than sleeping in the park.'

'Thanks, that's really sweet,' Gareth said. 'But I don't want to give Matt any more ammunition to use against you, so I'd best not.'

'It's got nothing to do with him,' said Ellie. 'This is *my* flat, and *I* decide who stays; so do you want to, or not?'

Grinning when he saw the steely look in her eyes, Gareth said, 'Well, if you put it like that, I suppose I'd be an idiot to say no, wouldn't I? But I'll ring the housing every day while I'm here; and I'll start looking for a job so I can pay my own way.'

'Don't worry about that,' Ellie said, doubting that he would be around for long enough for money to become an issue, because the council were sure to offer him something soon now he'd been made homeless again.

19

After spending all those weeks on her own, Ellie enjoyed having company again, and she began to look forward to going home after work, because she knew that Gareth would be there to greet her. It was good to have someone to cook for again, too, because she rarely bothered to do more than make a sandwich when there was just her to cater for. And Gareth liked all the same TV programmes, so there was never any conflict about what to watch when they settled on the sofa after dinner.

But as nice as it was to have Gareth around, there was always a niggling worry at the back of her mind that Matt might find out he was here and come round to cause trouble. So when somebody suddenly started hammering on the front door as she and Gareth were watching *Emmerdale* one evening, her heart leapt into her throat.

Telling Gareth to stay there, she went out into the hall, pulling the door shut behind her. Another thunderous round of knocking came before she reached the front door, and then the letterbox flap was raised, and a deep voice boomed: 'Police!'

Alarmed, she opened the door and gaped at the three burly officers standing in the corridor outside.

'Can I help you?'

'Eleanor Fisher?' one of them asked.

'Yes,' she confirmed, eyeing them nervously. 'Has something happened?'

'We need to speak to your husband in connection with a serious assault,' the man said. 'Is he here?'

Ellie shook her head. 'No. We split up a few weeks ago, and I haven't seen him since.'

'Mind if we come in and take a look around?'

Aware that it wasn't so much a request as an order when all three officers stepped forward, Ellie had no choice but to step aside. Dwarfed by the sheer size of them crammed into her tiny hallway, she watched as one of them went to check the bathroom, while another headed into the bedroom.

Almost jumping out of her skin when the third opened the living room door, and barked, 'Stay where you are, and keep your hands where I can see them! Are you Matthew Fisher?' she rushed after him.

'He's just a friend,' she said, scared when she saw the spray canister the man was aiming at Gareth's shocked face. 'That's my husband.' She pointed at a framed photograph on the sideboard, of herself and Matt signing the register on their wedding day.

Satisfied that Gareth was not the man in the picture, the officer lowered the spray and asked Ellie if she had any idea where her husband was.

'He told me he was going to stay with a friend,' she said, watching the other officers out of the corner of her eye as they checked the kitchen and the balcony. 'But my stepdad saw him in town with another woman last week, so he could be with her. I honestly don't know.'

'And your stepdad is William Thompson?' the copper asked.

'Yes,' Ellie replied warily, wondering how he knew that. 'But what's *he* got to do with this?'

'He's the one who was assaulted, and he gave your husband's name before he lost consciousness.'

'Matt wouldn't hurt Billy,' Ellie said, avoiding Gareth's gaze when his eyebrows shot up. 'He's got no reason to.'

'Your mum told us your stepdad saw your husband with another woman and they had a heated argument about it,' said the copper. 'Did you know about that?'

A knot formed in Ellie's stomach, and she folded her arms.

'Yeah, she told me. But he wouldn't have been bothered about me finding out, because he thought I was cheating on him.'

'Maybe it was a revenge fling?' one of the other coppers mused. 'He might have done it to get back at you, then regretted it when your stepdad caught him and he realized you were going to find out?'

'I can't see that,' said Ellie. 'He was really mad at me the last time we spoke, so he'd have wanted to hurt me like he thinks I hurt him.'

'Got a bit of an anger problem, has he?' the third copper asked.

'No.' Ellie frowned and turned to him. 'He's actually clinically depressed, so he can be very moody; but he's not violent.'

Aware that Gareth was staring at her, as if to say, *Are you being serious? Have you forgotten that he stabbed me?* Ellie avoided his gaze, and turned back to the first copper when he said, 'Well, I guess we won't know what happened, or why, until your stepfather's able to talk.'

'Is he going to be all right?' she asked.

'We're not dealing with that side of things,' he replied. 'Your mum's at the hospital, so she'll be able to tell you more. In the meantime, who's this mate your husband said he was staying with?'

'Dave Boyle,' she told him.

'Address?'

'I don't know, 'cos I never actually went to his house. We used to meet up with him and his wife at the pub near the building company where he and Matt worked.'

'Where was that?'

'Dale Street. But I walked over there on my lunch hour the other week to see if I could find Dave, and the business has closed down.'

'And I don't suppose you've got a number for him?'

Sensing that he was getting frustrated with her, Ellie shook her head.

'Sorry. He was Matt's friend, not mine, so I never needed it.'

'No worries,' the copper said. Then, nodding at the wedding photograph, he asked, 'How long ago was that taken?'

'Seven years,' said Ellie. 'But his hair's grown a lot since then, and he could have a beard by now.'

Asked if she had a more recent image they could take with them, she went over to the cabinet where the photograph album was kept on the shelf above Matt's music albums. There weren't many pictures of him, because he usually disappeared at the first sign of a camera; but Holly had managed to catch him on her phone at their mum's house the previous Christmas, and it had been so rare to see him actually smiling, Ellie had asked for a print copy.

Yeah, and now we know why *you were smiling, don't we?* she thought bitterly as she peeled the photo off its sticky backing. *Because your bit on the side was behind the camera, and you were probably reminiscing about the great sex you'd had with her!*

Angered to think that Matt and Holly had pretended to hate each other's guts for years so she wouldn't suspect they'd had – or were still *having* – an affair, Ellie shoved the photo into the officer's hand. He thanked her and slid it into a plastic bag. Then, holding out another, smaller photo, of a blue hat with a distinctive MCFC logo, he asked if she recognised it.

'Matt's got one like it,' she said.

'And did he have it with him when he left?'

Ellie frowned as she tried to remember details of that day. She didn't think Matt had been wearing the hat when he walked out, and she was pretty sure he hadn't packed it into the holdall, because she would have noticed that it was in the bedroom instead of the hall where he kept it. The last time she definitely remembered seeing it on his head was when he'd gone fishing on Christmas day, but she didn't know if he had still been wearing it when he came home a couple of hours later.

'I'm honestly not sure,' she admitted. 'Is it important?'

'This hat was recovered at the scene of the assault,' the copper explained. 'Do you have a hairbrush your husband used, so we can take a sample to compare to the hair we found inside the hat?'

Ellie went to the bathroom and came back with a comb Matt had left behind, which had several strands of his hair stuck between its teeth. The officer bagged it, and then he and his colleagues went on their way.

'Are you okay?' Gareth asked when Ellie sank down on the sofa after locking the door behind them.

'Not really,' she said quietly. 'I can't get my head round this. Why would Matt attack Billy?'

'Who knows why he's done *any* of the things he's done lately?' said Gareth. 'I know he suffers from depression, but what if it's more than that?'

'What do you mean?'

'Well, it's not exactly normal to go around stabbing people

because you think they've done something bad to you, is it? And I know he must hate your stepdad for what he did, but it's a bit extreme to put him in hospital for it.'

'This isn't about that,' Ellie said with certainty. 'Matt hasn't mentioned it since I first told him about it, so he's probably forgotten about it by now. I reckon it was revenge, like that copper said; 'cos Billy caught him with that woman and grassed him up.'

'Maybe,' Gareth conceded. 'But I suppose we won't know for sure till your stepdad comes round, or the police find Matt.'

'They won't hurt him when they catch him, will they?' Ellie asked, looking at Gareth with worry in her eyes. 'They always look like they're being rough when you see them arresting people on TV, and those three who were here just now are a lot bigger than Matt.'

'Well, they were going to use that spray on me when they thought I was him, so I'm guessing they're expecting him to react violently when they catch him,' said Gareth. 'He'll be sorry if he does, though, 'cos they're likely to zap him with the Taser, as well. You'd best hope they find him before . . .'

'Before what?' Ellie prompted when he tailed off.

Sighing, as if he hadn't meant to say that last bit, Gareth said, 'Look, I'm not trying to scare you, but people can do stupid things when they're in the kind of head-space he's in. I tried to fling myself off that bridge, and I wasn't even in as bad a state as he is. But when your head's twisted up like that, you think there's no other way out.'

'You think he did it, don't you?' Ellie asked.

Gareth shrugged, as if to say: *You know I do – and so do you, even if you don't want to admit it.*

Feeling suddenly drained, Ellie said, 'I'd best ring my mum and find out which hospital they're at.'

'Why?' Gareth frowned. 'You're not thinking of going over there, are you?'

'Of course I am,' Ellie replied, looking around for her phone. 'My mum needs me.'

'I'm not being funny, but if this happened last night, like that copper said, she's had plenty of time to let you know about it,' Gareth pointed out. 'Have you thought that she might not want you there?'

Irritated to think that he might be right when she checked her phone and saw there were no missed calls or messages from her mum, Ellie asked herself why she was so surprised. This was about Billy, after all, and her mum had put him first from day one.

That wasn't true, and Ellie chided herself as soon as the thought entered her mind. Her mum had never been the kind to hand out hugs and kisses, but she had always been fiercely protective of her daughters, and she'd have kicked Billy out without a second thought if she'd known about him going into Ellie's room that night. Kath and Billy had almost split up on several occasions before that, because of the trouble Ellie and Holly had caused between them in the early days. They had both resented him for trying to take their father's place, and

Holly in particular had hated him – and made sure that he knew it. She had eventually eased up on him when she realized she could get more out of him by making him think she liked him, and he'd become her personal taxi and bank after that. For their mum's sake, Ellie had followed suit and tried to get along with him, and things had settled down for a while. But when he came home steaming drunk that night and tried it on with her, that was the end of that.

Fifteen years had passed since then, and Billy hadn't come near her again – which had, at times, made her wonder if she might have over-reacted that night. But each time she decided to try and put it behind her, she would catch him giving her a sly look or making a snide dig, and she would go off him all over again.

But whatever she thought of him, Ellie would never have wished something like this on him, and she genuinely hoped he wasn't too badly hurt now. Not only because Matt would be in serious trouble if he was, but also because her mum would be absolutely devastated.

Silently praying for good news, she rang her mum.

'Hi, it's me,' she said when her call was answered. 'The police came round and told me about Billy, but I forgot to ask which hospital you're at . . . So I can come and sit with you . . . Of course I'm not too busy; you're my mum, so I want to be there . . . Okay, I'll see you in half an hour. Bye.'

'What did she say?' Gareth asked when she'd finished.

'She's worried sick, but she's coping,' Ellie said, checking that her keys and purse were in her handbag before going out into the hall to get her coat.

'Do you want me to come with you?' Gareth offered when she sat down to slip her shoes on.

'Thanks, but I'd best go alone,' she said. 'My mum can be a bit funny with people she doesn't know.'

'I can wait outside,' Gareth said, following when she went back out into the hall. 'I don't want you walking around in the dark by yourself.'

Touched that he cared, Ellie smiled as she opened the door.

'Thanks, but I've got no idea how long I'm going to be, and I'd feel terrible knowing you were hanging around in the cold. Don't worry, I'll be fine.'

'Okay, I'll wait here,' Gareth agreed. 'But if you see any sign of Matt, ring me and I'll come and meet you. I know you don't want to think badly of him, but he's not in his right mind at the moment, and I don't want you to get hurt.'

'He wouldn't do anything to me,' Ellie said. 'Anyway, go in before you let all the heat out. I'll ring you when I know what's happening.'

She could feel Gareth's gaze on her back as she walked away, so she kept her pace steady to show him that she was okay. But as soon as she turned the corner and was no longer in his sights, she slipped her keys out of her handbag and held them tightly in her hand to use as a weapon if Matt was lying in wait somewhere. She had told Gareth that he wouldn't hurt her, but he'd already attacked two people because of her, so who was to say he wouldn't do the same *to* her?

Too nervous to hang around at the bus stop, Ellie walked to the taxi rank at the end of the main road. Hurrying inside the hospital after paying the driver, she rode the lift up to the first floor where the critical care unit was located. Directed by a nurse to a small room at the far end of the ward, she got a shock when she opened the door and saw Holly sitting with their mother beside the empty bed.

'I said you didn't need to come,' Kath said, tugging a tissue out of her cardigan sleeve and blowing her nose.

'I thought you were on your own,' Ellie replied quietly as she pulled another chair up to the bedside. 'Where's Billy?'

'They rushed him into theatre about ten minutes ago,' Kath told her. 'I'm not sure what's going on. They keep telling me stuff, but I can't take any of it in.'

'That's because you're exhausted.' Holly squeezed her hand and gazed at Ellie over her head. 'Poor thing's been sat here all night. I tried to persuade her to go home when I got here, but she wouldn't budge.'

'And when *did* you get here?' Ellie asked frostily.

'About five this morning. Tony insisted on driving me over when Mum rang and told me what had happened, bless him.'

'How come you told her but not me?' Ellie asked Kath. 'I could have got here way faster than she did.'

'I called you first, but you didn't answer,' Kath said, shoving the tissue back up her sleeve. 'And I must have tried at least six times before I gave up, so don't say I never gave you a chance.'

'I didn't have any missed calls,' Ellie said. 'I checked after the police came round, and there was nothing. Are you sure it was my number you were ringing?'

'Oh, I'm sure,' Kath replied flatly. 'But I figured you were probably too busy trying to concoct an alibi for that bastard husband of yours to be bothered talking to me.'

'Now, come on, Mum,' Holly chided softly. 'You can't blame our Ell for what Matt did. They're not even together any more, don't forget.'

'I can speak for myself,' Ellie snapped, struggling to contain the rage that was bubbling in her chest as she stared at her sister's perfectly made-up face. *How long were you at it with my husband?* she wanted to yell. *How many times did you fuck him behind my back, you vain, money-grabbing, back-stabbing little whore?*

Kath released a weary sigh and slumped back in her seat.

'I'm not blaming her; I'm just lashing out 'cos she's the reason he did it.'

'What do you mean by that?' Ellie asked. 'It had nothing to do with me. I haven't seen Matt in weeks.'

'Billy told her that was what Matt said before he stabbed him,' Holly explained. 'Apparently, he jumped him in the alley behind theirs, and said *"This is for Ellie"*; then he stuck the knife in and legged it.'

'So Billy didn't actually see his face?' Ellie asked.

'It was him,' Kath said sharply. 'Billy recognized his voice. But even if he hadn't, we'd still know it was him, 'cos he dropped that City hat we bought him for Christmas the other year.'

'He's not the only City supporter in Manchester,' Ellie pointed out. 'It could be anyone's.'

'See what I mean?' Kath turned to Holly with a look of indignation. 'Didn't I tell you she'd defend him to hell and back? She'd knife the bloody lot of us in the heart for that bugger, and she wonders why none of us bother with her any more.'

'I'm not defending him,' Ellie said, acutely aware of how lame she must sound. 'I'm only saying you shouldn't jump to conclusions, 'cos that hat could be anyone's.'

'Well, we'll soon know after the police have done their tests,' said Kath. 'And *then* we'll see where your loyalties lie, won't we?'

Holly caught Ellie's eye and gave her a supportive smile, but Ellie didn't return it. Whatever Matt had or hadn't done, it wasn't her fault; but her mum clearly didn't agree.

The women lapsed into silence; Kath yawning every few seconds; Holly tapping furiously on her phone as she replied to a stream of text messages that had started to come through; Ellie struggling to cope with the realization that Matt really must have done this if Billy had recognized his voice, *and* his hat had been left at the scene.

'Tony's on his way,' Holly said, stretching her arms above her head after coming off her phone. 'He's just dropping our bags off at yours first.'

'That's good.' Kath smiled. 'I get nervous being in the house by myself, so it'll be lovely to have you both there. I only hope I'm not disrupting things too much for Tony? I know how important his job is.'

'You're *more* important,' said Holly. 'And if he needs to go back for meetings, or whatever, I'll still be here.'

'Thanks, love,' Kath said gratefully. 'I don't know what I'd do without you.'

Resisting the urge to gag, because these two had never been as close as they were acting right now, *and* their mother seemed to have forgotten all about Tony betraying Holly not so very long ago, Ellie said, 'There's no need for you to stay when I'm already here, Holly. I can stop at Mum's till Billy comes home.'

'No, you bloody won't,' Kath said before Holly could respond. 'I wouldn't be able to sleep for worrying about you letting Matt in to stab me in my bed.'

'How can you say that?' Ellie gasped. 'I would never do anything to hurt you.'

'I'm sure she didn't mean it,' Holly interjected. 'She's just stressed out about Billy.'

'Don't speak for Mum,' Ellie replied sharply. 'She's perfectly capable of telling me what she does or doesn't mean.'

'What are you shouting at *me* for?' Holly drew her head back as if she'd been slapped. 'I'm on *your* side, you daft cow.'

'Don't make me laugh,' spat Ellie. 'And you can drop the

holier than thou act, as well, 'cos we both know you're a two-faced whore!'

'What the hell's got into you?' Holly stared at her in disbelief.

'More like what's got into *you*,' Ellie shot back. 'Or should I say *who*.'

'I honestly haven't got a clue what you're talking about,' said Holly. 'But if you're trying to imply that I'm screwing around behind Tony's back, you couldn't be more wrong.'

'I'm talking about Matt!' snapped Ellie. Sneering when she saw the shock in Holly's eyes, she said, 'Yeah, that's right, I *know*. Gareth told me everything.'

'*Gareth?*' Holly screwed her face up. 'What's *he* got to do with anything?'

'You told him you'd screwed my husband, and *he* told *me*,' said Ellie. 'And don't bother denying it, because Matt's already admitted it.'

'He's lying,' Holly spluttered. 'They *both* are! Call him and ask him, if you don't believe me.' She thrust her phone at Ellie. 'Go on . . . call him. And put it on loudspeaker, 'cos I bet you a million quid he won't have the bottle to say it if he knows I'm listening.'

'You know damn well he won't answer.' Ellie pushed her hand away. 'Just like *you* didn't answer when I messaged asking you to ring me – because you probably knew I'd found out and you couldn't face me.'

'I swear on my life I have not been with Matt,' Holly said,

making the sign of the cross on her chest. 'Why the hell *would* I? He's not even my type.'

'Enough!' Kath barked, holding up her hands when Ellie opened her mouth to continue the argument. 'Holly said she hasn't done it, and I believe her, so drop it.'

Ellie glared at Holly. But Kath wasn't finished with her yet.

'My husband's fighting for his life, and you're sitting here squabbling over the man who flaming well put him there. You ought to be ashamed of yourself. And as for—'

Interrupted by the door opening, Kath looked round and gazed fearfully up at the doctor who walked in.

'Mrs Thompson?'

'Yes,' she said, in a shaky voice that contained none of the vim of moments earlier. 'Is Billy all right? Did the op go okay?'

'I'm afraid not,' the doctor replied gravely. 'There was a complication . . .'

Ellie sat in stunned silence and listened as the doctor told her mum that Billy's spleen had been so badly damaged by the knife it had ruptured during the operation, causing a massive haemorrhage.

'No . . .' Kath whimpered, shaking her head from side to side when he said they had done everything they possibly could, but that Billy hadn't survived. 'He can't be dead; he's only fifty-three. The cut wasn't even that deep.'

After explaining that it was the location of the wound rather than the depth that had caused the problem, the doctor offered his condolences before rushing off to deal with another emergency.

When the nurse who had come in with the doctor went off to get them all a cup of tea, Ellie turned to her mum, who was sobbing in Holly's arms, and tried to hold her hand.

'I'm so sorry, Mum.'

'No, you're not,' Kath howled, snatching her hand away. 'You never liked Billy, so don't start acting like you give a toss now. This is all your fault,' she went on bitterly. 'If you hadn't cheated on Matt, he wouldn't have gone off with that other woman, and Billy wouldn't have had to get involved.'

Hurt that her mum was blaming her, Ellie said, 'I haven't done anything. Matt's the one who cheated, not me.'

Kath ignored her and turned back to Holly.

'Someone needs to tell the police that it's murder now, and not just assault.'

Ellie's stomach twisted into a painful knot. She didn't want to believe that the man she had married and loved with all her heart was capable of such awful violence, but he had now stabbed two people; and her mum was right: it *was* her fault, because he would never have done it if she hadn't lied about Gareth in the first place.

'Are you okay, Ells?' Holly asked, gazing over at her.

'I need some air,' she muttered, jumping to her feet when the walls began to close in on her.

'Go home,' Kath ordered. 'Holly will look after me.'

Ellie didn't want to leave. As the eldest child, it was her duty to look after their mother if something bad happened. But her mum had made her wishes clear, and she had to respect them.

'Okay, I'll go,' she said. 'But please don't push me out, Mum. I love you so much, and I'm always here if you need me.'

'Go home and get some rest,' Holly said when their mum didn't reply. 'I'll ring you when we know what's happening.'

Aware that her mother neither needed nor wanted her there, a wave of sadness and pain washed over Ellie, and it was all she could do to keep herself from bursting into tears as she mumbled a quick goodbye before walking out.

20

Ellie ran down the stairs to the ground floor, lurched out into the cold night air and leaned against the wall to catch her breath. She may not have liked Billy, but he'd been in her life since she was twelve years old, so she couldn't pretend that she didn't care about him dying. Whatever he had done to her, he didn't deserve this, and it killed her that her mum was blaming her for it.

'Ellie . . . ?'

At the sound of Gareth's voice, Ellie snapped her head up and swiped the tears off her cheeks when she saw him hurrying toward her.

'What are you doing here? I thought I told you to stay at home?'

'I was worried about you,' he said, frowning when he reached her. 'What's wrong?'

'Billy's dead,' she told him, rooting in her bag for a tissue. 'They were operating on him when I got here, but his spleen ruptured, and they couldn't save him.'

'I'm so sorry.' Gareth touched her shoulder. 'Is your mum okay?'

'No.' Ellie blew her nose loudly. 'She's blaming me.'

'Why? It's not your fault.'

'Yes it is. Matt was fine until he found out I'd seen you behind his back.'

'Ah . . . So *he's* blaming *you*, and *you're* blaming *me*?'

'No, of course not,' Ellie said guiltily. 'I'm the one who lied.'

'Yeah, and with good reason, considering what he's done since he found out,' said Gareth. Sighing when she dipped her gaze, he said, 'Come on, Ellie . . . how long are you going to keep defending him?'

'I'm not,' she said brusquely, wishing that people would stop saying that.

'Yes, you are,' he argued. 'You didn't believe me when I told you he'd stabbed me, and then you argued with that copper when he told you he'd done the same to your stepdad. Now Billy's dead, but you'd rather blame yourself – or me – than admit that Matt's guilty. So what are you going to do next? Tell the police he was with you when it happened so he's got an alibi?'

'I would never lie to the police. I just . . .'

'Just what?' Gareth prompted when she didn't finish. 'Just don't want to believe that Matt's a murderer?'

'God, I don't know what I think,' Ellie moaned. 'My head's completely battered with all of this. Billy's dead and I'm getting the blame, and now Holly's sitting up there with my mum acting like butter wouldn't melt.'

'Holly's here?' Gareth frowned. 'I thought she'd gone back to London after Christmas?'

'She did, but she came straight here when she heard what had happened. My mum swears she tried to call me, as well; but you saw me check my phone earlier, and there were no missed calls were there?'

'Not that I saw. So what did Holly say? Did you ask her about her and Matt?'

'Yeah, but she denied it, of course.'

'You didn't believe her, did you?'

'I don't know,' Ellie admitted. 'She was so adamant she hadn't done anything, I did wonder if you might have got it wrong. But then I remembered the look on Matt's face when you told me about it after he went for you, and I knew she was lying. I'll get the truth out of her eventually, but I couldn't push it any more tonight – not with all this going on.'

'So what are you doing now?' asked Gareth. 'Are you staying with your mum tonight?'

'No.' Ellie shook her head and pushed herself away from the wall. 'She's got Holly to look after her so she doesn't need me. I just want to go home and have a drink.'

'Come on, then.' Gareth offered his arm to her. 'I'll flag a cab down on the main road.'

'I can't afford a cab,' Ellie said, linking her arm through his. 'We'll have to catch the bus.'

'No, we'll get a cab,' Gareth insisted. 'My treat.'

'I thought you were broke?'

'I was, but I found a tenner at the bottom of my bag when I was looking for clean socks. Lucky, eh?'

'Very,' Ellie said.

They started to walk, but after a couple of steps, Gareth stopped again. A thrill of anticipation rippled through Ellie's body when she saw the way he was looking at her, and she knew he was going to kiss her. To her surprise, instead of pushing him away, she found herself raising her lips to meet his.

A car turned into the hospital grounds a few seconds later, and Ellie pulled away from Gareth when the beam of its head-lights swept over them. Heart lurching when it drove slowly past and she saw who was behind the wheel, she said, 'Oh God, it's Holly's boyfriend. I think he saw us.'

'So what if he did?' Gareth shrugged. 'You're not with Matt any more, so you can do whatever you like.'

He was right, but that didn't make Ellie feel any better about it. Her mum was already mad at her, but she would go ballistic when she heard that Ellie had been seen kissing a man outside the hospital where her stepfather had died only a few minutes earlier. And not just any man, but the one Matt had accused her of having an affair with, which had been the catalyst for him losing his mind and stabbing Billy.

Tony had parked the car by then, and he hurried up the path toward them with a sombre look on his face. Walking straight past Gareth as if he hadn't even seen him, he opened his arms and pulled Ellie into an embrace.

'Oh, my love, I'm so sorry for your loss,' he said as he held her. 'Billy was a good man, and I know your mum and Holly are devastated, so you must be, too.'

'I'm okay,' Ellie said, wriggling free. 'You'd best go in; they'll be waiting for you.'

'That'll be Holly now,' he said, pulling his phone out of his pocket when it started ringing. 'She's probably wondering where I've got to. Are you coming?'

'No, I'm going home,' Ellie said, sure that Holly must have already told him that their mum had kicked her out when she'd rung to tell him about Billy.

Tony nodded and squeezed her arm. 'Holly's your sister, so it goes without saying that she'll always be there for you. But I'm here for you, too – I hope you know that? If there's ever anything you need, all you have to do is ask. Okay?'

Eager to get away from him, because his over-familiarity was grating on her, Ellie muttered, 'Thanks,' and looked round for Gareth, but he'd walked into a doorway some feet away to light a cigarette.

Tony cast a furtive glance in his direction, then turned to Ellie, saying, quietly, 'I'm not being funny, love, but do you really need someone like him hanging around at a time like this? I know I've only met him once, but I've come across his type before, and they're pure trouble. Holly says he gives her the creeps, as well.'

'Is that right?' said Ellie, guessing that he didn't know about his precious girlfriend following Gareth home on Christmas Day and throwing herself at him.

'I'm only looking out for you,' Tony went on sincerely. 'You're going through a hard time right now, and I'd hate to see you being taken advantage of.'

'Well, thanks for your concern, but I'm not the one who's in danger of being taken advantage of,' Ellie said coolly. Then, smiling tightly when he gave her a questioning look, she called: 'Gareth . . . let's go.'

Falling into step beside her as she marched out of the hospital grounds, Gareth said, 'Christ, what a tosser. Anyone'd think *you* were his girlfriend the way he was going on. No wonder him and Holly get on so well, 'cos they both think they're God's gift.'

'Don't talk about her like that,' Ellie said loyally. 'She's still my sister.'

'Are you serious?' Gareth stared at her in disbelief. 'Why are you defending her after what she did?'

'I don't want to talk about her, *or* him,' Ellie said tersely. 'All I want is to go home.'

'I'm sorry,' Gareth apologized, hurrying after her when she picked up speed. 'Ellie, wait . . .'

Forced to stop walking when he ran round in front of her, Ellie sighed. 'Look, I know you're trying to protect me, and I genuinely appreciate your support, but please don't slag my sister off. Whatever she's done in the past, we're still family, so I'm just going to have to find a way to deal with it.'

'I didn't mean to upset you,' Gareth said sincerely. 'I love you so much, I can't bear to see you hurting like this.'

'What are you talking about?' Ellie frowned. 'You hardly even know me.'

'I know you better than you think,' he argued. 'I know you like your coffee weak and your tea strong; and you take two sugars, but you think you're fat, so you cheat by having a heaped one instead. I know you hate football and rugby, but love tennis, and you'd rather watch a good soap than read one of those trashy gossip magazines your sister probably loves. I *also* know that you deserve to be treated way better than Matt ever did, and if you let me, I'll treat you like a queen.'

A little disconcerted that he'd noticed all those things about her in such a short space of time, *and* seemed to think he was in love with her, Ellie said, 'I can't cope with this right now, Gareth. My stepdad's dead, and my husband's wanted for murder. All I want is to go home.'

'Okay, let's go, then,' Gareth said.

Sensing that he was pissed off when he shoved his hands into his pockets and started walking off without waiting for her, Ellie sighed and traipsed wearily after him.

After a silent journey home in the taxi Gareth had flagged down around the corner from the hospital, Ellie was desperate to go to bed so she could think things over in peace. But when they turned into the car park at the flats, and a police van and two cars pulled in behind them, she had a horrible feeling the night wasn't over yet.

A chunky red-headed man was sitting in the passenger seat of the first police car, and he stared at Ellie when she and Gareth got out of the cab. Stomach already churning, she felt her legs begin to shake when the man and several uniformed officers climbed out of the vehicles.

'Mrs Fisher?'

'Yes,' she replied, clutching the strap of her handbag tightly.

'Detective Inspector Collins.' He flashed an ID badge at her. 'We have a warrant to search your property, so could you open the door, please?'

'Yes, of course,' she said, her hands shaking now as she reached into her bag for her keys. 'Is this about Matt? Because if it is, I haven't seen him.'

'We'll talk when we've had a look around,' Collins said, waving for her to go ahead of him.

As they entered the foyer, Ellie saw the detective flash a penetrating glance at Gareth and guessed that he was probably wondering who he was. In no mood for making introductions, she kept her mouth shut and her gaze on the floor as the three of them went into the lift while the others climbed the stairs.

Taking the keys from her when they reached her floor, Collins handed them to a copper and told her and Gareth to stay clear of the door.

'He's not here,' Ellie told him, hugging herself when the

copper opened the door and yelled, 'Police!' before the rest of them piled inside the flat. 'I made him give me his keys back the last time he was here.'

'We'll see,' Collins replied – as if, Ellie thought, he didn't believe her.

'I hope they're not making a mess in there?' Gareth muttered when he heard doors being opened and closed, and a copper shouting, 'Nothing in here . . .'

'I'm sure I don't need to explain the procedure to you,' Collins replied flatly without looking at him.

Already embarrassed, because she sensed that the detective disapproved of Gareth being here, Ellie wished the ground would open up and swallow her when one of her neighbours came out to see what was going on.

Glad to get inside when one of the coppers came out to tell Collins it was all clear a few minutes later, Ellie perched on the sofa, clutching her handbag in her lap.

Collins took a seat on Matt's chair and raised an eyebrow at Gareth when he sat beside Ellie.

'Could you give us a minute?'

'It's okay,' Ellie said quietly to Gareth when she saw a spark of anger flare in his eyes. 'Go and make yourself a brew, or something.'

Sighing when he stalked into the kitchen, slamming the door shut behind him, Ellie turned back to Collins.

'Sorry about that. It's been a difficult night, and he's tired. We both are.'

'I'll try not to keep you too long,' said Collins. 'I take it you're aware this has been escalated to a murder inquiry?'

'Yes, I know. I was at the hospital when the doctor told my mum.'

'I'm very sorry for your loss.'

'Thank you,' Ellie murmured, sniffing softly when tears unexpectedly pricked her eyes.

Back to business, Collins said, 'I believe you told the officers who visited you earlier that you haven't seen your husband in several weeks? Is that still true?'

'Yes.'

'And you haven't had any contact with him by phone, through another person, or on social media . . . ?'

'No, nothing. I called him a couple of weeks ago and left a message asking him to ring me back, but he didn't.'

'And this friend you said he was staying with – Dave Boyle, was it?'

'Yes. But as I told your colleague, I've got no idea where he lives – or *if* Matt even went there. My stepdad saw him with another woman, so he could be with her. I honestly don't know.'

'And were you aware of any issues between your stepdad and your husband before that night?'

'No.' Ellie guiltily dipped her gaze. 'We, um, didn't really speak to Billy all that much, to be honest; apart from wishing him a happy Christmas, or birthday, or whatever.'

'Oh? And why's that?' Collins raised an eyebrow. 'Only I was told he moved in with your mum when you and your sister were still children, and you all got along fine?'

'Not at the start,' Ellie said, shifting nervously in her seat. 'Me and Holly didn't take to him at first, because we'd not long lost our dad and we didn't want another man taking his place. It did get a little better as we got older, but we were never what you'd call close. At least, *I* wasn't.'

'But your sister was?'

'Closer than me, I suppose.' Ellie shrugged. 'But she lets go of things faster than I do.'

'And was there something to let go of?' Collins asked. 'Something you might have mentioned to your husband that would have made him want to hurt your stepdad? An argument that might have got out of hand when you were younger, maybe?'

'No, nothing like that,' Ellie muttered, unwilling to tell him about the night Billy had come into her room, because that would open up a whole new can of worms. 'We just didn't gel. He – *Billy* – could be a bit . . . sarcastic, and Matt's depression makes him hyper-sensitive to things like that, so I was always on eggshells whenever they were together. I guess Matt must have picked up on that.'

'It's interesting that you just referred to your stepdad in the past tense and your husband in the present,' Collins said, peering at her thoughtfully.

'He's dead.' Ellie frowned. 'I'm hardly going to talk about him as if he was still here, am I?'

Collins didn't reply to that, but Ellie could see that his suspicions had been aroused – although she genuinely didn't know why, because she couldn't see anything wrong with what she'd said.

'Look, is any of this relevant?' she asked. 'I thought you came to see if Matt was hiding here, and now you know he's not, I don't get why you're questioning me.'

'I'm trying to build a picture of your husband's relationship with Mr Thompson, to see if we can establish a motive,' Collins replied evenly.

'I'm not being funny,' said Ellie, 'and please don't think I'm defending Matt, because I'd be the first to condemn him if I knew for certain that it was him who'd done this. But you don't, do you? Know for certain, I mean.'

'Your stepdad gave his name to the paramedics,' Collins reminded her. '*And* he told your mum that he'd recognized your husband's voice. We also have the hat – which, incidentally, we believe *is* your husband's, because the hair we recovered from it matched the hair from the comb you gave us. And we have this . . .' He took a rolled sheet of paper from his pocket and opened it up.

'What is it?' Ellie asked, peering at it.

'A still taken from the CCTV footage of a shop not far from where the attack took place,' Collins told her. 'The man you can see in the alley . . .' he pointed to a barely visible figure in the shadows, 'appears to be wearing a hat like the one we found at the scene.'

'I can hardly see anything,' said Ellie. 'So how can you possibly know that?'

'We were able to enhance it, so I've seen a clearer image than this,' Collins said as he re-rolled the paper. 'The face is obscured by a scarf, so it's not possible to make a positive identification at this stage. But we're working on it.'

Ellie shivered as the last of her doubts began to evaporate. It had to be Matt who had done it, and it wasn't going to take long for the police to prove it.

Turning his head at the sound of a loud bang coming from the kitchen, Collins said, 'He doesn't sound very happy in there. Can I ask how long you've known him?'

'A few months,' said Ellie. 'He, um, helped my sister out at Christmas, and she brought him round to have dinner with us.'

'And is he the one your husband thought you were having an affair with?'

'Yes, but it wasn't true. Matt's not well, and he tends to imagine things and then blow them out of proportion.'

'I see,' said Collins, giving her that look again, as if he didn't believe a word she'd said. 'About your husband's illness . . . depression, was it?'

'Yes, that's right.'

'Has he been prescribed any medication for it?'

'Prozac,' Ellie said, frowning as she added, 'but he didn't take it with him when he left. The packet's still in the bedroom.'

'Could he have had a spare?'

'No.' She shook her head. 'The doctor only gives him enough

for a couple of months to start with. He wanted to review him after that, to make sure it's working.'

'And was it working, in your opinion?' Collins asked.

'Not really,' Ellie admitted. 'I think it might have been making him worse . . . '

Gareth had calmed down by the time Collins had finished questioning Ellie and gone on his way, and he handed Ellie a cup of drinking chocolate he'd made for her.

'It went cold while I was waiting, so I had to reheat it,' he told her. 'It might taste funny, 'cos the milk gets a skin on it when it's been in the microwave.'

'It'll be fine,' she said, gratefully taking it.

'So what was with all those questions?' Gareth asked, watching as she sipped her drink. 'It sounded more like an interrogation than an interview.'

'It felt more like it as well,' she muttered. 'But it's done now.'

'For now,' Gareth said ominously. 'But don't think that's the last you've seen of them, 'cos they could turn up at any time to do another search.'

'I don't care,' Ellie said wearily. 'They're not going to find him here, so they can come as many times as they like.'

'Well, I'll be here to keep an eye on them and make sure they treat you right if they do,' Gareth said, reaching for her hand.

'I don't need protecting from the police,' Ellie replied irritably, jerking her hand away. 'And I'm perfectly capable of looking after myself, so please stop mollycoddling me.'

A hurt look came into Gareth's eyes and he held up his hands.

'I'm sorry if you think that's what I'm doing. I'm only trying to make things easier for you.'

'I appreciate that,' said Ellie. 'But it's all the other stuff.'

'What stuff?' He frowned. 'You mean like telling you I love you? Well, I'm sorry but I *do*.'

'No, you don't.' Ellie sighed. 'You're just grateful because I was there when you needed help.'

'Do you really think that's all this is?' Gareth asked. 'After everything we've been through together?'

'I need to get some sleep,' Ellie said, rising stiffly to her feet.

'That's right, run away to avoid talking to me,' Gareth sniped. 'It's not like I'm important, or anything.'

Tutting softly, Ellie said, 'That's not what I'm doing, and you know it. I just can't cope with anything else tonight, and I need to go to bed.'

'Don't let me stop you,' he grunted, crossing his legs and jiggling his foot.

'We'll talk in the morning,' she said. 'Goodnight.'

He didn't reply, but she didn't have the energy to try to coax him out of his mood, so she left him there, with his face like thunder, and went to her room.

21

Ellie had thought she wouldn't be able to sleep, but she went out like a light as soon as her head hit the pillow. Woken by the sound of tapping on her bedroom door the next morning, she prised an eye open and squinted at the clock. Shocked to see that it was almost 10 a.m., she was struggling to sit up when Gareth popped his head round the door.

'I forgot to set my alarm,' she croaked. 'I'm late for work.'

'It's okay, you're not going in today,' he said, walking over to the bed and placing a cup of coffee on the table. 'I rang your office earlier and told them you've had a death in the family.'

His words brought the events of the previous night back in a sickening rush, and Ellie reached for her phone to check if her mum or Holly had tried to get in touch while she was sleeping. Groggy and uncoordinated, she hit the cup with her hand and cried out when hot liquid splashed onto her skin.

'Careful,' Gareth said, reaching out to steady the cup. 'Did it scald you? Let me see.'

'I'm okay,' she insisted, flopping back against the pillow and rubbing her hand on the quilt. 'Mustn't have woken up properly yet.'

'It'll be the shock of everything catching up with you,' he said, picking her phone up and wiping it on his jumper. Hesitating before handing it to her, he said, 'Look, don't get freaked out, but I must have pressed the home button when I was cleaning it, and I'm sure I saw Matt's name on the screen.'

'*What?*' Ellie felt as if a bucket of ice-water had been tipped down her back.

Gareth passed the phone over, and watched as she typed in her password.

'He tried to call me at half three this morning,' she said. 'And then he sent a text.'

'What does it say?' Gareth asked, sitting on the edge of the mattress.

Ellie opened the message, and inhaled sharply when the words leapt out at her.

You lying whore! You tried to make me think I was crazy, but I knew you were fucking around behind my back, and you're gonna get what that pervert Billy got when I get my hands on you. And tell that cunt you're screwing that he'd best keep looking over his shoulder, 'cos he won't be so lucky next time!

'He says he's going to do the same to me as he did to Billy,' she said when she'd finished reading. 'So he *must* have done it.'

'Hate to say it, but you're the only one who doubted it,' said Gareth. 'And now he's showed his hand, you need to let the police know ASAP.'

In no rush to face the detective and go through another grilling, Ellie said, 'I'll do it later; when my head's a bit clearer.'

'No, you'll do it now,' Gareth ordered. 'I've got an appointment with the housing this morning, but I'm not going until I know this had been dealt with, so it'll be on your head if they were about to offer me a place and I miss out 'cos I was late.'

'Okay, I'll do it now,' Ellie conceded, reaching for her handbag to get the card the detective had given her with his number on it. Gareth had been stabbed because of her, and he had to be nervous knowing that Matt was still out there somewhere, waiting to finish the job. But instead of running for the hills, as she would probably have done in his place, he was still here, supporting her, so she owed it to him to do the right thing.

Listening as she made the call, Gareth gave her a reassuring smile when she was done.

'I know this isn't easy, but you had to tell them, because they'd have found out anyway, and then they'd have wondered why you were trying to hide it from them. They already think you know more than you're telling them.'

'I know, but it still feels like I've betrayed him.'

'He killed your stepdad and threatened both our lives,' Gareth reminded her. 'And you've stood by him for longer than most people would have considering how badly he treated you, so you've got absolutely nothing to feel guilty about. This is his fault, not yours, and it's time you stopped trying to protect him.'

'I'm not,' Ellie argued. 'But he's not well, so I can't help worrying about him.'

'Well, you need to stop, because he isn't worrying about you, or he wouldn't be putting you through this shit,' Gareth said bluntly. 'Now stop thinking about him and let the police deal with it.'

'Okay,' Ellie agreed, desperate for him to stop talking, because her head was starting to ache.

'Good girl,' Gareth said approvingly. Then, glancing at her alarm clock, he said, 'Right, I'd best get going. You'll be all right on your own for an hour, won't you?'

'I'll be fine,' she said, reaching for the coffee. 'Go on . . . get yourself off.'

As soon as she heard him leave the flat, Ellie put the cup down and jumped out of bed to click the deadlock into place. She'd said she would be fine on her own, but it was a lie. She was scared – *terrified*, in fact – that Matt would turn up before Gareth got back and carry through with his threat to do to her what he'd done to Billy. The police had told her they would be watching the flats in case he tried to gain entry, but what if he came in disguise and they didn't recognize him? They only had that old photo she'd given them to go on, and he looked completely different now; especially when he hadn't shaved or washed his hair, which he probably wouldn't have been able to do if he was hiding out somewhere.

Scared and jumpy, Ellie had a quick wash and got dressed, and then made her way into the living room – where she stayed for the rest of the day; sitting by the window, so she could see who came in and out of the block.

It was late afternoon before Gareth strolled up the path, and Ellie was so relieved to see him, she couldn't get to the door fast enough. Watching through the spyhole, she waited until he'd turned the corner before opening the door.

A look of concern came onto his face when he saw how pale she was, and he rushed up to her, asking, 'Are you okay? He didn't turn up after I went out, did he? If he's hurt you, I swear to God—'

'He hasn't been here,' Ellie interrupted, stepping aside to let him in before quickly closing the door. 'I've been a bit jumpy, but I'm fine now, honestly.'

'I should never have left you on your own. I'm so sorry.'

'There's no need, honestly. Anyway, forget about it. How did you get on at the housing?'

'Yeah, it was good,' Gareth said, slipping his jacket off and hanging it up before following her into the living room. 'Better than good, actually, 'cos they've offered me a place. They drove me over to see it. That's why I'm late.'

Ellie's heart had sunk a little, but she forced a smile.

'Really? Wow, that's fantastic. Where is it?'

'Cheetham Hill. It's classed as a flat, but it's more like a bedsit, it's that small; and the walls are so thin I could hear every word the neighbours were saying – or should I say *shouting*, 'cos they were having a full-on domestic while I was there. The ones on the other side must have been able to hear it as well, 'cos they turned their music up so loud the windows started rattling. Oh, and did I mention the cockroaches?'

'You're kidding? There's no way they can expect you to live in a place like that. I hope you told them where to stick it?'

'It doesn't work like that when you're homeless. You either take what you're offered or go to the back of the list. And I can't afford to do that, 'cos it might be years before they offer me anything else.'

'Surely they can't expect you to take any old dump, just because you're homeless?'

'Yeah, they can. But it's okay. I've lived in worse places.'

Horrified to think of him being forced to live in those conditions, Ellie said, 'Why don't you stay here until something better comes up? Unless you *want* to get away, obviously. And I wouldn't blame you if you did after the way I spoke to you yesterday.'

'Of course I don't want to get away from you,' Gareth said earnestly. 'I only said I'd take the flat because I thought you were sick of me being here. But if you really don't mind, I'd love to stay – at least until they've caught Matt and I know you're safe.'

'Thank you,' Ellie said gratefully as a wave of pure relief

washed over her. Yesterday, she would have been happy for him to go, because he'd made her feel so uncomfortable with his claim that he was in love with her. But after seeing that text from Matt, the thought of being alone terrified her.

'No, thank *you*,' Gareth said, reaching for her hand. 'For showing me that, no matter how difficult it gets, there's always something better around the corner. And I know you didn't believe me when I said I loved you last night, but I do. You're amazing, and I wish you could see yourself through my eyes because you're beautiful inside and out. And I reckon my nan thinks so, too,' he added, grinning as he reached into his pocket and pulled out a tiny white feather. 'I found this outside the front door when I let myself out this morning, and my nan used to say that's the angels letting you know you're on the right path. She must have put this there knowing I'd find it. There's no other explanation, is there?'

Ellie smiled but didn't reply. She thought it more likely that one of her neighbours had carried the feather in on their clothes and it had dropped off when they'd passed her door. But if it gave Gareth comfort to believe that his grandmother was watching over him, who was she to disillusion him?

'Anyway, I've thought about what you said,' he went on, 'and I know it's my fault you got annoyed with me last night, because I was rushing you. But I'm not going to do that any more. You mean too much to me, and I don't want to lose you, so we'll take it at your pace from now on. And if you decide you only want to be friends, then I'll respect that. All I ask is that you don't completely write me off because I acted like a love-sick idiot. Please, give me a chance to prove that I'm worthy of you.'

'It wasn't about that,' Ellie said when he'd finished. 'And it's never even entered my mind to think that you're not worthy. You're a lovely man, and any woman would be lucky to have you. I'm just not ready to start thinking that far ahead yet.'

'As long as you haven't ruled it out, I'm happy to wait, because you're worth it,' Gareth said sincerely. Then, grinning, he said, 'Right, I'm going to nip out and get a bottle of wine so we can celebrate me telling the council where they can stick that dump.'

'No, don't, you can't afford it,' Ellie said. 'And I can't either, 'cos my wages won't be going into my account until the end of next week.'

'My JSA came through today, so it's my treat,' said Gareth. 'And I got back-pay 'cos they cut me off after I left the hostel, so I can afford it. And now I'm going to be sticking round for a while longer, I want to help you out with the shopping, as well.'

'You don't have to do that,' Ellie protested. 'I'd be buying it anyway, so—'

'Sshhh . . .' Gareth placed a finger on her lips. 'As long as I'm here, we split everything down the middle. Okay?'

'Okay, you can help with the shopping, if you insist,' she conceded. 'But I'm not having you help me with the rent, or anything like that, because you'll need to save to buy stuff for your new place when you get it.'

'Let me worry about that,' Gareth said, walking back out into the hall to get his jacket. 'See you in a minute.'

Ellie went into the kitchen to make a start on dinner when he'd gone. There wasn't a lot of choice, because she hadn't done a proper food shop since Christmas and the cupboards and freezer were almost empty, but she managed to scrape enough together for a fry-up.

When Gareth came back, he was carrying two bottles of wine.

'They were on special offer: two for the price of one,' he told her. 'This day just keeps getting better and better.'

Glad that he was happy again, because she'd felt guilty for upsetting him when all he had done was try to help her, Ellie finished cooking and carried their plates through to the living room. But her newly elevated mood was shattered in a flash when she switched the TV on and saw the photograph of Matt that she'd given to the police on the screen. No longer hungry, she put her plate on the coffee table and listened intently as the presenter outlined that Matt was wanted in connection with murder, and was considered to be a danger to the public, so anyone who saw him should contact the police and not, under any circumstance, try to approach him.

'Oh, God, all the neighbours will have seen that,' she moaned, switching the TV off when the segment had ended. 'What if they think I was involved?'

'Don't be daft,' Gareth said, putting his plate down next to hers and reaching for her hand. 'You haven't got a bad bone in your body, so they'll know this has got nothing to do with you.'

'But the neighbours don't really know me,' Ellie said despairingly. 'Apart from saying hello in passing, I've never had an actual conversation with any of them in the whole time we've lived here, because Matt didn't want them knowing our business. They already think we're standoffish, but now they'll probably think we're one of those weirdo couples who go around murdering people for kicks.'

'No, they won't,' Gareth said firmly, raising her chin to force her to look at him. 'They'll think exactly what *I* think: that you're as much of a victim in this as your stepdad was, because you've been living under Matt's control for years. It's not your fault he went off his head, and if anyone says different they'll have me to deal with.'

Ellie breathed in deeply and then nodded.

'I know you're right, I'm only panicking because I don't know what's going to happen next.'

'Nothing bad's going to happen,' Gareth assured her, getting up and going into the kitchen to pour a couple of glasses of wine. 'Not to you, anyway,' he added when he came back. 'I'm here, and I'll stay as long as you need me, so stop worrying.'

'I'll try,' Ellie agreed, conscious that her hand was shaking when she took her glass. 'I wish I knew where Matt was, though, and what he's thinking.'

'You know what he's thinking, because he told you in that text,' said Gareth. 'But you're safe with me, so drink that, and then I'll pour you another. And when you relax, we're going to forget about Matt and talk about the future, because this will all be over soon, and you've got to start looking forward.'

Ellie wished she could believe that this was going to come to an end, but she had a horrible feeling that it was going to get a whole lot worse before it got better. Now that everybody knew what Matt had done, they were bound to wonder if she'd played a part in it – or had known and tried to cover for him. He was okay, because he'd done a runner and couldn't be got at, but there was nowhere Ellie could go to escape the inevitable gossip and suspicion.

'Drink,' Gareth ordered, watching as she sank into her gloomy thoughts. 'It'll help.'

Ellie very much doubted that, but she did as she'd been told and raised the glass to her lips.

'Good girl,' Gareth said, stroking her hair back off her face as she swallowed a mouthful of wine. 'Everything will get easier soon, I promise.'

22

It was dark in the bedroom when Ellie woke up the following morning, but the glowing digits on the alarm clock told her that it was almost 7 a.m. Glad that she hadn't overslept again, because she needed to go back to work, she stretched her arms above her head and was about to roll over when she heard the soft sound of breathing coming from Matt's side of the bed.

Jerking upright, terrified that Matt had broken in while she'd been sleeping, she was about to leap out of the bed and run, when Gareth's face emerged from beneath the quilt.

'Morning, beautiful.'

Flooded with a mixture of relief that it wasn't Matt, and shame, because she couldn't remember a thing after her second glass of wine, Ellie muttered, 'Morning,' and hurriedly covered her exposed breasts with her arm before snatching her T-shirt up off the floor.

'You're not getting up, are you?' Gareth pushed himself up onto his elbow.

With his hair tousled, and his eyes still half-closed with

sleep, he looked even more handsome that he usually did. Embarrassed, Ellie averted her gaze and turned her back to him to pull her T-shirt over her head.

'I need to get ready for work. I've had too much time off lately, and I can't afford to get sacked on top of everything else.'

'Aw, don't go,' Gareth moaned, leaning forward and wrapping his arms around her waist. 'Stay here and keep me warm.'

Wriggling free when he tried to pull her under the covers, she said, 'I can't.'

'No, what you *can't* do is go out there while Matt's still on the loose,' Gareth argued, no longer smiling. 'I'm sure your boss will understand when you tell him your psycho ex has murdered your stepdad and threatened to do the same to you. And I hope *you're* taking that seriously, now you know he's capable of doing it.'

Ellie chewed on her lip and mulled over what he'd said. As moody and verbally aggressive as Matt could be, she had never in her wildest dreams imagined that she would one day be in fear of her life because of him. But that day had come, and there was no use sticking her head in the sand and trying to pretend that this wasn't real, because it was.

'Okay, I'll ring the office and let them know what's happened,' she agreed. 'I just need to nip to the loo first.'

'That's my girl,' Gareth said, grinning as he lay down and slotted his hands behind his head. 'Now, hurry up and get yourself back in here. I'll be waiting.'

'Actually, I, um, think we should probably get up now we're

both awake,' Ellie said, modestly tugging the hem of her T-shirt down to cover her thighs when she stood up.

'Why?' Gareth frowned. 'You're not regretting what we did, are you?'

'No,' she lied, afraid that she might upset him if she told him that she actually didn't have a clue what they had done; although she could guess, because her inner thighs were aching.

'So what's the problem?' he asked.

'It doesn't feel right, being in here with another man so soon after Matt,' Ellie said. 'It's not that I don't like you, because I do,' she went on when his frown deepened. 'But it would never have happened if I hadn't got so drunk last night, and now I'm sober, I—'

'It's okay, you don't have to explain,' Gareth interrupted, shoving the quilt aside and dropping his feet to the floor. 'I hear you loud and clear.'

'Please don't be upset with me,' Ellie said guiltily when he snatched his jeans up off the floor and started dragging them on. 'You must understand this isn't easy for me. I've been with Matt for a long time and never thought I'd end up in a situation like this, so I wasn't prepared for how it would make me feel.'

'And how *do* you feel?'

'I don't know? Guilty, I suppose. And . . .' Tailing off, scared of offending him any more than she already had, Ellie shrugged. 'I just don't think I'm ready for this yet. Please don't be mad at me.'

Gareth pursed his lips for a moment. Then, smiling, he got up and walked round to her.

'Of course I'm not mad,' he said, looping his arms around her waist. 'And this is exactly why I love you: because you're not an easy lay like all the other girls I've been with. You've got morals, and I respect you for that.'

Glad that he was taking it so well, because she genuinely did like him, Ellie breathed a sigh of relief when he held her to him and stroked her hair.

When they were both dressed a short time later, they went into the kitchen, where Gareth made coffee while Ellie called the office to let them know she wouldn't be going in. That done, she wrote a quick shopping list before pulling her coat on.

'I'm only going to Abdul's, so I won't be long,' she told Gareth. 'I just hope there's enough left in my account to cover it, 'cos Matt withdrew most of it when he left. It'd be a lot cheaper to go to the supermarket, but I don't want to risk going that far in case he's watching and comes after me.'

'He'll have to get past me if he does,' Gareth said, reaching for his own jacket. 'He caught me off guard last time, but I guarantee he won't get that lucky again.'

'You don't have to come,' Ellie said, secretly pleased that he'd offered. 'I know how much you men hate shopping.'

'Do *not* compare me to other men!' Gareth snapped.

Shocked by the sudden switch in his mood, Ellie jerked back

from him. Looking guilty, Gareth reached out and cupped her cheek with his hand.

'Hey, it's okay, I'm not angry with you. I'm not Matt, and I'd never hurt you, or try to control you like he did. Forgive me?'

Ellie nodded, but she was frowning as they made their way out. She didn't like to admit it, even to herself, but Gareth was right about Matt controlling her. Since the accident, her life had become a constant battle not to upset him in any way. She'd walked on eggshells around him for years, monitoring every little thing she said or did; but her efforts hadn't got her anywhere, because Matt was never completely satisfied, no matter how hard she'd tried.

'Hello . . . ? Earth to Ellie?'

Brought out of her thoughts by Gareth's teasing voice, Ellie smiled. 'Sorry; I was miles away.'

'I can see that, but you've got to snap out of it,' Gareth chided. 'Matt's gone, and you need to forget about him and start concentrating on yourself.'

Again, he was right, but Ellie knew it wasn't going to be as easy for her to shake this off as he seemed to think it should be. She had spent the last nine years of her life with Matt and had thought they would be together forever, and she couldn't stop loving him overnight. But he had committed a serious crime for which he would serve a very long prison sentence when he was caught, so she had to face facts and accept that there was no way back from this.

*

Three elderly female residents who lived on the ground floor were coming in through the main door when Ellie and Gareth came out of the lift. They had been loudly gossiping about one of their other neighbours, but they abruptly stopped talking when they spotted Gareth, and Ellie blushed when she saw the disapproval in their eyes.

Unfazed, Gareth gave them a cheery smile, and said, 'Morning, ladies,' before looping an arm around Ellie's shoulder and herding her out through the door.

Mortified, because she had no doubt that she was going to be the new topic of gossip on everybody's lips from now until Matt was caught, Ellie kept her head down as they made their way over the road to the bus stop outside Abdul's.

To Ellie's relief, the bus arrived within seconds of them getting there. As they left the estate – and any chance of being followed by Matt – behind, she finally began to relax.

Conscious that she didn't have much money to play with when they reached the supermarket a short time later, Ellie worked her way slowly around the aisles, searching out bargains and special offers. She didn't realize that Gareth was no longer with her until she reached the freezer aisle and turned to ask which kind of pizza he preferred. Guessing that something must have caught his eye in a different section and he'd gone to check it out, she opted for the Meat Feast that she usually bought.

Finished with that aisle, she was turning the corner to move on to the next when she spotted Gareth talking to a woman a couple of rows along. He had his back to her, but it was obvious from the way he was gesticulating that he was agitated about something.

Afraid that he might think she was spying on him when he suddenly turned round and started marching in her direction, Ellie quickly dragged the trolley back into the aisle and pretended to be rooting through the frozen chips cabinet.

'We need to go,' he said when he reached her.

'Why, what's up?' she asked innocently.

'I've just seen Lynn, and I need to get out of here.'

'Lynn?' Ellie gazed blankly up at him for a second. Then, remembering, she said, 'Oh . . . you mean your *ex* Lynn?'

'Yeah, her,' he muttered. 'Only you wouldn't think she was my ex the way she was talking. Can you believe she actually had the cheek to ask if we could try again, even after I'd told her I was with you now? Shows you how shameless she is. And that's why I need to get out of here – before she sees you and causes trouble. I've never hit a woman in my life, but I won't have any choice if she starts on you, 'cos she's an absolute psycho.'

Ellie had never had a serious fight in her life, and she didn't fancy having a run-in with this violent-sounding woman, so she didn't argue when Gareth pushed her half-filled trolley away and, clutching her by the arm, started marching her toward the door.

Spotting his ex before they got there, she glanced back over her shoulder – at the exact same time the woman looked at her. It was only the briefest exchange of glances before Gareth hustled her out of the store, but Ellie could have sworn it was fear and not anger she'd seen in the other woman's eyes. But, then, she reminded herself that Gareth knew the woman; and if he said she was dangerous, Ellie wasn't about to stick around to find out.

23

There was no further contact from Matt over the next few weeks, and, apart from one crank who claimed to have witnessed him being abducted by aliens on the Yorkshire Moors after his picture was featured on the news, there were no reported sightings of him.

The police had spoken with his old workmate Dave by then, and he'd told them that Matt *had* been staying at his place, but that he had left the day before the stabbing, telling Dave that he intended to go home and try to sort things out with Ellie.

The police had also managed to find the woman who'd been with Matt on the night he'd told Billy that he intended to divorce Ellie, and she'd told them that she and Matt had met in the pub only that night, and she had been on the verge of inviting him back to her place when Billy turned up. She claimed they'd had a heated argument and had almost come to blows, but then Billy had walked out, followed shortly after by Matt – which, she'd told the police, had been a huge relief, because she'd seen something evil in his eyes and truly believed he would have slaughtered her in her sleep if she'd taken him home.

Ellie thought the woman was lying about that last bit, and had only said it because she'd recognized Matt on the news and realized that she had almost slept with a murderer. But it proved that Matt hadn't cheated on Ellie, and that pleased her – although she wasn't sure why since there was no chance of them ever getting back together. It was just nice to know that he hadn't completely stopped loving her, and had wanted to try to repair the damage he'd done to their marriage.

She didn't share those thoughts with Gareth, though, because Matt was the one subject that was guaranteed to upset him. He thought she ought to be glad to be rid of Matt, and in some respects she was, because it had been peaceful in the flat without him going into a mood every two minutes and blaming her. She and Gareth had started to get a little closer during this time, and she couldn't deny that her feelings for him were growing. But she was determined not to rush into anything, so they were taking things slowly. *Very* slowly.

With each day that passed, Ellie began to feel a little safer, and by the end of the third week, she decided it was time to go back to work. Gareth didn't agree, and he tried to talk her out of it; arguing that, just because Matt hadn't been seen, that didn't mean he wasn't still out there somewhere, waiting for an opportunity to ambush her. But, while she understood his concern, and was truly grateful that he cared, Ellie had made up her mind.

As she'd feared might happen, she received a frosty reception from her co-workers when she walked into the office that morning, and it soon became clear from the snippets of whispered conversations she overheard whenever she left the room, that they would have preferred it if she'd stayed away and Louise – the temp Richard had hired to cover for her – had taken over permanently. They didn't say it to Ellie's face, but she knew, and it made her feel as if she'd gone right back to square one with them.

Relieved to escape the unpleasant atmosphere when lunchtime came around, Ellie pulled her collar up high around her throat when she walked outside and found that it was raining. Hurrying to the cafe, she jumped when a bus drove past and sprayed her legs with filthy puddle-water. Tutting when she saw a female passenger swivel her head and stare at her as the bus drove on, she muttered, 'Yeah, go on, take a good look, why don't you?'

Unable to eat outside, as usual, she ordered her lunch when she reached the cafe, and carried it to a table in the corner. About to take a bite of her sandwich, she glanced up when a shadow passed the window, and froze, with her mouth still open, when she saw the woman from the bus standing in the doorway and realized it was Gareth's ex.

'I don't want any trouble,' she said, standing up when Lynn walked over. 'Whatever happened between you and Gareth, it's none of my business, so let's keep this civil. Okay?'

A flicker of confusion flashed through Lynn's eyes. 'Sorry, I don't know what you're talking about.'

'I saw you arguing with him in the supermarket, so I know it's you,' Ellie said, as calmly as her pounding heart would allow. 'And you must have recognized me, as well, or you wouldn't be here. But, just so you know, there's a camera in the corner, and they *will* call the police if you kick off.'

Lynn held up her hands, and said, 'I only want to talk. Please . . . it's important.'

Surprised to see that Lynn looked as nervous as she herself felt, Ellie sank back down onto her seat.

'Okay, we can talk,' she agreed. 'But I haven't got long, so it'll have to be quick.'

Lynn nodded her agreement, then cast a nervous glance at the door, before asking, 'You're not expecting Gareth, are you? Because I don't want him to see me talking to you.' Visibly relieved when Ellie shook her head, she said, 'Okay, great. I'll get a coffee. Won't be a sec.'

Lynn went to the counter to order her drink, and Ellie studied her profile. She looked to be in her early twenties, and she was very pretty, with long, glossy red hair tied in a loose ponytail, amber eyes, and a delicate smattering of freckles that added warmth to her make-up-free-complexion. It was easy to see why Gareth had fallen for her and had wanted to marry her before he'd found out about her aborting his baby and caught her in bed with another man. But those two acts had almost caused him to take his own life, and Ellie knew that, even if he still loved her, he would never be able to forgive her.

When Lynn came back, Ellie noticed that her hands were shaking as she placed her cup and saucer on the table before taking a seat. She didn't look like she was putting on an act, but Ellie hadn't forgotten the picture Gareth had painted of her, so she wanted to get this over with as quickly as possible.

Taking the bull by the horns, she said, 'I'm guessing you want to talk about Gareth, but before you start, can I just say that I didn't meet him until *after* you'd split up.'

'I'm not here for an argument, honestly,' Lynn replied. 'I've come because I felt I ought to warn you.'

'Warn me?' Ellie repeated. *Or warn me off?* she thought, bracing herself for the threats she was sure would follow when Lynn heard something she didn't like and dropped the mask of civility.

'About Gareth,' Lynn said, clutching her cup tightly as she cast another nervous glance at the door. 'I don't know how long you've known him, but if you're already engaged, like he told me that day, I think you need to know what you're letting yourself in for.'

Ellie didn't correct her about the engagement, because she guessed that Gareth had probably told her that in order to prove that he'd moved on. Instead, she said, 'I've known him for a few months, but that's long enough to know that he's a decent man with a good heart, so if you're going to try and turn me against him, don't bother. He's already told me what you did.'

'What *I* did?' Lynn's eyebrows shot up.

'Like I said, it's none of my business, and I don't want to get into it with you,' said Ellie. 'But, woman to woman, I think you need to accept that he doesn't want to be with you.'

Lynn's mouth fell open now, and she gasped, 'Oh, my God, is that what he told you – that I was trying to get back with him? That's an absolute lie! I was terrified when I saw him that day, 'cos I thought he'd started again.'

'Started what?'

'Stalking me,' Lynn said quietly.

'*What?*' Ellie drew her head back in disbelief. 'Don't talk rubbish.'

'It's true,' Lynn insisted. 'It went on for a year, and it nearly destroyed me.'

'So you're telling me you weren't in a relationship with him?'

'I did date him a couple of times, but I realized pretty fast that I didn't want to take it any further. I tried to let him down gently, but he refused to accept it, because he reckoned we were meant to be together. I had to change my phone number to stop him from calling and texting all the time, but then he started turning up at my flat in the middle of the night, demanding to come in.'

'Why didn't you call the police if it was that bad?' Ellie asked.

'I did,' Lynn said. 'But he always disappeared before they got there, and then he'd come back as soon as they'd gone. It got so that I couldn't go out on my own, because I was terrified he'd follow me. And I even got nervous about going out in daylight, which nearly cost me my job. I thought it was never going to end, then one day, a few months ago, he suddenly stopped coming round. It was such a relief, I actually prayed he was dead.'

Ellie didn't say anything when Lynn paused to take a sip of coffee. The woman sounded sincere, but Ellie didn't know her from Adam. She *did*, however, know Gareth, and she was more inclined to believe his version of events than that of a woman she'd never spoken to in her life.

'I was made up when Gareth told me the two of you were engaged,' Lynn went on after putting her cup down. 'Because it meant he'd turned his attentions onto someone else and wouldn't start bothering me again. But then I saw you, and I couldn't help wondering if you knew what he was like; or if he'd fooled you, like he fooled me at the start.'

'I'm a pretty good judge of character,' Ellie said. 'And, to be honest, if I hadn't seen you talking to him that day, I'd swear you were talking about somebody else, because this sounds nothing like the Gareth I know. He's been living with me for weeks, and I think I'd have noticed if he was anything like you're describing.'

'Not if he hasn't turned on you yet,' Lynn replied bluntly. 'I know how lovely he can be when you first get to know him;

and he's so handsome, you can't help being flattered that he's interested in you. But, believe me, that doesn't last long.'

'Sorry, but I can't listen to any more of this.' Ellie pushed her chair back. 'You're very pretty, and you probably can't believe that he turned you down for someone like me, because I'll admit that I'm struggling with that one myself now I've seen you up close. But I know Gareth, and I believe him, so if you're saying all this to get me to finish with him so he'll come back to you, it's never going to happen.'

'I'm sorry if I've upset you, that honestly wasn't my intention,' Lynn said earnestly when Ellie rose to her feet. 'But please think about what I've told you, and if you see any sign of him starting to behave like that with you, get him out of your life before it's too late.'

'Thanks for the concern,' Ellie said coolly. 'But me and Gareth are fine.'

'I genuinely hope he never turns on you, because you seem like a nice lady,' Lynn said. 'Please don't tell him you saw me, because I honestly don't think I could cope if he started coming after me again.'

'Fine, I won't tell him,' Ellie agreed. 'But don't approach me if you see me again, because I don't like keeping secrets from him.'

Back at her desk a short time later, Ellie thought about what Lynn had told her. She claimed to have only had two dates with Gareth, but he'd told Ellie that they had been engaged and were planning their wedding when he'd caught her with the other man. And then there was the baby Lynn was supposed to have aborted. She hadn't mentioned it, but Ellie remembered how cut-up Gareth had been when he'd told her about it, and she was certain she would have sensed if he'd been lying. And why would he lie about something as traumatic as that? He had nothing to gain from it, whereas Lynn had *everything* to gain from making Ellie doubt him. In fact, the more Ellie thought about it, the more likely it seemed that Lynn was the one who had been stalking Gareth, and not the other way round. She could have heard that he was seeing someone else and gone out of her way to bump into him at the supermarket that day, to try and persuade him to give her another chance. And when that hadn't worked, she'd approached Ellie instead, and made him out to be some kind of twisted weirdo in the hope that Ellie would call things off and kick him out.

Well, if that *was* her game, Ellie wasn't about to fall for it. Gareth had stood by her when even her own family had turned their backs on her, so she would judge him on *that,* she decided, and not on the words of some bitter ex who couldn't – or wouldn't – let go.

Determinedly pushing Lynn out of her mind, Ellie made an effort to concentrate on her work as the day wore on. But just as she was finally beginning to get back into the swing of things, Richard stalked out of his office with a grim expression on his usually jovial face, and yelled, 'Everybody out!'

'Is everything all right?' Ellie asked, rising from her seat as the other girls did the same.

'No, it isn't,' he said, already heading back into his office. 'And I need a word before you go.'

Worried that he was about to sack her, Ellie followed him into his office and closed the door.

'Have I done something wrong, Richard? If it's about those mistakes I made in the Slater document, I've already—'

'It's not about that,' he interrupted, unhooking his suit jacket from the back of his chair and shoving his arms into the sleeves. 'It's about the disturbing conversation I've just had with your husband.'

Ellie sucked in a sharp breath and gripped the edge of his desk when her legs turned to jelly.

'M-Matt's here?' she croaked. 'Please tell me he's not, because I can't—'

'He isn't here,' Richard cut in when he saw the panic on her face. 'He rang me and told me to tell you that he's been watching you, and he's furious with you for moving on so fast. He also said I was to fire you immediately, or he's going to petrol bomb the building with everybody in it.'

'No . . .' Ellie shook her head slowly as the last of the blood drained from her face. 'He wouldn't do that.'

'He's already wanted for murder, so I can't afford to take the risk,' Richard said, tugging a tissue out of the box on his desk and passing it to her when a tear trickled down her cheek. 'I've reported it to the police, and they're sending a unit over to search the area, but they advised me to close up for the day.'

'I'm so sorry,' Ellie apologized, wiping her cheeks. 'I would never have come back if I'd known he was still around, but I honestly thought it was safe.'

'You should have told me you were at risk,' Richard chided. 'Now, because you didn't, we *all* are.'

'I know, and I feel terrible about it,' Ellie murmured, twisting the tissue in her hands. 'Do – do you want me to hand in my notice?'

'No, of course not.' Richard sighed. 'Although, that said, I can't guarantee the board will be as understanding once they get wind of this. They're already grumbling about the amount of time you've taken off, so they won't be too happy when they hear I've told you not to come back until the police have caught your husband. Temps don't come cheap, and that's an expense we could do without right now.'

'I'm so sorry for putting you in this position,' Ellie said guilt-ily. 'But what if they never catch him? I can't expect you to keep my job open forever, so maybe it'd be better if I resign before you're forced to sack me? I'm sure the girls would be happy if it means they could have Louise back permanently.'

'That's never going to happen,' Richard snorted, sucking his stomach in so he could button his jacket before reaching for his bag. 'The girl was bloody useless; couldn't seem to understand a word I'd dictated. Anyway, there's no point making plans until we know what's what,' he went on, guiding Ellie to the door with his hand on her elbow. 'Right now, we just need to get out of here.'

Terrified by the thought that Matt was out there somewhere, Ellie hesitated when they entered the foyer, and peered out through the glass.

'What if he's waiting for me to come out? The train station will be deserted at this time, and if he catches me on my own . . .'

'Don't worry, I'll give you a lift,' Richard said, pushing the door open and waving her out ahead of him.

When Richard dropped her off a short time later, Ellie thanked him and then ran inside. She could hear Gareth moving around in the living room when she let herself into the flat, and she rushed in to tell him what had happened. Hesitating when she spotted his partially packed rucksack standing on the coffee table, she said, 'What's going on?'

'Ah . . . you caught me,' he said, giving her a sheepish look when he turned round. 'I thought I'd be gone by the time you got home.'

Already shaking, Ellie walked over to the sofa and sank down on it.

'You're leaving?'

'It's for the best,' Gareth said, squatting beside her and reaching for her hand when he saw the tears in her eyes. 'Hey, come on . . . it's not the end of the world. We'll still be able to see each other; you just won't have to put up with me mooching off you any more.'

'Where are you going?' she asked. 'Have you found somewhere else to stay?'

'Not yet, but I will,' Gareth said, rising to his feet and looking around. 'I don't suppose you know where I put my Stone Roses jumper, do you? I've looked everywhere, but I can't find it.'

'I put it in the wash last night,' Ellie told him. 'Your jeans are in there, as well, so you'll have to wait until they're washed and dried before you can go.'

'Or I could take them out of the machine before they get wet and save you the bother.'

'I don't mind.'

'Well, I do,' said Gareth. 'You've been taking care of me for so long, I'm starting to get used to it. And that's half the reason why I've decided to go: because I don't want you to think I'm taking you for granted.'

'What's the other half?' Ellie asked. 'Of your reason for leaving, I mean.'

Gareth shrugged, as if he didn't want to discuss it, and started shoving the clothes he'd already packed further down into the rucksack to make room for more.

'Don't you think I deserve to know?' Ellie persisted when he didn't answer.

'I think it's time, that's all,' he replied quietly. 'I still love you, so don't ever doubt that. But . . .'

'But what?' Ellie demanded. 'Have you met someone else?'

'No, of course not. I've told you I love you, so how could you think I'd leave you for someone else?'

'Well, what is it, then? Please tell me.'

'Don't worry, it's nothing *you've* done,' Gareth assured her. 'But I think you were right when you said it was too soon for us to get into a full-on relationship.'

'I thought you were okay with us taking it slow?' she said.

'I was,' Gareth replied. 'And, believe me, I'd be happy to wait another ten years if I thought there was a chance that you'd choose me at the end of it. But you've still got feelings for Matt, and I think you need space to work out if it's him you want.'

Unable to contain her emotions any longer at the mention of Matt's name, Ellie burst into tears and dropped her face into her hands.

'Hey, come on, it's not that bad,' Gareth said, sitting down and putting his arm around her. 'All I want is for you to be happy, and if that means letting you go so you can be with Matt, that's what I'll do. He'll get out of prison eventually, and you'll be able to put all this behind you and—'

'He's going to kill me,' Ellie sobbed, cutting him off mid-sentence. 'He rang my b-boss this afternoon and threatened to petrol bomb the building if he didn't sack me.'

'You're kidding?' Gareth drew his head back and gazed down at her. 'Why?'

'Because of us,' she cried. 'He said he's been watching me, and he's mad at me for moving on so fast.'

'I hope your boss called the police?'

'Yes, and they told him to clear the building, so he sent everyone home.'

'Good,' Gareth said. 'But you know this wouldn't have happened if you'd listened to me in the first place, don't you? I did try to warn you, but . . .'

'I know,' Ellie said when he tailed off. 'And it won't happen again, because Richard's told me not to go back until the police have caught Matt. But they can't keep my job open forever.'

'They can't sack you for obeying orders,' Gareth assured her. 'And if they try, we'll sue them.'

'It's not that simple,' said Ellie. 'I haven't been there for a full year yet, so I'm still in my probationary period, and there'll be nothing I can do if they decide not to renew my contract.'

'This is Matt's fault, not yours,' Gareth pointed out. 'And they must know you've got no control over what he does.'

'I just want it to stop,' Ellie moaned. 'I can't keep living like this; it's killing me.'

'I blame the police,' said Gareth. 'They need to stop arsing around and catch Matt before he does anything else.'

'They're doing the best they can,' Ellie said, rubbing her temples when they started to throb.

'Don't kid yourself,' Gareth snorted. 'I know how those bastards work, and they won't give a toss if he gets to you before they catch him. They'll probably think you deserve it for cheating on him and sending him over the edge.'

'But I didn't cheat,' Ellie protested. 'He'd already left before anything happened between you and me.'

'*We* know that, but they clearly don't,' said Gareth. 'I saw the way that fat bastard Collins looked at us the last time he was here; like *we're* the criminals for falling in love. I wouldn't put it past them to try and use you as bait to lure him out of his hiding place.'

'They wouldn't do that, would they?'

Gareth frowned when he saw the fear in her eyes, and said, 'No, of course they wouldn't. Ignore me, I'm only mouthing off because I'm angry that they haven't caught him yet. I've had my share of run-ins with them in the past, so I don't exactly trust them; but I'm pretty sure they wouldn't deliberately put you in danger, so don't start worrying about that.'

'How can I not worry?' Ellie asked. 'I'm terrified Matt's going to kill me the first chance he gets.'

'Okay, look, if it makes you feel any safer, I'll stay for a while longer,' Gareth said, pulling her closer. 'And don't worry about Matt, because I'll kill him before I let him get anywhere near you. And that's a promise.'

24

Ellie didn't set foot out of the flat again for the next few weeks, and she started to go a little stir crazy with a routine that consisted of nothing but getting up in the morning, watching TV, cooking, eating, watching more TV, then going back to bed . . . only to do it all over again the next day.

The only time she felt truly safe was when Gareth was home, but he'd been going out every day searching for work so he could take care of the bills when she was no longer able to. And that day was bound to come, because the longer this went on, the less likely it was that Ellie's contract would be renewed at the end of her probationary period.

Gareth was out on another interview today, and Ellie was already on edge, so when the intercom suddenly buzzed, she leapt to her feet and ran to the window to see who it was. Half expecting it to be the police, she was shocked to see Holly standing down below. It was the first time Ellie had laid eyes on her since the night Billy had died, and neither she nor their mum had answered any of Ellie's calls or replied to her messages. They hadn't even bothered to tell her the date of Billy's funeral, when they must have known she'd have wanted to go, and she had been deeply hurt to see it featured on the local news after the fact.

Curious to know what her sister wanted, Ellie went out into the hall and pressed the door-release.

Waiting at the door when Holly strolled around the corner a couple of minutes later, she said, 'What's brought you here? I thought you'd forgotten where I lived?'

'Nice to see you, too,' Holly said breezily, giving her a quick hug. Pulling back then, she looked Ellie up and down, and said, 'Have you lost weight, 'cos you don't feel as pudgy as you were last time I saw you?'

Sighing when Holly walked into the living room without waiting for an answer, Ellie closed the front door and followed her in.

Holly dropped her expensive-looking handbag onto the coffee table and, slumping down on the sofa, kicked her high-heeled shoes off.

'God, that's better. They were killing me.'

'You haven't answered my question,' Ellie said, perching on the chair she usually avoided because she still thought of it as Matt's.

'Can't you even try to look pleased to see me?' Holly complained, flashing Ellie a disapproving look as she rubbed one of her feet. 'And a drink would be nice – thanks for offering.'

'I've only got tea, and that's not alcoholic enough for you,' said Ellie. 'And I *am* pleased to see you,' she added grudgingly. 'But I'm curious to know why you're here when you haven't bothered with me in ages. I thought you'd have gone back to London.'

'I did, and I've been so busy I haven't had a chance to call,' said Holly. 'But I'm here for the week, and I had a free morning, so I thought I'd best come round and tell you the news before you heard it from someone else.'

'News?'

'Yeah, Mum's sold the house, and she's coming to live with me and Tony.'

'In London?' Ellie frowned.

'Well, that's where we live, so, *duh*!' Holly said sarcastically. Then, narrowing her eyes when she spotted a sweatshirt hanging over the radiator behind Ellie's chair, she pointed at it. 'What's that doing there?'

'What?' Ellie twisted her head to look. 'Oh, that? I've just taken it out of the wash, so I hung it there to dry.'

'For who?' Holly narrowed her eyes, instantly suspicious. 'It's way too big for you, and it's not your style. Here, it'd better not be Matt's,' she went on accusingly, ''cos if I find out you're hiding him here after what he did to Billy, I swear to God I'll grass you up!'

'Of course he's not here,' Ellie spluttered, shocked that her sister could think she would harbour him. 'What do you take me for?'

'You've been defending him and lying for him for years, so

you can't blame me for asking,' said Holly. 'Why are you still washing his clothes if he's not here?' she demanded. 'And please don't tell me you've started wearing them because you're missing him, 'cos that'd be too creepy for words.'

'You don't half talk rubbish sometimes,' Ellie said irritably. 'If you must know, it's Gareth's.'

'Gareth?' Holly pulled a face. 'Why the hell are *his* clothes here?' Then, widening her eyes, she said, 'Oh, God, please don't tell me you've shacked up with him? Tony said he thought something was going on when he saw you together outside the hospital that night, but I said no way; she's too stuck in her ways to cop off with someone else the minute Matt's back is turned.'

'Matt's been gone for months,' Ellie reminded her. 'And I'd hardly welcome him with open arms if he tried to come back, would I?'

'Hard to tell with you,' Holly snorted. 'He's always known how to pull your strings.'

'Is that what he did with you?' Ellie replied tartly. 'Pulled your strings and got you to drop your knickers and open your legs? And how long was that going on, by the way? I didn't get a chance to ask you at the hospital, but I'd really like to know.'

'God, I knew you'd do this,' Holly said, as if Ellie was out of order for bringing it up again. 'You can never let anything go, can you? You've always got to keep pecking and pecking at the wound till it bleeds all over you.'

'I think I've got a right to know, seeing as he's *my* husband,' Ellie retorted.

'Oh, so that's how you still think of him, is it?' Holly pounced, a victorious smirk on her heavily glossed lips. 'I wonder what *Gareth* would say if he knew you were still thinking about your ex while you're screwing him? And where is he, by the way? Down at the dole office, or has he started begging in town now, like all the other tramps?'

'He's gone for an interview, actually,' said Ellie. 'And don't talk about him like this, because he's done nothing to deserve it.'

'Apart from jump into Matt's shoes the first chance he got, like the scrounging low-life he is,' sniped Holly.

'You didn't think that when *you* were trying to get off with him,' Ellie argued. 'It must have put a massive dent in your ego to know he fell in love with me after rejecting you.'

'You reckon he's in love with you?'

'I don't reckon, I *know*. And if you've got nothing nice to say about it, I suggest you go back to your perfect life and forget all about me – *again*!'

Holly pursed her lips and peered at Ellie's angry face for several moments. Then, sighing, she said, 'Okay, I'm sorry. I didn't come for an argument, so let's drop it, eh? I've done shit in the past, and so have you, so there's no point pretending that either of us are angels. But we *are* sisters, and I do care about you.'

Ellie took a deep breath in an effort to calm down. Holly had been the bane of her life for as long as she could remember, but however badly she'd behaved in the past, she was Ellie's little sister, and Ellie loved her. But that didn't mean she was going to allow her to start treating Gareth the way she'd treated Matt.

'Gareth's been good to me,' she said. 'He stood by me when I had no one else to turn to, and I honestly don't think I'd have got through these last few months if I hadn't had his support. And he's not scrounging off me, by the way. He contributes to the shopping, and when my wages stop in a couple of months, he'll be paying for everything until I'm free to start looking for another job.'

'So he's moved in, then?' Holly raised an eyebrow.

'Not into my bedroom, if that's what you're thinking,' said Ellie. '*Yet*,' she added quietly.

'Fair enough.' Holly shrugged. 'Matt did the dirty on you, so why not? I just hope Gareth's not playing you, 'cos you're not exactly the best judge of character when it comes to men, are you?'

'Obviously not, or I wouldn't have married a man who was more interested in my sister,' Ellie replied. 'I still can't get my head around you betraying me like that, but I suppose our interpretation of loyalty is as different as we've always been.'

'Look, I'm not proud of myself for going with Matt,' Holly said, sounding guilty for the first time. 'But if you're going to keep throwing it in my face, you should know that he's the one who started it, not me. I turned him down loads of times before it happened, and I was only with him for a few months, 'cos I broke it off as soon as he started talking about finishing with you and marrying me instead. I couldn't do that to you; not when you were already planning the wedding.'

Shocked, because she'd genuinely thought it had been a one-off thing, twice at the most, Ellie's mouth fell open. 'A few months?' she gasped. '*Before* we got married?'

'Yeah, well, like I said, I'm not proud of it,' Holly muttered. 'I was barely out of my teens, and he was proper fit back then – and he knew it, so you can't blame me. Anyway, I wasn't the only one.'

'What's that supposed to mean?' Ellie demanded.

'Oh, come on, you don't need me to spell it out.' Holly sighed. 'He told me I was special, and I'm ashamed to say I believed him. But then I found out he was shagging that Poppy bird from the newsagents at the same time, so I told him to sling his hook.'

'You said you broke it off because of *me*,' Ellie reminded her. 'But I should have known you only did it because you were jealous. What I don't understand is why you didn't tell me.'

'You'd already ordered your dress, and I didn't want to ruin everything when you were so happy,' Holly explained, as if she'd done something noble. 'Anyway, Mum would have kicked me out if she'd found out about it, and I had nowhere else to go.'

'I doubt that very much,' Ellie snorted. 'You've always been her favourite, so she'd have taken your side – like she did at the hospital that night,' she added bitterly, remembering how their mum had turned on her, telling her to drop it because she believed Holly.

'Well, now you know everything, can we forget about it and move on?' Holly asked hopefully when Ellie sank back in her seat. 'You and Matt are finished, so it shouldn't bother you what he did in the past. Best that you forget him and concentrate on us, 'cos we're blood, and that means more than *he* ever did.'

'It's a pity you didn't think like that when you were screwing him behind my back,' Ellie said wearily. 'And I can't pretend it's going to be easy to forgive you, but I'll try.'

'You will?' Holly's pretty face lit up.

Unable to look at her, because all she could see was the better-looking, more vivacious sister that Matt had wanted to marry before plumping for second best, Ellie said, 'I'll *try*, but I'm not making any promises. You've really hurt me, and it'll be a long time before I get over it. I'm just glad I won't have to see you very often when you go back to London.'

'You'll be coming over for the wedding next year, though, won't you?' Holly asked. 'I know Mum isn't ready to talk to you yet, because she still blames you for what Matt did to Billy; but this is about me and Tony, and we both want you there, so please say you'll come?'

Hurt all over again to have it confirmed that her mother *did* blame her for Billy's murder, Ellie shook her head sadly. Then, flapping her hands in a gesture of surrender, she said, 'Fine, whatever. But make sure Mum knows you've invited me, 'cos I don't want her kicking off when she sees me.'

'Don't worry about her,' Holly said dismissively. 'She'll be living with us by then, so she'll do as she's told.'

'So you say she's sold the house?' Ellie asked.

'Yeah.' Holly grinned. 'To me and Tony.'

'Why?' Ellie frowned. 'You're settled in London, why do you want a house up here?'

''Cos it's a good investment,' said Holly. 'Mum let us have it for the same price she paid the council for it, and it's worth ten times that now, easy.'

'Lucky you,' Ellie muttered, annoyed that her mum hadn't thought to offer it to *her* when she knew how much Ellie had always longed to have a house of her own. It didn't even matter that she'd have struggled to get the money together; it would have been nice to be considered for once.

'Right, I'd best get going,' Holly said, glancing at her watch before sitting forward to slip her shoes on. 'Tony'll be here in a minute, and then we're off to pick Mum up from the hairdresser's.'

'Are you taking her out to dinner, or something?' Ellie asked, standing up when Holly did.

'Kind of,' Holly said evasively. Then, looking a little sheepish, she said, 'Actually, we're going to Aunt June's to celebrate our Hayley getting engaged. I'd invite you to come, but it's not my place. You understand, don't you?'

Ellie was shocked to hear that her cousin had got engaged and nobody had thought to tell her. But, then, why would they bother when her own mother wanted nothing to do with her?

'Yeah, course,' she said, trying to make it sound as if she wasn't bothered about this latest slap in the face. 'Tell our Hayley I'm really happy for her.'

'Will do,' Holly said, walking out into the hall.

Turning to Ellie before opening the door, she said, 'I'm glad we got all that Matt business out in the open at last. It's been on my conscience for years, so it's a massive relief to get it off my chest. And thanks for forgiving me.'

Ellie distinctly remembered saying that she would *try* to forgive her, but it was obviously a done deal in Holly's fickle little head, so she saw no point in replying.

'I'll try to pop round again before we go,' Holly promised, giving her a quick hug. 'And don't worry about Mum; I'll work on her.'

Ellie nodded, although she didn't hold out much hope of Holly being able to change their mother's mind, because the woman was as stubborn as a mule.

Holly was about to open the door when Gareth unlocked it from the other side. Frowning when he saw Holly, he gave Ellie a questioning look.

'What's *she* doing here? I thought I told you not to answer the door when I was out? What if it had been him?'

'I saw her from the window,' Ellie told him, feeling guilty, although she wasn't sure why. 'And I thought I'd better let her in, in case there was something wrong with my mum.'

'Why would you care if there was?' he demanded. 'She

hasn't been worrying about you while she's been ignoring your calls, has she?'

'She's still my mum,' Ellie said quietly, embarrassed that he was arguing with her in front of her sister. 'And me and Holly have managed to resolve some of our issues, so that's good, isn't it?'

'Well, it *was* good before you turned up with your slap-arse face,' Holly interjected sarcastically, giving Gareth a dirty look. Tutting when Ellie flashed her a look of warning, she said, 'Right, I'm off before I get myself into trouble.'

She stepped outside, then turned round and pointed her finger at Gareth, saying, 'You make sure you treat my sister right, 'cos she's been through enough shit already.'

'Most of it caused by *you*,' he replied tersely as he placed a proprietorial arm around Ellie's shoulders. 'But, don't you worry, I'm looking after her. She's my world, and I'd do anything for her.'

'My, my, we are smitten, aren't we?' Holly drawled.

Ellie slipped out from under Gareth's arm when she felt his body stiffen, and pushed him toward the living room, saying, 'Why don't you go and put your feet up? I'll make you a coffee when I've seen Holly off.'

Sneering as she watched him do as he'd been told, Holly waited until he'd closed the door behind him then turned to Ellie and said, 'What *are* you doing, Ells? He's exactly like Matt.'

'No, he isn't,' Ellie argued. 'He's *nothing* like him. He's kind, and gentle, and he makes me feel good about myself.'

'If you say so,' Holly sighed. 'I can see why you're so keen to hold onto him, 'cos he's even more gorgeous than I remembered. Pity I can't remember if he was any good in the sack, 'cos I was out of my head that night; but I'm guessing from that little blush that *you're* more than satisfied. Am I right?'

Embarrassed, because she had never felt comfortable discussing intimate details of her life with Holly, or anybody else, Ellie shushed her and glanced back to make sure that Gareth wasn't listening. Holly couldn't remember sleeping with him because it had never happened, but with her track record for stealing Ellie's men, Ellie wasn't about to tell her what she'd missed and have her start thinking about him in that way again.

After one final hug, Holly went on her way, and Ellie headed back inside to make Gareth the coffee she'd promised and find out how his interview had gone.

But Gareth didn't want to talk about the interview; he wanted to know what she and Holly had been talking about. And he particularly wanted to know if Ellie had invited her round – and, if so, why she hadn't told *him* about it.

'I didn't invite her,' Ellie told him truthfully. 'But I *was* glad to see her, because I've missed her. And at least I know the truth about her and Matt now.'

'See, that's what I don't get,' Gareth said coolly. 'How come you don't want to rip her scheming little face off? I would if it was me, but the way you were talking to her just now, it's like it never even happened.'

'Matt was as much to blame as she was,' Ellie said defensively. 'More, in fact, because he was a grown man and she was practically a child. But it doesn't matter any more. We've made our peace, and that's the end of it.'

Gareth shook his head in disgust. 'I can't believe you've let her talk you round so easily. And that makes me wonder if you'd let Matt do the same if he ever turns up when I'm out?'

Ellie was beginning to feel how she'd felt whenever Matt accused her of cheating on him, and she decided to nip this in the bud before it escalated.

'Look, I don't know where this is coming from, or why you're suddenly feeling so insecure when I've done nothing wrong,' she said. 'But you need to stop this before you say something you regret. Holly's my sister, and I love her, and it's my business if I choose to forgive her.'

Gareth's cheek muscles twitched, and a spark of anger flared in his eyes.

'Is that right?' he said quietly. 'Well, fuck you, Ellie. *I'm* the one who's been supporting you while your so-called family have been ignoring your calls and slagging you off behind your back – or have you forgotten everything I've done for you; the sacrifices I've made?'

'Gareth, stop. I'm sorry.' Ellie held out her hand in a conciliatory gesture. 'I honestly didn't mean it like that. I only meant that me and Holly talking again shouldn't affect me and *you*, because it's a completely separate relationship.'

'Yeah, well, it seems like you'd rather have her than me,' said

Gareth. 'So I might as well leave you to it and let *them* take care of you from now on.'

'You're over-reacting,' Ellie said, following when he went out into the hall and hauled his rucksack out of the cupboard. 'Can't we talk about this? You know it's been killing me not seeing my family, so I thought you'd be pleased that I've managed to patch things up with Holly.'

'And *I* thought I'd be slightly more important to you than her and your mum obviously are,' Gareth replied tersely as he marched into her bedroom and yanked open the drawer she'd told him he could use. 'But, like you said, it's your business, not mine.'

'You're important, too,' Ellie insisted, watching helplessly as he began to stuff his clothes into the rucksack. 'If you'd come home a few minutes earlier, you'd have heard me telling Holly how amazing you've been, and how much I appreciate everything you've done for me. Go after her and ask her, if you don't believe me.'

Back still turned, Gareth paused what he was doing and took a deep breath. Then, raking his hands through his hair, he turned round and gave her a sad look.

'I thought we had something special, Ellie; something that nobody else could ever touch. But seeing you and her acting like the best of friends just now, it made me feel like . . .' He tailed off and shook his head, as if he couldn't find the right words to describe it. 'Nothing.'

'I'm so sorry if I've hurt you,' Ellie apologized, going over to him and touching his arm. 'I know you're only trying to protect me, but you've nothing to fear from Holly, because we've been through too much for her to come between us. I *am* glad I spoke to her, though; I'm not denying that. But I'm not holding out any hope of seeing her again any time soon, because she'll be too busy helping my mother pack her stuff for the move.'

'Move?' Gareth repeated.

'Yeah, I was going to tell you.' Ellie sighed. 'Holly said Mum's going to live with them now. That's why she came round: to tell me before I heard about it from someone else. It seems Tony's bought my mum's house, and she's going to live with them in London.'

The anger fell from Gareth's face when he saw the bereft look on hers, and he said, 'I'm so sorry, sweetheart. You must be gutted, and there was me ranting on like some jealous prick.'

'It's okay,' Ellie said, resting her cheek against his chest when he put his arms around her. 'I've survived without her for this long while she's only a bus ride away, so a few more hundred miles won't make any difference.'

'I can't believe how strong you are,' Gareth said, stroking her hair. 'I'd be in bits, but you're taking it so well.'

'I've got no choice,' Ellie replied simply. 'There's nothing I can do about it.'

'Well, they might have deserted you, but I'm going nowhere,' said Gareth. 'Unless you want me to?' He drew his head back and gazed down at her. 'And after that little meltdown, I wouldn't blame you.'

Smiling, because that 'little meltdown' as he'd called it had been nothing compared to the enormous ones she'd regularly suffered from Matt, Ellie shook her head.

'No, of course I don't. And, while we're in here, I was actually thinking . . . maybe it's time we put the spare quilt back in the cupboard.'

'What do you mean?' He frowned.

'You know what I mean.' Ellie gave him a shy smile. 'And, seeing as you're going to be sleeping in here from now on, you might as well put your stuff back in the drawer.'

'Are you serious?' Gareth asked. Laughing delightedly when she nodded, he scooped her up off her feet and rained kisses on her neck. 'Oh, God, you don't know how happy you've made me; how long I've been waiting for you to commit to me.'

'I just thought it was time we moved on to the next level,' Ellie said, laughing herself now, because his happiness was contagious. 'It was talking to Holly that did it. She looked at me like I was an idiot when I told her you were in love with me, and I thought, you know what . . . screw you; and screw anyone else who's got anything to say about it. I'm happy for the first time in ages, and that's because of you, so why shouldn't we make a proper go of it?'

'Hallelujah! She finally gets it,' Gareth chuckled, putting her down. 'I've been trying to tell you that for ages.'

'I know, and I'm sorry for dragging my heels,' Ellie said, straightening her skirt when he let go of her. 'But I needed to be sure that it was right.'

'And do you think it is?'

'Yeah.' She nodded. 'I think I do.'

'Don't say that yet,' Gareth grinned. 'Save it for when your divorce comes through.'

'Is that a proposal?' Ellie laughed.

'What do *you* think?' he asked, dropping down onto one knee and reaching for her hand. 'So, what's your answer, Eleanor Louise Fisher? Will you marry me, or what?'

Ellie's joy of moments earlier fizzled out. They'd only just decided to make a go of it, and he was already talking about getting married. But even if she was ready for that, surely he knew that it would take at least two years for her to get divorced. And that was only if the police managed to find Matt between now and then – *and* he agreed to it.

'Let's see how it goes,' she said carefully, praying that he wouldn't take it the wrong way. 'I'm happy as we are, for now – aren't you?'

'Yeah, course.' He grinned and stood up. 'But now we know it's *going* to happen, we're doing it properly. And that means getting rid of these.' He grabbed her hand and started pulling at her wedding and engagement rings.

A wave of sadness mixed with panic washed over Ellie at the thought of taking them off. They were the physical representation of the vows she had made on her wedding day, and they symbolized the hopes and dreams she and Matt had shared for the future. That all lay in tatters now, and it couldn't be repaired, so she knew she would have to let go of these last threads that bound her to Matt at some point. But it felt like a bereavement, nevertheless, and she wasn't sure she was ready yet.

Pausing when he saw tears in her eyes, Gareth frowned.

'What's wrong? You do want to be with me, don't you?'

'Yeah, of course. It's just . . .'

'What?' he demanded. 'You either do or you don't, so which is it? 'Cos I'm telling you now, there's no way I'm sleeping in this bed if *his* ghost is lying between us.'

Ellie swallowed deeply. Then, nodding, she slid the rings off and laid them on the dressing table.

'You're right; I need to let go of them. But that doesn't mean you have to go out and buy me a new one, because we need to be careful with money, and we can do without that kind of expense. Are we agreed?'

'Ah, now that might be a problem,' Gareth said, smiling sheepishly as he unzipped the pocket at the front of rucksack and reached inside. 'I've been waiting for ages to give you this, but I had to be sure you were ready, because it's really special.' He pulled out a shabby little box and flipped the lid open. 'It was my nan's, and I've been saving it for the right one. So, would you do me the honour . . . ?'

'It's lovely,' Ellie said, gazing at the ring with its cluster of tiny, dull diamonds. 'But don't you think we should wait?'

'Why?' Gareth asked. 'We're engaged, so what's to wait for?'

'It doesn't seem right, so soon after taking the others off,' Ellie said.

'Oh, not this again,' he groaned. 'First it was too soon for me to sleep in here because of *him*, and now it's too soon to replace his shitty rings with mine. I wish you'd make up your mind.'

'I have,' Ellie insisted. 'But . . . well how do you think it's going to look to everyone else? You already said DI Collins was giving us funny looks that day, and he's not the only one who'll think I'm moving on too fast. My mum won't like it, for starters.'

'She's pissing off to London, so she won't even know about it,' Gareth reminded her sharply. 'As for Collins, I don't give a shit what *that* tosser thinks. And you shouldn't, either. Not if you love me.'

'Okay, fine, I'll wear it, if it means that much to you,' Ellie relented, holding out her hand.

'You could try looking more excited about it,' Gareth sniped. 'Anyone would think you'd didn't want to be with me.'

Irritated because he was acting like Matt again, Ellie said, 'I've said I'll wear it, isn't that good enough for you?' Then, sighing when he looked hurt, she said, 'I'm sorry, I didn't mean it like that. Of course I want to wear it, so will you please put it on my finger?'

'Only if you're sure? I don't want you to think I'm forcing you.'

Ellie wasn't sure at all, and she dreaded to think what her mother would say when she found out about this, because she already thought that Ellie had cheated on Matt with Gareth, and that was what had caused him to flip out and kill Billy. If she got wind of this, it would confirm her suspicions, and she would never forgive Ellie. Her neighbours were bound to think the same; as would the police. But, more importantly, so would Matt – and God only knew what that would do to him in his current frame of mind. He hadn't taken his medication when he left, and the police would have been alerted if he'd turned up anywhere trying to get a new prescription, so he had to be in a seriously unbalanced state right now.

But Gareth wouldn't understand that *that* was why she was reluctant to wear his ring; he'd assume that she was trying to delay things because she still had feelings for Matt. So, because she didn't want to risk losing him – *and* because there was no real danger of anybody seeing the ring on her finger since she wouldn't be going out until Matt had been caught – she held out her hand again.

'I'm sure.'

Happy again, Gareth pulled the ring out of the box and slid it onto her finger. It was a tight fit, and he had to force it over her knuckle, but he managed it eventually.

'Right, we need a picture,' he said, pulling his phone out of his pocket. 'Stand there under the light . . .' He manoeuvred her into position. 'Then hold your hand up so I can see the ring properly. And smile, 'cos I want our grandkids to see how happy we were when I show them this picture.'

A little taken aback by that, because it hadn't even occurred to her that Gareth might want children, Ellie did as she'd been told and fixed a smile onto her lips as he took the photograph. Her finger was starting to throb from the force he'd used to get it on, but she supposed it would fit better when she'd lost some more weight – which, if it carried on dropping off her at the rate that it had been doing since the start of this nightmare, shouldn't take too long at all.

25

'See how happy she looks?'

Gareth held out his phone to show off the picture he'd taken of Ellie.

'She was so ecstatic when I proposed, she burst into tears. How sweet is that, eh? And, do you know why? Because she knows she's with the right man at last. All that pain you put her through, with your miserable, selfish, soul-sucking moods – that's all gone now, and she's happier than she's ever been. And that's down to *me*, because I'm more of a man than you'll ever be. And that's not just me saying that, by the way; they're the words *she* said when she chucked your worthless rings in the bin.'

The tears in Matt's eyes didn't dilute the pain and rage behind them as he thrashed against the cords that were tightly binding his wrists to his ankles.

'*I'm gonna kill you, you fucking bastard!*' he roared, but the words stuck to the glue of the gaffer tape covering his mouth, so nothing but muffled noises came out.

'Yeah, I know, mate; I reckon she's better off with me, an' all. And so does she, since I convinced her that you stabbed me and killed her stepdad,' Gareth grinned, rolling Matt onto his side and shoving one end of a straw through the tiny hole he'd pierced in the gaffer tape. 'The sex is already amazing,' he went on as he stuck the other end into a carton of juice, 'so think how good it's going to be when we're married. That thing she does when she squeezes her thighs together just as you're about to come . . . Man, that's good. Remember that, do you? Yeah, course you do. It's way too fuckin' hot to forget. In fact, it's giving me a hard-on thinking about it, so hurry up and finish your drink so I can go home and give her one.'

Matt's shoulders convulsed and the tears streamed down his cheeks and gathered in a pool at the edge of the tape. Choking on the juice he hadn't been able to resist sucking up through the straw, he cried, 'Why are you doing this?'

'What's that?' Gareth cocked his head to one side. 'You're very happy for us? Wow, mate, thanks! That's really generous of you, under the circumstances.'

Removing the carton when Matt thrashed his head, Gareth laid it to one side, and said, 'See, now, if you'd done the decent thing in the first place and set her free to be with the real love of her life, you and me could probably have been buddies. But you were never going to let that happen, were you? You took one look at me and wrote me off, like I'm some piece of shit you'd walked in and wanted rid of. That hurt, that did; got me right here.'

He thumped his chest with his fist.

'I'm a decent bloke, but I've had that kind of shit from people all my life, and I'm not having it any more. And, don't worry, you're not the only one who's gonna regret treating me like that. I've got a list, and the rest will soon be getting what's coming to them – just you wait and see. That's if you're still here, by then, of course. I mean, it's fun punishing you like this, but who knows how long it'll be before I get tired of you?'

When Matt squeezed his tearful eyes shut, Gareth stood up and brushed the dirt off his jeans.

'Right, best get home before my fiancée starts missing me. See you tomorrow – if I can be bothered.'

Laughing nastily, he pushed the carton of juice over with his foot, then blew out the candle and made his way up the stairs, leaving Matt howling in agony as he struggled to break free of the bonds.

PART TWO

26

Gareth dipped down in front of the dressing-table mirror and straightened his tie before turning to Ellie.

'How do I look?'

'Nice,' she said, smiling to disguise how uncomfortable she felt, seeing him in Matt's jacket. He'd found it in the wardrobe, and had decided to wear it for the interview he was going for that morning. His shoulders were broader than Matt's, so it was tight at the seams, but he thought it looked great. And Ellie couldn't deny that he *did* look smart, even with the faded patches on the shoulders. But she couldn't help but wonder if he'd be so keen if he knew it was the jacket from the suit Matt had worn on their wedding day.

'I'll be home as soon as I'm finished,' Gareth said, kissing her on the forehead before walking out into the hall. 'But ring me if anything happens, and I'll come straight back.'

Already on edge at the thought of being alone in the flat, Ellie nodded. Two days after Gareth had proposed, Matt had sent another message telling her that she was fooling herself if she thought he was going to let her live to wear another man's ring. She had no idea how he'd found out about it, but the vile language he'd used to describe the ways in which he intended to punish both her and Gareth before killing them had chilled her to the bone. Even in his lowest, most rage-filled moments, she had never heard Matt talk like that, and it had unnerved her so much that she'd taken to carrying a knife around the flat, in case he was hiding somewhere and jumped out on her.

'Are you sure you're okay with me going?' Gareth asked, gazing down at her as the fears flashed through her eyes. 'I can ring them and cancel the interview if you want me to stay?'

Ellie would have liked nothing better, but she didn't want him to think she was a pathetic little woman who needed protecting, so she shook her head.

'No, they're expecting you, and it'll look bad if you pull out at the last minute.'

'Are you sure?' Gareth asked again. 'I don't mind, honestly. I probably won't even get it anyway.'

'I'll be fine,' she insisted. 'And, you never know, this could be the one, so go and knock 'em dead.'

'Will do.' He grinned, leaning down to kiss her on the lips. 'Okay, I'll be back before you know it. Don't be answering the door while I'm out.'

'I won't,' she promised, forcing a smile.

The smile dropped as soon as he'd gone, and she deadlocked the front door before going into the living room. Too scared to even go out on the balcony, she opened the window

and sat down on one of the dining chairs before lighting a cigarette. Gareth emerged from the main door a minute later, and
she was struck by how much he reminded her of Matt as he
strolled down the path in that jacket. And what must Matt be
thinking if he could also see him? Judging by the tone of his
latest message, he'd be raging that the man had not only taken
his wife, but was also now wearing his clothes.

Finished with the cigarette, she was stubbing the butt out in
the ashtray when the intercom buzzed, and she eased the net
curtain aside. Surprised to see Holly standing down below,
because she hadn't expected her to honour her promise to call
round again before she returned to London, Ellie bit her lip.
Gareth had only been gone a few minutes. What if he'd seen
Holly coming and had hidden somewhere to see if Ellie
answered the door after promising that she wouldn't?

Unwilling to risk upsetting him, because he'd been happy for
the past few days and things had been good between them,
Ellie decided to ignore the door. She would ring Holly later,
when she was sure they were on their way to London and there
was no danger of her turning back.

It was too late. At the exact moment Ellie was about to drop
the net curtain, Holly looked directly up at her and waved.

Annoyed with herself for taking so long to make a decision,
Ellie went out into the hall and pressed the door-release,
already mentally rehearsing the excuses she would make to
Gareth if he had been watching and came back.

At the thought of Gareth, she remembered that she was

wearing his ring, and rushed into the kitchen to grease it off her finger before Holly spotted it and started asking questions. She would have to tell people about the engagement eventually, but not yet. She wasn't ready.

Holly looked as chic as ever when she reached the flat a couple of minutes later, and she left a trail of expensive perfume in her wake when she strolled into the living room after giving Ellie an air-kiss.

'Guess who's got to stay in the shit-pit for another week?' she said, flopping down on the sofa after placing her handbag on the coffee table.

'Oh?' Ellie frowned, picking the bag up and placing it on the floor. 'How come? I thought you were supposed to be leaving today.'

'We were, but then Mum decided she couldn't leave without saying goodbye to Whatserface next door; and *she's* on holiday till next week. I tried telling Mum it's only a two-hour train ride so she can come and see her another time, but she won't budge – stubborn auld bitch.'

'You and Tony can still go, though, can't you?' Ellie asked, praying that she would say yes, because that would give Ellie the opportunity to pay their mum a visit while she was on her own and try to sort things out with her.

'Tony's flying to Dubai in the morning to do a business deal that'll make him an absolute fortune, so he's got to go,' Holly said boastfully. 'But he wants me to stay, so Mum can keep an eye on me.'

'Why?' Ellie frowned. 'Doesn't he trust you?'

'Course he does, silly.' Holly grinned. 'We've been getting on great. So well, in fact . . .' she added coyly, 'we've decided to have a baby. In six and a half months, to be exact.'

'What?' Ellie's eyebrows shot up. 'You're pregnant?'

'Well, I didn't get this fat from overeating,' Holly chuckled, stroking her ironing-board-flat stomach.

Wondering how their mother had taken the news that Holly and Tony were going to have a baby out of wedlock, because she'd always threatened to disown her girls if they ever shamed her by having a bastard child like Vicky Slut Jones from down the road, Ellie was about to ask when the intercom buzzed again.

'What's up?' Holly asked when Ellie almost jumped out of her skin. 'Are you expecting someone you don't want to see? You haven't got the bailiffs after you, have you?'

'No, I haven't,' Ellie muttered, rushing over to the window. 'I'm scared it might be Matt.'

'I thought he'd disappeared off the face of the earth?'

'So did I, but he sent me another message the other day.'

'You're kidding? Saying what?'

'The usual . . . how much he hates me, and how he's going to kill me and Gareth to punish us for getting engaged. And—'

'Excuse me?' Holly cut her off. 'Did you say you're *engaged*?'

Cursing herself for letting it slip, Ellie mumbled, 'Er, yeah. It happened after you left last time you were here. I was going to tell you.'

Not even trying to disguise her shock – or was it disbelief? Ellie couldn't quite decide – Holly said, 'So let me get this straight . . . *he* proposed to *you*?'

'Well, I certainly didn't propose to him, if that's what you're implying,' Ellie replied tersely. 'Now, shush, 'cos I need to see who's at the door.'

'And I need to see the ring,' Holly said, coming over and grabbing Ellie's left hand. Dropping it again in disgust when she got margarine on her finger, she wiped her hand on the curtain. 'So he hasn't got you one yet, why doesn't that surprise me? What's he doing? Waiting for you to buy your own?'

Ellie ignored her and peered down to the path below. Frowning when she saw DI Collins and a female police officer standing at the main door, she muttered, 'What does he want now? He was only here the other day.'

'They might have caught Matt,' said Holly, following when she went out into the hall. 'Wouldn't it be funny if he's been hiding in the block the whole time the police have been looking for him?'

'I wouldn't find that very funny,' Ellie said, shuddering at the thought of Matt being that close all along. It would certainly explain how he'd known that she went back to work that day, but it didn't explain how he'd known about her getting engaged to Gareth, considering she hadn't set foot out of the flat since putting the ring on.

Unless he'd had a spare key cut and had been letting himself in when she and Gareth were in bed.

Reminding herself that they always put the deadlock on before they went to bed, so Matt wouldn't be able to get in even if he did have a key, Ellie peered out through the spyhole until the detective and his colleague came around the corner.

'Have you found him?' Holly asked as soon as Ellie opened the door.

'Sorry?' Collins looked puzzled.

'Ignore her,' Ellie said, pushing Holly into the hall and giving her a warning look. 'Come in,' she said then, stepping aside to give them room to enter.

Seated on Matt's chair a few seconds later, Collins said, 'Sorry for calling round out of the blue like this. I hope it's not an inconvenient time?'

'No, it's okay,' said Ellie, wondering why he was apologizing when he didn't usually.

'So, has he been spotted?' Holly asked, sitting forward with her hands clasped between her knees. 'Has he attacked someone else?'

Irritated with her for behaving like an excited child, Ellie said, 'Why don't you stop interrupting and let him tell us why he's here?'

'I'd like you to take a look at something,' Collins said to Ellie when Holly rolled her eyes and sat back. 'Someone tried to sell a mobile phone to a local pawnbroker this morning, and he got suspicious that it might be stolen when the man couldn't produce ID or proof of purchase. There was an altercation, and the owner called us when the bloke did a runner.'

Ellie's heart leapt into her mouth. 'Wa-was it Matt?'

'The man had already left by the time we arrived, but the CCTV footage isn't very clear, but he was the right height and build, so I'm not ruling it out,' said Collins. 'Fortunately, the shopkeeper managed to hold onto the phone.'

He snapped his fingers at the female officer, who stepped forward and handed a clear plastic bag containing a mobile phone to him.

'Take a look, and let me know if you can recognize it,' he said, shifting his bulky frame forward to place the bag on the table.

Ellie peered at it for several moments and bit her lip. 'I'm not sure. Matt was always quite protective of his phone, so I didn't see it very often.'

'He was probably having an affair and didn't want you to see the sexts,' Holly sneered. Then, looking guilty when Ellie gave her a dirty look, as if to say, *Well, you'd know that better than most, wouldn't you?* she said, 'I just mean it's a pretty classic sign when someone starts hiding their phone from their partner.'

'If you could take another look, Mrs Fisher?' Collins said to Ellie. 'It'll save us a lot of time and money getting it checked over by forensics if it's not even the same model.'

'Maybe?' Ellie said. 'But Matt's had a black fold-over cover on it; and, like I already said, I didn't get to see it very often.'

'Can't you find out by checking his phone records?' Holly suggested. 'In fact, couldn't you have done that while he still had it? I thought you lot could track people down by tracing their phone signal?'

'I'm no expert,' Collins admitted, 'but I don't think it's that easy. And when someone's in the kind of mental state we're assuming Mr Fisher's in since he hasn't had access to the medication he needs, he's probably extremely paranoid and taking great care to cover his tracks.'

'So you're saying nutters are better at evading the police than sane people?'

'In a way, yes, because they don't do the expected, and that makes it harder for us to pre-empt their movements.'

'You're making it sound like you don't think you're going to catch him,' Ellie said.

'We *will*,' Collins replied, holding her gaze to reassure her that he meant it. 'Anyway, the phone . . .' He shoved the bag closer. 'Do you think there is a chance it might be his?'

'If it is, it'll have a little gouge on the side,' she said when a memory popped into her mind. 'He had a pretty bad episode a couple of years ago and convinced himself that the government had bugged his SIM card. He couldn't get it out, so he stuck a knife into the gap, but it slipped.'

'Freak,' Holly sneered. 'Why would anyone want to bug a boring bastard like him?'

'That's the way he thinks when he's in one of his moods,' Ellie said defensively. 'But I don't expect *you* to know that, because you only ever saw the best side of him when you were busy—'

'Don't start banging on about that again, 'cos I've already apologized,' Holly interrupted, flashing a hooded glance in Collins's direction. 'All I'm saying is, if you knew he was that bad you should have had him sectioned. At least then he'd have got the help he needed, and Billy might still be here.'

'I hope you're not blaming me for what he did to Billy?' Ellie said sharply. "Cos if you are, you can—'

'What's this?'

Jumping at the sound of Gareth's voice, Ellie snapped her head round and swallowed loudly when she saw him standing in the doorway.

'God, you scared the life out of me! I didn't hear you come in.'

'That's not very good, is it?' he said disapprovingly. 'If I can keep letting myself in without you hearing me, Matt could easily do the same.'

'I know, and I did put the dead-lock on when you went out,' Ellie replied guiltily. 'But I forgot to put it on again after Holly and DI Collins came round.'

'You came together?' Gareth raised an eyebrow at Collins. 'You must have important news if you thought Ellie would need her sister here when you told her? So is he dead, then?'

'You don't have to say it like that,' Ellie chided.

'Like what?' he asked, as if he could see nothing wrong with it. 'Like I'd be glad if he was? Sorry, but I *would*, 'cos until he is, or they catch him and chuck away the key, you're not safe.'

'We haven't found him,' Collins interjected. 'But I can assure you we won't stop looking until we do.'

'Well, I wish you'd hurry up,' Gareth said, perching on the arm of the sofa and putting his arm around Ellie's shoulders. 'My fiancée hasn't been able to go out in weeks because of him, and she hardly sleeps, because she's terrified he's going to kill us both.'

'*Fiancée*?' Collins switched his gaze to Ellie. 'When did this happen?'

Ellie looked down at her hands as a blush seared her cheeks, and mumbled, 'A few days ago.'

'I knew she was the one when I first laid eyes on her,' Gareth expanded. 'But she was still with Matt at the time, so I thought I'd have to be satisfied with being friends. Then Matt walked out on her and did what he did, and Ellie realized her marriage was over, so we decided to give it a go – didn't we, darling?'

'Mmmm,' Ellie murmured, acutely conscious of Holly pulling a scornful face to her right while Collins studiously maintained a neutral expression to her left.

'I gave her my grandmother's ring,' Gareth went on proudly. 'Show him, Ellie.'

'I, um, had to take it off 'cos it was getting tight,' she lied. 'I was going to put it on again later, when my finger's not quite as swollen.'

'Okay . . . we'd best be on our way,' Collins said before Gareth could respond. 'There is a mark on the phone, Ellie, so it looks like it could be his. I'll be in touch as soon as I have more news, but in the meantime, let me know immediately if you receive any more messages or calls from strange numbers, because there's every likelihood your husband will try to get his hands on another phone to replace this one.' He picked up the plastic bag as he spoke, and handed it to the policewoman.

'What's this?' Gareth asked, peering at the bag as if this was the first time he'd noticed it.

'Someone tried to sell it at a local pawnbroker's this morning, and he kicked off when the shopkeeper asked him for ID,' Ellie explained. 'DI Collins thinks it might be Matt's, so he brought it round to see if I could identify it.'

'Wait, you're saying Matt tried to sell his phone round here, but you lot still can't find him?' Gareth frowned.

'We're working on several lines of inquiry,' Collins said, rising stiffly to his feet. 'And we'll have more of an idea what's going on once forensics have checked the phone out.'

'Will you let me know?' Ellie asked, also getting up.

Collins assured her that he would. Then, nodding goodbye to Holly, he followed the female officer into the hall.

When Ellie returned after showing them out, she sighed when she saw the daggers flying between Gareth and Holly.

'I hope you two haven't been arguing again, because I'm under enough pressure right now without you two adding to it.'

Gareth stared at her for several seconds, as if he wanted to say something. But then he turned and walked into the bedroom, slamming the door behind him.

Holly looked at Ellie and raised an eyebrow. 'And you still reckon he's nothing like Matt? Open your eyes, Ells, he's *everything* like him. Worse, in fact, 'cos at least Matt was consistently moody, whereas he *pretends* he's easy-going – until he can't get his own way.'

'I think you'd better go,' Ellie said wearily.

'Why? Because I've hit a raw nerve and you can't face the truth?'

'No. Because I need you to respect my relationship, but you're clearly not willing to do that.'

'So you're putting him before your own family – exactly like you did with Matt?'

'*You* put Tony before me and Mum when you moved to London to be with him, so what makes you any different?'

'I moved to London *before* I met Tony, actually. But even if I had moved there to be with him, at least he's a decent man, not an argumentative, scrounging homewrecker.'

'Yeah, so decent he cheated on you with the wife he forgot to tell you about.'

'Well, at least he didn't seduce my own sister behind my back, which is way worse in my opinion,' Holly spat, jumping to her feet and snatching her handbag up off the floor. 'And now you've landed yourself another moody control freak. Well done, our kid; I'm sure you'll be very happy – *not!*'

'Gareth's not a control freak,' Ellie argued. 'He might be a bit over-protective, but that's only because he's worried about Matt getting to me.'

'You keep telling yourself that it if makes you feel better,' said Holly. 'But I'm telling you now, there's something not right about him. So don't say I didn't warn you when he shows his true colours. And he *will*, I guarantee it.'

'Not this again,' Ellie groaned. 'I know it must be killing you that he chose me after rejecting you, but it's time you got over it.'

'Oh God, you actually believe that, don't you?' Holly spluttered. 'He didn't reject me, you silly cow; I slept with him – *twice*. And both times it was shit,' she added nastily.

'Strange how you've suddenly remembered that, when you reckoned you couldn't remember a thing because you were so pissed that night,' sniped Ellie.

'Bring him out here if you don't believe me,' Holly challenged, putting her hands on her hips to show Ellie that she wasn't messing around. 'If you know him half as well as you think you do, you'll be able to tell if he's lying when I confront him about it, won't you?'

Ellie breathed in deeply when she remembered Gareth's ex warning her to get him out of her life if she noticed any sign of him changing toward her. She recalled thinking at the time that Lynn had sounded and looked sincere – exactly as Holly looked and sounded now. So could it be possible that they were both right and she was wrong?

Holly's phone suddenly beeped, and she tutted when she pulled it out of her bag and read the message on the screen.

'Tony's downstairs, so I've got to go,' she said. Then, sighing, she gave Ellie a regretful look. 'Come on, Ells; I don't want to leave it like this. You're my sister, and I honestly don't mean to upset you; it just pisses me off when I see you falling over yourself to make excuses for *him* like you always did for Matt. I know you don't want to believe it, but I'm telling the truth about sleeping with him. I'm not apologizing for that, because you weren't with him when it happened, but please don't mention it to Tony, 'cos I haven't told him about it, and I don't want him to find out. I honestly do love him, and I can't bear the thought of losing him now we've got the baby to think about.'

Ellie had forgotten about that, and it changed the answer she was about to give. She'd once read that babies, even when still in the womb, were affected by their mother's emotions, and she didn't want to be responsible for traumatizing her niece or nephew by breaking Holly's heart.

'I won't tell him,' she promised. 'But you need to stop slagging Gareth off, because he's been good to me.'

Holly's expression told Ellie that it would be a struggle, but she quickly changed it into a mischievous grin and, lifting her hand, stuck her little finger out.

Smiling when she remembered how they had made pinky promises as children, Ellie hooked her own finger around Holly's, and they chanted, 'I won't tell if you don't tell,' before giggling and giving each other a hug.

'Love you, Sis,' Holly said.

'Love you, too,' said Ellie.

As soon as she had shown Holly out, Gareth appeared in the

bedroom doorway, and Ellie felt a ripple of apprehension in her stomach when she saw the sneer on his face.

'*Love you, Sis,*' he mimicked nastily. '*Love you, too, kissy kissy . . .*'

Aware that he must have been eavesdropping to have heard that, Ellie said, 'She's my sister.'

'So you keep reminding me,' he drawled. 'And here we are again . . . me trying to protect you; you siding with the enemy against me.'

'Matt's the enemy, not Holly,' Ellie reminded him. 'And I've just asked her to stop talking about you like this, so now I'm telling you the same thing.'

'Oh, so you *asked* her, but you're *telling* me?' He narrowed his eyes.

'I didn't mean it like that, so don't make a big thing of it,' Ellie replied coolly, determined not to let him turn this on her as he'd done the last time they had argued about Holly. 'I've not long got away from a man who made me believe that everything was my fault, and I won't let you start doing the same, so—'

Gareth lunged at her before she could go on, and seized her by the arms.

'Don't you *dare* compare me to that waste of fucking space!'

Crying out in pain and fear, Ellie struggled to free herself, but he held on tight.

'I've done everything for you,' he went on angrily through bared teeth, 'and I've asked for nothing in return, 'cos being with you was reward enough. But I'm starting to see that you don't really care about me at all. *Do you?*'

Terrified, because she'd never seen him as angry as this before, Ellie forced herself to meet his angry gaze with a steady one of her own.

'Let go of me right now, Gareth. You're hurting me, and I've done absolutely nothing wrong. And if you don't like being compared to Matt, you'd better stop acting like him, because this is what I'd expect of *him*, not *you*.'

Her words had the desired effect, and Gareth immediately released her.

'I'm sorry,' he said, raking his hands through his hair. 'I don't know where that came from, I honestly don't. It just feels like everyone's against me.'

'Nobody's against you,' Ellie lied, rubbing her arms. 'DI Collins is only doing his job, and Holly's worried about me because of what's going on, that's all.'

'It's not just that,' Gareth argued. 'She hates me, and he looks at me like I'm scum.'

In no mood to reassure him, because she was still angry with him for putting his hands on her, Ellie said, 'Maybe if you tried being more civil to Holly, she'd be nicer to you. As for Collins, I told you people would think we were moving too fast, so he probably thinks *I'm* scum, as well. But you've told him now, so there's no point worrying about it.'

'It's no one else's business what we choose to do,' Gareth

said sulkily. 'But you could have backed me up, instead of making it look like it was all my idea.'

Tired of being forced to justify herself, Ellie said, 'I didn't make it look like anything, and I'm not doing this any more, 'cos I had nine years of it with Matt. You can think what you like, but you're wrong about me siding with Holly against you, because I've taken your word over hers about the two of you sleeping together. Same as I took your word over Lynn's when she said—'

She abruptly stopped speaking when she realized what she'd said, but it was too late.

'What did you say?' Gareth demanded, staring at her. 'Have you spoken to Lynn?'

'No, of course not,' she lied, desperately back-tracking. 'I was talking about what you told me about her.'

'But I didn't tell you anything she'd *said*,' Gareth replied suspiciously. 'I only told you what she'd done.'

'Yes, and I took your word for it,' said Ellie. 'That's all I meant.'

'I don't believe you,' Gareth said quietly. 'I know you, and I can tell when you're lying.'

Ellie sighed. Then, flapping her hands, she said, 'Okay, fine, so maybe I did speak to her. But it didn't change anything between you and me, so I don't know why you're angry about it. And I didn't go looking for her,' she added, in case he thought she had. 'She went past on a bus when I was walking to the cafe on the day I went back to work, and she recognized me and got off to talk to me.'

Gareth's breathing had become increasingly ragged as he listened to her account, and Ellie took a step away when she noticed that his hands were clenched into fists.

'I know you're angry, but you've honestly got no reason to be, because I didn't believe a word she said – and I told her that. If I had, don't you think I would have confronted you about it when I got home?'

'The fact that you didn't tell me *anything* is what's bothering me,' Gareth replied tersely. 'Don't you think I've got the right to know if my psycho ex is spreading malicious lies about me?'

'I hardly even listened to her,' Ellie assured him. 'And the reason I didn't tell you about it is because I *forgot*. It was the day Matt threatened to petrol bomb the office block, so I had more important things to think about than anything your ex had said. Anyway, I knew she was only saying it out of jealousy, because she thought she could make me doubt you. But it didn't work – and *that's* what you should be taking from this.'

'I don't know what to take from it,' Gareth said flatly. 'I thought I could trust you, but you're the same as all the other dirty liars I've had in my life, and I'm not sure I want to be with you any more.'

Ellie sighed when he snatched his jacket off the hook, but she didn't try to stop him when he yanked the door open and walked out. Instead, she went back into the living room.

Sliding a cigarette out of her pack, she sat by the window

and lit up. Gareth emerged onto the path a short time later, and she watched as he marched down the path in the direction of the canal. She'd told him that she had taken his word over Holly's about the two of them sleeping together, but it wasn't true. Just as Gareth had said that he could tell when *she* was lying, *she* could tell when her sister was, and she honestly didn't think Holly had been.

As she struggled to put her jumbled thoughts into order, Ellie sucked the cigarette down to its stub and immediately lit another. Gareth claimed that his grandmother had instilled a deep respect for women in him, so when Lynn had told Ellie that he had terrorized her for a year, Ellie had dismissed it out of hand, because it hadn't sounded anything like the Gareth she knew. But after his latest outburst, she wasn't so sure. She had been genuinely scared, and it made her wonder if she knew him as well as she'd thought she did. He could be lovely when it was only the two of them here, but as soon as anyone else came into the picture, he changed. So was the nice side the act and the nasty side the real him? She honestly didn't know any more.

27

Gareth didn't come home until three in the morning, by which time Ellie was fast asleep on the sofa. She woke with a start when she felt her hair being stroked, and inhaled sharply when she saw him squatting beside her in the dark with a smile on his lips.

'You scared me,' she croaked.

'You've nothing to be scared of with me,' he crooned, stroking her cheek now as he gazed into her eyes. 'You know I'd never hurt you, and I'm sorry for what happened earlier. I've never behaved like this with any other woman, but I thought it over while I was out and I think it's because I'm in love for the first time in my life. I've thought I was before, but it wasn't real, I know that now. And I know you feel the same, because there's no way you could have loved Matt as much as you love me.'

Ellie sensed that it was a question rather than a statement, but she couldn't tell him what he obviously wanted to hear, because the truth was, she had loved Matt deeply.

'I think we need to talk,' she said, pushing herself up onto her elbows.

'No, we don't,' Gareth said, resting his arms on her knees when she swung her legs down.

'*Yes*, we *do*,' she insisted, beginning to feel claustrophobic. 'This is moving way too fast, and I think we both need some space to think about what we really want.'

'No . . .' He shook his head. 'We're meant for each other; my nan told me.'

'Your nan's dead,' Ellie reminded him sharply. Instantly regretting it when she saw pain in his eyes, she said, 'I'm sorry, I shouldn't have said that.'

'No, you shouldn't,' he agreed. 'Because she isn't dead. Not to me . . . not in here.' He slammed his fist into his chest. 'In here she lives *forever*.'

'I know, and that's how it *should* be,' Ellie said carefully, trying to bring him back down before his anger escalated again. 'A lot's happened today, and we've both said things we don't mean, so why don't we get some sleep and talk properly in the morning when we're both rested?'

Gareth peered at her and pursed his lips. 'Okay, I can see you're tired, so I'll let you get some sleep.'

'And you'll get some yourself?' Ellie asked, afraid that he might work himself up again if he stayed up and brooded about the argument.

'In bed?' Gareth asked.

Ellie had been about to ask if he'd mind sleeping on the sofa but, scared that he wouldn't take it well, she decided that it would be wiser to let him sleep in her bed tonight, and then tell him that she had changed her mind about being in a relationship with him in the morning.

'Okay, if that's what you want,' she said, forcing a little smile as she added, 'but I really am tired, so I don't want to have sex.'

'Make love,' Gareth corrected her.

'That's what I meant.' She maintained the smile with difficulty and reached out to switch the lamp on. 'I'm going to make myself a drinking chocolate to help me drop off. Do you want one?'

'I'll do it,' he offered, standing up.

Frowning when she noticed blood on the sleeve of his jacket, Ellie said, 'Have you hurt yourself?'

Gareth shook his head and shrugged the jacket off.

'Don't worry, it's not mine,' he said as he carried it into the kitchen and ran water into the sink to wash the blood off. 'I saw a gang of lads laying into a drunk bloke in the park when I was on my way home, so I chased them off and called a taxi to take him to hospital. The blood's his.'

'That's awful,' Ellie said from the doorway. 'Is he going to be all right?'

'Yeah, I think so,' said Gareth. 'Now go and get into bed. I'll make you that drink as soon as I've done this.'

Ellie was too tired to argue, so she changed into her pyjamas and climbed into bed. Joined by Gareth a few minutes later, she sipped the sweet hot chocolate he'd made and felt herself gradually begin to relax. By the time she'd finished the drink, her eyes were so heavy she could barely keep them open.

When he noticed, Gareth took the cup out of her hand and placed it on the bedside table and then gently pulled her into his arms.

'This is all I've ever wanted,' he crooned as he listened to her breathing becoming heavier. 'And I'm all *you'll* ever need,' he added quietly. 'So I'm never going to let anyone come between us again. And that's a promise.'

28

After her fall-out and subsequent make-up with Ellie, Holly hadn't been able to stop thinking about her. She had given Tony an edited version of the argument, omitting the part about her telling Ellie she had slept with Gareth. Tony didn't know about that, and she had no intention of ever telling him, because he was a bit of a traditionalist in that sense, and it was one thing for him to sleep with his ex-wife behind *her* back, but quite another for *her* to have cheated on *him*.

If any other boy had dared to pull a stunt like that, she'd have gone straight out and screwed somebody else to spite them – and then gone home and told them all about it in minute detail. But something had shifted inside her when she'd found out that she was pregnant, and she'd realized that she genuinely did love Tony and didn't want to risk losing him over a no-mark like Gareth.

She'd also realized that she loved her sister, and wished she could make up for some of the horrible things she'd done to her over the years. She'd lied when she had said that Matt had pursued her, because it had been the other way round. But that was the way she had operated back then: if she wanted something, she wouldn't stop until she got it. Matt hadn't put up too much of a struggle, but it hadn't been Holly who'd finished it, as she'd told Ellie, it had been him, because he'd decided that Ellie was the one he wanted, after all. Holly had hated him for that, and she had resented Ellie for years afterwards.

Her infatuation with Matt had abruptly ended after the accident, because the idea of having a cripple who couldn't even wipe his own arse hanging round her neck like a lead weight had repulsed her. Being the selfless little carer was Ellie's forte, not Holly's, so Holly had happily left her to it.

In the years between then and meeting Tony, Holly had lost count of how many lads she'd slept with, but Tony was the first one she'd stayed with for longer than a month. Him having his own place in London had certainly been a factor in that decision, but mainly it was the money she'd been attracted to. Now, it was so much more than that. She loved him, and she couldn't wait until his divorce came through and she was able to marry him. And when that day came, she wanted her sister to be standing by her side.

And that was why, as soon as Tony had left for his trip to Dubai, she embarked on a mission to persuade her stubborn mother to stop blaming Ellie for what Matt had done and allow her back into the family. And now, finally, two exhausting days later, her mum had agreed to let Ellie come round to talk things over.

Determined to strike while the iron was hot, Holly rang Ellie's phone, but it rang several times and then went to voicemail. Assuming that Ellie must be in another room and hadn't heard it, she waited a couple of minutes and then tried again. And then again. Giving up after the third time, she rang for a taxi and set off to tell Ellie in person.

Gareth had just finished breakfast and was washing his bowl when the intercom buzzed. Ignoring it, he dried his hands and switched the kettle on before taking a cup and a small plastic bag containing tablets out of the cupboard. Crushing two of the pills with the back of the spoon, he scooped the powder into the cup before adding three heaped spoonsful of drinking chocolate. After mixing the powders into a paste with cold milk, he switched the almost-boiled kettle off and filled the cup.

'Ellie . . . ?' he said softly, tiptoeing into the bedroom with the cup in his hand. 'Are you awake?'

'Ummana . . .' she croaked, struggling to open her eyes. 'Whazzadaamon?'

'Oh, you poor thing, you're still not well, are you?' he crooned, placing the cup on the bedside table before sitting on the mattress and slipping his arm beneath her to raise her up. 'Come on, let's get some of this into you so you can get a lovely sleep while I nip out.'

Ellie spluttered when he put the cup to her lips.

'Careful,' he chided. 'We don't want to waste this lovely

chocolate, do we? I made it specially, 'cos I know it's your favourite.'

'Srrr,' Ellie murmured.

'Good girl,' Gareth said when she took a little sip. 'I'm the only one who really loves you, you know that, don't you? Matt just used you, and your family have treated you like dirt. That's why I'm keeping you safe in here, so they can't get to you and poison your mind against me. That's what they were trying to do, and it was starting to work, wasn't it? But, don't worry, I won't hold it against you. You're weak, but I'm strong, so we'll get through this.'

Ellie muttered something unintelligible in reply, and Gareth poured a little more liquid between her lips. When it dribbled straight out and streamed down her chin, he set the cup down on the table and picked up her limp hand to check her pulse. Satisfied, when he felt the slow beat, that she was out of it, he eased himself up off the bed and covered her with the quilt, before leaning down and kissing her softly on her open lips.

'Won't be long, sweetheart; just need to take care of some business,' he said, opening the drawer of her bedside table and reaching to the back for the engagement and wedding rings he knew she'd stashed there.

Holly had intended to pick Ellie up and take her to their mum's, so she'd asked the taxi driver to wait in the car park. Returning to the car after buzzing Ellie's flat and getting no answer, she was about to climb in when she spotted Gareth coming out of the flats. She waved and called his name, but he carried on walking as if he hadn't heard her. Aware that Ellie wouldn't have gone out without him while Matt was still on the prowl, she wondered if her sister was at home, after all. If Ellie and Gareth were as loved up as Ellie reckoned they were, they could have been having sex when she'd buzzed the intercom, in which case they wouldn't have heard, or had chosen to ignore the door – just as she and Tony had done on numerous occasions.

Asking the taxi driver to give her another five minutes, Holly made her way over to the block to try the buzzer again. As luck would have it, somebody was coming out as she got to the door, so she was able to go straight in.

When she reached the flat, she knocked, and then waited a few seconds before calling through the letterbox: 'Ells, it's me. Are you up yet?'

Silence came back to her, and she frowned, wondering if Ellie was ignoring her. She wouldn't have thought so, considering they had made friends the last time she was here; but who knew what that twisted little freak, Gareth, might have said to change her sister's mind since then?

Well, fuck him, she thought, yanking her phone out of her bag. *Ellie's my sister, and I'm not letting that little weasel come between us.*

She called Ellie's phone and immediately heard it ringing inside the flat. Irritated when Ellie didn't answer it, she waited until it went to answerphone.

'I know you know I'm at the door,' she said tartly after the beep, 'and I'm not impressed, because I thought we'd got past all that shit. But clearly not, eh? Well, just so you know, I only came to te—'

'I thought that was you I saw sneaking in here,' Gareth said quietly into her ear. 'No mistaking that brassy hair and those whore shoes, is there?'

'Jeezus!' Holly squawked, almost jumping out of her skin, because she hadn't heard him come up behind her. 'What do you think you're doing sneaking up on me like that, you idiot? I nearly had a heart attack.'

'Only nearly?' He smirked. 'That's a shame.'

'You're such a dickhead,' she hissed, wondering what she had ever seen in him, because his nasty personality made his handsome face ugly. 'I can't wait till Ellie sees through you and kicks you into the gutter where you belong. Where is she, anyway? And don't bother telling me she's out, 'cos I could hear her phone ringing in there, and she'd never go out without it.'

'Maybe she's ignoring it because she doesn't want to talk to you?' Gareth sneered. 'Can't say I'd blame her. I mean, who'd want to admit they were related to a tramp like you?'

'You're lying,' Holly said. 'We left things on a good note last time I was here, and she'd tell me to my face if she'd fallen out with me again.'

Casting a wary glance along the corridor when he saw a male neighbour come out of his flat and look in their direction, Gareth lowered his voice.

'Look, she's ill, if you must know; and she was fast asleep when I left, so that's why she didn't answer your call. Now if you're done playing detectives, I'll walk you downstairs.'

'What do you mean, she's ill?' Holly frowned, staying put when he gestured for her to start walking. 'She was absolutely fine last time I saw her. How could she have got ill between then and now? What's wrong with her?'

'I don't know, I'm not a doctor,' Gareth replied irritably. 'She felt sick after you left and decided to have an early night, but she was worse the next morning, so I've been looking after her.'

'I want to see her.'

'You can't. Like I said, she was asleep when I left, and I don't want you to disturb her.'

'She's my sister, and I need to make sure she's okay,' Holly persisted. 'If she's as ill as you say, she needs someone with her; and you're on your way out, so I'll look after her till you get home.'

'I'm only going to the pharmacy to see if they can recommend anything,' said Gareth. 'And I won't be more than a couple of minutes, so there's no need for you to stay.'

Determined not to let him fob her off, Holly said, '*I'll* decide what she needs when I see her. And I'm not leaving till I do, so you might as well quit stalling and let me in. Unless you want me to start making a scene?'

Gareth's cheek muscles twitched, and Holly physically felt his animosity when he glared at her. But just as she thought he was about to tell her to sling her hook, he said, 'Right, fine, you can see her. But don't you dare disturb her, because it took her ages to get to sleep, and she needs as much rest as she can get.'

Following him into the hallway when he unlocked the door, Holly squinted to see in the darkness of the bedroom when he pushed that door open. As her eyes began to adjust, she frowned when she saw Ellie lying as still as a rock in the bed.

'I told you not to disturb her,' Gareth hissed, using his arm to block her path when she made to enter the room. 'You wanted to see her, and you have, so now you can go.'

'I'm going nowhere till I know what's wrong with her,' Holly argued. 'She's my sister, and you've got no right to stop me.'

'You're really pushing it now,' Gareth snarled, looming over her.

'Don't you dare try to bully me,' Holly replied tartly, injecting strength into her voice to disguise the fear she was suddenly feeling. 'I don't know why you're trying to keep me away from her, but I'm not having it. If she's that ill, she needs to be seen by a doctor, and if you won't call them, I will.'

Still glaring down at her, Gareth held his stance for several seconds. Then, stepping aside, he said, 'You've got two minutes, after that I want you out of here. I'll call the doctor when you've gone.'

'Thank you,' Holly muttered grudgingly.

'Don't wake her,' Gareth warned, rushing to the bed ahead of her and planting himself by Ellie's side – as if to stand guard, Holly thought.

Ellie's breathing was shallow, and her forehead was clammy

when Holly gently laid her hand on it; but she wasn't burning up as Holly had feared she might be.

'What are her symptoms?' she whispered to Gareth. 'Has she been sick? Does she have a cough? The runs?'

'All three,' he said. 'But I'm doing what the pharmacist told me, and making sure she's getting plenty of fluids. Now, if you've seen enough . . .' He nodded at the door, letting her know that it was time to leave.

'Okay, I'm going,' Holly said reluctantly, remembering that she'd asked the taxi driver to wait – and the meter was still running. 'But you'd better call the doctor when I've gone – and ring me to let me know what he says. Okay?'

When Gareth nodded his agreement, Holly took one last look at Ellie and then left the room. Something was niggling at the back of her mind, and it was making her feel uneasy, but she couldn't put her finger on it. When she reached the front door, she hesitated and reached up to the top of the electricity meter box, where she remembered Ellie had kept a spare key. Glancing nervously over her shoulder to make sure Gareth was still in the bedroom when she felt the cold metal of the key beneath her fingertips, she grabbed it and then let herself out.

She would give Gareth the benefit of the doubt for tonight, she decided as she made her way down to the taxi. But if he hadn't been in touch by tomorrow morning to tell her what the doctor had said, she would return tomorrow and wait for him to go out, then let herself in.

29

It was almost lunchtime when Gareth emerged from the main door of the flats the following day, and Holly darted behind a bush and watched as he strolled down the path and headed over the road to the bus stop. He'd had all night and most of this morning to update her about Ellie's condition, but she still hadn't heard from him; and Ellie's phone had gone straight to answerphone without even ringing when Holly had tried to call her, which made her wonder if Gareth had switched it off to stop her from leaving any more messages.

When she was feeling better, he would tell Ellie that nobody had given a toss about her, Holly thought bitterly as she loitered behind the bush, waiting for Gareth to board his bus. He was such a possessive freak, that was exactly the type of stunt he'd pull to make Ellie fall out with her family again. She'd thought Matt was bad, but he had nothing on Gareth in that respect, because Matt would never have dreamed of trying to stop Ellie's family from visiting if she was ill.

As soon as the bus pulled away with Gareth safely aboard,

Holly came out of her hiding place and hurried over to the main door. The niggling feeling that had troubled her the previous day was still there. She'd thought about it all night, and had even discussed it with Tony when he'd rung to say goodnight; but she still hadn't worked out what it was that her instincts were trying to tell her. Tony had suggested that it was probably Gareth's general freakiness that was unnerving her, but she thought it was something Gareth had said that had rung an alarm. That, and the sound of Ellie's breathing; as if she wasn't just sleeping, but was actually unconscious. It was possible that Ellie hadn't been sleeping and desperately needed rest, as Gareth had said; but Holly had been to enough raves and seen enough people off their heads to know the difference between a natural sleep and a drug-induced one.

Conscious that she needed to get inside before Gareth returned, Holly pressed a random bell and told the man who answered that she was delivering a surprise bouquet of flowers to somebody on the fifth floor. The moment he buzzed her in, she rushed upstairs.

Ellie's flat was in silence when Holly let herself in and, even though she had seen Gareth get on the bus, she was still nervous of him coming home and catching her, so she headed straight for the bedroom. The sour-smelling air brought back an unwelcome memory of what her grandmother's hospital room had smelled like on the day she had died, and Holly swallowed a rush of nausea before tiptoeing to the bed.

Ellie was lying exactly as she had been the previous day: flat on her back with the quilt pulled up to her throat. Her eyes seemed to be rolling in their sockets, and Holly realized that the sour smell was coming from her open mouth. Her forehead felt hotter today, so Holly gently eased the quilt off her to give her some air.

'What the *fuck* . . . ?' she gasped, gazing down in horror when she saw that her sister's hands were bound together with gaffer tape. No longer worried about waking her, she yanked the quilt the rest of the way off, and cried, 'Oh, no . . . what has he *done* to you?' when she saw that Ellie's ankles were also bound.

'This can't be fucking happening,' she muttered, shaking wildly as she struggled to tear the tape off her sister's wrists. 'Don't worry, Ells, I'm gonna get you out of here before he comes back, I promise!'

Unable to loosen the tape sufficiently with her fingers after trying for several moments, Holly ran to the kitchen to get a knife. But as she was returning to the bedroom, the front door opened, and she stopped in her tracks when Gareth walked in.

'How the fuck did you get in here?' he demanded, kicking the door shut when he saw her. Then, grinning slyly when he spotted the knife in her hand, he said, 'Oh, I see . . . I take it you've seen her, then? So what were you going to do? Rescue her from the big bad wolf? Good job I came back for my phone, or you might have succeeded.'

'Don't come anywhere near me, or I swear to God I'll stab you,' Holly warned when he walked toward her. 'I mean it, Gareth . . . I don't know what shit you've got going on in that sick head of yours, but I will not let you keep my sister hostage. Now, back off and let me go to her, because this stops now!'

'Nice speech,' Gareth said, clapping his hands as if he was applauding her. 'And the Oscar for best performance of a sister who suddenly gives a flying fuck goes to . . .'

'If you come any closer, I'll scream,' Holly warned, stumbling into the living room. 'You know how thin these council flat walls are, so someone's bound to hear me and call the police.'

'Don't you fucking dare!' Gareth hissed, lunging at her and covering her mouth with his hand. 'Quit fighting,' he ordered, dragging her into the kitchen as she tried to gouge his face with her nails. 'I said fucking *QUIT!*' he yelled, slamming her up against the ledge.

Pain flared in Holly's eyes, and her knees buckled beneath her. Still holding her tightly, Gareth yanked a drawer open and took out a roll of gaffer tape, then flipped her round so that her back was against his stomach. Unrolling a strip of tape, he broke it off with his teeth and slapped it over her mouth before throwing her down onto the floor. Sitting on her when she started to buck, he yanked her arms up behind her and wrapped tape around both wrists before turning to do the same to her ankles.

When he'd finished, he stood up and laughed when she started flip-flopping on the floor.

'You look like a fucking slug on crack,' he said. 'Wait there while I get my phone to film you.'

Holly screamed when he ran out to get his phone, but no sound came out. Terrified, because she had no idea what he intended to do with her, she forced herself to stop panicking so she could figure out a way to get him to set her free. This was a completely different level of crazy from anything she had ever encountered before, and she would need to stay cool-headed if she were to stand any chance of getting out of here alive. Tony was flying home from Dubai in the morning, and he knew she'd been planning to sneak in here to see Ellie today. The first thing he'd do when his flight landed was try to ring her, and if he couldn't reach her, he'd ring her mum. He'd be bound to get worried when he heard that she hadn't gone home, and this was the first place he would come looking for her.

Unless his flight got delayed and he decided to stay in Dubai for another night.

Oh, God, please don't let his flight get delayed, she prayed. *Please, please, please . . .*

'Why have you stopped?' Gareth demanded, his voice ringing with disappointment when he returned with his phone and saw that she was no longer struggling. 'I was going to put it on Facebook and make you a star. I thought you'd like that, seeing as you make so much effort to attract attention to yourself?'

'Fuck you!' she spat, tears of anger and frustration burning her eyes.

It came out as a grunt, and Gareth squatted down beside her

and tilted his head. 'What was that? You want me to kill you now?'

Terrified for the baby she was carrying, Holly shook her head.

'Don't worry, I won't,' Gareth said, gently wiping the tears off her cheeks. 'Not yet, anyway. I need to figure out how to get your body out of here without being seen first. In the meantime, me and you are going to have some fun.'

Holly screamed behind the tape when he flipped her onto her back and trailed his gaze down her body. Her short skirt had ridden up during the struggle, and she knew her flimsy see-through panties must be on display when his gaze came to rest on her crotch.

'*Don't!*' she pleaded silently with her eyes. 'Please, don't . . .'

Gareth pursed his lips as if he was trying to decide what to do next. Then, snapping his head round when he heard a noise coming from the bedroom, he hissed, 'Now look what you've done,' as he raised himself up.

Holly looked around the room in search of something she could use to cut the tape while Gareth rushed to the bedroom. The knife she'd been holding when he came home was lying on the carpet outside the kitchen door, if she could only reach that . . .

She had almost wriggled over to the door when Gareth appeared. He immediately guessed what she was doing and kicked the knife out of reach. Breathless from the effort it had taken to make it that far, Holly glared at him when he squatted down beside her again.

You wait till Tony gets here, she screamed in her mind. *He's going to kill you for this, you freak!*

Gareth chuckled softly when he saw the hatred in her eyes. 'You know, you're not half as good looking as you think,' he told her amusedly. 'Ellie's way more beautiful than you, and it amazes me that she can't see that. But that's your fault, isn't it; 'cos you destroyed her confidence when you screwed all of her boyfriends behind her back. You even tried to steal Matt, but that clearly didn't work out quite as well as you'd hoped, considering he went ahead and married her after getting what he wanted off you. But shall I tell you *why* he chose her over you . . . ? It's because she's beautiful on the inside as well as the outside, whereas you're nothing but a cheap little tart who spreads her legs at the drop of a hat. And you actually thought you'd be able to steal *me* off her, as well, didn't you? That's why you've been telling her all those lies about us sleeping together when you know damn well I didn't touch you – because you're hoping she'll finish with me. Well, tough, 'cos she loves me, and I love her, and we're not letting a cheap little skank like *you* ruin things for us. And that, my dear, is why you've got to go.'

Holly's heart leapt into her mouth as any lingering doubt that he intended to kill her evaporated, and the panic made her start struggling to free herself again.

'You know you're wasting your time, don't you?' Gareth snorted as he slid his hands beneath her and lifted her up off the floor. 'But it's probably best if we get you out of here before you start knocking chairs over and making noise. Don't want that nosy bastard next door suspecting that something's going on and calling the police, do we?'

Sure now that he was actually insane when he carried her into the bedroom and laid her in the bed next to Ellie, Holly followed him with her eyes when he walked round to her sister's side and picked up the cup that was sitting on the bedside table before leaving the room.

Not even trying to speak, because she knew no words would come out, and she also didn't want Gareth to come running in, she wriggled closer to her sister and bumped her several times with her shoulder. Her sister's hands were tied at the front of her body, while Holly's were behind her, so if she could rouse Ellie enough to get her to loosen the tape on Holly's wrists, Holly would be able to free her own feet and run for help.

Ellie didn't respond, and Holly stopped what she'd been doing the moment Gareth came into the room carrying the same cup, which now had a tiny bloom of steam rising from it.

'I've brought you a drinking chocolate,' he told her, placing the cup on the table and pulling a straw and a screwdriver out of his pocket. 'It's your sister's favourite, so I'm sure you'll like it, seeing as you always want what she likes.'

Holly squealed with fear when Gareth sat down on the edge of the mattress and placed the pointed tip of the screwdriver in the centre of the tape covering her mouth.

'Stop being such a baby,' he chided, twisting the screwdriver to make a hole for the straw. 'Oops!' he grinned when she jerked her head away and a drop of blood appeared on the jagged edge of the tape. 'Did I cut your lip? Oh, well, you should have kept still, shouldn't you? But, no worries, the drink will make it all better. Ask Ellie, if you don't believe me,' he went on as he slotted the straw into the hole he'd made before reaching for the cup. 'Don't hear her complaining, do you?'

Guessing that the drink had been spiked, Holly twisted her head to one side when he stuck the other end of the straw into the cup.

'Pack it in!' he barked, seizing her chin tightly in his hand to force her head round. 'Now drink it, or I'll get a syringe and inject it into you instead. Is that what you want?'

Sobbing by then, Holly shook her head, and once again tried pleading with her eyes for him to stop. But, again, it didn't work, and Gareth shoved the straw deeper into the hole in the tape.

Giving in, because she had no doubt that he would follow through with his threat and inject her if she didn't, Holly reluctantly sucked the drink up through the straw. It was overly sweet, and there was a hint of something bitter which she assumed must be the drug he'd laced it with. Praying that her years of hard partying had given her a higher tolerance than her clean-living sister, Holly told herself to stay calm and ride out whatever effects came from it when Gareth eventually withdrew the straw.

Gareth didn't take his eyes off her, and Holly guessed that he was waiting for the drink to knock her out. Drawing on the memory of an embarrassing video an ex-boyfriend had filmed of her after a particularly heavy drug binge, she forced herself to breathe more deeply and let her eyes slide into the back of their sockets. This was a nightmare, and she had never imagined that anything like this would ever happen to her, but she intended to fight it with every fibre of her being.

As darkness began to descend, Holly's eyes drifted shut, and she felt the mattress dip and rise again when Gareth got up. The last thing she heard was the door closing behind him as he made his way out of the room.

30

Holly didn't know how long she'd been sleeping, but it was pitch-dark in the bedroom when she woke up. Twisting her head round on the pillow, she was relieved to see that Ellie was still lying beside her. Her head was banging, and she felt groggy, as if she was on a come-down after a massive binge. She just prayed that the baby hadn't been affected by whatever that bastard had given her, because she would kill him with her bare hands when she got free if it had. And she *would* get free, she was determined about that.

A red glow caught her eye in the darkness on the other side of the bed and, guessing that it was an alarm clock, she attempted to lift her head so she could see past Ellie. It was difficult with her arms secured behind her, and she winced when pins and needles started to prickle painfully in her hands, but she craned her neck until she was able to make out the clock's digits. It was almost 6 a.m., and a wave of relief washed over her at the thought that Tony would soon be back in the country.

Tensing when the door suddenly opened, she snapped her eyes shut again. But it was too late, Gareth had seen that she was awake, and he came over to her.

'Sleep well?'

Like you care! she wanted to scream, but she knew it wouldn't come out, so she didn't bother trying.

'*I* did, thanks for asking,' Gareth said, grinning when she glared at him. 'It's amazing how comfortable it is when you're the filling in a sister sandwich.'

Nauseated by the thought that he had crawled into bed and slept between her and Ellie while they were unconscious, Holly swallowed loudly.

'Don't worry, I didn't touch you, if that's what you're thinking,' Gareth went on. 'I'm not like you, and I'd never cheat on Ellie the way you cheated on Tony. And while we're on the subject . . . you really should have put a more difficult password on your phone, 'cos it was easy as piss to open it when your man started messaging you last night. He's got quite a temper on him, hasn't he?'

Holly stared at him, waiting for him to elaborate.

Clearly enjoying himself, Gareth said, 'He didn't take it too well when I told him – well, I say I, but he thought it was you, so I should say when *you* told him you'd met someone else while he was away.'

Holly's breath quickened, but he hadn't finished yet.

'I had fun telling him how much better in bed your new man is, and how much younger and better-looking he is. He wasn't happy about that, but he got really mad when he tried to ring you and you kept declining the calls. I think he understood when you explained that you couldn't speak to him 'cos your new man had his head between your legs. Strangely, he didn't seem to believe you at first; seemed to think you would never do that to him – at least, not now you're having a *baby*.' Gareth paused and gave her a questioning look. 'Is that true? Are you pregnant?'

Holly nodded, hoping that it might make a difference. But she should have known better.

'Great.' He sighed. 'I've never had to kill a baby before. But I suppose there's a first time for everything, eh?'

A tear trickled from Holly's eye, and Gareth wiped it away, crooning, 'There, there; no need for that. I was going to do it last night, but I'm afraid you're going to have to wait a little longer, 'cos you'll only stink the place out if I do it before I've got the tools to dispose of you properly. And we don't want anyone catching a whiff of you and putting two and two together, do we?'

Ellie began to stir on the other side of the bed, and Gareth glanced at the clock.

'Oh, oh . . . time for my princess to have her medicine. Now you behave yourself till I get back and I'll take you to the loo. I know you pregnant women are always bursting to go, and we can't have you wetting the bed, can we?'

When he'd left the room, Holly wriggled closer to Ellie and nudged her with her shoulder. Yesterday, Ellie hadn't stirred when Holly had done the same thing; but the drugs Gareth had given her were clearly wearing off, because she groaned and turned her head round on the pillow.

Willing her to open her eyes, Holly brought her legs round and repeatedly nudged Ellie in the thigh with her knees. After a while, Ellie's eyes flickered open, and she blinked a couple of times as if she thought she was dreaming when she saw Holly.

Aware that Gareth would return any minute, and that she didn't have the time to make Ellie understand that she wanted her to try and free her hands, Holly stared into her eyes, trying to telepathically reassure her that she would get them both out of this if it killed her.

31

Tony's plane landed at 9.30 a.m., and he couldn't get out of the airport and into a taxi fast enough. His text conversation with Holly in the early hours of that morning had deeply disturbed him. He hadn't expected her to be awake when he'd sent his first message, he'd just wanted her to wake up and read that he'd missed her and couldn't wait to see her. So when, a few minutes after sending it, she'd replied, telling him that she'd met someone else and no longer wanted to marry him, he'd thought she must have been drinking. But it had soon become clear that she was stone-cold sober, and some of the things she had written had truly shocked and angered him. He'd tried to call her, several times, but she'd refused them all, and had then sent another message telling him that she was too busy getting pleasured by her new stud to be bothered talking to a boring old fart like him. It was at this point that Tony had reminded her about the baby and the fairy-tale wedding she had been planning, in the hope that it would bring her to her senses and make her realize exactly what she was putting at risk. But she had replied that she didn't want either of them, and had already booked herself in for a termination to remove every last trace of him from her life.

Tony was an old-school kind of man, who considered crying a weakness, but Holly's words had made him sob like a baby. Several brandies later, he had calmed down enough to review her messages from a more objective viewpoint, and he'd come to the conclusion that he had been right first time and she was steaming drunk. Or – and he preferred this theory – somebody had got hold of her phone and she hadn't sent those messages at all.

Clinging to that latter theory on the journey to his flat, he tried to call Holly as soon as he got home. Assuming that her battery must have died when it went to voicemail without ringing, he called her mum's landline instead, hoping that Kath might be able to throw some light on whatever was going on.

Dismayed when Kath told him that her daughter hadn't come home the previous night, he gave her a brief rundown of the text conversation he'd had with Holly. But if he'd expected reassurance, he was in for a shock, because Kath said, 'I can't say I'm surprised, love. I'm actually *more* surprised that you've lasted this long, to be honest, because she gets bored very quickly.'

And then, as if this were of far more importance than her daughter calling off the wedding and declaring that she intended to abort her baby, she'd said, 'I hope you're not going to kick me out of my house over this? You know I only let you have it cheap because I thought I'd be living with you and Holly; but if you're splitting up, I'm going to need to buy it back – at the same price.'

Unable to even think about something as trivial as that right then, Tony had told her that they would talk about it when he'd had a chance to speak to Holly.

After showering and drinking a gallon of coffee to dilute whatever booze was left in his system, Tony locked up the flat and took the lift to the underground car park to make the long drive to Manchester.

Three hours later, Tony pulled up outside Kath's house.

'Is she home yet?' he asked when Kath answered the door.

'Good morning to you, too,' Kath said huffily, stepping aside to let him in. 'And, no, there's no sign of her. I tried ringing her after I spoke to you, but she's not answering.'

The faded living room carpet was still in place, as was the shabby three-piece suite Kath had owned since before Ellie was born. But apart from those items and the curtains at the window, everything that had once made this house a home was now packed inside a stack of boxes in the dining room. It felt cold and devoid of life, and it occurred to Tony as he followed Kath through to the kitchen that this was what his future was going to feel like without Holly and the baby in it.

'You look tired,' Kath said, glancing at Tony over her shoulder as she switched the kettle on and dropped teabags into two of the three cups she hadn't yet packed. 'Don't you think you'd have been better off getting your head down for a bit before driving all this way? Billy used to tell me horrendous stories about the crashes he'd seen on the motorway when he was a truckie, and he reckoned most of them were caused by people falling asleep at the wheel.'

'I needed to see Holly and get this sorted,' Tony sighed, glancing at his watch as he took a seat at the kitchen table. 'Did she mention me while I was away? Any hint that she was thinking of calling the wedding off; or mention of another fella?'

'To be honest, she spent most of her time banging on about our Ellie,' said Kath. 'She reckons I'm wrong to hold what Matt did against her, and she said I'd better sort it out before the wedding 'cos she was having her there – whether I liked it or not.'

'So she was still talking about the wedding going ahead, then?' Tony said hopefully.

'Well, yeah, but you know what she's like for changing her mind at the drop of a hat, so I wouldn't take anything she says as gospel,' Kath said, pouring water into the cups when the kettle switched itself off.

'So where did she say she was going when she left the house yesterday?' Tony asked. 'Did she tell you she'd been to see Ellie and was worried about her?'

'No.' Kath frowned as she handed a cup to him and took a seat on the opposite side of the table. 'She was supposed to be fetching her here the other day so we could talk, but I assumed Ellie mustn't have wanted to come when Holly came home on

319

her own. I didn't ask what had happened, because I wasn't in the mood for another lecture. But you say she was worried about her?'

'Yeah, apparently, she's not too well,' said Tony. 'But that Gareth tried to stop Holly from seeing her.'

'Gareth?' Kath repeated.

'Er, yeah, I think he's a friend of Ellie's,' Tony said diplomatically, sensing that Kath wouldn't approve if she knew the truth, which might jeopardize any chance of her and Ellie settling their differences in the future.

Kath wasn't as daft as she allowed people to believe, and she narrowed her eyes when she smelled a rat.

'Try pulling the other one; it might play "Jingle Bells",' she said as Tony sipped his tea. Pursing her lips when he looked up at her with guilt in his eyes, she said, 'Our Holly mentioned that name when she was talking to you on the phone the other night. That's the fella Matt accused her of cheating on him with, isn't he?'

'Yeah, but I honestly don't think she was seeing him then,' Tony said. 'I think it happened after Matt left.'

'He's only been gone two minutes,' Kath said disapprovingly. Then, sighing, she said, 'Ah, well, it's her life, and I'll get no thanks for interfering. But it would have been nice to be told instead of making me work it out for myself.'

'Sorry, but it wasn't my place to tell you,' said Tony.

'Is that why you haven't mentioned the baby yet?' Kath asked casually. Tutting when he gave her another guilty look, she said, 'I bloody knew it. I asked her outright if she was pregnant the other day, and she looked me in the eye and said no. She must think I was born yesterday. I can recognize the signs, you know. So when's it due, then? Before or after the wedding?'

'Probably after, the way things are going,' Tony said apologetically. 'My ex keeps delaying things.'

'I knew she was a piece of work the first time I clapped eyes on her,' Kath snorted. 'So, what's she after now? More money?'

'And the rest.' He sighed. 'She's already got the house, two cars, and over a grand a month in child maintenance, but now she wants a portion of my future earnings, as well.'

'I hope you told her to bugger off, 'cos you're going to need all you've got for the new baby,' Kath huffed.

'I haven't dared tell her about that yet,' he replied wearily. Then, giving Kath a questioning look, he said, 'Does this mean you don't mind – about us having the baby before we're married, I mean? Holly thought you'd disown her.'

'What, and miss out on seeing my grandchild grow up?' Kath frowned. 'I'm not that bad. Mind you,' she added ominously, 'you'd better hope you and her have managed to patch things up before it's born, 'cos you don't want it calling some other bloke Daddy.'

'Don't say that,' Tony groaned. 'I've already messed things up with my other kids, and I really wanted to do a better job with this one.'

Kath reached across the table and placed her hand over his when she heard the anguish in his voice.

'If it's any consolation, I think Holly will be making the biggest mistake of her life if she lets you go,' she said kindly. 'I wasn't your biggest fan after all that nonsense in Barbados, but I've seen how hard you've been trying, and I know how much you love her. So if you want her and that baby, you'd better fight for her. Do you hear me?'

'What if it's too late?' Tony asked. 'I can't force her to stay with me if she doesn't want to. You know how stubborn she is.'

'I'm twice as stubborn as her, but she managed to talk me round about our Ellie, so I'm sure you can talk *her* round about this – whatever *this* is.'

'I can't talk her round if she won't take my calls.' Tony sighed. 'I might drive over to Ellie's to see if she's there.'

'She won't have stayed there if Ellie's ill,' Kath said with certainty. 'She's a bit OCD about germs. Always has been.'

'I know,' Tony said, smiling as he recalled the one and only time he'd been ill enough to take to his bed during his and Holly's relationship. She'd slept on the sofa for a full week in order to avoid catching anything, and she'd be even more cautious now she was pregnant.

'Why don't you give her a couple of days to think things over?' Kath suggested. 'Whatever's going on, she won't thank you for chasing after her; and it might even make things worse.'

'Yeah, I know,' said Tony. 'I went after her at Christmas, when she flew back from Barbados and went to Ellie's, and she tried to make me jealous by telling me she was going out with that Gareth.'

'It wasn't true, though, was it? And chances are, this one isn't, either,' Kath said encouragingly. 'It's probably a touch of cold feet. Happens to everyone at some point.'

'I hope that's all it is,' Tony murmured.

Kath patted his hand and drank some of her tea. Then, resting her arms on the table to let him know it was time to talk business, she said, 'Anyway . . . about the house . . .'

'Don't worry about it,' Tony said wearily, wondering if her display of support had been designed to butter him up for this. 'If me and Holly end up calling it a day, the house is yours.'

'I knew you'd do the right thing,' Kath said, swivelling in her seat and taking a pen and a little notebook out of her handbag. 'But would you mind putting that in writing . . . ?'

32

Ellie's stomach was hurting, and the pain dragged her up through the darkness of the nightmare she'd been having about Matt. He'd been dressed in filthy old clothes, and his hair and beard had been longer and more straggly than she had ever seen them before. A crowd of jeering people had been following as he was dragged along by his rope-bound feet behind a motorbike, and they had all started hurling bricks at him when her eyes fluttered open, saving her from the horror of witnessing his inevitable death.

Her head felt like it was stuffed with cotton wool, and she was confused when she tried to raise her hand and found that the other once seemed to be stuck to it. She heard the sound of breathing in the darkness beside her, and her heart skipped a beat. Was it Matt? Had he come home while she was ill?

She turned her head, and peered at the figure lying as still as a rock on Matt's side of the bed. Confused all over again when the fuzzy features began to take shape and she realized it was Holly, she thought she must still be dreaming.

'Holly . . . ?' she croaked, weakly nudging her sister with her elbow. '*Holly . . . ?*'

Getting no response after several attempts, Ellie winced when another dull pain rippled through her stomach. Her tongue was bone dry and her mouth tasted foul, and she rolled onto her side in desperate need of a drink. The glowing red digits of her alarm clock told her that it was 2:45 a.m.

A sliver of light under the door caught her eye, and Gareth's name flashed into her mind, followed by a series of hazy visions. Gareth stroking her hair . . . Gareth lifting her up to give her a drink . . . Gareth talking softly in the dark, telling her that everything was going to be all right . . .

But hadn't she told Gareth that she wanted to end their relationship? Or had she dreamed that, like she'd dreamed that Matt was in danger and Holly was here?

Feeling sick again, she tried to sit up, but her arms felt numb, and she couldn't seem to separate her hands. With effort, she managed to swing her arms round and grope for the switch on the cord of the lamp. The light seared her eyes, and she squeezed them shut again until the pain had passed.

Able to see more clearly when she opened them again, she looked round and was shocked to see that Holly really was there. Confused when she saw that her sister's mouth was covered by a strip of dull silver tape with a jagged hole in the centre, she snapped into full consciousness when she saw more of the same tape wrapped around her own wrists and realized that was why she hadn't been able to separate them. She had no idea what had happened, or why they were both tied up like this, but she needed to get that tape off Holly's mouth, so she swung her arms round and desperately clawed at the tape with her fingernails.

Even when her mouth was uncovered, Holly still didn't move and, terrified that she might be dead, Ellie started tearing at the tape around her wrists with her teeth. But the door opened before she'd managed to free herself, and she cried out in fear when Gareth appeared with a roll of bin-bags and a hacksaw in his hand.

'Oh, no . . . when did you wake up?' he asked, rushing over to her. 'I didn't want you to see any of this.'

'Wh-what's going on?' she spluttered, pushing herself further up the bed with her heels. 'Why are we tied up?'

'One question at a time, sweetheart,' Gareth said calmly as he laid the hacksaw and roll of bags on the floor beside the bed. 'Let's get you comfortable, then I'll explain. Okay?'

'Explain what?'

'All in good time,' he said, checking to make sure she hadn't done too much damage to the tape around her wrists. Satisfied that it would hold until he'd had the chance to re-do it, he slipped his hands beneath her and laid her on her back before covering her over with the quilt. 'Stay there . . . I'll be with you in a minute.'

Feeling as if she had slipped into some sort of alternate universe where nothing made any sense when he rushed out of the bedroom and she heard him switch the kettle on in the kitchen, Ellie sat up and peered down at the hacksaw and bags, wondering what he intended to do with them.

'Oops, sorry, my mistake,' he said, running into the room at that exact moment and snatching the hacksaw up off the floor. 'Wouldn't want you getting hold of it and cutting yourself by accident, now, would we?'

'I'm going to be sick,' she said, bringing her bound hands up to cover her mouth.

'Hang on,' Gareth said, grabbing the small wastebin from under the dressing table and tipping the rubbish onto the floor. 'Do it in this.'

'Get away from me!' she cried, swinging her hands at the bin when he thrust it under her chin. 'I SAID *GET AWA*—'

Gareth clamped his hand over her mouth when her voice rose, and he threw his weight onto her to wrestle her onto her back, hissing, 'Stop it! They're the enemy, not me! I'm only trying to help you.'

Ellie shook her head violently, and sank her teeth into the tender, fleshy part of his palm.

Crying out with pain and rage, Gareth lashed out with his free hand, striking the side of her head.

'See what you've made me do now?' he hissed when her body went limp and her eyes rolled to the back of their sockets. 'That was *your* fault, not mine! All I'm trying to do is help you, so why did you have to start fighting with me?'

Snapping out of his rage when she groaned, he sat down and pulled her into his arms, crooning, 'Oh, thank God you're okay. I'm so sorry, I didn't mean to hurt you; please forgive me . . .'

33

Tony hadn't slept well. He was missing Holly, and couldn't get Kath's words about his child growing up calling another man Daddy out of his mind. Having spent the entire night veering from pain to anger and back again, he got up before the sun had fully risen the next morning and, after a quick wash, headed down to the kitchen.

After making a cup of coffee, he unlocked the back door and stepped out into the tiny garden to have a cigarette. He'd no sooner lit up than he heard the chimes of the doorbell echoing in the hall. Hoping that it would be Holly; that she'd been out on a bender and lost her keys along with her phone, he dropped the cigarette and ran inside to answer the door.

Dismayed to see a chunky red-headed man in an ill-fitting suit on the doorstep, and not Holly, Tony said, 'Yes?'

'DI Collins,' the man said, flashing a badge at him. 'I believe we have met.'

'Ah, yes, of course,' Tony said. 'You're leading the investigation, aren't you? Sorry, it's a bit early, and I'm not quite with it yet. Are you here to see Kath?'

'If she's available?'

Telling him that she was probably still sleeping, Tony invited him in and showed him into the living room before going upstairs and tapping on Kath's bedroom door.

'What's up?' she grunted, peeling a sleepy eye open when he popped his head round the door.

'DI Collins is downstairs.'

'What?' No longer sleepy, Kath jerked upright. 'What's he doing here at this time of the morning? Has something happened?'

'He's here to see you, not me, so I didn't ask,' said Tony. 'Anyway, I've just made myself a coffee, so the kettle's still hot if you want one?'

'Tea, one sugar,' she muttered, dragging her nightgown off over her head in her haste to get dressed and find out what news the detective had for her.

Quickly averting his gaze when she exposed her drooping breasts, Tony withdrew his head and made his way down the stairs.

Collins had taken a seat on the sofa, and he shook his head when Tony asked if he'd like a cup of tea or coffee.

'I'm okay, thanks. Not planning on being here that long.'

They were interrupted by the sound of Kath clattering down the stairs.

'What's going on?' she asked. 'Have you caught him?'

'Not yet, but we have had a breakthrough,' said Collins. 'I'm sorry for coming round so early, but I was hoping you might know where Ellie is? I need to speak to her, but I haven't been able to reach her by phone, and she didn't answer the door when I went round to her place earlier.'

'I believe she isn't very well, so she was probably in bed when you called,' Kath told him as she sank down onto a chair. 'Is there anything I can help you with?'

'There might be, actually,' Collins said. 'I don't suppose you'd know how long Ellie's known Gareth Wilkinson, would you? Only he was at her place the last time I was there, and he told me they were engaged.'

'That's news to me!' Kath said, her eyebrows shooting up in alarm. 'Did *you* know about this?' She stared up at Tony when he walked in with the cup of tea he'd made for her. 'Detective Collins reckons Ellie and that man have got engaged.'

'Erm, I think Holly might have mentioned something about it,' he replied guiltily.

'And I'm the last to hear about it *again*,' Kath said angrily. 'I swear this family's going to hell in a bloody handbasket; all these secrets and lies.'

'Sorry,' Tony mumbled.

Tutting at him, Kath turned to Collins. 'Go on, then . . . you might as well finish what you were saying.'

'I'd gone round there that day to ask if Ellie could identify a mobile phone somebody had tried to pawn, which we believed might belong to her husband,' Collins continued. 'She wasn't sure, so we did tests which confirmed that it *is* Mr Fisher's phone. We were also able to establish that, on each occasion it was used *after* Mr Fisher went missing, it was in the vicinity of the flats where Ellie lives.'

'So what are you saying? He made those calls from inside the block?'

'We can't be that precise, I'm afraid; but he was certainly close by.'

Kath frowned and pursed her lips thoughtfully. Then, narrowing her eyes when something occurred to her, she said, 'What if the calls were made from inside her flat, because she's been hiding him there this whole time?'

'I really don't think so,' Tony said before Collins had a chance to respond. 'Holly told me Ellie's been too scared to go out because of the threats Matt's been making; and she can't even go to work because he rang her boss and threatened to set fire to the place if he didn't sack her. Anyway, Matt hates Gareth, because he thought Ellie was having an affair with him, so I can't see him agreeing to let Gareth move in if he's still there himself.'

'Oh, so now that fella's living there?' Kath said tartly. 'This just gets better by the flaming second.'

Avoiding her accusing glare, Tony turned back to Collins. 'Can I ask why you wanted to know how long Ellie's known Gareth? Only, I don't see how that's got any relevance to this case.'

'Mr Wilkinson is known to us,' Collins explained. 'And I

asked because we found his fingerprint on the phone, and I need to establish if he might have had an opportunity to touch it prior to Mr Fisher leaving.'

'Actually, yes, he could have,' said Tony. 'Holly met him on Christmas Day and took him to Ellie's to have dinner with them; and Matt was still there, so it's possible he might have let Gareth use it.'

'Ah . . . well, I guess that clears that up,' said Collins. 'I'll get going and leave you folks in peace, then.' Standing, he looked down at Kath, and said, 'Don't worry about Ellie. We'll be keeping a close eye on the flats now we know the phone was definitely used there.'

Tony escorted Collins to the door, and stepped outside to have a quiet word with him before he left.

'I hope you don't think I'm being nosy, but can I ask why you've got Gareth's prints on file? Is he a criminal, or something?'

'I'm afraid I can't discuss that,' said Collins. 'But I will say this . . .' he added, lowering his own voice and glancing into the hall to make sure Kath wasn't listening. 'Keep an eye on Ellie while he's around.'

'Why?' Tony frowned.

'That's all I can say, and I shouldn't even have said that,' said Collins. 'Just keep an eye on her, that's all.'

Still frowning, Tony watched as the detective walked to his car and climbed behind the wheel. Waving when the man nodded goodbye through the window before setting off, he thought about what Collins had said – and, more importantly, *how* he'd said it; as if to insinuate that Gareth Wilkinson was a potential danger to Ellie.

Holly had always said that she thought the man creepy, and Tony couldn't say his own opinion had been all that different on the couple of occasions they had met. But being creepy didn't necessarily mean he was dangerous – did it?

'If you've finished out there, come in and close the door before you let all the heat out,' Kath said as she came out into the hall. 'I'm going to have a bath, so if you need the loo, you'd better use it now.'

Telling her that he didn't need it, Tony went out into the garden to finish his coffee and the cigarette he'd started before Collins had arrived. She had told him to give Holly space to think things over, but he needed to know where her head was at, so he decided to drive over to Ellie's place – to see if she could tell him what Holly was up to, *and* to make sure that she was all right in light of the detective's warning.

34

Gareth lit a cigarette as he paced the living room floor. It had taken him ages to get Ellie to drink her hot chocolate after she'd come round from the blow he'd dealt her, and he knew it wouldn't be long before he had to go through it all again with her whore of a sister.

If only Ellie hadn't woken up when she did, he could have killed Holly and smuggled her chopped-up body out of the flat in the suitcase he'd found in the cupboard. But it was too late now, because the block was coming to life all around him; TVs blaring, toilets flushing, parents shouting at their kids to hurry up and get ready for school . . .

No, he couldn't do it now; he would have to wait until the early hours, when the neighbours were sleeping and he could do what needed doing without raising suspicion.

Frustrated that he'd been forced to delay his plans, and all too aware that if it happened again he'd run out of tablets and wouldn't be able to keep both women sufficiently sedated, Gareth pulled Ellie's wedding and engagement rings out of his pocket and gazed at them thoughtfully. He needed to buy more drugs, but he'd already spent the money out of Ellie's purse, and there hadn't been much actual cash in Holly's, so he would have to sell the rings. But not round here where somebody might recognize him and ask questions; he needed to go to one of those shady backstreet places on the outskirts of town, where they didn't give a shit who you were or how you'd come by the stuff you were trying to sell. But he had to be able to get there and back before either of the women woke up again.

Decided, he was about to set off when the intercom buzzed, and he cursed under his breath when he saw Holly's boyfriend standing at the door below. What was he doing here? Did he suspect something?

Don't be ridiculous, he chided himself as soon as the thought entered his mind. Tony didn't know Holly was here. Gareth had read all the messages he'd sent to her after Gareth, pretending to be her, had told him it was over, and the idiot definitely believed she'd gone off with another man. If anything, he'd probably come to beg Ellie to speak to her sister on his behalf again.

Itching to know how much damage he'd done, Gareth went out into the hall and answered the intercom in a sleepy voice, as if he'd just woken.

'Hello?'

'It's Tony,' the man announced. 'Holly's fiancé,' he added, as if he thought Gareth might have forgotten who he was. 'Is it possible to speak to Ellie, please?'

Gareth felt a kick of excitement in his gut when he heard the man's grovelling tone, and he said, 'Just a minute,' before pressing the door-release button. This cunt had looked down his nose at Gareth the last time their paths had crossed, but he'd obviously realized that Gareth was the king of this castle now, and if anyone wanted an audience with the queen, they needed his permission.

'Thanks for letting me come up,' Tony said when he reached the flat a couple of minutes later to find Gareth waiting in the doorway. 'Holly told me Ellie hasn't been very well. Is she feeling any better yet?'

'Not really,' Gareth said, waving for him to come inside. 'She's sleeping at the moment,' he went on, struggling not to grin as Tony walked up the hall ahead of him, unknowingly passing the door behind which his beloved fiancée and her sister were trussed up like a pair of prize turkeys. 'But we tell each other everything, so I might be able to help with whatever you were going to talk to her about?'

'It's about Holly,' Tony said, taking a seat on the sofa. 'I wanted to ask if Ellie's spoken to her recently, only I've been away on a business trip, and Holly . . . well, she was acting a bit funny last time I spoke to her. She's not answering her phone now, and she didn't go home to her mum's last night, so I wondered if Ellie might know what's going on?'

Perched on the arm of Matt's chair, Gareth dipped his gaze and chewed on his lip, as if he knew exactly what was going on, but didn't want to say anything.

'If you know something, please tell me,' Tony implored. 'I can handle it.'

Frowning, as if he hated to be the bearer of bad news, Gareth said, 'Okay, but you can't tell her it was me who told you, because Ellie made me promise I wouldn't.'

'I won't,' Tony assured him.

'She *was* here last night,' Gareth said. 'But she wasn't alone.'

'A man?' Tony asked, his expression telling Gareth that he was fully expecting an affirmative reply.

Gareth gave a regretful shrug.

Tony breathed in deeply and clasped his hands together between his knees. 'How did she look?' he asked after a moment. 'With the bloke, I mean? Did she look happy?'

'Aw, mate,' Gareth groaned. 'Don't ask me that.'

'I need to know,' Tony insisted. 'Who is he? Where did she meet him? How long has it been going on?'

'Look, all I know is it's some lad she was crazy about at school,' Gareth said. 'He emigrated to Australia when they were fifteen and broke her heart, but she bumped into him the other day when he came over to visit relatives, and she's been with him for the last few nights. She brought him round last night, 'cos she's thinking about going with him when he goes home to Australia, and she wanted to ask Ellie's advice about it.'

Tony's head was spinning. He couldn't believe Holly had done this so soon after telling him about the baby. She'd been so excited about it, and they had already discussed names and talked about moving to a bigger place in a better area to give their child the best start in life. And now, because of some chance meeting with a childhood crush, she was willing to turn her back on the future they had planned. It didn't make sense. Unless it was payback for him not telling her about his wife and kids? But she'd forgiven him for that. Or, at least, she'd *said* she had.

'Can I get you a drink?'

'Sorry?' Tony snapped out of his thoughts and looked up at Gareth.

'Drink?'

'No, thanks; I think I'd best go,' Tony said, standing up, and holding out his hand. 'Cheers for telling me. I appreciate your honesty.'

'Wish I hadn't had to,' Gareth said, shaking his hand. 'But you had a right to know.'

Tony nodded sadly and walked out into the hall. Hesitating when he heard a noise coming from the bedroom, he looked back at Gareth, and whispered, 'I think Ellie might be waking up.'

'Sounds like it,' Gareth agreed, quickly stepping in front of the door. 'She probably needs her medicine.'

'You go and see to her; I'll let myself out,' Tony said. 'Give her my love, and tell her I hope she's feeling better soon.'

'Will do,' Gareth said, nodding goodbye when Tony opened the door.

*

In desperate need of air, Tony trotted down the stairs and burst out through the main door. After pausing to light a cigarette, he was on his way to his car when a vision flitted through his mind and brought him to a stop. Holly's shoe, one of the pair of Louboutins he'd bought her a few weeks earlier with their distinctive red soles, had been poking out from under the sideboard behind the chair Gareth had been sitting on. He'd caught a glimpse of it on his way out, but it hadn't registered until now. She loved those shoes, so there was no way she'd have given them away; and they were far too expensive for Ellie to have bought a pair, so what had it been doing there?

Unless Holly was there, too, and that noise he'd heard as he was leaving was actually her trying to stifle her laughter after hearing him fall for Gareth's lies? For all he knew, her new man had been in there, as well; all three of them listening and laughing as his heart was being smashed to pieces.

He turned and stared up at the flats, torn between marching up there and demanding to see Holly, or leaving the heartless bitch and her new man to it.

The latter won and, taking a deep drag on his cigarette, he flicked it away and marched to his car, thinking, *Fuck her*! as he climbed behind the wheel. If she was willing to sacrifice the life they shared and the future they had planned for some old flame who had already abandoned her once – and probably would again – then good luck to her. He just hoped she *did* bugger off to Australia, because at least then he wouldn't have to watch some other man bring up his child.

Gareth had been watching Tony from the window, and the buzz he'd been feeling about having him here, so close to Holly, had long gone. His ego had made him invite the man in, and he was furious with himself for being so reckless. His nan had always said he was his own worst enemy, and she was right, because things could have worked out very differently just now. One of the girls might have woken up and escaped from the room while Tony was here; or Tony could have opened the bedroom door when he'd heard the noises coming from inside. Anything could have happened, and Gareth couldn't believe he'd been so stupid.

Well, that decided it, he thought, making his way into the kitchen when Tony had gone. One way or another, he had to get Holly out of here tonight.

When the drinks were ready, Gareth carried them into the bedroom. It was Holly who had woken up, and she glared at him when he walked toward the bed. Her eyes were far sharper than the last time she had come round, and Gareth guessed that she was building a tolerance to the drugs he'd been feeding her and he would have to up her dosage if he hoped to keep her sufficiently sedated until he was able to dispose of her.

Furious when she kicked out at him as he approached the bed, almost knocking the cups out of his hand, he placed them out of reach and then punched her hard in the face.

Blood exploded from her nose, and her eyes shot up into their sockets. Aware that she was choking when she started convulsing and making gurgling noises, Gareth pulled her up by her shoulders and tore the corner of the tape off her mouth so she could catch her breath.

She inhaled sharply and then retched a couple of times, but as soon as her breathing settled, Gareth slapped the tape back over her mouth.

'Don't make me do that again!' he hissed. 'It's not time yet, so quit fighting me and do as you're told.'

Ellie had started to come round, and Gareth dropped Holly back onto her pillow and rushed round to the other side of the bed when he heard her whimper.

'It's okay, darling,' he crooned, slipping his arm beneath her to raise her up. 'I'm here, there's nothing to worry about. Let's just get you into a better position so you can have your medicine.'

Gareth had weakened the tape's effectiveness when he'd pulled it off Holly's mouth, and she had been desperately pushing at it with her tongue while he was tending to Ellie. When the edge popped free, she let out a blood-curdling scream, almost causing Gareth to drop the cup he'd been about to feed Ellie from.

'Shut your mouth!' he hissed, clambering over Ellie to deal with Holly.

She screamed again, louder this time, and Gareth clamped his hand over her mouth and looked around for the roll of tape.

Remembering that he'd taken it into the kitchen, he kicked off one of his trainers and peeled his sock off with his free hand. Holly's eyes bulged when he shoved the damp material into her mouth, and she bucked beneath him.

Looking at Ellie, who was shaking her head from side to side and pleading with her tearful eyes for him to stop, Gareth said, 'I'm sorry, darling, I know this isn't nice for you; but I can't let her ruin everything when we've come so far. It won't be long now. A few more hours and she'll be out of our hair forever . . .'

35

It was gone midnight when Debbie Makin and Lee Jones made their way across the lane and into the field facing the derelict cottage they had just burgled. Unable to see when the moon disappeared behind a dense bank of clouds, plunging them into pitch darkness, Debbie clung to the bottom of Lee's jacket as he forged a path through the undergrowth and debris.

Relieved when they made it out the other side, she squinted in the dirty yellow glare of the streetlamps and looked nervously around. The estate was a run-down litter-strewn wasteland by day, but it took on a far more sinister atmosphere by night, when the younger gangbangers had gone to bed and the older, more dangerous ones came out to play. Scared that they might get jumped before they got home, Debbie quickened her pace to keep up with Lee when he marched on ahead with the heavy bag in his arms.

Rushing inside when they reached their block, the pair rode the piss-stinking lift up to the tenth floor, and hurried into their equally unpleasant-smelling flat.

'Hurry up and open it,' Debbie ordered, rushing into the living room ahead of Lee and switching the light on. 'I want to see what we've got.'

'Give us a fuckin' minute,' he grunted, dropping the bag onto the floor, sending a cloud of dust, cigarette ash and crumbs off the rug into the air.

'I'll do it,' Debbie said, dropping to her knees when he started shaking his arms to loosen his cramped muscles.

'Get the fuck off it!' he barked, kicking her out of the way. 'I'm the one who carried it, so I get first dibs.'

'Selfish bastard,' she muttered, rubbing her thigh where the kick had landed and giving him a hateful look.

'I'd shut my mouth if I was you,' he warned, flopping down on the shabby sofa and tugging the bag toward him. 'Go get us a drink while I check it out.'

'In a minute,' she said, edging closer. 'Come on, stop messing about; I want to see what's in it.'

Lee unzipped the bag and pulled a face when he saw that it was stuffed with clothes. 'What a waste of fuckin' time.'

'Some of this looks all right.' Debbie pulled out a jumper and held it up against herself. 'There's no holes in it, so I bet Neil from downstairs would give us a couple of quid for it.'

Unimpressed, Lee pulled out the rest of the clothes and tipped the bag upside down.

'It's shite,' he said, jumping to his feet and kicking the clothes aside before heading into the kitchen.

Still sure that she could get a few quid for some of the

clothes, Debbie carried on rooting through the pile. Tugging a pair of jeans out, she felt something hard in the back pocket, and her eyes lit up when she pulled it out and saw what it was.

'Lee . . . I've found a wallet!'

'You what?' He came in with a can of Tennent's Super in his hand and snatched the wallet off her.

'Hey, I found it,' she protested, struggling to get to her feet. 'Give it back.'

Shoving her roughly aside when she tried to grab it, Lee opened the wallet and rifled through it.

'There's nowt in it apart from receipts and bus tickets,' he grunted, chucking it at her in disgust before sitting down.

Debbie sniffed it, and said, 'It's real leather. We could give it to my dad for Christmas.'

'Why?' Lee sneered. 'He's ain't got nowt to put in it.'

'Hey, you missed something,' she said, sliding her finger into one of the pockets. 'Look . . .' She pulled out a credit card and grinned at him. 'It's still in date.'

'So what if it is?' he said, taking a swig of beer before pulling his tobacco pouch out of his pocket to roll a cigarette. 'We haven't got the pin, so we can't use it.'

'You only need them for debit cards,' Debbie informed him knowledgeably. 'You can use these to buy stuff online; as long as you don't go crazy, 'cos they'll block it if they get suspicious.'

'We don't need shopping, we need gear,' Lee reminded her as he licked the Rizla to bind his cigarette. 'And I've never seen any dealers walking round with a credit card machine, have you?'

'We can buy trainers, and watches, and perfume, and shit like that off eBay,' Debbie persisted, pulling her phone out of her pocket as she spoke. 'That kind of stuff sells on dead easy round here; Sue from the fifth floor does it all the time, and she's got a car, and everything.'

'Go on, then; order summat,' Lee said, watching as she connected her phone to their next-door neighbour's Wi-Fi signal.

'I'll have to make an account first, but I can't remember the password for my old email address.'

'That's 'cos you're thick,' Lee sniped, taking another swig of beer.

'Shut up, I'm trying to think.'

Before she had a chance to input the initials and date of birth of her ex-boyfriend, which she had a feeling was what she had used when she'd set up the old Yahoo account, someone started hammering on the front door.

'Go and see who it is,' Lee hissed, jumping to his feet. 'If it's for me, I'm not here.'

'They might have seen us coming in,' Debbie hissed back, shaking as she followed him out into the hall. 'What am I supposed to say?'

'Just deal with it,' he ordered. 'Fuck 'em if you have to; just don't let them come into the bedroom.'

Debbie crept up to the front door and peeped through the spyhole. Recoiling in shock when she found herself staring into a massive eyeball, she swallowed nervously when the eye moved and she saw that it belonged to Jez Benson – one of the dealers they owed money to.

She was backing quietly away, intending to ignore it, when a heavy kick landed on the wood.

'Okay, okay, I'm coming!' she yelped.

'What took ya?' Jez grinned, sauntering inside when she'd unlocked the door.

'You didn't have to kick it so hard,' she complained, dismayed to see that he'd damaged the lock. 'The council charge fifty quid to replace them, you know.'

Jez ignored her and walked into the living room. 'Where's dickhead?' he demanded, looking around.

'Lee . . .' Debbie yelled, annoyed that he'd left her to deal with this. 'Jez is here, and he wants to see you.'

Jez was looking at the pile of clothes when Debbie joined him. 'What's all this shit?' he asked. 'Hope you ain't planning to do a moonlight flit before you pay me what you owe me?'

Lee had come out of the bedroom by then, and he flashed Debbie a dirty look before asking Jez: 'What you kicking the door for, man? I thought it was a fuckin' raid.'

'It is,' Jez smirked. Then, looking at Debbie, who had sat down on the floor by then, and was typing something into her phone, he said, 'What you up to, Debs? Sexting your other man? No need, Babes; I'm already here.'

Debbie didn't reply, but her hands started shaking when she

felt Lee staring at her, and she prayed he wasn't about to offer her to Jez to pay off their debt. She'd prostituted for drugs in the past, but this man was a beast.

'What's that?' Jez narrowed his eyes when he spotted the credit card lying on the floor beside her.

'Nothing,' she muttered, sliding it under her leg.

'Pass it over.' He held out his hand. 'Or are you gonna make me take it off you?'

Too scared to argue, Debbie reluctantly handed it to him.

'It's no good, 'cos we haven't got the pin,' she said, hoping he'd be as clueless as Lee when it came to the difference between credit and debit cards.

'Someone'll buy it,' he replied, slotting the card into his pocket.

'Aw, come on, man, we need it more than you,' Lee moaned.

'I think you're forgetting you still owe me,' Jez reminded him.

'I told you you'd get it on Monday when my giro goes in,' said Lee. 'Come on, mate, be fair.'

'Nah, you're a piss-taking cunt, so I'm having this as part payment,' Jez said. 'Unless you wanna try and take it off me?' He stood over Lee with his arms outstretched and a menacing grin on his lips.

'Keep it,' Lee muttered, shrinking into his cushion.

'Pussy!' Jez jeered. Then, turning to Debbie, he grabbed her by the hair and stuck his tongue down her throat while fondling her breast with his other hand. Laughing when he looked round and saw Lee still sitting there with his eyes downcast, he shoved Debbie's head away and wiped his hand on his leg, saying, 'Later, losers.'

'Have you got anything on you?' Lee asked when he turned to leave. 'I'll pay you on Monday, I swear.'

Smirking, Jez pulled a little wrap out of his pocket and flipped it to him. 'Now you owe me seventy.'

'But you've got the card,' Debbie complained.

'You what?' He turned and stared at her.

'Nothing,' she muttered.

When Jez had gone, Debbie scrambled to her knees and watched as Lee sat forward to open the wrap.

'What you looking at?' he barked, flinging his beer can at her head. 'You ain't getting none!'

'Yeah, I am,' she argued, snatching the can up off the floor where it had landed and hurling it back at him.

'You wanna bet?' he growled. 'You're the one who handed that fuckin' card over, so you ain't getting klish.'

'Fuck you!' she yelled, looking around for something else to throw at him.

'Go on, I dare you,' he challenged, lurching to his feet and balling his hands into fists.

'I'm sorry!' she cried, covering her head with her arms. 'I've got the number!'

'What number?' Lee hesitated.

'The one off the credit card,' she said, lowering her arms and eyeing him warily. 'That's all you need when you're ordering stuff online: that, the expiry date, and the three numbers off the back. I was copying them into my phone when Jez saw the card. And I've remembered my password.'

'Yeah, well, it's no use now, is it?' Lee grunted, sitting down to prepare his fix. 'He's probably already sold it.'

'We can still use it till it gets cut off,' she insisted, her gaze riveted to the powder he was loading onto a strip of silver foil. 'So can I have my bit now?'

'I'll think about it,' Lee said grudgingly. 'Order me some trainers while you're waiting.'

36

DI Collins had been sleeping, but he roused when his mobile began to vibrate under his pillow. Sliding it out without opening his eyes, he answered it quietly, hoping not to wake his wife.

It was DS King, one of the detectives from the late-shift team, and Collins's eyes snapped open when the man told him that Matt Fisher's credit card company had just alerted them to recent activity on Fisher's account. Telling him he would be there in ten, Collins climbed carefully out of bed, lifted his suit and shirt off the chair where he'd draped them, and tiptoed out onto the landing to get dressed.

The previous morning, he had interviewed the man who'd been caught on CCTV trying to sell Fisher's phone – although it had turned out to be a fifteen-year-old boy from one of the local estates, and not a man, as they'd thought. The kid, armed with fake ID this time, had returned to the same pawnbrokers to sell a stolen bicycle. But the broker had recognized him and locked him inside the shop before alerting the police.

Like so many of the kids Collins encountered these days, the boy had been a mouthy little prick who thought he knew the ins and outs of the law better than all the coppers at the station put together. But he'd soon seen his arse when Collins had explained that the owner of the phone was wanted for murder, and that he would be charged with obstruction – or, worse, conspiracy – if he didn't start cooperating.

Scared shitless by the thought of getting dragged into a murder investigation, the kid had admitted to finding the phone under a pile of bricks in one of the unused garages beneath the flats in Ellie's block – although he swore he would never have touched it if he'd known who it belonged to. He claimed he'd seen a shifty-looking bloke in a hoody coming out of the garage, and that he'd found the phone after the bloke had gone.

The boy hadn't seen the man's face, so he hadn't been able to give any kind of description, which was disappointing; but Collins thought it was a fair bet that it had been Matthew Fisher, and that he had made the calls and sent the threatening texts to Ellie from that garage. It was a shame there were no cameras covering that estate, because it would have been useful to know which direction the man had come in from and gone out by – or even, as Ellie's mother had suggested the last time he'd visited her, if he'd been coming out of the block of flats to use the phone, because he'd been hiding in there the whole time they had been looking for him.

Still, the activity on Fisher's credit card ought to provide a clue to his whereabouts, because the person who had used it to order goods online would have had to provide a delivery address. And even if that didn't turn out to be Fisher himself, the purchaser must have been in contact with him to have got their hands on his credit card.

DS King had assembled a raid team by the time Collins arrived at the station, and Collins joined them in the briefing room.

'What do we know?' he asked.

'Delivery address came in as flat fifty-eight, Jackson House,' King told him, slipping a stab vest on as he spoke. 'Tenant is a Lee Jones; lives there with his girlfriend.'

Collins knew them well. They were both addicts, and Jones had form for burglary. But they weren't the sort of people he'd expect a man like Matt Fisher to be associated with. According to his wife, Fisher had never done drugs in his life, apart from those prescribed by his GP; and he didn't associate with any of the neighbours in his own block, never mind getting friendly with anyone from the rougher side of the estate, like Jones.

Still, Jones had got his hands on that card somehow, and Collins wanted to know how and from whom.

37

Debbie had flaked out on the living room floor after taking her share of the smack Jez had given them. Waking with a start now when she heard a loud bang on the front door, she crawled over to Lee, who was sprawled on the couch, and shook his arm roughly, hissing, 'Lee, wake up . . . someone's breaking in!'

Lee's eyes snapped open, and he rolled off the sofa and scrambled behind it.

The front door came in before Debbie could follow, and she cried, 'What's going on?' when several uniformed coppers swarmed in.

'We're looking for Matthew Fisher,' one of them told her as the others spread out and started searching the flat.

'I don't know anyone called Fisher,' Debbie replied truthfully. 'You've got the wrong place.'

Another copper had just spotted Lee's feet sticking out from beneath the clothes he'd hidden under behind the couch, and he shoved the sofa aside, barking, 'Come out with your hands where I can see them!'

'Don't shoot him!' Debbie squawked when the man aimed a Taser at Lee. 'He's got a bad heart.'

At the mention of shooting, Lee shuffled out of his hiding place and threw his hands into the air.

'Matthew Fisher?' the copper asked.

'That's not him,' Collins said, walking into the room.

'What's going on?' Debbie asked, shaking wildly. 'I swear down we haven't done nothing.'

'You ordered some goods online earlier tonight, using a credit card,' said Collins.

'No, not me.' She shook her head. 'We haven't got no credit cards. They won't let us have one. You can search us, if you want?' She held out her arms. 'But you won't find no credit card in here.'

One of the coppers had spotted a wallet sticking out from the middle of the pile of clothes on the floor. It looked empty when he flipped it open, and he was about to put it back down when he noticed a tiny speck of white sticking out from a corner of one of the card slots. Easing it out, he saw that it was a photo-booth picture.

'Guv,' he said, extracting the photograph and passing it to Collins.

It was a picture of Ellie Fisher; much younger than she was now, and smiling, which Collins had never seen her do on any of the occasions he had spoken with her; but it was definitely her.

'Who's this?' He showed the photo to Debbie and Lee.

'My cousin,' Lee lied.

'Really?' Collins raised an eyebrow. 'So you're related to the man whose credit card you used tonight, are you? The man we're looking for in connection with a murder?'

'Nah . . .' Lee shook his head. 'You ain't dragging me into nothing like that.'

More scared of being implicated in a murder and going through the hell of withdrawing in prison than she was of Jez right then, Debbie said, 'Jez Benson's got the card! He came round earlier tonight and forced us to order that stuff!'

'Shut your mouth,' Lee hissed, glaring at her.

'I don't believe you,' Collins said flatly. 'You used the card, and you've got the wallet which links you to Matthew Fisher, so I'm arresting you on sus—'

'We found it in the old cottage over the lane,' Debbie blurted out, ignoring Lee when the blood drained from his face and he told her to shut it. 'No one lives there, so we didn't break in or nothing. We only wanted to see if there was anything in there, and he – he saw a body in the cellar. But we didn't do it, I swear . . .'

'Body?' Collins's ears pricked up.

'I didn't see it,' Debbie said truthfully. 'I didn't even go in; it was Lee who did it.'

'I didn't do nothing!' Lee protested. 'It was already dead when I got there. I didn't even touch it; I just grabbed the bag and got the fuck out of there!'

38

Ellie's head was banging. She remembered Gareth forcing her to drink more of the sickly hot chocolate, but she had no idea if that had been today, or yesterday, because time had ceased to have any meaning. She'd been dreaming again, but it hadn't been a nightmare about Matt, this time; it was Holly who been in danger. A vision flashed up in a murky corner of her mind, but she couldn't keep hold of it for long enough to gauge if it was an image from the dream, or something she had seen in a waking moment.

As she stared into the darkness, Ellie's eyes began to focus, and her gaze was drawn to the thin sliver of light at the bottom of the door. Someone was moving around in the living room. Among the muted bangs and clatters, she heard what sounded like a female cry, and a jolt of fear skittered down her spine.

Nauseous, her heavy head aching, she winced when she tried to sit up and a dull ache shot down both arms. Confused to find that her hands were tied together behind her back, and that she couldn't open her mouth, she lay still for several moments and blinked rapidly in an effort to clear the fog in her brain.

She could hear a man talking quietly in the other room now, and she swallowed dryly when the vision floated into her mind; clearer this time. Holly . . . lying here in this bed, with blood on her face and something covering her mouth. Then someone had come into the room and carried her out . . .

Gareth!

He'd been in here and hurt them both, and now he had taken Holly into the other room to . . .

Unable to bear the thought of what he might be doing to her sister, Ellie forced her body to move when the muffled crying became louder and more panicked. After a couple of attempts, she managed to sit up and, shuffling to the edge of the mattress, dropped her feet to the floor. A wave of dizziness washed over her, and she forced herself to breathe slowly and evenly through her nose until it had passed. Then, shifting her body round until her fingertips connected with the bedside table, she groped for the drawer handle and slid it carefully open. Praying that the drawer wouldn't fall onto the floor and alert Gareth that she was awake, she reached inside and felt around for the small nail scissors she kept in there. Almost crying with relief when she found them beneath a pile of tissues, she carefully turned round so that her hands were over the bed in case she dropped the scissors and made a noise.

It took several attempts before she managed to dig the pointed ends of the scissors into the tape that was binding her wrists, and her fingers ached as she struggled to push them through the sticky material. When, at last, she had made a tear, she pulled her hands in opposite directions until the tape gave way.

Free, she ripped the tape off her mouth and then cut through the tape around her ankles before gingerly standing up and creeping to the door. Biting down hard on her bottom lip to keep from crying out when a muffled scream reached her, she reached out to open the door, but it didn't move. Desperate by then to get to her sister, she tugged harder, and this time it opened an inch. The hall light was on and she could see what appeared to be a pair of tights wrapped around the handle on the other side of the door. She couldn't see the other end but, guessing that it was probably tied to the handle of the bathroom door, she used the scissors to cut through the nylon.

Gareth hadn't heard the bedroom door creaking open; he'd been too busy trying to keep Holly from wriggling off the sheet of taped-together bin-bags he'd laid on the floor to contain the blood.

'Keep fucking *still*!' he hissed, striking her across the face. 'It's your own fault I've got to do this while you're awake, you stupid bitch! If you hadn't been such a disgusting junkie when you were younger, there would have been enough drugs to keep you quiet, but now you've made me run out, so just shut up and let me get on with it!'

'Stop it!' Ellie cried, staggering into the room and clutching onto Matt's chair to support herself when her legs threatened to give way.

'Aw, no . . . what are *you* doing up?' Gareth wailed when he turned his head and saw her. 'Go back to bed; you don't need to see this.'

'Let . . . her . . . *go* . . .' Ellie said breathlessly, afraid that she was about to pass out when her head started to swim. 'Please, Gareth . . . I'm begging you.'

On the floor, her eyes now covered with tape along with her mouth, Holly heard Ellie's voice and cried out, trying to tell her to get out and bring help.

'She's my sister, and I love her,' Ellie said when Gareth pressed his elbow into Holly's throat. 'Stop it now, Gareth, or I'll hate you for the rest of my life!'

'Don't say that,' he replied sharply, frowning up at her. 'Don't ever say that, because I'm doing this for *you*!'

'No, you're not,' she argued, readjusting her grip on the scissors before taking a hesitant step toward him. 'I never asked you to do this, but I *am* asking you to stop – now, before it's too late.'

'Go to bed,' he yelled, struggling to keep Holly in position when she started bucking beneath him.

'Let her go or I'll kill you!' Ellie screamed, raising the scissors above her head and staggering around the chair.

His neck was exposed, and she lunged at him, but he swung out his arm and knocked her to the floor.

Adrenalin began to course through her body, giving her

strength, and she scrambled to her knees and groped for the scissors she'd dropped. Gareth kicked them out of reach before she got to them, and then fell back onto Holly and kicked Ellie in the stomach when she made to lunge at his face with her nails. She flew across the room, smashing into the coffee table, and slumped to the floor when her head struck the corner.

Crying out when he saw blood from a cut on her temple seep into the carpet, Gareth crawled over to her and lifted her up by the shoulders. 'Don't leave me,' he sobbed, holding her in his arms. 'I'm doing this because I love you and want to be with you for the rest of my life, so why did you have to fight me and make me hurt you? Why couldn't you stay asleep and let me get this over with so we could have been happy?'

Ellie began to stir, and he held her tighter, murmuring, 'Oh, thank God!'

Guided by the sound of his voice, Holly twisted her body round and drew her knees up, then shot her feet out as hard as she could. Furious when she caught him flush in the back, Gareth laid Ellie down and scrambled over to her.

'Leave her alone!' Ellie croaked, clutching onto the edge of the table to pull herself up when he grabbed Holly by the hair and tried to manoeuvre her into the centre of the sheet he'd made. 'Gareth, stop it! She's pregnant!'

'I know, and it'll be better off dead, like *her*,' Gareth hissed, punching Holly in the face and chest when she continued to struggle.

Ellie grabbed the table lamp and tugged it, trying to yank the plug out of the socket. It didn't work, so she dropped it and threw herself onto his back instead, tearing at his hair.

A massive booming suddenly echoed around the hallway, followed by the splinter of wood as the front door crashed against the wall. Crying out with relief when DI Collins ran into the room along with four uniformed police officers, Ellie let go of Gareth's hair and threw herself on top of Holly to protect her as Collins hauled Gareth to his feet, saying, 'Gareth Wilkinson, I am arresting you for the abduction and false imprisonment of Matthew Fisher . . .'

Epilogue

It was two weeks before Matt was able to breathe on his own again, and Ellie watched nervously as the doctor switched off the machine that had been keeping him alive ever since Collins and his men had rescued him from the cottage.

'I think he's waking up,' she said hopefully when Matt's eyelids fluttered.

'Don't expect too much,' the doctor cautioned. 'He's done well to get this far, but there's still a way to go, and we'll need to monitor him very carefully for the next few days.'

'He's stronger than he looks,' Ellie replied quietly, her gaze still riveted to Matt's gaunt face. 'I know him, and if he's got this far, he'll make it all the way through this.'

Collins appeared in the doorway at that moment and gave the doctor a questioning look. Replying with a shrug, as if to say it could still go either way, the doctor excused himself and left the room.

'How are you bearing up?' Collins asked Ellie, pulling a chair up beside her as the nurse diplomatically checked Matt's notes to give them the illusion of privacy.

'A bit better, now I know he's going to be all right,' she said, clutching one of Matt's unresponsive hands between both of hers. 'He will be, won't he?'

Sensing that it wouldn't matter what he told her right then, because she needed to believe that Matt would pull through, Collins said, 'I reckon so. How could he not, with a wife like you waiting for him?'

'I'm a terrible wife,' she murmured, sniffing when a tear fell from her eye and landed on her wrist. 'This is all my fault.'

'No, it isn't,' Collins said, rubbing her back in a fatherly gesture. 'Wilkinson's to blame, not you, and don't you ever forget that. And I'm not entirely without blame myself,' he added guiltily. 'I should have told you about Wilkinson when I had the chance. But I never dreamed he was capable of . . .'

He tailed off and released a weary breath, then gazed at Matt, saying, 'At least this will never happen to anyone else, eh? Wilkinson might only have got a few years for what he did to you and your sister, but now we know he murdered your stepdad and kept Matt hostage, the judge will throw the book at him.'

'I hope so,' Ellie said, shuddering at the memories that were always hovering at the edge of her consciousness. 'I only wish I'd listened to his ex when she tried to warn me about him that time.'

'You weren't to know, so stop beating yourself up about it,'

Collins counselled. 'I realize it won't be easy, but you need to forget about Wilkinson and concentrate on getting your husband back on his feet.'

'That's if he still wants to be my husband when he hears what I've done,' Ellie replied miserably. 'I knew he was depressed, and I should have supported him; but I let that . . . *man* worm his way into my head and destroy us. How could I even think Matt would do something like that?'

'It's not your fault,' Collins reiterated kindly.

'Yes, it is,' Ellie argued. 'And I'm going to have to live with that for the rest of my life. But it doesn't matter what I go through, as long as Matt gets better.'

A tiny tap came at the door, and Collins stood up when Tony pushed Holly into the room in a wheelchair.

'I'll get out of your way,' he said, stepping aside to make room for the chair.

'How's she doing?' Tony asked Collins quietly when Ellie fell sobbing into Holly's arms.

'Still blaming herself,' Collins said, sighing as he looked at the bruises and scars on the sisters' faces. 'I've told her it's not her fault, and I'm sure she'll start believing it in time, but it's still too raw right now.'

'We'll look after her,' Tony assured him. 'And thanks for taking the time out to come and see her; it means a lot.'

'I was passing when I got the call saying they were taking him off life-support,' Collins said, as if he hadn't made the nursing staff promise to ring him when the time came. 'Anyway,

I'd best get going,' he said then, glancing at his watch. 'I'll pop round to Kath's as soon as we have a court date. Is Ellie still staying there?'

'Yeah, and thanks,' Tony said, extending his hand. 'And let's hope he never gets out, eh?'

'It'll be a long time, that's for sure,' Collins said, shaking his hand before leaving.

The nurse excused herself shortly after, and Tony took the seat she had vacated on the other side of the bed. Taking advantage of them being alone, Holly eased Ellie away from her.

'Right, now you listen to me,' she said sternly. 'I know you're worried; we all are. But you don't want Matt waking up to a hysterical mess, so you need to pull yourself together.'

'He's going to hate me,' Ellie sobbed.

'No, he is not,' Holly argued. 'And you need to stop acting like he's some kind of saint, when we all know he's not. If he'd trusted you, you wouldn't have got involved with that psycho in the first place, and if Matt dares to blame you when he comes round, he won't just have *me* to deal with, he'll have Tony and Mum on his case as well. *And* DI Collins,' she added, as if that added weight to her argument.

'He wasn't well, and I lied to him,' Ellie said quietly, her gaze drifting to Matt. 'And I wouldn't blame him if he never wants to see me again, because I let him down in the worst possible way when I took another man into our bed. He'll never forgive that.'

'Er, remember me?' Holly raised an eyebrow. 'I didn't want to bring it up, but you're not the only one who's done that, are you? Anyway, Matt walked out and told you it was over, so, technically, you weren't cheating when you went with . . .' She pulled herself up short before the name slipped out of her mouth, and said, 'That maniac,' instead.

Ellie didn't reply. She knew that what Holly was saying was true, but that didn't make her feel any better about it, and she hated herself for allowing Gareth to creep into their lives and cause a rift when she'd known that Matt was at a low ebb and wouldn't be able to cope with it. And she hated herself even more for allowing herself to start falling for Gareth. Now, she felt nothing but revulsion whenever an unwelcome memory of having sex with Gareth forced its way into her mind, and she could only imagine how Matt would feel about it when he came to and started asking questions.

As if he'd sensed that she was thinking about him, Matt's eyelids fluttered again, and Tony sat forward when he saw them flicker open.

'Hey, matey; welcome back.'

'Matt . . .' Ellie cried, leaping to her feet and gazing down at him. 'Can you hear me? It's Ellie . . .'

Matt's dry lips cracked as he opened his mouth, but no words came out.

'I'll fetch the nurse,' Tony said, getting up from his seat.

Matt blinked a few times, and then licked his lips.

'Do you want a drink?' Ellie asked. 'Shall I just wet your lips first?'

Matt squeezed her hand weakly, and she turned and reached

for the jug of water that was standing on the bedside cabinet. Dipping her fingers into the warm water, she gently touched them to his lips.

'Thanks,' he whispered. 'Love y . . .'

'See,' Holly said, squeezing her sister's arm when Matt's voice faded and his eyes drifted shut again. 'He just tried to tell you he loves you. I said he wouldn't blame you.'

'Did you hear him?' Ellie asked uncertainly. 'Was that really what he said?'

'Clear as a bell.' Holly smiled.

A moment later Tony returned with the nurse. After checking Matt over and making a few notes on the clipboard at the end of the bed, she said, 'He'll probably drift in and out a lot before he comes to properly, but give me a shout if you have any concerns. I'm right outside.'

Holly thanked her, and watched as she went back to her station. Then, turning to Tony, she said, 'Why don't you wheel me to the canteen so Ellie can have some time alone with Matt? I found some new shoes on that website I was telling you about, so you can get your credit card out while I'm having my brew and treat me to a few dozen pairs to make up for being stupid enough to believe I'd ever cheat on you.'

'You, my love, can have whatever your heart desires,' Tony said softly, leaning down to plant a kiss on her lips.

'He's such a pushover,' Holly giggled when Ellie smiled at them. 'And if he's this easy for me, just imagine what this little one'll get away with when it's born.' She stroked her stomach.

Feeling suddenly tearful again at the mention of the baby, Ellie reached for Holly's hand before Tony could turn the chair around, and said, 'I'm so sorry for what he did to you. If anything bad had happened, I would never have forgiven myself.'

'Well, it didn't,' Holly replied gently. 'Baby's fine, I'm fine, you're fine, and Matt's going to be fine, so stop thinking about the what-ifs and start thinking about the what's-going-to-be's instead. Okay?'

'Okay,' Ellie agreed, struggling to hold the fresh batch of tears at bay.

When the others had left the room, Ellie turned back to Matt and rested her cheek on his hand, murmuring, 'I'm so sorry, Matt. Please forgive me.'

Feeling him move, she snapped her head up.

'You're awake,' she said, jumping up when she saw that he was staring at her. 'I'll go and get the nurse.'

'Wait . . .' he croaked, holding onto her hand when she went to stand up. 'Need . . . to say . . . sorry.'

'I *am* sorry,' Ellie said guiltily, sinking down onto her seat. 'This is all my fault, and I'll never forgive myself for what that monster did to you.'

'Not your fault,' Matt argued. 'He . . .'

Scared that he was about to die when his voice faded, Ellie cried, 'Don't leave me, Matt, *please* . . . I hate myself so much for hurting you, just stay with me and give me a chance to—'

'Sshhh . . .' He squeezed her hand. 'Doesn't matter.'

The door opened and the nurse walked in.

'Well, hello, sleepy head,' she said, smiling when she saw that Matt was conscious. 'How are you feeling?'

'A bit weak, but my wife is strong so she'll get me through this,' he said, gazing into Ellie's eyes as he added, 'That's why I love her.'

'I love you, too,' she sobbed, her tears now tears of joy. 'Always have, always will.'

Matt smiled and, still holding tightly onto her hand, closed his eyes and drifted back to sleep.